GETTING HIS GAME BACK

A Novel

GIA DE CADENET

DELL

New York

A Dell Trade Paperback Original

Copyright © 2022 by Gia de Cadenet

Book club guide copyright © 2022 by Penguin Random House LLC

Excerpt from *Not the Plan* by Gia de Cadenet
copyright © 2023 by Gia de Cadenet

Published in the United States by Dell,
an imprint of Random House, a division of
Penguin Random House LLC, New York.

DELL and the HOUSE colophon are registered trademarks
of Penguin Random House LLC.

RANDOM HOUSE BOOK CLUB and colophon are trademarks
of Penguin Random House LLC.

This book contains an excerpt from the forthcoming book
Not the Plan by Gia de Cadenet. This excerpt has
been set for this edition only and may not reflect
the final content of the forthcoming edition.

ISBN 978-0-593-35662-3
Ebook ISBN 978-0-593-35663-0

Printed in the United States of America on acid-free paper

randomhousebooks.com
randomhousebookclub.com

2 4 6 8 9 7 5 3 1

Book design by Alexis Capitini

Pour mon Roux
For believing in me when I couldn't believe in myself

GETTING HIS GAME BACK

CHAPTER ONE

April

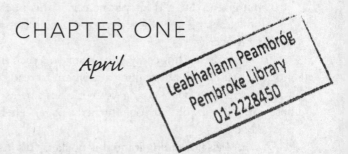

Maybe he was becoming obsessive.

Khalil shifted in the hard plastic seat. While aesthetically pleasing, it clearly wasn't made for guys over six feet who wanted their asses not to hurt while they sat in waiting rooms. He squinted, focusing again on the potted plant next to the far window. It had to be fake. He counted the little white flowers again. There were seven. Were there seven last month? He was sure there were seven two weeks ago. Before that, he couldn't remember. And it was spring, but still that seemed like a lot of flowers for the time of year. Maybe he was making something out of nothing.

"Mr. Sarda."

The low rumble of his doctor's voice bounced off the empty seats, rolling over the modern concrete floor.

"Dr. E," he said, standing to shake his hand and follow him into his office.

"What's new?" Dr. Edwards asked from his leather armchair, smiling at Khalil as he settled into a much more comfortable seat on the other side of the coffee table.

Khalil took a deep breath, sliding his palms together. This was always the strange part, the transition from wherever his head was in the waiting room, to focusing on what he wanted to talk to Dr. E about. But this was part of his new normal. Talking openly to people he'd met after his breakdown six months ago was a challenge.

"Well. It's been a good couple of weeks, I think. Work's been busy, but good." He slid his phone out of his pocket, opening it to his mood tracking app. "I've been on a nice trend lately," he said, handing it over.

"If you're being honest, you've been on a nice trend the past two months," said Dr. E after taking a moment to read. "You haven't had a relapse; you've been taking your medication as prescribed. Last time you told me you felt you'd turned a page." He handed Khalil his phone back.

"Yeah," he said, sliding it into his pocket. "It's just . . ." He ran his hands down his jeans. "Karim brought it up. Me still not dating."

Dr. Edwards leaned back in his chair, his hands relaxed on his khaki-covered thighs.

"What did he have to say?" he asked.

"It was a joke, him ribbing me, you know? But he made a good point."

Dr. Edwards kept listening, his expression neutral. Khalil stifled an urge to call his therapist Uncle Phil; certain other patients already had.

"It's been ages since I've been interested in a woman. Don't know the last time it's been this long."

It had taken a while, but Khalil was finally comfortable with Dr. Edwards's nod, his silent response. Khalil caught himself readjusting his watch and the friendship bracelets his niece had made for him. His watchband easily covered the scar, but there wasn't any harm in being careful. The "Khalil the Player" joke always made him uncomfortable. He knew it came from a good place, from both his twin and his best friend, Darius. And yeah, from the outside looking in, he could admit that it might once have seemed like he fit that description. He loved women; he'd never treat them as disposable. But since he hadn't been able to keep his sadness in check, and Nia had left him, and things had gone . . . bad, he'd lost interest. Which, now that he was doing better, felt really strange. Though after the past few months he'd had, he wasn't sure what was supposed to be normal and what was supposed to be strange anymore.

"Maybe it's a good thing," Khalil continued.

"What's that?" Dr. Edwards asked.

"That I'm noticing, that I'm missing having someone in my life. Maybe it's a sign that I'm getting back to myself," he said, shrugging. "I don't know."

Dr. Edwards nodded, but remained silent.

"And like we've talked about, maybe I was hiding. Maybe I was turning to relationships to stay away from feeling sad."

"How do you feel now?" Dr. Edwards asked.

"About?"

"Are you having those same feelings? Do you feel you have a reason to hide?"

Khalil hesitated before replying. Enough time to realize he already had the answer in his pocket.

"No. Like you said, my mood's been great for months." He rested his forearms on his thighs. "But still, all this, my *stuff* is here." He gestured to the space between them. "What woman would want to deal with a man whose emotions get the better of him?"

Dr. Edwards raised a hand.

"Is it possible that you're getting ahead of yourself? First, I think it's important to recognize that it's good you're interested in meeting someone. Just meeting them. You don't have to share all of your challenges right away."

Khalil nodded. Darius and Karim were still in the dark and they were the closest people in his life. No reason to behave differently with someone right off the bat.

"If you cross paths with someone, just exchange a few words. Start small, no expectations," Dr. E said.

Khalil nodded, keeping his doubts to himself. All his time was spent in his barbershops, and sometimes on basketball courts. It would be tough for him to naturally cross paths with a woman in either place.

———

"I will see your 'the darker the berry, the sweeter the juice' and raise you an 'aye, mami, how 'bout you try a white papi,'" Ana Garcia said, raising her glass to Vanessa Noble. The other women around the high table laughed, taking a sip. Then it was Helen Hsu's turn.

"Okay, okay," she said. "I got one. 'The best thing about you Asian chicks is how docile you are, how servile. You really know how to treat a man.'"

"Ewww," Vanessa said, her skin crawling. "That one definitely deserves another sip." They lifted their glasses in unison, knocking back a little more wine.

"My turn," Jill Santos said. "'But where are you *really* from?' Oddly enough, when I say Florida, that's not the right answer for them."

"God," Ana sighed.

Time to pull out the big gun, Vanessa thought.

"'I like black girls,'" she said.

Ana, Helen, and Jill remained silent, eyebrows raised or smiles frozen. Vanessa picked up her glass and took a sip.

"Then what?" asked Jill.

Vanessa shrugged. "That's it. That was the whole pickup line."

Ana frowned. "You're shitting us, right?"

"Nope. That was it. He just walked up to me, said 'I like black girls,' and stood there grinning. Guess that was supposed to make me get naked for him right then."

"How do we tolerate this?" Helen asked. "It's a wonder none of us has ever committed a felony."

"We tolerate it," Vanessa said, sitting up straight and raising her glass, "because we are some badass women, killing it in STEM and in everyday life."

"Hear, hear," Ana said as they clinked glasses. "Now we just have to get through one more day of this conference, without any creepy—"

"Well, well, well, what do we have here?"

The women sighed as one, turning to face four dudebros, led by one of the rising stars in renewable energy, Greg Cavana. "Looks like a Benetton ad of Hot Chicks in STEM." Greg and his friends laughed as the four women looked at one another and knocked back some more wine.

"So, ladies, mind if we join you?" asked Greg, sliding between Vanessa and Ana.

"Actually, we were just leaving," Helen said, scooting out of the way before one of the guys "accidentally" brushed his arm against hers.

"Oh no," Greg said. "Taking the party elsewhere?"

"Nope." Ana shrugged. "Early start tomorrow. See you on the panel, Mike?"

The tallest guy nodded, his gaze over Vanessa's shoulder at another group of women.

"Come on, Vanessa, let's kick it for a while." Greg winked at her.

Yeah, no.

"Have a good evening, boys," Vanessa said, linking arms with Jill as they left.

Vanessa and Jill could have walked back to their hotel, but there was a chill in the air, and it was late.

"Am I an ass?" Jill asked, looking out the window of their Lyft.

Clearing her inbox, Vanessa didn't look up. The update she'd been expecting about the suite of business management software and related apps that her company was designing for Alphastone Technologies in New York had yet to come through. While she knew that her team lead was on top of things, this was a make-or-break project for her reputation. She wanted time to assess the progress during her flight home. But she didn't want to be rude to Jill.

"What do you mean?" she asked, resting her phone in her lap.

Jill sighed. "I don't know. It's like, I don't want to be rude . . . it just gets old, having to put up with their shit, then have them be shocked if we take precautions."

"Like what?" Vanessa asked.

Jill glanced at the driver, then shifted closer to Vanessa.

"Maybe this sounds bad, but I can't take white guys seriously. Actually, almost no guys seriously. At least not guys who aren't Filipino

American. Don't tell my parents, they'll start looking for eligible bachelors right now. I don't want to just refuse to date whole groups of men—"

"'Cause it makes you feel like you're being as racist as they are."

Jill grimaced. "Yeah. Do you hate me?"

"Can't hate you for something I do myself," Vanessa said.

"Really?"

"Yeah. I can't see myself dating anyone who isn't black. It's not because I don't want to. It's just . . . relationships are hard. There's already so much to deal with, why add an extra layer of difficulty by being with someone who's never been confronted with the same shit you have to put up with every day? And worse, does that shit to you too?" She looked out the window. "I've tried. And it really, really didn't work. So now . . . that's just my policy. No white guy has ever shown me that he could truly see me as a real person, an individual. As an equal, not just the stereotype he had in his head." She sighed, hesitating to share a recent example that still stung. "A couple months ago, I went on a few dates with this white guy. Works for a nonprofit. Volunteered for the Peace Corps in Liberia. 'Woke,' right?"

Jill nodded.

"He invited me over for dinner. While I'm admiring a photo on his wall, he puts on a recording of wild animal sounds. Roaring lions, stuff like that. I made a joke, saying it would be tough to relax and eat while it sounded like we were about to be eaten. He was surprised. Said he thought it would make me feel more comfortable."

Jill frowned, eyebrows coming together.

"More comfortable?" she asked.

Vanessa nodded.

"Because he wanted me to feel 'safe,' 'at home' with him, he said. He pointed to the African fabrics he'd draped over his furniture. There were even animal print placemats. When I asked him what he meant, he said black people like that stuff. Animal prints and sounds of roaring lions. He didn't want me to feel uncomfortable in a"—she raised her hands to do air quotes—"'regular person's' apartment."

Jill's jaw dropped.

"I'm sorry?" she asked.

"Yep," Vanessa said. "I'm not a regular person, apparently. Only white girls are, I guess. And that's hardly the first time a white guy has pretty much told me that I'm different, that I'm 'other.' And it stings the same each time. So why keep setting myself up to get hurt?"

CHAPTER TWO
May

Three weeks later, spindly heels clacking on the pavement, Vanessa sped up as much they'd allow her to. But early was on time, and on time was late. Rounding the corner, she froze. The salon's light was off. After a quick glance up and down the street, she crossed the intersection, concern slowing her steps. The handwritten sign taped to the inside of the glass made her stomach drop.

"Closed due to fire."

Vanessa cupped her hands to the glass, peering inside. Misshapen shadows stared back, over blackened, melted bottles of creams and conditioner visible near the soot-covered door. She was as frozen as the charcoal-black salon seats she could barely make out. Cars passed on the street behind her, music loud, breaking her out of her shock. She fished her phone out of her pocket and scrolled through her contacts.

"Hey, Tanya, this is Vanessa. I'm in front of the salon. What happened? I hope you and the girls are all right. Lemme know when you can?"

She hung up, tapping the corner of the phone to her chin. Closing the shop, even for a little while, would be a major blow for Tanya. Vanessa knew that she'd already been operating at a tight margin, eager to up her social media presence and get new customers. Speaking of . . . Vanessa googled the shop and flipped through its social media accounts. Not one word about the closing or a fire. Even worse. She'd have to call Kyle. She'd recommended him to Tanya to get her media right, and here was plain evidence he wasn't doing his job. Vanessa switched back to her contacts, eyes narrowed. Kyle had some serious explaining to do. And she wasn't about to wait until she got back—

Shit!

She still had to get her hair cut. Her flight was in a couple of hours and everything was set except her hair. She couldn't be the only woman on the panel with the dudebros and have her hair not looking right. Scanning the storefronts, she couldn't remember if there was anything nearby. Returning her attention to her phone, she did a quick search. There was a new barbershop a few blocks down the street. Their website was clean and modern. A quick scan of their Instagram showed photos of old-school barbershop chairs and a black and white checkerboard floor. The vibe was masculine, which made her pause, but she'd gotten good cuts in places like that, and, in terms of the amount of time she had, beggars couldn't be choosers.

At least someone's taking their online presence seriously.

"I just need a shape-up."

Women's voices were few and far between in his shop, so Khalil stopped sweeping and took a step out of the back room to see what was going on. He immediately regretted not taking a glance at himself in the mirror first. The woman standing in the doorway was maybe five feet tall without those heels, light jacket open, revealing a streamlined figure that went with her streamlined hair. Everything about her was polished, well put together. Flawless, deep copper skin. Full brows arched perfectly over dark, doe-shaped eyes and a slim nose ending in a gentle curve. Her round lips probably formed a little heart, and their sexy pucker had Khalil's heart racing, but at the moment she was waiting for Darius, his business partner, to reply. Khalil held his breath and tried to slide back out of sight long enough to check he wasn't covered in the hair his previous client had left behind. Then Darius betrayed him with a glance.

"My next client will be here any minute, but Khalil can hook you up." He nodded in Khalil's direction, and she looked straight at him.

There was a falter in the intensity of her gaze, one he knew well. She hid her surprise, clearing her expression.

"Can you? Just a shape-up with a V in the back," she asked. Even her little shrug was charming.

"Got you, fam," he said, intentionally not reacting to her surprise at his choice of words. He looked away long enough to lean the broom against the wall, then stepped over to his chair and turned it toward her. He wanted to make a little joke but looking at her again took away the thought. She thanked him and slid out of her jacket, which he still had the presence of mind to step forward and take from her. Hanging it on the rack near the front of the shop gave him a second to collect himself. He glanced at Darius's reflection and caught the laugh he was holding in.

"It's Khalil?" she asked as he draped a cape over her.

"It is," he said. "And you are?"

"Vanessa; nice to meet you. Listen, um . . . Do you have a lot of experience? I, uh . . . I've never—"

"Had a white boy cut your hair?" he asked, keeping his grin at bay.

"Well, yeah, but . . ." She scrunched her eyebrows as she looked at his reflection, and he was sure he'd embarrass himself by blushing. "Are you . . . white?" Sliding a perfectly manicured hand out from under the cape, she clapped it over her lips. "This is completely out of line. I'm sorry. Clearly you're here, you're certified." She nodded at his license beside the mirror. "You know what you're doing."

He pumped the pedal of the chair, almost as much as when he cut his niece's hair. He leaned over so their reflections were almost eye to eye.

"Technically, I'm Algerian and French. So no, not a white boy–white boy. But I understand."

He caught the warmth in her cheeks before she covered them with her hands. He couldn't hold in his laugh.

"I'm sorry!" she said. "Please don't mess up my hair! I'm giving a talk in Vancouver tomorrow; my professional image is in your hands."

He'd always had a weakness for a woman's smile. But Vanessa's right then nearly killed him. She wasn't being polite. She was genuine, open, and radiant. She clearly had a sense of humor and probably didn't take herself too seriously. Not if she smiled like that with someone she'd just met. He didn't temper his smile in return.

"I told you," he said, giving her shoulder a gentle squeeze. "I got you, fam."

Vanessa Noble, "the App Goddess," CEO of Oshun Communications. Khalil had had a tech celebrity in his shop that day and hadn't known it. Scrolling farther down in his Google search of Vanessa and forgetting his aching eyes, he watched her talk from the previous year. Scanning a linked article, he learned that her TEDx Talk on the future of business management software had gotten so many hits she'd been invited to the home of TED Talks to give one the next day—that was the "talk" she had mentioned. He liked her choice not to tell him it was a TED Talk, that decision not to show off. He liked it because he'd done something similar with her, in not telling her that the Fade was his shop, the third he and Darius had opened in the past four years.

Wanting to see what else was out there, he googled and got rewarded with another article: a presentation she'd given earlier that year. It was too technical for him to follow, but that didn't matter. She'd had room to walk across the stage. And he couldn't get enough. Her heels were stratospherically tall, but simple. He marveled at her strides, looking as comfortable as if she were barefoot. She'd mentioned her professional brand that afternoon, that her hairstyle was part of it. He imagined the shoes were as well. He smiled, recognizing that the couple inches they gave her probably didn't hurt. The camera angle changed, giving the viewer a glimpse of the audience, rapt and focused. But Khalil's attention was drawn to Vanessa's silhouette: svelte and petite. She was a sexy pixie of a thing and he couldn't wait to see her again.

He'd been nervous at the register, hands shaking a little as he'd shifted the card machine toward her.

"So," he'd managed to say. "Should I put you down for an appointment two weeks from now? Say ten A.M.?"

"Two weeks?" she asked. "Trying to keep me looking sharp?"

He shrugged. "What can I say? I'm invested now."

He thought he caught a little smile as she looked down to put her wallet back in her purse. She backed up a few steps toward the door and made eye contact with him again.

"Do you flirt with all your clients?" she asked.

He smiled, feeling his cheeks warm.

"Just being friendly," he said. "Besides, flirting with my usual clients doesn't work if I want them to come back."

She laughed, free and open. He couldn't help smiling along.

"I'll see you at ten A.M. in two weeks, Khalil." She winked at him. "Have a good day."

He nodded as she pushed the door open and left, flashing that amazing smile.

Headed to bed after brushing his teeth, Khalil got there in time to catch his phone on the last ring before it went to voicemail.

"Just the man I need to talk to," he said, stretching out on his bed.

"'Sup, bro?" The background noise settled, and Khalil figured Karim had shut himself away somewhere.

"When was the last time you changed your glasses? I've been fine with my contacts, but it's like my glasses don't wanna work anymore."

"I guess three or four months ago?"

"Right. Forgot." He pulled the sheets down and shoved a pillow against the headboard. "Ran out of contacts around the same time and had a checkup before I could get new ones. Never got around to updating my glasses."

"I think we've reached the age where people can tell us apart without the old 'glasses, no glasses' thing," Karim said.

"Yeah, I think it's more the 'wife, no wife' thing now."

Karim grunted. "Next subject."

"Things are that good?" he asked.

"She's been in a mood lately. I don't know why. And whenever I ask, she says there's no specific reason."

"Sounds fun. You guys still trying? Maybe she's stressed about that."

"God, please, next subject. Seriously."

"Okay . . ." Khalil was excited to be an uncle again, and he knew Karim had been ready to start a family of his own. He guessed the holdup was Karim's wife, Laila, but his brother shut him down every time the subject came up.

"Let's talk about you," Karim said. "How are things back home? How's the new Fade?"

After an hour on the phone with Karim, Khalil checked in with Mo, Rachid, and Amir. Their mom always encouraged Mo, as the oldest, to take the lead in making sure that the boys spoke frequently, but it wasn't his personality, while it was second nature to Khalil. Maybe because he was the middle child, even though Karim would never accept that. But what could Khalil do? Three minutes older was still three minutes older. Rachid would have to leave his laboratory long enough to remember that other people existed in order to initiate a call, and Amir was still in college. Family was central for Khalil; he couldn't help but check on them. He shot a quick text to Darius about some details for the block party they were planning and asked about his parents before he could let himself relax.

After popping his meds, he plugged his phone in and clicked off the light. Under the covers, everything calm and still, one person came back to him: Vanessa Noble and her intimidating shoes. Women had enthralled him since he'd gotten that first big hit of testosterone in his teens. Every single one of his girlfriends had tortured themselves with high heels, and while he appreciated the result, he wasn't oblivious to the discomfort. But Vanessa seemed different. He'd never met a woman who looked so light and at home in shoes like that, as though they'd been made for her. He smiled, letting himself imagine sliding those heels off her, running a hand up the back of her calf, skittering higher. But he might not be her type. Or she might have a boyfriend. Rather than let himself get excited now and make it awkward when he saw her again in two weeks, he'd better start thinking of her as a client, instead of wondering how her skin felt, or if that hint of lavender around her came from her lotion, her perfume, or her body wash.

But she'd been on his mind off and on all evening. Head cradled in his palms, he relaxed his gaze at the ceiling, trying to track the last time he'd spent as much time thinking about a woman. The past few months he'd spent hours upon hours ruminating. He'd dissected, looked for clues, tried to understand all his *stuff*. Nia had left him after he'd fallen apart. But why had he fallen apart in the first place? He shuddered, frustration rolling through him. All his ruminating had made it hard to think about the future. He had way too much work to do on himself before he could entertain the possibility of a new woman in his life. But now . . . thinking about her this much had to mean something. Maybe Dr. E was right. He cleared his throat and rolled over, bunching up a pillow and tugging it against his chest as he willed himself to sleep.

CHAPTER THREE

B aby, is that you?"

"Hey, Ma-Max," Vanessa called out, stepping into the house from the garage. She paused beside the door to switch into her slippers. The scent of crisp apple cinnamon wrapped around her as she turned the corner, headed toward the kitchen. Her grandmother's house was always fresh and full of light, a welcome reprieve on days like today when the thirty-minute drive stretched closer to forty-five. Crossing the threshold, Vanessa immediately relaxed.

"There you are," her grandmother said, arms spread. Vanessa snuggled in and hugged her. She'd hoped to speak first to avoid the habitual line of questioning, but she should have known better. Her grandmother brushed a graceful swoop of relaxed hair off her forehead as she stepped back and looked Vanessa up and down.

"You've lost weight," she said.

"Have I, ma'am? I don't think so," Vanessa said, keeping her tone light.

Maxine squinted, the corners of her mouth turning down. She appraised again. "You have. You've been traveling too much. Stresses the body." She lifted a glass of sparkling water off the counter. "You should come home more," she said, turning toward the patio and crooking a bejeweled finger to tell Vanessa to follow.

My weight and my work. Not even in the house two minutes yet.

She carefully schooled her features as she closed the sliding glass door behind her. The serviceberry tree was in bloom, its feminine aroma filling the air. Arletta, her grandmother's best friend, was under it, talking on her phone and finishing a cigarette. She waved at Vanessa.

Lunch was laid out on the patio table. Vanessa took her seat, sliding her phone out of her pocket, arranging it beside her plate. Her grandmother sighed.

"Must you?" She tipped her head at Arletta. "She's getting as bad as you, being on her phone all day. I will never understand. How can people possibly communicate through those things? Face-to-face communication. That's how it should be—"

"Lord, Max. The girl just got here. You aren't gonna start already?" Arletta joined them, taking her usual spot across from Maxine. "Please spare us the 'playing on your phone all day' speech. You don't become the App Goddess by sticking to outdated perspectives on—"

"Outdated? Letta, you are trying my patience today. Did you come for lunch, or to work my last nerve?"

Arletta reached over and squeezed Vanessa's crossed knee.

"I came to see my girl, you know that." She winked at Vanessa. Her smirk was always the same when she was going to pick at Maxine. Vanessa appreciated the warning not to laugh too hard. She fixed her gaze on the waterfall at the edge of the pool, raising her sparkling water for a sip. Arletta continued.

"Besides. You wanna talk outdated, let's talk about that getup. Hostess pajamas went out with the Twist."

Vanessa swallowed hard, fighting down her laughter at her grandmother's clucking, while Arletta egged her on. Harold the gardener passed at the end of the yard, shaking his head. He was well accustomed to the bickering. Vanessa slid forward for a cherry tomato. She had fuzzy memories of her grandfather, Papa Joe. He'd passed away when she was ten, after years of working hard to ensure his family's future in a Michigan strongly opposed to a black man's success. Her grandmother had picked up the reins of his insurance business, managing it as well as she'd managed her family's industrial support operations. Vanessa knew all of the stories of her grandparents' business acumen, but she didn't know what their relationship had been like. She imagined that they had set the example her parents were following—out saving the world together. But if Vanessa couldn't have a relationship like that, she'd be good with a best friend for the rest of her life. Like Ma-Max and Arletta. Then her grandmother turned her attention on her, as though she'd read Vanessa's mind.

"Of course Vanessa knows I'm proud of her. What I want to know is when I'm gonna get some great-grands."

Vanessa did not roll her eyes. Instead, she picked up the serving utensils next to the sliced pork roast.

"Auntie Letta, I'm starved. You?"

"I am; thank you, baby." She lifted her plate and Vanessa avoided eye contact. She got a helping of potato salad on the plate before Arletta remembered their last conversation. "Wait a minute. Ness, didn't you just get back from Vancouver?"

"She did," Maxine said. "How did your talk go? What is it again? A Teddy?"

"TED Talk, Ma-Max. Just TED. And everything went great. Made some good connections."

Ma-Max's eyes lit up. "Speaking of connections, did you see Andrew? Debra's grandson?"

Vanessa served herself, then cut off an unladylike chunk of pork roast and shoved it into her mouth.

"Please, Ness, do tell. Did you have a good time on your date with Andrew?" Arletta singsonged. She pulled the bottle of Chardonnay out of its chiller and poured Vanessa a large glass. Vanessa raised an eyebrow. Arletta winked.

Guess I have backup.

She took a fortifying drink of wine and smoothed her napkin on her lap.

"He begged me not to say anything, Ma-Max."

"Say anything? Did he get too fresh with you, Vanessa? Try to take advantage?"

"Take advantage?" Vanessa asked.

"Yes. Debra promised me he wouldn't, but if he's anything like his father—"

"Like his father?" Arletta asked, laughing. "You can't be this blind."

"What?" Maxine looked back at Vanessa. "Is that what happened? Did he try anything?"

"No, Ma-Max. Nothing like that. He was the perfect gentleman."

"You'll see him again, then?" Maxine asked.

"Um . . . no." Vanessa picked up her utensils, wishing she were anywhere else. Andrew's secret wasn't hers to tell.

"Vanessa. I fail to see the problem. He's one of the few eligible young black men in our social group with an MBA, a strong family background, and his own thriving business. Plus, he is handsome and dresses well."

Arletta snickered.

"What is the problem?" Maxine asked, glaring at her friend. "He is quite the catch."

Vanessa relented. "He was, Ma-Max. For his husband."

Arletta cackled. "Better than I thought!"

"Repeat that, please," Maxine said.

"Everything you said is true. Young, attractive, educated, accomplished. Attributes that snagged him an equally attractive man."

"Man?" Maxine asked.

"He's gay, Max," Arletta said. "You owe me fifty bucks."

Vanessa balked. "You all bet on him being gay?"

"No, sweetie," Arletta said. "I bet your gran that the date would be a flop. Because she refused to believe what everyone's known since forever and what Debra won't accept. Did you really go out?"

Vanessa shrugged. "We met for coffee, with his husband, Nick—who is stunning, by the way. They showed me around the city. And because things are so tense in his family about him being gay and with a white man, he begged me not to say anything other than that we had seen each other. Please keep everything to yourselves, especially the fact that they got married."

Maxine huffed, taking a bite of her pork.

"Pay up," Arletta said.

"You know I'm good for it," Maxine said, cutting her eyes at Arletta. "Shame. You two would have made some beautiful babies to-gether."

Vanessa rested the tines of her fork on the edge of her plate. Ma-Max's great-grandbaby mania was new. After years of encouraging Vanessa to excel in her career, her grandmother's advanced age might have shifted her focus to convincing Vanessa to start a family.

"Promise not to say anything, please?" she asked.

"Not a word from me," Arletta said.

"Me either," Maxine said. "Though I can understand Debra being upset."

"You understand her being upset that Andrew is gay?" Vanessa didn't check her tone.

Her grandmother scrunched her nose.

"No! I don't care what he does with his dick."

"Blegh, Max," Arletta said. "Don't put that in my mind."

Maxine rolled her eyes. "I mean, I can understand Debra being upset about him being with a white man."

Vanessa let her head loll back to rest on her chair. Then she thought better of it, picked up her glass, chugged a good mouthful, and let her head fall back again.

"Ma-Max," she sighed. "Do we have to do this today?"

Arletta retrieved the Chardonnay, topped off Vanessa's glass, then her own. Vanessa lifted her glass to clink with Arletta's but didn't raise her head.

"Look," her grandmother said. "You know I am all for people being with who they want. But my lived experience—and yours, Ness—bears out that interracial dating is unwise."

Vanessa schooled her features, her love and respect for her grand-mother outweighing her annoyance. It had been almost a decade since the only experience Ma-Max knew about, and she still felt the sting of her own stupidity. But that was unfair. She'd been too young to understand all the dynamics at play, and now, with time, she'd for-given Tony for being a kid, at the mercy of his parents. Though for-giveness didn't erase the hurt. She knocked back another mouthful, not looking at either woman. Arletta sighed.

"Max, when are you gonna let this go?" she asked. "Two men—one a boy, actually—were assholes. When in the history of human life have most men *not* had asshole tendencies?" She sat up in her chair, making a show of looking out over Maxine's yard, shielding her eyes as though she were searching the horizon. "If I threw a rock right now, I'm sure I'd hit at least three assholes, so at some point you're gonna have to give this a rest."

"Yes, Ma-Max," Vanessa said. "I think it's time to leave the past in the past. At least for me."

"You were broken, baby. You can't expect me to forget that," her grandmother said. Arletta sighed again. Maxine shot her a look, continuing. "It pays to be vigilant in matters of the heart. And based on the standing of the families at that school, I'd have expected more gallantry."

"Money buys class now?" Arletta asked. "Better not tell Ness's parents. All these years with Doctors Without Borders must have knocked them down several social pegs."

Vanessa's eyes nearly shot out of her head. Arletta wasn't pulling any punches. Maxine's eyes narrowed to slits.

"What did you say?" she asked.

Arletta relaxed into her seat and folded her arms.

"You're being an idiot. Been going on about that boy for years, as though Vanessa went looking to get hurt."

Vanessa tried to melt into the pattern of her patio chair.

Maxine gave Arletta another hard glare, then turned to Vanessa, features softening. "Baby, I know you didn't do anything wrong. Other than hiding that boy from your parents and me at first. You should never feel like you have to hide things from your family. Having to hide means the person isn't good enough for you anyway."

"Yes, Ma-Max. I know. We've been over this a few hundred times."

Maxine covered Vanessa's hand with hers and squeezed.

"You're right, baby, we have. I'm sorry. You know how I get when I worry."

"I know. Although I'm sure you can understand if I don't drag a man home the second we've met, right? I'm picky. It's gonna take a lot for me to be sure I like him enough to bring home." *Thank God I never introduced Rick to Ma-Max. That latest foray into interracial dating was a nightmare.*

"Picky. Acorns don't fall far from the tree," Arletta said.

"What are you implying now, Letta?" Maxine asked.

"You're picky, your son is picky, so naturally your granddaughter is picky. A trait that can get downright insufferable with age."

Vanessa barely got her mouthful swallowed before she choked.

Maxine squinted. "Are you trying to say I'm difficult?"

"I'm not trying to. I'm saying flat out: You're a pain in the ass, Max."

Vanessa took a slow breath to tamp down her laughter. She returned to her meal as the bickering started up again. Apart from managing Andrew's discomfort, the trip to Vancouver had gone quite well. She was proud of the balance she'd struck—a successful TED Talk and some time for herself. She'd scheduled one day more than necessary, a choice she intended to repeat. For the past two years, she'd been going a mile a minute between app design and business management software consulting. It was time to slow down, to savor what she was doing and the lifestyle it allowed her. And while it was fun, jetting around, proving that people's notions of who belonged in tech were outdated, she was starting to miss having some time at home. Well, home for her. She cringed, glancing at Ma-Max. She'd disown Vanessa for referring to Detroit as "home." At least she'd returned to the family home in Bloomington today. With her parents still on their most recent mission, maybe it was time to get back into the rhythm of Sunday Lunches with Ma-Max every two weeks. Her fork wavered as she relaxed her grip, itching to pick up her phone and check her agenda, but she didn't want to get caught.

Kathryn, Ma-Max's housekeeper, came by to clear the plates for dessert and Vanessa snatched the few seconds of distraction to take a look. Things were pretty open in two weeks' time, maybe . . . She stopped on the appointment for her next haircut and couldn't help but smile. Her next haircut with Khalil.

What's the deal with that guy?

Wavy, dark hair, golden-olive skin. Tall and broad-shouldered: her absolute catnip. She should have picked up on the fact that he wasn't a "white boy—white boy" before he'd said so. She might have guessed Latino but wouldn't have placed him correctly. Not with those green eyes that got so intense while he focused on cutting her hair. Beautiful and professional. She'd nearly memorized every inch of decor in that shop to avoid staring at his reflection in the mirror. Hot and masculine, he might as well have been a model with that angular jaw, those dimples, and those crazy-sexy lips. She pursed hers, letting out a stream of calming air, thinking of his yet again. Made zero sense for a man to be so blessed in the lip and eyelash department when so many women were wandering around without.

". . . want to, Ness."

Maxine's voice snapped her back to the present. She glanced at Arletta, hoping for a clue, but she was relishing the first bite of her chocolate mousse. Vanessa tucked her phone under her thigh.

"I'm sorry, Ma-Max?"

"There's still time to join us on the cruise this autumn," Ma-Max said.

"Oh. Don't think I can take that much time off." A transatlantic crossing was tempting, but Ma-Max would only do a roundtrip, and Vanessa wasn't ready to spend three weeks at sea. Although, if her developers stayed on schedule and Alphastone kept following her advice, she'd close on the biggest deal of her life and have more than enough reason to celebrate.

"All right," Ma-Max said. "But let me know soon if you change your mind."

Vanessa nodded, retrieving her spoon for dessert. The corner of her phone poked into her thigh, and she shifted to reduce the pressure. She couldn't do a cruise, but she could certainly enjoy the view the next time she got her hair cut.

CHAPTER FOUR

Vanessa checked the clock over her monitor for the fifth time in as many minutes, then turned her attention back to the end of quarter review for her London investors.

Louis, her team lead, began winding the meeting down, and she returned her notepad and pen to their places.

"Thanks again for your time. You'll have the updated report by the end of the week," Louis said, wrapping up the chat.

Vanessa nodded and clicked her microphone back on. "Yes, thanks, everyone. I'm here if you have any questions." She finished the rest of her responsibilities on autopilot. After replying to her mom's latest email about the antiviral work she and Vanessa's father were doing in Cambodia, Vanessa was ten minutes ahead of schedule to get to see Khalil—to get to her appointment—but her anxiety started to inch up.

Would be better to be a couple minutes late. Don't want to look too eager.

A two-toned chime announced Vanessa's arrival. It was midmorning and the shop's first appointment, a time she'd been happy he suggested as she liked avoiding the rush of a busy barbershop. Black barbershops had always been places where she could get a quality cut, though she disliked intruding on the male-dominated domain. It went both ways: She'd be annoyed if some random guys crashed her time at the nail salon.

"Morning, Vanessa."

Khalil was in his chair, angled toward the door, sliding his phone back into the pocket of his vest.

"Morning, Khalil," she said, hoping her voice didn't sound as strained as it felt. How was it possible for him to be even sexier than she remembered? He stood, unfolding those long legs, showing off his broad shoulders with the way he supported himself through the movement with a hand on each armrest. She froze as he took a few steps toward her, his hand extended for an awkward shake. His smile sparkled, the corners of his eyes crinkling.

"Can I take your jacket?" he asked, his hand still out.

"Oh, right. Yes," she said, snapping out of her stupor. Sliding it off her shoulders gave her an excuse to look away and catch her breath.

"How are you?" he asked as he hung it up.

"Good, you?"

"Great. Ready?" he asked.

She nodded and conspicuously did not look at his butt as he led the way back to his chair. Her peripheral vision had a mind of its own, but thankfully she didn't follow it. Once she'd reached the chair, she remembered that there were mirrors in front of and behind her; no way he wouldn't have caught her checking him out.

"How was your trip?" he asked, draping the cape over her. "Vancouver, right?"

She smiled. "It was good, kind of you to remember."

The chime sounded again and the other barber stepped inside, two cups of coffee in a carrier, a brown paper bag in the other hand.

"Morning, Dare," Khalil said. "Put mine there?" He tipped his chin at the edge of his station.

"Got it," he said. "Hey, how are you?" he asked Vanessa.

"Good. It's Darius, right?"

"It is." He looked at Khalil. "Didn't realize you had an appointment first thing. Could have given me a heads-up so I could have brought something for the lady." He put Khalil's cup down, looked at Vanessa's reflection, and shot her a wink. "Sorry I can't offer you a coffee; our maker's broken. Haven't had any of mine though, want to split it?"

"I'm good," she said. "Thanks." Adjusting herself on the seat, she almost missed the glare Khalil shot Darius. And the shrug and smirk he got in return. Khalil tracked his colleague as he went into the back, eyes narrowed. Vanessa asked herself what sort of magical barbershop she'd landed in with two hot guys working there, and at least one with a sense of humor. Then Khalil caught her attention, a hand on each of her shoulders, his voice soft and warm.

"Shape-up like last time, or are you in the mood for something different?"

I could definitely be in the mood for something different. Tall, broad-shouldered, French and Algerian . . . Stop it. You can look. Nothing wrong with enjoying the sight of a handsome man. But you are not in the mood for anything.

"Um . . . why don't you surprise me?" she asked. His eyes widened and she caught a tint in his cheeks.

"Really?" he asked. "You trust me that much already?"

And she failed—completely and totally failed—at not running her gaze down his chest and arm, her treasonous eyes even shooting a look over her shoulder at the reflection of his ass in the mirror behind her. She ran the tip of her tongue inside her bottom lip and looked back up at him, not missing the surprise in his eyes. She tilted her head to the side, trying to play it off as though she'd been thinking.

"I shouldn't trust you?" she asked.

He smiled, definitely blushing, and averted his gaze.

"I hope you do," he said in his deep, intoxicating voice.

"You design apps, right?" he asked, coming around to her left side, his attention on her hair.

"I do," she said. Had she mentioned what she did the last time? Probably; she couldn't remember. His hands caught her attention as he pulled a pair of gloves out of a box and began working them on. His really sexy, very masculine hands. Without a wedding band in sight. She cleared her throat.

"Darius and I have been thinking about getting one to work alongside our website," he said. "For our staff, but also for our clients. Easier to make appointments, choose cuts, stuff like that."

"Ah," she said. If he wanted an app, she'd feel even worse about ogling him. It was bad business to look at a client that way. He turned his wrist a little, and the friendship bracelets on each side of his watch caught her eye. On one hand, it was kind of cute—such an attractive guy his age not too full of himself to wear something silly. On the other hand, maybe his daughter had made them for him. That thought severely dampened Vanessa's fun. Maybe he had a kid—and a baby mama. She glanced at the photos tucked into the edge of his mirror. There was one of Khalil and Darius when they'd been much younger, and a slightly faded one at the highest corner with a group of guys, maybe college age. There may have been a family resemblance, but she wasn't sure. In another Khalil was smiling, wearing graduation regalia. She was pretty sure it was master's level and that the man and woman on either side of him were his parents. It was a really sweet photo, and he'd clearly gotten his height from his dad but his looks from his mom. Only photos of friends and family. No women, no kids. Then she realized the clippers had gone silent and he was standing right behind her, looking at her reflection with an open expression in his eyes and a little smile. *Shit*.

"Um . . . sorry," she said. "Did you ask me something? I was kind of lost in my thoughts."

"No problem," he said. "I, well, Darius and I, were wondering if you could help us out. With designing an app. For our business. If . . . you have the time, and if that's even the type of app you make . . . um, you know."

A little part of her registered that he sounded nervous asking. But a larger part had to hide her disappointment. She always drew a strong line between business and pleasure. And she wasn't about to let a little attraction change her practices.

"Sure," she said. "We work with small businesses all the time. I can set up a meeting for you with one of my staff, get the ball rolling."

"Oh," he said softly, suddenly intent on the chair. "Cool. Thanks."

He finished up and she nodded her approval, very impressed with the light fade he'd given her. She followed him to the register to pay and flipped the cover of her phone case open to see when she could link him up with her assistant. Then she paused and looked at him, her gaze tripping on his lips. He smiled. She smiled back. No reason she couldn't handle things. She could be professional while enjoying some eye candy.

"You know, it would probably be easier for us to work on this together . . . I mean . . ." She took a quick breath. "It's been a little while since I worked directly with a client, designed a project myself. Do you mind being my refresher?"

He grinned, and she discovered he was adorable when he was shy. "I'd like that," he said. "How do we get started?"

Timing presented a challenge. Vanessa's travel schedule didn't leave a lot of free time, and Khalil's work schedule required him to be in his shop most business hours. Her office on Jefferson off Shelby would be too far away for him to get to on a busy day. She was about to ask about using his back room, so they could work between his clients, until he suggested a coffee shop a couple of miles away.

"Day after tomorrow, I've got the afternoon free to take my niece to the dentist. We could meet before I have to pick her up from school."

"Oh," Vanessa said, concealing how cute she found his involvement in his niece's life. "That could work. We'd need about an hour, is that okay?"

"Perfect," he said, flashing her that bashful grin.

"No," Lisa, Vanessa's best friend, said, sitting at the bar counter overlooking Vanessa's kitchen. She hadn't taken her eyes off of Vanessa's laptop since they'd finished dinner and Vanessa had introduced her to Khalil and Darius, courtesy of the photos on the Fade website.

Vanessa chuckled, putting the leftover salad in the fridge.

"Yes," she said.

"No," Lisa repeated. "I'm sorry, but no. There cannot be this much hotness in the same space. They're business partners?"

"And longtime friends, I think," Vanessa said, joining her at the bar. "Come on, let's get your room set up."

"I'm bringing them with me," Lisa said, picking up the laptop and following Vanessa out to the garage.

"So, an app," Lisa said. "That's . . . very noncommittal." She finished stuffing her pillow into its case. Vanessa stopped working on the other one to look Lisa in the eye.

"Who says I want him to be committal?"

Lisa shrugged, grabbing the blanket off the chair and unfolding it on the bed.

"You have not been talking about this guy like he's some random barber. Or a potential client. You have definitely been using words that could lead to commitment-based ones."

Tossing the freshly cased pillow on the bed, Vanessa flopped into the armchair. She'd have to take a second pass at decorating it, but the little guest room over her garage-turned-art studio looked pretty good and was coming in handy for the last week of renovations at Lisa's apartment.

"Like what?" she asked.

"Hot, professional, sexy, intelligent . . ." She trailed off. "Actually, it's less the specific words than the quantity. You've been talking about him nonstop since I got here."

"Have not."

"Have too."

Vanessa squinted at her. Lisa smirked back and went into the bathroom with her toiletry kit. Lisa was off base. Vanessa hadn't been talking about Khalil that much. Pushing herself out of the chair, she grabbed Lisa's bag off the floor. She'd put half the clothes in the dresser drawer by the time Lisa returned.

"Sorry," she said, bumping her hip against Vanessa's. "Maybe I'm just ready for you to have someone in your life."

Vanessa laughed. "*You're* ready? How do you think I feel?"

"He sounds hot, but other than where he works, do you know

anything about him? Like, could he check some boxes on The Basic Requirements?"

"The List? You just gave me grief about it last week. Now you want me to use it?"

Lisa scooped up the remaining clothes she'd brought, and Vanessa took the empty bag to fold and toss in the closet.

"You know how I feel about The List. You're gonna use it no matter what I say. Not that big of a surprise. I see you've even put together a list of anything your guests may need."

"The stuff in the bathroom?"

"Hope you didn't buy all that just for me," Lisa said. "Though it's good to know there are condoms on hand if I get lucky." She waggled her eyebrows.

Vanessa rolled her eyes. "You better not bring anyone back here."

"If you don't want anyone gettin' freaky in here, why are there condoms?" Lisa asked, tossing a pillow at Vanessa.

"Because I don't want any gross surprises when I change the sheets!" She laughed, chucking the pillow back. "And excuse me for trying to be hospitable. I appreciate having a few necessities when I check into hotels. Thought I'd do the same for houseguests."

"What kinda hotels you stayin' in that provide condoms?"

"Oh my God." Vanessa rolled her eyes again and fell back into the armchair.

Lisa grabbed the laptop off the dresser and stretched out on the bed.

"Speaking of condoms, back to Hottie Barber and The Basic Requirements," she said. "You think he just wants an app?"

"Maybe he checks a box or two. And why wouldn't he just want an app?" Vanessa asked.

Lisa arched an eyebrow.

"A box or two? One: He's hot. Two—"

"Being attractive is not number one on The List," Vanessa said.

"Please. It's either number one or two. I'll save you from yourself if you forget the importance of good genes. Two: He owns his own business. And it's doing well. Three: He has a master's or an MBA?"

Vanessa nibbled the inside of her lip.

"Saw a photo at the shop. Pretty sure he has one or the other."

"Okay. Well-mannered?"

Vanessa shrugged, fiddling with a loose thread on the arm of the chair. "Yes."

"Guess it's too early for you to know if he's got a good relationship with his family."

"See?" Vanessa said. "It's too early for all this. And what do you mean about the app?" she asked.

Lisa side-eyed her. "What do you think I mean? You're attracted to him; you said he might be attracted to you. You really think an app is all he's interested in?"

"Even if he were attracted to me, and even though I do find him cute—"

"Cute, sexy, handsome," Lisa cut her off without looking up from the screen.

"Even though he's cute, he's off-limits. If I take him—them—on as clients," Vanessa said.

Lisa rolled her eyes, then flipped the laptop around, the screen facing Vanessa. She'd zoomed in on a close-up of Khalil, a candid shot taken of him and a client laughing together.

"Why in the world would you want him, that smile, to be off-limits?" she asked.

"You know precisely why," Vanessa said. "Bad for business." She glanced at her hand, checking her fingernails. "Plus, I've got so much on my plate right now," she said. "This Alphastone project deserves all my focus. Not some man who is not only a potential client but might not be on the market—and he might not date black women."

Lisa sighed, then turned the screen back to herself.

They sat in amiable silence for a few minutes, Vanessa's mind trailing to the meeting she had the following morning and the need to check her inbox.

"Well . . ." Lisa brought Vanessa back to the present, then didn't say anything.

"Well?" Vanessa asked.

"Mr. Darius is super fine himself. Any sparks there?"

Vanessa let her head roll to one side, strumming her fingertips on the arms of the chair.

"If you have to think about it," Lisa said.

"There's no spark," Vanessa finished. "He seems like a great—" Vanessa straightened, grinning.

"No," Lisa said. "We're talking about you right now, not me."

Vanessa leaned back.

"For the moment," she said.

Lisa returned to the laptop. "This Khalil guy might be okay, Ness. He's not Rick."

Vanessa narrowed her eyes at Lisa. Rick, her most recent ex, was the reason she'd added "has to be a black man" to her list of Basic Requirements. They'd been together for eight months, and while things had started off well, the clueless microaggressions built up to a point that she just couldn't take.

"Rick was the last straw," she said.

"You're letting that fool live rent-free in your head, Ness," Lisa said.

"I made a fool out of myself for him."

"How so? All you did was be an open-minded, caring person. And apart from a couple clueless gaffes, I don't think he was mean-spirited."

Vanessa crossed her arms.

"He added 'Jungle Fever' to his sex playlist," she said.

"Like I said, a clueless gaffe that he corrected and apologized for when you pointed it out."

"After a lot of educating him. And his snide comments about my diversity program at work. And his joke about me looking like a slave with my sleep scarf on. He even got mad when I said that he was white. Though he sure had no problem describing me as black. The small things add up. As you know so well."

Lisa sighed. "I do."

"And yeah, he was cute and kind at first. But I can never forget how he made me feel like I was just one of a mass. 'Black girls this' and 'black girls that.' He didn't even see a problem with his friend suggesting I cut his hair, 'cause 'all black girls know how to do hair.'

Come on, what was that even about?" She sighed, leaning back against the chair. "Same 'black people are a monolith' I have to deal with in my field, that blackface nonsense in college. It even goes back to Tony in high school."

"Please do not let Mr. High School Basketball Star have an impact on your grown-ass life," Lisa said. "You were both young and learning about the whole concept of dating. Anyone who looks back on their first boyfriend is going to cringe."

"He kept me a secret from everyone. Didn't want people, or more important, *his parents* to know that we were dating, to know that he even liked me. Why should I be someone's dirty little secret? It's part of a pattern. Time after time, the men I've dated who *aren't* black make me feel like I'm not a real person. I'm a secondary character in their story."

"Okay. Let's talk black men. What about Tyrone?" Lisa asked.

"What about him?"

"Technically, he checked all the boxes."

Vanessa squirmed.

"He did," she said. "And there was so much I didn't have to say. I didn't have to explain simple things, like why I was sure I was getting screwed with that business loan. He understood being discounted."

"Tyrone was an undercover hotep. Pro-black, but just for men. Didn't he also call you a traitor for 'trying to get the white man's money' when you needed that loan?"

"Not in so many words."

"He wasn't good for you. Don't see how he's good for anyone but himself. And he's proof that being with a black man isn't the be-all, end-all."

Vanessa chewed that over. There'd been a lot about Tyrone she'd just let slide, and Lisa was right: He hadn't been good for her.

Lisa was quiet, lips pursed to the side as she scrolled down the screen.

Vanessa sighed.

"Listen, you get me. I hate how it looks, rejecting a guy because of the color of his skin. But ultimately, it's not about that. I just want to be seen as an individual, treated as a person. Not some 'other.' And I have yet to cross paths with a man who isn't black who's shown me he can do that."

Lisa stopped scrolling and rubbed her chin.

"I know. You're right. But look," she said, pointing at the laptop again.

The About the Team page filled the screen, Lisa having scrolled down to Khalil's bio.

"He went to Morehouse," Lisa said. "You never ran into him when you were at Spelman?"

Vanessa squinted, reading the relevant line.

"No, I'd have remembered him."

"And he works in a black neighborhood. Two of his three shops are in black neighborhoods," Lisa said. "He made the choice to invest in them."

"Um . . . okay?" Vanessa looked straight at Lisa. "Where are you going with this?"

Lisa went to a page of photos, scrolling down fast, and back up again. Then she nodded and angled the screen toward Vanessa.

"What do you see?" she asked. There were different shop interiors, close-ups of cuts, a few shots from sporting events and bake sales. Vanessa was lost.

"A small business with a good vibe?" she asked. "I like the choice to run things that way."

Lisa looked disappointed. "You said he and his business partner seem to go way back?"

"Yeah. Saw an old photo of them at the shop."

"Kay. He went to an HBCU. His partner is black. He works and has invested in black neighborhoods. Nearly all the people in these pictures with him are people of color—he is literally surrounded by people of color, mostly black people."

Vanessa took a second look. Lisa had a point.

"I seriously doubt he's some clueless white boy who doesn't understand that being black in America comes with specific challenges," she said.

Vanessa shrugged. "Spicy white boy."

"So?" Lisa asked.

Vanessa looked again, enjoying his easy smile.

"I can admit that appearance and personality wise, he is very attractive. But he's a potential client. Gotta focus on that."

Lisa sighed. "Can't say I didn't try."

CHAPTER FIVE

Khalil compared the train-station-style clock on the wall to the time on his phone again. The wall clock was definitely his style, but not the way the second hand was dragging, each tick slower than the last. He rolled his eyes. Both clocks showed the same time, neither taking his impatience into account. Getting to the coffee shop early kept him from being late, not antsy.

The door swung open and there she was, outfit accented with a light scarf that coordinated with another pair of those sexy heels. She shifted the attaché case on her shoulder, caught his gaze, and smiled. He smiled and waved. She pointed to the counter and he nodded. Then he kicked himself. He should have waited in his car, paying attention so he could have walked in with her. From where he was sitting, there was no way to offer to pay for her drink. He uselessly checked his phone again before tucking it away in his pocket and running his hands down his thighs.

"Hi," she said as he stood to greet her. He returned her handshake.

"Hey," he said. "Thanks for meeting me."

She shook her head, sitting down.

"Glad to. Like I said, it's good for me too. Gotta keep my skills sharp. Have you been waiting long?"

"No." He wanted to say something else, but his mind went blank.

"Well," she said, surprising him as she pulled out a leather document holder and flipped it open to reveal a legal pad. He would have expected a tablet and stylus. She pulled a pen out of its loop holder and clicked it once. "Guess we'd better get started; I don't want to make you late for your niece."

He smiled. "No worries; it's not far."

"Gotta say, I was surprised when you told me that."

"What?" he asked.

"Don't know many men involved enough in their nieces' lives to take them to the dentist," she said, blowing across her coffee to cool it.

He shrugged. "Family's important. And she's a cool little lady. Hope I have one just like her someday."

"Oh." She blinked once, in sync with a quick jump of her eyebrows. He couldn't help but lean forward, curious as to what that expression meant. He crossed his forearms at the edge of the table and caught her glance at his watch. Instinct made him curl his wrist inward a bit.

"Did . . . um, did she make those for you?" Vanessa asked.

He followed her gaze again.

"Ah, my bracelets. She did. Guess it's kind of weird, a twenty-eight-year-old guy wearing them," he said.

Vanessa shot him that devastating smile, and he caught himself smiling too.

"I don't think it's weird," she said. "It's really sweet. Kinda shows you don't take yourself too seriously."

He glanced away as his cheeks heated.

"No," he said to Vanessa. "Not *too* seriously. And Maddie was so cute about making them for me—Madison, my niece. It would have been cruel to not wear them."

Heat shot up his neck as Vanessa puckered her lips into a little heart, sighing out a brief stream of air, attention firmly on her legal pad.

"You're . . . unexpected," she said, looking up at him.

He gulped. Then he tried to smile. "What do you mean?"

"I'm used to men my age pulling away from family ties or the idea of kids. Going after that all-important independence." She took another sip.

"I get it," he said. "But those guys are crazy. I can't wait to start a family of my own someday. Now that my shops are good, I have something to offer, you know? Before . . ." He shrugged. "Maybe they're not so crazy. It would have been really difficult to have kids much younger. Building a business takes drive, as you're well aware," he said. She returned his smile. "I was so focused on that, I'd have made a rotten husband or father. But now, things are coming together pretty well. All that's missing is the right person." He flashed hot, embarrassed, and unusually angry with himself. Something he'd need to note in his mood tracking app. "Umm . . . sorry. Didn't mean to say all that."

"It's cool," she said, taking a much longer sip and gazing off to the side.

He took a drink as well, happy for the excuse to shut himself up since he was buzzing with nerves and was going to start babbling again if he didn't relax. He really needed to get this attraction in check. He'd been off the market for so long that he felt like a goofy teenager around a beautiful woman. Plus, they were meeting for professional reasons, not personal ones. His attraction to her had no business in the situation.

"So, um, you're single?" Vanessa asked, and his attention was one hundred percent back on her. Hers was on the zipper on her document holder, then the edge of her paper. A blast of adrenaline almost shot his heart out of his chest. He leaned forward again, inching his chair closer to the table.

"I am," he said. "Are—"

"I'm sorry, Khalil. Excuse me. That was inappropriate." She sat up straighter in her seat, shoulders back, gaze firmly on his. "You're my client, well, a potential client. Let's get down to business, shall we?"

"Um, okay," he said, confused. She unfolded a printed sheet from a pocket in her document case and wrote the date at the top of her legal pad.

"So," she said. "According to your website, you have three shops, is that correct?"

The shift in mood and even in her tone made him pause. Friendly, then all business. And then it clicked. Maybe she didn't date clients? He took a second look at her, assessing, ticking through the information he'd gathered from his borderline stalking online. Now that he thought about it, there'd been a Facebook page with her name on it, but all it had was posts from business-related events. Her relationship status hadn't been noted. Her Instagram had also been business only. *I bet she doesn't mix her professional and personal lives.* Maybe for the best. His personal life was barely stitched back together.

"Yes," he answered. "Three shops."

"And you aren't currently using your website for scheduling purposes, right? I couldn't find that option online."

"No, we aren't," he said. "But we would like to."

He answered each of her questions mechanically, beating himself up for his cluelessness. He should have listened to Darius and stuck to the original timeline. Even if that meant finding a different excuse to talk to her. She was efficient and professional in each detail; the possibility of getting to know her personally was slipping away. And then another detail cropped up. She was already his client, and maybe her resistance to mix business and personal went both ways—whether she was the client or the service provider. He might not have ever had a chance for something more. He didn't know what to do.

"Hmm," she said, scanning her notes. "Give me just a second."

She flipped the page up and started to sketch. Some bullet points, a drop-down menu.

"Have to admit I'm surprised," he caught himself saying as he watched.

A smile lit up her face and she glanced up at him.

"Why's that?"

"Figured the App Goddess didn't do pen and paper."

Her hand stilled. When she looked up at him again, the red undertones in her cheeks seemed to deepen. He was almost sure she was blushing.

"'The App Goddess'?" she asked, cringing a little.

"Uh, yeah," he said. "That's . . . not your nickname?"

She shrugged. "It is in the industry. But it's always seemed a bit much. I appreciate the intent behind it, though."

"Oh. Well, that's why I thought to ask for your help. Saw you were the best in app design when I googled you."

"Before you knew what I do?"

"Well, yeah. It was kind of . . . at the same time . . ." he said. Then flushed hot again. He'd told on himself. He gulped. "Um, sorry. You're right, I—"

"Did research on a potential service provider," she said, looking away. "That's normal." She turned her attention back to her paper.

She was sweet, to let him save face. But he was sure she'd figured out that he googled her before knowing anything about her work. "It's just that . . ." he said. "I was curious . . ." He stopped and cleared his throat. That was about to get too personal. "*We* were curious. We'd originally planned to look into an app in about a year. I had to convince Darius that now might be a good time, so we did some research, like you said."

She slid her pen back into its spot.

"You had to convince him?" she asked, looking up.

He stifled the urge to hide his face in his hands. Every word was a mistake. Never in his life had he had so much difficulty talking to a woman. Maybe he was screwed for good.

"Um, yeah. We're a good team, help each other see things clearly." He decided it was best to shut up and wait.

She nodded. "Having the right business partner is key."

"Yeah," he said. "How did you get started?" *Good, Khalil, that wasn't weird. Just keep not being weird.*

"The apps grew out of a grad school project. Software consulting developed naturally out of that," she said, relaxing back into her seat, her coffee in both hands. "Though I ended up doing it alone. Not everyone is comfortable with a woman of color leading in tech."

He nodded, relief washing over him.

"I can get that," he said. She arched an eyebrow and he realized how many shades of wrong that sounded. "Sorry! No. What I mean is that I really know what it's like to understand that you aren't wanted where you're comfortable, where your skills and interests align."

"Yeah, something like that."

He wanted to know more, to know exactly what her experience

had been. But maybe it would be pushing too much. Maybe she wouldn't want to . . . *Fuck it.*

"Did something happen?" he asked.

She looked up from her notes, nose crinkling.

"It's not the nicest story," she said.

"I'd still like to hear it."

She cocked her head, assessing him. After a deep breath, she placed her coffee on the table.

"How do you feel about blackface?" she asked, squaring her shoulders.

"Blackface? You mean, like white people using makeup to look black?"

"Mm-hmm."

"Uh, it's definitely not cool. Racist. Othering."

"'Othering'? Cool that you see that. Well, when I was in college—I went to Spelman, I did the dual degree program with Georgia Tech—things went pretty well. When I was on the GT campus, I felt like my classmates respected me, and no one was ever openly negative with me. Then there was this event, student-sponsored, and someone went as Tiger Woods. It wasn't enough to dress like him, they decided to go in blackface. The guy was interviewed on the student channel—GTCN. It became a thing. Of course, there were two opinions—that it had only been a joke, and that it was downright racist. My lab partners asked my opinion, and I gave it to them honestly. Suddenly, I wasn't a team player anymore. I was making everything about race, when they were the ones who asked me. I didn't know what they expected me to say. But the rest of the semester was tense. One guy, who'd already invited me for a drink, made a bunch of comments that I was racist because I wouldn't go out with him and that I couldn't take a joke. It wasn't that at all. Until he got all bent out of shape about race, he'd had absolutely no personality. After all that, it was almost impossible to get any of them to work with me. I had to practically beg for partners on assignments." She paused, then sighed. "I'm sorry to dump all that on you."

"No, don't apologize," Khalil said. "I'm really sorry that happened to you. Blackface is just wrong. Putting pressure on you to excuse it is worse."

"So you can understand why it wasn't the most comfortable environment for me?"

"Of course. But are things different now? In your field?"

She brought her cup to her lips, then shook her head.

"It's just under the surface. In general, we treat each other professionally. But I'd be a fool to believe that I'm accepted as an equal."

She looked crestfallen a moment, then took a deep breath, a pleasant smile lightening her features. And he recognized that—the masking of the hurt, having to cover up the feeling of rejection for something that she had no control over. He knew it well enough from Darius's experiences, and he had tried his best to support his ex, Nia, through the same thing. He hoped that she could tell he saw her as a person, saw beyond the outside. But for her to understand that, he'd have to offer a deeper connection than just being her client. Maybe he should share too.

"I kind of get it. I get feeling like people see me as 'other.' Like I told you, I'm Algerian and French. For some people, that's too white; for others, it's not enough."

"Okay," she said, looking wary.

"I went to Morehouse."

"I know," she said. Then her eyes got big and she was blushing again. "Um, I mean—"

He tempered his grin.

"That you did research on a potential client," he said. "That's normal." And he winked, without thinking. Her shy grin was emboldening. "So, um, Morehouse. While it was absolutely the best college experience I could have imagined, it was tough in the beginning. A lot of people felt like I didn't belong there, and they let me know."

Her brow knitted together, and she shot him a sweet smile.

"I'm sorry you had to go through that," she said.

"Thanks, but I got through it. By junior year, it wasn't something I had to deal with anymore. You still have to. Almost every day, I imagine."

She looked out the window, and he was sure he'd crossed the line. He was so nervous, and he'd messed up before, trying to empathize, not equate, and had failed. Sure he had again, he was searching his thoughts for an apology. Then she gave him that devastating smile, and his brain stopped working.

"Thank you for recognizing that," she said. "A lot of people don't."

"Sure," he said, glancing at the table because he couldn't keep looking at her.

"How did you get into barbering?" she asked. "Was it something you were always interested in?"

"No." He shook his head. "Getting out of school, my primary goal was my own business. Darius and I knew we wanted to do something, but it took a little while to decide on what. His uncle was a barber and taught him a few things when he was still in high school. Said it was always good to have a trade, no matter what sort of studies you pursue."

"I get that. Even if my company were to fall apart one day, I could still program. All the more reason to keep my skills sharp. Thank you for the chance."

He shook his head again, smiling.

"No, thank you," he said. "It's pretty clear that you're doing well for yourself. I know our little app won't be bringing in that much for you. I'm surprised you agreed to take it on at all."

She tilted her head to the side, eyebrows crinkling slightly. And again, he found himself wondering what that expression meant.

"It's been a couple years since I worked on a project for a small business," she said. "But the skills transfer to all sorts of things. What made you follow Darius's uncle's advice?"

"First off, he's a wise guy. He gives great advice about life in general. I think he'd make a great psychiatrist." *Shit. Don't give her a reason to think you'd know what makes a good psychiatrist.* He cleared his throat. "Of course, Dare and I wanted to make a good living, and we looked at a lot of career opportunities. We met in undergrad but got more serious about starting something together in the first year of our MBAs."

"Where did you get your MBA?" she asked.

"Michigan Ross. Wanted to get back closer to home."

"Oh. Where's home?" she asked.

"Grosse Pointe," he said.

She nodded.

"It was important to me—well, to us—that we have a good impact on the community. Not be too far removed. What's nice about being a barber is that I get to talk to people from different walks of life every day. I'm not stuck behind a desk, punching keys on a keyboard . . ." *Shit, shit, shit.* He swallowed hard. "I'm sorry, I'm not criticizing it. I just . . . I really need to connect with people every day. And I guess I get antsy; it's hard for me to sit still for long periods of time." He stopped again, running a hand through his hair. "Wow. Okay. I'm running my mouth too much."

She rolled her lips, then smiled.

"I'm not insulted. It's important to be comfortable with what you're going to do every day. I like speaking, making a connection with people. But I've also always loved getting lost in code, building something sharp and efficient. I know it isn't for everyone."

"Okay," he said. "The very last thing I'd want is to offend you, Vanessa."

She smiled.

"Don't worry, Khalil. You haven't offended me at all. But . . . um, can I ask you something?"

He nodded.

"You said the community. Did you specifically mean the black community? I . . . uh, noticed that you have two locations in black communities and one in Midtown. Was that intentional?"

Without thinking, he mirrored her head tilt.

"Did I say that?" he asked.

She nodded.

"Well, yeah. The black community is what I meant. When D's uncle taught me the first few things, it was in his shop, with his clients. That just felt like home. Of course, getting licensed, I learned to cut all sorts of hair. And in Midtown we cater to everyone. But being in black neighborhoods just felt right. It wasn't even something we questioned, I don't think." He shifted his wrist, to be sure the bracelets were in place. "Plus, how can we give back if we aren't in the community?"

"Oh," Vanessa said. "I see. That's . . . that's cool."

He turned his cup slowly in his hands, unsure what to say next. A lull in the conversation wasn't a bad thing, and it gave him a moment to appreciate the fact that she'd shown an interest in him, in the way that he thought. Maybe she was having as much trouble separating the professional and the personal as he was.

"Right," she said. "So the app. Do you know anything about how they're designed?"

"Not a thing."

"Well, today I'll get an idea of what you and Darius need. I've already looked into similar applications, for scheduling and other personal care services. We can start with the basics of those and you let me know what's most important for you all, what features you feel you need."

He caught himself frowning.

"What is it?" she asked.

"To be honest," he said. "I'm not sure what we need. You're probably right, looking at other apps would give me a good idea, but I don't even know what sort of specifications to ask for."

She shook her head gently.

"That's not a problem at all. We'll have at least two more meetings, and you can let me know if my ideas are heading in the right direction. It's not a one-shot thing. And once it's implemented, we can always tweak it. If there are functionalities that just aren't working for you, or if you get feedback from your clients that they'd like something different, we can make adjustments."

"Okay, cool."

"One thing to keep in mind: It takes about three months from start to finish. Is that a timeline that works for you?" she asked.

"Yeah, that works. We'd only planned on looking into it next year. Having one set to go in the next few months is far ahead of our schedule."

"Great. So, naturally, I won't be working alone on this. My programmers and I will work together, so although it's been a while since I've been personally involved in a project, you're in good hands."

He nodded, smiling. As intelligent and professional as she was, he didn't have any concerns.

"I'm sure you've got this," he said. "But would our project take you away from other responsibilities? I'm totally cool with working directly with someone else. Don't want to take up too much of your time."

She smiled back.

"You're not taking up too much of my time, Khalil."

His cheeks got warm. And he decided he loved the way she said his name. He felt a little dopey thinking that, but maybe he really could be interested in someone again.

She tore off the sheet of paper she'd been writing on and pulled three printed pages out of the document holder. Spreading them out as much as possible on the small table, she turned them toward him.

"My sketch here is based on the ideas I got from these other examples. This first one is from a hair salon—thought that would be a good place to start. But there isn't the option you mentioned about— Oh! It's almost been an hour," she said. He glanced over his shoulder and mentally cursed the clock on the wall.

"It has," he said.

"Do me a favor," she said. "Take a quick look at these and put a check mark beside the things you like." She handed him her pen. "An X on things you don't think you'll need."

He accepted the pen, focusing on the first page. He liked what he saw, thinking that maybe all they needed was the exact same app.

"This looks really good," he said. "Could we pretty much do the same thing?"

"I'd change the appearance a little, make it more masculine. But what do you think of the setup on the second page?"

He flipped to it, realizing he liked it just as much. He wasn't sure how to choose.

"Um . . ." He looked up at her. "Maybe I should just trust you.

These look fine to me, scheduling is the main thing. And access for our employees, I suppose. So they can manage their schedules too and get in touch directly with clients if there's a problem."

"This gives me a good idea for a start. Let's meet again next month. I'll have a first version for you to check out."

"Cool," he said.

She began putting her things away.

"Better let you go. Can't have you be late for Madison," she said, standing.

"Yeah," he said, standing too.

"I'll call you at the shop to schedule our next meeting? Or we could just talk about it when I come in for my next haircut?"

"Works for me," he said. He wanted to say more but wasn't sure what. And she was right, he did need to get to Madison. He followed her to the door, tossing his cup and taking a few quick steps so he could open it for her.

"Thanks for meeting with me today," he said once they were outside.

"Glad to. Thanks for giving me the chance to design again. It's been a while. I missed it."

He nodded. Not wanting to leave her yet, but unsure of what to do, he slid his hands into his pockets. She glanced away, then back at him as she readjusted the strap of her bag on her shoulder.

"So, um, have fun with Madison," she said, then her eyes widened. "Sorry, that was weird. I mean, I hope you have a good afternoon."

"Yeah, uh, thanks. I'll be thinking of you, Vanessa," he said. He gulped. That was too much. "I mean, I'll be thinking of the app. You know."

Her smile was shy as she nudged at a pebble with her toe, adjusting her bag again.

"Me too," she said. "About the app."

He had to get out of there. He was feeling way too flustered.

"Have a good one?" he asked, turning toward his Jeep.

"You too."

They parted ways with him still feeling awkward, but he'd see her again soon. He'd have another chance to be smooth.

It wasn't until he was about to back out of his parking space that he caught the opportunity he missed. He could have given her his personal number instead of her calling him at the shop.

Amateur.

CHAPTER SIX
August

Even though he'd seen her several times over the past two months, Khalil still felt nervous around her as Vanessa walked him to the bank of elevators across from her offices at the end of their third and final app meeting. Maybe because they were back on her turf instead of his.

"As always, it's been good to see you, Vanessa," he said. She smiled at him.

"You too, Khalil. I'm glad you're happy with the app. Guess now we'll just see each other at the Fade."

"Yeah," he said, then stalled out. *Is she saying she'd like to see me away from work?*

Stepping out of a restroom across the hall, Darius joined them again.

"Thanks again, Vanessa, the app looks great," he said.

"Sure thing," she said as the elevator arrived.

Khalil followed Darius into it, waving goodbye to Vanessa as the doors closed. The meeting had gone well, and Darius had come along so that they could sign off on the final changes together.

"Gotta say, you were right, man," Darius said.

"About what?"

"Good timing. It'll be great to get rid of the old scheduling system now that we've got something specific to our needs. We'd have been squeaking by for at least a year without your crush on Vanessa."

Khalil's ears burned hot. He turned to his friend, whose lips were jumping like he was fighting back a smile.

"A crush?" Khalil asked. "Is this high school?"

"What would you call it, then?" Darius asked.

"I wouldn't call anything anything. She walked in the shop one day, I happened to find out that she makes apps, and she happened to be willing to build one for us. And now we have one. You're welcome."

Darius faced the closed doors again, nodding.

"Right," he said. "It all just happened to come together. It's not like you were looking for an excuse to talk to her."

The elevator slowed and the doors opened. A man and a woman got in. Khalil nodded a hello to them but held his tongue. He shot a harsh look at Darius. Once they'd reached street level, Khalil had calmed himself down from the teasing. But he was worried about how he'd made things look.

"Do you think it seemed like a pretense?" he asked as they walked back to Darius's car. "I mean, we went ahead and bought a whole-ass app."

"You're good, man," Darius said. "And I mean it, you were right. I'm glad we have one now. It's just a shame that for all of your time spent together, you don't know that much more about her."

Khalil chewed on that as he buckled his seatbelt. He had gotten the opportunity to get to know Vanessa better than he would have if she'd only been his client. And he was encouraged by the questions she'd asked him. She seemed genuinely interested in knowing more about him. However, she'd been the very image of professionalism the whole time. He'd reflected that back. Now that the app was complete, the only time they'd be able to see each other would be in the shop. Likely with other clients around. Part of him wanted more, which surprised him. He wanted to ask her out, see her in a social setting, not a professional one. But would that be wise? In the past he wouldn't have hesitated about at least asking. Now, though . . . he didn't know if he was ready to actually go out on a date with someone. The thought was like a bucket of cold water over his head. However . . .

"What if we invited her to the block party?" Khalil asked.

"Vanessa?"

"Yeah. We've been inviting all our other clients. I hadn't mentioned it to her yet, have you?"

Darius grinned and shot him a glance.

"I have never spoken to her outside of your presence. Wouldn't want you to feel like I was moving in on your girl."

Khalil rolled his eyes.

"She's not my girl."

"Not yet. I don't know if this is some new maturity or something, but Khalil the Player wouldn't have been caught slippin'. If you want to invite her, invite her."

"Think she'd come?"

"Only one way to find out."

Khalil slid his phone out of his pocket. He pulled up the last email she'd sent him about the app. But then the words wouldn't come to him. Should he just reply directly to the email? Or send a separate one? Should he even email her at her professional address about something personal? Was this personal? Maybe he should invite her whole team? He rested the phone in his lap as he looked out the window. *Why the hell am I being so indecisive? I* fucking *hate this.*

"You good, man?" Darius asked, glancing at him from the driver's seat.

"Yeah, yeah. Fine."

"Still want me to drop you off at the Original?" Darius asked. "Pax texted me this morning, said things seem better; Rod's finding his groove as manager."

Khalil kept his gaze out the window. He hated lying to his best friend.

"Yeah, I still want to swing by. Haven't been in a couple weeks. Went to Fade Two just a couple days ago."

"Aight," Darius said.

"There's no way she could ever see me as anything more than a client. Or just her barber," Khalil said, rubbing his face in his palms as he leaned over on the couch in Dr. Edwards's office. Dr. E was silent until Khalil looked up at him.

"What makes you say that?"

Khalil shrugged.

"I . . . it's like I can't talk anymore. I never used to be like this. I couldn't even email her to invite her to our block party when I was in the car on the way over here. Oh, and I lied by omission to Darius again. He dropped me off thinking I was going into the shop. I can't even bring myself to tell my best friend that I'm seeing you, but I'm supposed to be able to talk to an intelligent, inquisitive woman?" He sat up straight, groaning in frustration. "I am really getting on my own nerves right now."

"Okay," Dr. Edwards said. "Let's just take a step back. Everything went well with the app. You've spoken to her multiple times at your workplace and hers, and you are satisfied with the work she provided for your shops."

"Yes, that's true."

"Just a few months ago, you were telling me that you didn't even think you could talk to a woman anymore, and here you have proof that you were able to work together to meet a goal. Is that correct?"

Khalil nodded. "I was."

"And you feel that your conversations went well? You previously said that she asked you about yourself," Dr. E said.

"She seemed surprised about where we chose to open our shops, or, well, surprised that I wanted to do business there. And she asked about my studies."

"Did you feel that she was just being polite, or were those genuine questions?"

Khalil sat with that a moment. She didn't seem like the type to ask questions just for the sake of asking them. But how could he know? He still barely knew his own mind; how could he guess at someone else's?

"I mean . . . I think they were genuine. But what if it's weird to invite her to the block party?" he asked.

"Why would it be?"

"I dunno." Khalil shrugged. "We're inviting all of our clients. And it'll be before the next time she comes in for a haircut. I'd forgotten to bring it up in her office, but thought about it in the car. I guess it's not weird if we're inviting everyone."

"But you feel different about her potentially attending," Dr. Edwards said.

"Yeah. I do."

Dr. Edwards didn't say anything. And for a few moments, Khalil let his mind go blank. He was doing it again. Making a thing out of nothing.

"I guess I just need to try and see what happens, huh?" he asked.

"That sounds reasonable."

Khalil pulled his phone out while Dr. E reached for his prescription pad. Copying Vanessa's address into a new email, he simply wrote "Party on Woodward" in the subject line. Before he could think about it too much, he wrote a couple of quick lines, informing Vanessa that they were having a block party on the fifteenth, where to park to avoid the madness of the Woodward Dream Cruise, and that their clients were special guests. He said she was welcome to bring some friends but avoided saying anything about her team. Hopefully that would be enough to get the shift to personal across. He hit "send" and stuffed his phone back into his pocket as he released a deep breath.

"So," Dr. Edwards said as he handed Khalil the prescription. "Did you invite her?"

Khalil nodded.

"And how do you feel? Having faced something you were nervous about but did anyway?"

Khalil ran his palms down his thighs.

"Anxious but good, I guess. It was a step."

"Right. Just keep taking them."

CHAPTER SEVEN

Khalil closed the industrial fridge, rubbing his hands together. "Thanks again, Mrs. Clayton," he said.

Turning from her desk, the older woman smiled back.

"Glad to help," she said. "Wasn't sure about this block party idea, but you're right, should drum up some business for all of us. Will your girlfriend be there tomorrow?"

Khalil hid his cringe. He hadn't corrected his neighbor at the Original Fade when she'd assumed that his sister-in-law was his girlfriend. Honesty was long overdue, especially for someone he thought of as his Detroit grandma.

"Actually, Mrs. Clayton, I . . . um . . ."

"Say no more, dear," she said. "If it isn't meant to be, it isn't meant to be. Handsome thing like you won't be single for long." She winked at him. "And don't worry, I'm done trying to push you and Audrey together."

He measured his exhale, not wanting to offend.

"Not good enough for her, huh?" he asked.

"Please. You know better." She stood. "Come on, let's see if Mo and Henry have been able to communicate."

Khalil didn't offer her his arm. He'd only needed to get thumped with her cane a half dozen times before he'd learned his lesson. Instead, he followed close, but not too close, out of the kitchen, through the front of the bakery, and out the door.

The Highland Park streetlights had come on, and he caught the distant grumble of his brother's voice down the street.

Mo and Henry were three shops away, disagreeing about the placement of one of the barrel barbecues Mo had forged for the party.

"You put it here and if there's a line, it'll flow onto the dance floor," Henry said. "I'd think a young man like yourself would want enough space to dance." Mo's arms remained crossed. He was the last Sarda brother to try to persuade with an argument about dancing.

"Easterly breeze tomorrow." Mo grunted.

"What does that have to do with anything?" Henry shrugged and caught his wife and Khalil approaching. "Khalil, help me out. Can't get Mo to see reason about this grill."

Shooting a quick frown at Mo, Khalil smiled at Mr. Clayton.

"Well, sir," Khalil said, "I'm guessing Mo's objection has something to do with smoke?" He looked at his brother. Mo nodded once.

"Smoke? All the grills are gonna smoke. Why should it matter?"

Mrs. Clayton made her way over to Mo. He immediately unfolded his arms and bent his lips at her. Khalil appreciated his brother's attempt at looking pleasant. Mrs. Clayton patted his arm.

"Mo, is my husband giving you a hard time?"

"Ma'am," he said. "The wind changes like it's supposed to; you won't have a break from the smoke."

"How? We'll be out in front of the shop, like everyone else," Mr. Clayton said.

"Your A/C," Mo said.

Khalil sighed. "If I understand," he said, "putting the grill any closer to the bakery means that the window unit in the office will pull in a lot more smoke. If we move it farther up the block, that should reduce the problem."

Mo rolled his eyes at Khalil with his perpetual exasperation at explanations.

"And Mrs. Clayton can take a break if she gets too hot," Mo said.

"Thank goodness you're looking out for me, Mo," she said,

squeezing his arm. "Henry, leave the boy alone. He knows what he's doing."

Henry frowned at his wife, then looked back at Mo. "Okay," he said, crossing his arms. "Where should it go?"

"Four feet, nine inches that way." Mo gestured up the street. "Smoke down that alley with no windows. The third grill, smaller, seven feet, two inches inside the barricade. Smoke collects behind Mama Paul's Daycare. Once the wind picks up tomorrow night and through Sunday, it'll clear by Monday."

"That's precise," Mr. Clayton said. "Did you measure it out? Get it on paper?"

Mo shook his head. "Don't need to."

"He doesn't need to," Khalil said.

"Henry, let the boys work in peace. I'm tired; it's time to go home." Mrs. Clayton gripped her cane a little tighter, reaching out for her husband. He joined her, glancing back at Mo over his shoulder.

"Sorry, Mo," Henry said. "Shoulda known you wouldn't be stubborn for no reason."

Mo shook his head. "No problem, sir."

Khalil turned to his brother. "You know, words are free. Doesn't cost extra to use more of them when you're trying to get your point across."

Mo scowled. "Doesn't cost *you*." He grunted, returning to the grill.

Khalil reached him in a couple of steps, and they worked together to get the grill into place.

Tired-wired wasn't Khalil's favorite state, but he tried to relax himself into accepting it. He tapped a quick goodbye on his horn, leaving Mo to spend the night in the Original Fade so he could keep an eye on his grill babies. Khalil felt obligated to spend the night with him, but Mo had made his decision and actually pulled rank as the oldest, sending Khalil to go sleep in his own bed.

After getting home, he showered and texted back and forth with

Darius, making sure everything was ready for the next day. After bringing up the instructions for the security team for the third time, Darius got annoyed and told him to go to bed too. Khalil didn't appreciate getting treated like a kid twice in the same night. It wasn't until he was standing in front of his closet, stuck between two shirts for the next day, that he recognized he wasn't acting like himself. He never thought twice about what he was going to wear, and he'd changed his mind four times already. He relented, facing what he was worried about.

Vanessa had thanked him for the invitation to the party, but she didn't say she was coming. She didn't say she wasn't either. That was a good sign. He opted for the olive linen button-down, closing his closet with a grin. He flicked off the light and got into bed, then his grin faltered.

What if she's bringing a guy? Maybe she has a boyfriend. The grin dissolved into a scowl. How had he not considered that possibility? A woman like her probably had a man in her life. He rolled his eyes at himself. *Of course she's seeing someone. Okay. Just be cool tomorrow. If she shows, that's great. And if she brings her man, that's great too.* But she hadn't given off the vibe that she was with someone. She'd even asked if he was single at the coffee shop. His thoughts wandered back to his conversation with Dr. E. He'd cleared a hurdle, getting to know Vanessa professionally over the course of the past few months. He was curious about Vanessa personally, interested. That showed progress; he should have been proud. And now it was more than that; he wanted to get to know her, but the possible rejection was a barrier. He'd met plenty of women who were curious about dating someone outside of their race, but he'd been scorned by plenty who refused to. Vanessa might fit into that latter category. And he was still working through some things—maybe she couldn't handle him or wouldn't want to try. A guy in therapy wasn't usually a big turn-on for women. It would be wise of him to be careful, not to put too many emotional eggs in one basket. He grabbed his phone and opened his mood tracking app. His finger hovered between "okay-ish" and "good." Just the thought of Vanessa would shift him into the "good" category. But the possibility that he might not be her type because of all his *stuff* tipped the balance more toward "okay-ish." He put the phone down. This was too much weight to be placing on someone he just found attractive. Maybe he could get some clarity the next day if she showed up. He balled up his pillow and pulled it against his chest, committing himself to some much-needed sleep.

CHAPTER EIGHT

T his is another benefit to a TWA," Vanessa said, watching Lisa's
mounting frustration with her hair.

She glanced at Vanessa in the mirror. "Teeny Weeny Afros are not
for everyone. There's a reason I keep my ears covered up."

"There's nothing wrong with your ears, other than the fact that
working to keep them covered is making us late." The block party
had started an hour earlier, and while Vanessa didn't want to show up
too early, she felt they were slipping into impolite territory. Lisa rolled
her eyes.

"Are you gonna make your excuses to the host? Perhaps leave a
calling card if he is indisposed upon our arrival? It's a block party,
Ness."

"It is. But we still have to get Bibi and drive across town."

"Okay, okay." Lisa dabbed two fingertips of holding gel on her
edges and washed her hands. "Let's go."

The party was in full swing when they arrived. The heat of the day
hadn't crested, and it took a moment to recover from the slap of it
once Vanessa opened her door. Then she and Bibi had to wait while
Lisa fussed with her hair in the side mirror.

"I thought we were here to check out Hottie Barber for Ness, not
try to catch him for ourselves," Bibi said, running an elegant hand
through her box braids. No matter how hard she tried, Vanessa knew

she could never capture the baba-cool of her bohemian cousin. Never rushed, never pressed, Bibi exuded a level of zen Vanessa aspired to. Maybe it was her willowy height. Vanessa nodded toward the party, and she and Bibi left Lisa behind.

Lisa sighed, catching up. "Of course we're here to check him out for her. But he has friends. You never know."

"True," Bibi said. "Hope he also has vegetarian options. I can smell death from here."

"You promised," Lisa said.

"I did. I'll keep my opinions to myself. As long as there's something I can eat."

The music drew them in, the rhythm from a band on stage at the far end of the block picking up, encouraging Vanessa to walk faster, even as she tried not to look too eager.

"I didn't expect live music," Bibi said.

"Me either. He was casual about it. I didn't anticipate all this."

The barricades blocking off the end of the street dripped with balloons and streamers, a riot of color that Vanessa would have found tacky, if not for the adult-sized poster beside the entryway.

"Welcome to the party, from the kids at Mama Paul's Daycare," Lisa read, smiling.

Getting closer, little handprints in a rainbow of colors were splattered all over, even on the black shirts of the security guards checking bags at the entrance. The two young men ahead of Vanessa handed one of the guards their tickets and her breath caught.

"We need tickets?" Lisa asked.

"I guess so," Vanessa said. "He didn't mention that."

She was next in line, so she plastered a cute smile on her face as she opened her clutch.

"Hi," she said to the guard. He flashed his teeth in what she guessed was a smile. "Do we need tickets?"

He nodded, glancing in her bag. "Unless you're on the list."

"Oh. Maybe we are."

"Name?"

"Vanessa Noble."

He checked a clipboard and nodded again. "Gotcha."

"Great," she said. "But I didn't know if my friends were coming. I doubt they're on your list."

The guard shook his head. "You're Khalil's guest. You can bring in as many people as you want."

Bibi smiled approvingly at Vanessa, and Lisa winked.

"Oh . . . that works out well," Vanessa said, impressed at Khalil's thoughtfulness. She thanked the guard and stepped through the barricade.

Laughter and shouting exploded out of a bounce house to the left. Vanessa, Lisa, and Bibi stopped short when a gaggle of excited children charged past to a water play area on the right. A group of older children took turns shooting hoops beside a booth for the Boys & Girls Club of Metro Detroit. Banners above thanked corporate and local sponsors, including the shops on the street and the Original Fade.

"Now, this is a block party," Lisa said. Vanessa nodded. Then something caught her eye. She nudged Bibi.

"Look."

"What?" She followed Vanessa's gaze. "Is it your man?"

"He's not my man. I meant the barbecue up ahead. Sign says it's vegetarian only."

Bibi grinned. "I like the way your man thinks, and I haven't even met him yet."

Vanessa sighed. "He is not my man."

Bibi shrugged. "Own business. MBA. Exceptionally attractive. That's most of the boxes on your list."

Vanessa glared at Lisa, who was feigning interest in a booth they were passing. They'd gotten deeper into the crowd; Vanessa stepped to the side to let a couple pass.

"You approve of The Basic Requirements now?"

"I can respect your attachment to something without approving of it," Bibi said. She looked over Vanessa's head at Lisa. "Come on, I'm starved." They linked arms and headed toward the vegetarian barbecue.

Vanessa's phone had already buzzed once as they'd been walking from the car, and now it was buzzing again. She stopped, letting Lisa and Bibi get ahead of her as she slid the phone out for a quick glance. She frowned. A client was asking a question she was pretty sure her team had already answered. Unlocking the phone, she started a quick reply.

"Why so stressed, Little Mama?"

She looked up from her phone, holding her breath against a waft of Black & Mild smoke. The man in front of her smiled, stepping closer into her personal space.

"What's the matter? I catch you by surprise?"

"I'm sure she's coming." Darius hid a smile behind his red Solo cup, sidling next to Khalil under the canopy in front of the Original Fade. Khalil finished his water, his attention on the passersby. The block party had been going for a couple hours, but he had yet to see Vanessa. And he didn't appreciate Darius's tone.

"Who?" he asked, facing the party again.

"Right, we'll just pretend you don't know who I'm talking about," Darius said. Two of their newest employees reached the canopy with their friends. Khalil and Darius took a few minutes to catch up, making sure that both young men knew they could reach out if they had anything on their minds.

"Fine, man," Khalil turned to Darius when they were alone again. "If she shows, do me a favor?"

"If who shows?" Darius teased as he cast his gaze over the party.

"Seriously?"

Darius waved to someone halfway down the street. He nodded at a young woman walking by. "Her?" he asked.

"Fine. If Vanessa shows, I need your help."

"Need me to tell her you think she's cute?" Darius fluttered his lashes.

"Cut that shit out, man," Khalil said. "And she's more than cute. She's clever."

"I mean, it's not like she doesn't know."

Khalil's hands got shaky as he swallowed against a wave of nerves. "Doesn't know what?" he asked.

"That she's cute. Even if she didn't, I'm pretty sure brother over there is tryna let her know." He nodded and Khalil followed his gaze.

And there she was. The sexy, intriguing App Goddess, talking to a man Khalil didn't recognize. His happiness at seeing her was tempered by her posture: one arm across her stomach, shoulders hunched. Her lips were tight together as she glanced over the man's shoulder. Khalil looked in the same direction and saw two women walking away, toward the veggie grill.

"I don't think she likes that guy," Khalil said.

Darius grunted. "Me either. You know him?"

"No." Khalil left the shade of the canopy, headed toward Vanessa, Darius beside him.

"I'll deal with him. What did you want me to do?" he asked Khalil.

The man caught Vanessa's wrist, and she pulled away. He got closer, and she jerked her arm down. Khalil smirked as the guy teetered off-balance.

"Let me know if I get weird."

"Get weird?" Darius asked.

"Yeah. She just . . . I don't know. Throws me off. I want to make sure she has a good time. It's important. But I don't want to hover over her either. If I'm hanging around her too much, come grab me or something, man."

Darius chuckled. "Since when do you worry about being too much?"

Since I had a fucking nervous breakdown, but you don't know about that.

"I'm just giving you shit," Darius said. "Don't worry about it. I doubt she's going to disappear."

"Huh?"

They were almost to her, and while he wanted to listen to Darius, Khalil was getting more and more annoyed by the man refusing to read Vanessa's signals.

"You don't see how she looks at you sometimes," Darius said.

Khalil lost his breath for a second but couldn't enjoy the thought; the guy was back in Vanessa's space again. Far too close.

"Hey, partner, y'all good?" Darius asked as they reached the man.

Relief washed over Vanessa's face before she schooled her features into cool and controlled.

"Hey." Khalil stepped to her side. "Glad you could make it."

Darius spoke directly to the guy across from her. "Time to call it a day, huh?"

"What? Nah, man, we're just getting started." He shot a look past Darius at Vanessa.

"Is he a friend of yours?" Khalil asked Vanessa.

"No. Yours?" She looked up at him with those doe eyes and he wanted to melt into a puddle.

"Nope. Wanna grab a bite with me?" He offered her his arm and couldn't help returning the smile that lit up her face.

"I'd love to." She slid her hand into the crook of his elbow, setting off little sparks across his skin. He was aware of Darius saying something to the guy as he and Vanessa left them behind, but he couldn't have cared any less what it was.

With her safely by his side, he led them into the thickening crowd. He caught sight of the two women again.

"Are those your friends?" he asked, nodding in the direction of the veggie grill.

Trying to see around the people ahead of them, she leaned to one side, then tugged on his arm as she strained upward. He tucked in a grin and glanced ahead.

"Erykah Badu with box braids and the curvy silk press," he said. She gave him a sly smile.

"Yes, but what do you know about box braids, Badu, and silk presses?" she asked.

"Hair is my specialty."

The crowd got even thicker and she started to pull away to let people pass between them, but he bent his elbow tighter, making sure she stayed close. He looked down at her again and couldn't help but return her smile. The party faded away. The music, the people bumping past, the smell of barbecue, the thousand and one details he had on his mind—everything dimmed. There was only Vanessa, and her smile, and her glance at his lips. His breath caught.

"Hey, Mr. S." Chris, his newest barber, stopped in front of them. Khalil tempered his frown. He hated being called "Mr."

"Oops. Forgot," Chris said. "Khalil."

"What's up, Chris, you good?"

"Yeah. Just wanted to say thanks, for earlier. Means a lot that you were willing to hear me out."

Khalil nodded, but talking to Chris again about his tension with Rod at the Original would have to wait. He didn't want any background drama to distract him from making sure Vanessa enjoyed the party.

"No problem, man," he said to Chris. "You got my number if you need anything else?"

"Yeah."

"Don't want to rush you off, but we're starved. You tried the smokehouse?" He gestured farther up the street.

"Not yet," Chris said. "I'll check it out. Thanks again."

"Sure thing."

Chris disappeared into the crowd and Khalil smiled at Vanessa, clearing his head of work stress and steering them up the line for the veggie grill until they'd almost reached her friends. Vanessa tugged on his arm.

"Everything okay?" she asked.

He shrugged. "No big deal. Do I get to meet your girls?"

Vanessa nodded and slipped her hand out of the crook of his arm.

"Nice leaving me behind," she said, touching her shorter friend on the shoulder.

The two women turned as one and looked at Vanessa for less than a second. Both immediately looked up at him. The taller one's eyes widened, but the shorter one went slack-jawed. Khalil's cheeks flashed hot and Vanessa cleared her throat.

"Bibi, Lisa, this is Khalil," Vanessa said. She turned to him. "Khalil, this is my best friend, Lisa, and my cousin Bibi."

"Great to meet you, ladies," he said, offering Bibi his hand, pretending not to notice Vanessa nudging Lisa.

"Thanks for having vegetarian options," Bibi said.

"Glad to have something for everyone," he said. "There's a new café opening up the block. They provided the food here, but they're also open today if you'd prefer to sit down."

"I'd like that," Bibi said. "Ness? Lisa?"

Khalil led the way. The trip was slow and winding due to the size of the crowd, and the people constantly stopping Khalil to congratulate him on the success of the party or to give him logistical details. By the time they reached the terrace in front of the café, Vanessa was pretty sure Khalil wasn't just a barber, or co-owner of the Fades.

"Girl," Lisa said under her breath as Khalil found them a table. "Your man is handling it! Think he's running this thing himself."

"He is not my man!" Vanessa hissed back.

"He wants to be," Bibi whispered.

"You can't know that," Vanessa said.

Lisa and Bibi exchanged a glance but smiled at Khalil when he returned with three menus.

"You're not going to join us?" Vanessa asked, accepting hers. He held her seat for her, and his smile was too gorgeous not to return.

"I'd love to, but I got a couple fires to put out." He squatted down beside Vanessa, lowering his voice. "The food is great here, but I have to recommend Mrs. Clayton's for dessert." They followed his nod to a stand farther up the street. An older black woman sat in the shade behind a bakery display case, laughing with a man who seemed to be her husband. She caught Khalil looking at her and waved. He smiled and waved back, Vanessa and the girls following suit.

"Anything we should try?" Vanessa asked.

"That's a tough call," he said. "I'm partial to her sweet potato pie and red velvet cake, but really—"

A boy jogged up to the table, his short locs bouncing.

"Hey, Khalil," he said. "Need your help."

Khalil stood, clearing his throat and tipping his head at Vanessa and her friends.

"Sorry," the boy said, looking at them. "Excuse me for interrupting."

"Ladies, this is Jalen," Khalil said.

"Hello, Jalen," they said in unison.

"How do you know Khalil?" Bibi asked.

"He used to be my big brother," Jalen said with a wide smile.

Lisa and Vanessa shared a quick glance, Bibi's attention remained on the boy, though she did raise an eyebrow.

"Sorry if I missed the family resemblance," she said.

Khalil smiled, resting a hand on Jalen's shoulder.

"Big Brothers Big Sisters," he said. "We were matched up a couple years ago. Still get to hang out."

"Oh," Lisa said. "I noticed the booth when we came in. You volunteer with them?"

Khalil nodded. "Jalen," he said. "These are some friends of mine. Vanessa, Lisa, and Bibi. Was there something you needed?" he asked him.

"Nice to meet you ladies," Jalen said. He turned to Khalil. "Mo told me to come find you."

"Did he say why?"

Jalen's forehead scrunched up.

Khalil laughed. "Sorry. Tell him I'll be right there."

"'Kay." He turned to go.

"Jalen!"

The boy turned around and Khalil frowned, nodding toward Vanessa and her friends again.

"'Scuse me," Jalen said. "Goodbye, ladies. Have a nice day." He smiled and waved.

"Goodbye, Jalen," Vanessa, Lisa, and Bibi said in unison.

Khalil smiled at the women. "Better go. My brother is great with metal—he forged all the grills for today with the Folk Arts foundation—but he's not so great with people. I'll come back and check on you in a little while?"

"Don't worry about us, Khalil," Vanessa said. "Take care of whatever you need to; we'll be fine."

"Thanks." He winked at her as he jogged away.

"Well . . ." Bibi unfolded her menu, scanning the contents.

"Well, well, well," Lisa echoed.

Vanessa narrowed her eyes at her friends, snapping her menu open.

"Go on, get it off your chests," she said.

"He's a fan of sweet potato pie," Bibi said, perusing her menu.

"And red velvet cake," Lisa said.

Vanessa shrugged. "Lots of people like those things."

"That's true," Bibi said.

Vanessa nodded.

"Big Brothers Big Sisters," Bibi said. "Quite a commitment on Khalil's part."

"It is. And he's gonna come back and check on us," Lisa said. "Even though he has his hands full. Think I'll try the chicken and quinoa salad."

"Sounds good," Bibi said. "I should go for something light. So I'll have enough room to try that sweet potato pie he suggested while giving Vanessa the puppy dog eyes."

Vanessa scowled at her menu, refusing to rise to the bait. She'd process and appreciate how sweet he was in her own time. But she couldn't help being impressed right then that he would take a young person under his wing like that.

"You know, that's a good idea," Lisa said. "This tropical salad also looks good. But I'm not a fan of papaya."

A passing waitress overheard Lisa and stopped.

"We can take the papaya out," she said.

"You don't mind?"

"Not at all," she said. "Khalil said to make sure that you all get whatever you want. And he already took care of the check."

Lisa and Bibi's heads swiveled to Vanessa, grins a mile wide.

"Did he now?" asked Bibi.

"Yes, ma'am," the waitress said before returning to her duties.

Vanessa's face caught fire.

"Last time a man paid for me and my friends, well . . . he was trying to be my man," Lisa said.

"Me too," Bibi said. "Interesting."

As promised, Khalil came by to check on Vanessa, Lisa, and Bibi twice during their meal. Vanessa wanted to express her appreciation for him covering the check, but he'd been with another person each time, and she didn't know if he wanted to share that detail with just anyone. The meal even met Bibi's high standards, so much so that she broached the idea of coming back across town to eat there in the future. Vanessa felt the same but was more curious about Mrs. Clayton across the street. The older woman had caught her eye several times, especially after Khalil's brief visits.

"Don't know that I can eat red velvet right now," Lisa said as they crossed the street, fanning herself. "But I'm curious."

"Me too," said Vanessa.

The Clayton Family Bakery itself was closed, but the proprietors manned two large refrigerated cases at the edge of the street under a canopy. Unfortunately for Lisa, there were only crumbs left behind a tag marked "Red Velvet Cupcakes." Bibi frowned at a large metal baking dish that had only half a serving of banana pudding left. As Mrs. Clayton doled out cookies to a raucous group of boys ahead of them, Vanessa wondered if there'd be anything left. The boys rushed off, thanking Mrs. Clayton through full mouths.

"Henry!" Mrs. Clayton called over her shoulder. "They're here!"

Vanessa and her friends looked at one another, then around. They were the only patrons nearby.

"Come on, come on," Mrs. Clayton waved them closer. "I hadn't anticipated quite so much demand today. Hid a stash in the back for you."

"For us, ma'am?" Bibi asked.

"You're Khalil's friends, aren't you?"

"Yes, ma'am," Vanessa said.

"Good." Mrs. Clayton smiled and stood, leaning on her cane. "Henry! Where are you?"

The older man Vanessa had noticed before backed out of the bakery's glass door, a heavy catering pan in his hands. He returned Vanessa's smile, then turned to his wife.

"I am right here, woman. Wasn't sure what to bring, so I got them all." He put the pan on the table and slid the cover off. "We've got red velvet cupcakes, cookies, some zucchini bread, banana pudding. What's your pleasure, ladies?"

Vanessa and Lisa took a cupcake each, Bibi opting for a small bowl of pudding.

Mrs. Clayton put the rest of the treats into two bakery boxes, and Mr. Clayton tied them closed.

"I'll keep them right here until you're ready to go," she said, returning to her seat.

"That's very kind of you, but we couldn't take all that," Vanessa said. "I'm sure there are other customers who'd love them."

Mrs. Clayton shrugged. "That may be. But Khalil wanted them set aside for you." The crinkles around her eyes spread along with her smile. She readjusted herself on her seat, gripping the purple sphere at the top of her cane. "The Khalil Sarda treatment," she said.

"Ma'am?" Lisa asked.

"You girls aren't blind. Khalil is quite the looker. But he's also a gentleman. After he and his last girlfriend broke up, she was sniffin' after him for months, moping about it. Who wouldn't be? She said the whole time they were together she never touched a door handle or her own seat, never walked anywhere by herself if she didn't want to, and never, ever paid for anything. Very little gallantry left like that nowadays. All her friends were green with envy. One even tried to steal Khalil for herself, but he wasn't having it. Caused quite a ruckus, but I only found out about all the drama when I went to the salon. When Khalil is with a young lady, she's the center of his world."

She was quiet until Vanessa looked up.

"If I were forty years younger, I'd give you a run for your money," she said, looking her in the eye.

"I'm still here, Yvonne," Henry called out from the alley beside the bakery.

"Don't I know it," Mrs. Clayton said.

"Vanessa's sure Khalil doesn't like her like that," Lisa said, ignoring Vanessa's glare.

Mrs. Clayton snorted. "He spent the whole day making sure this party was a success, spent time with friends, people I know he enjoys being with. But he didn't crack a genuine smile until I saw you all sitting down for lunch over yonder." She nodded in the direction of the restaurant. "When he was squatting down talking to you."

"Oh," Vanessa said.

"And he made me promise to give you the last of my red velvet cupcakes, the ones he knows I set aside 'specially for him. Knew you had to be someone special because when he comes by he mopes around all sad until I make him some."

"Glad you made it," Khalil said, walking her back to her car several hours later.

"Thanks for inviting us. And sorry if we monopolized your time." She glanced back over her shoulder, watching her friends return to the party for the baked goods from Mrs. Clayton. Bibi had Lisa return with her to "help" when Khalil offered to walk them to Vanessa's car.

"No reason to apologize," he said. "I can think of much worse ways to spend an evening." His grin was adorable: a little friendlier than she was used to, in a sweet and shy way. "I hope *I* didn't monopolize *your* time too much."

She paused before answering, not sure if he was teasing her or genuinely concerned that she wouldn't want to spend time around him. Her hesitation lasted long enough that they were at her car before she'd decided what to say. She changed course.

"I've been thinking about something you said at the coffee shop that time—not being accepted where you're comfortable," she said. "That hasn't been a challenge for you here?" She unlocked her door and he opened it for her. She leaned against the back passenger door, not wanting to sit while he was still standing.

He smiled again, broad and kind. Then he shrugged.

"There was a difficult period and I had to prove myself, but since then it's been cool. I . . ." He looked away. A flash of sad went over his features.

"What happened?" She jumped at the volume of her own voice. "Sorry, that's none of my business."

He looked back at her, the corners of his eyes crinkling, then gave her a sad smile.

"It's okay. Can I share something? Don't want to be a downer, but I think you might get it."

"I'm all ears," she said.

"Like I mentioned before, there were a lot of people who had no problem letting me know that I didn't belong at Morehouse."

She nodded.

"But there were also . . . others . . . who let me feel more than welcome."

She wasn't sure she followed.

"Um . . ." he said, shoving his hands in his pockets. "Women. Well, Spelman and Clark women."

"Ah."

"And naturally, I appreciated the attention at first. But around mid-sophomore year I caught on that it was less about me as a person and more about me as an experiment. As something to 'try.' And that felt—"

"Horrible," Vanessa finished for him. "Objectifying."

He nodded. "Still feel like I sound self-centered, though. I'm not holding a grudge from years ago. Just kind of pulled back, focused on school, kept to myself. It was easier to stay single, hang with my frat brothers, rather than feel like I was a thing."

"What fraternity?"

"Phi Beta Sigma," he said.

She didn't cover her surprise.

"What?" he asked, teasing smile in place. "I can't be a Sigma?"

Shaking her head, she smiled back.

"I'm just surprised is all. Didn't expect you to be in the Divine Nine."

"I get it," he said. "Don't exactly look the part."

She squirmed, wanting to probe but nervous about how he'd feel.

"Does that ever bother you?" she asked.

He turned to face her, resting his arm on the roof of her car.

"Does what ever bother me?"

"Being the only one in the room? I think I saw four other white people in the crowd today. Your work keeps you surrounded by a variety of different people, different races. And Morehouse? You eventually got comfortable, felt like you belonged. But do you feel out of place sometimes?"

A half-frown pulled his lips to the side. She kicked herself.

"Don't answer," she said. Her cheeks burned and she clasped her face to cover them up. "I'm treating you exactly the way I hate to be treated—people asking me if I belong where I am. I'm sorry."

"Don't apologize," he said. "I like that you want to know more about me, how I see things. The most uncomfortable part is the time it takes some people to accept me, to stop acting like I'm encroaching, don't belong. No matter what you do or enjoy or like, there's always going to be someone with a problem with it, you know? But this is who I am, where I feel at home. So what if I am the only one in the room? Being accepted may not happen right away, but I just turn on my natural charm and eventually everyone loves me." He winked and she smiled, shaking her head.

"You do have a lot of charm," she said.

He looked down a moment, blushing.

"I'm glad you think so."

She wanted to touch him. Reach out a hand and caress his arm, just for that contact, that understanding. But she kept her hands to herself.

"Back to what you said about objectification. I've had more than one guy make me feel that way," she said. "Like being with a black woman was an experiment to try. Something on his bucket list."

He chuckled. "I feel you. Even after college, I found myself on too many dates with women who were 'always curious.' Don't get me wrong, I love black women." His eyes bugged out and he sealed his lips together. "Sorry. That sounded exactly like what I'm complaining about."

She gave him a playful nudge.

"Don't worry about it," she said. "I'm sure the feeling's mutual." Then it was her turn to seal her lips out of embarrassment.

His cheeks flushed then he glanced back at her, an eyebrow arched.

"You think so?" he asked.

She let out a slow breath, heat flashing thick over her skin.

"Do you . . . Have you dated many black women? Since school, I mean," she said.

"Yeah. My most recent ex was black. I'm sure part of it's just my social circles, who I hang with. But also . . . I don't know. We clicked. Genuinely. Right from the start."

"It wasn't a challenge for you? No cultural differences?"

"Cultural differences?" He shrugged. "What do you mean?"

She didn't know what to do with her hands. If her dress had had pockets, she would have slid them in. Instead, she smoothed the fabric along her thighs.

"Well, like, I don't know what she did for a living, but how could you understand the frustration that comes with having to balance being seen as an 'angry black woman' when she was just trying to defend her ideas at work? Or having her skin color trigger all sorts of assumptions even before she could show who she is? Those are common experiences for any black woman and it's just confusing to me how you could understand."

"I can only understand a little. I know what it's like being the only one in the room and having people be wary of you or making sure you get the impression that your ideas shouldn't have space. But the intersection of being both a woman and black? Of course there's no way I can truly get that. I can respond with as much empathy as possible, though. I imagine it's been difficult for you at work. Especially in such a male-dominated field. But have I ever experienced having to prove myself again and again in that way? No. Like I said that day at the coffee shop, by junior year I didn't have to worry about that anymore. And now that I've proven myself to just be Khalil, not the weird-ass white guy trying to prove something, things have been pretty smooth sailing as an adult."

Vanessa tried to take it all in, to understand how his experience of being the other was similar to her own.

"Have you ever dated women who aren't black?" Vanessa asked. She hoped he wasn't rejecting all other women out of some internalized racism against himself.

"My first girlfriend was Algerian American, like my mom," he said. "Granted, we were only in high school, but our families knew each other. My parents supported us, but it wasn't like we were getting married. High school, you know? And my girlfriend before last was white. We were together for a while. But it wasn't meant to be. We had a lot of fun together." He looked down and chuckled, then shook his head. "I'd thought she might have been the one, but she wanted to travel, and I wanted to start the Fades. We just weren't on the same page. Learned a lot from each other, though."

Vanessa wanted to learn more, but she already felt like she was interrogating him. Didn't think it was polite to pry.

"I guess we have a lot in common, then," she said.

He smiled, turning a little toward her, his side against her car.

"I think we—"

"Hey, Ness!" Lisa called from far down the road. "Got the desserts!"

She and Bibi held up a bakery box each. Vanessa laughed and Khalil smiled.

"Guess they're giving us a heads-up," he said.

"Guess so." She cleared her throat, stepping closer to her still-open door. "Thank you again. I had a great time and you've given me a lot to think about," she said, taking her seat. He pressed her door closed. She started the engine and rolled down the window. Lisa and Bibi were almost there. "Khalil?" she asked.

He leaned down.

"Yes?"

"I'm sorry that happened to you. The feeling of being an experiment to try." She gave in and let herself touch him, laying a hand across his on the window frame. "I really understand how it feels." After a quick squeeze she let go, trying to ignore a wave of tingles in her fingers.

"I'm sorry too," he whispered. "That you know how it feels to be treated as different." He stood and took a step back as Lisa and Bibi arrived. "Thanks for coming," he said, loudly enough for her friends to hear. "Lisa, Bibi, it was nice meeting you."

"You too, Khalil," they said in unison.

"See you in two weeks?" Vanessa asked him, getting her car in gear.

"Looking forward to it." He stepped back and waved as they drove away.

CHAPTER NINE

Khalil could admit when he was wrong. He'd thought Darius was far too optimistic about the block party, but looking at the bottom line on his spreadsheet, the end result was much closer to Darius's estimation than his own.

"All right man," he said, leaning back from his desk. "You were right. I was wrong."

Darius smacked his lips together at the other end of the line.

"Never gets old," he said.

"Yeah, yeah. Still wanna see if we can sell the last grill. Don't want Mo to walk away with a loss."

"Thought Jamar called you. He wants it. I'll send you his number."

"Perfect," Khalil said. "You think we're good at the Original? I still have the feeling things are tense among the staff."

"I'll swing by tomorrow. Now about the actual party, you still haven't told me how things went with your girlfriend."

Khalil tugged at his collar.

"She's not my girlfriend." He turned off his desktop, scooting the receipts and invoices back into their folder. Switching off his desk lamp, he headed into the kitchen.

"Not yet," Darius said.

"Don't. I'm not even sure she's interested."

Darius's silence made Khalil pull the phone away from his ear to check they hadn't been cut off.

"You still there?" he asked.

"Uh, yeah. I'm just tryna figure out since when you aren't sure if a woman is interested in you. Especially with the way you two were practically holding hands as you walked her back to her car."

Khalil frowned, both at the dishes in his kitchen sink and the fact that Darius had been watching.

"Do we have to talk about this?"

"I think we should. Where'd Khalil the Player go? That guy's kind of an asshole, but he is my best friend, so . . ."

"I have never been a player." *And Vanessa's got me acting like Khalil the Nervous.*

"Nah, you just got women throwing their panties at you since freshman year. And since when is that a bad thing?"

Khalil thought about turning on the water and getting to the dishes if only to shut Darius up, but he knew he'd call back later, so he sat on the couch. "Look, chief, you know this isn't gonna go well."

"Maybe not, but it's gonna go."

"Fine," Khalil sighed. "When have I ever done a woman wrong?"

"From her perspective or yours?"

"Seriously?"

He was pretty sure Darius was only giving him a hard time, but it nagged at him. Sure, when they were in college Khalil had made a lot of mistakes, breaking hearts and getting his own broken.

"I've never intentionally played anyone," Khalil said. After nearly a year, he was . . . out of practice? That was all. This particular woman had him blushing and acting like a kid again because he'd been on the sidelines for too long.

"You're right. You've always done your best to come correct," Darius said. "Everyone knows that. But what's the deal right now? Am I crazy? You *are* into Vanessa, right?"

He let himself think about her and his smile bloomed on its own. He hadn't forgotten a single detail of how she'd looked at the party— her smile, the way her earrings sparkled and danced, the bright teal dress that contrasted so well with the radiant depth of her skin. He'd meant to tell her that she was beautiful, but then he'd gotten all shy and couldn't do it. He rolled his eyes at himself, then let them close, flipping through the catalog of Vanessa images he'd created since the day she'd walked into the shop.

"Yeah," he said, not keeping his smile in check. "I'm into Vanessa."

"From the outside looking in, she's into you," Darius said. "So what's the problem?"

"Dunno," Khalil said. As much as he wanted to, he couldn't say it out loud. He mentally repeated what he'd learned from Dr. E. Even if Nia had thought he wasn't a real man because he couldn't control his emotions sometimes, that didn't mean another woman would see it the same way. But how could he know? His old confidence was gone. He had no idea how to get it back.

Darius sighed. "All right man. I was talking to the rest of the boys, looks like Thursday nights are the best for practice, and everyone's clearing their Saturdays for games. Spoke with Carol from the League and our team is set to go. We can get Joel and Pax to cover for us on the Saturdays we play."

Khalil sat up. "Shit."

"What shit?" Darius asked.

"I forgot."

The familiar creak of one of Darius's kitchen cabinets echoed through the receiver, followed by the sound of a bag being torn open.

"What did you forget?" Darius asked, crunching.

"About the team."

Darius stopped crunching.

"What do you mean you forgot about the team?"

Khalil ran a hand down his face, leaning over to rest his elbow on his knee.

"Not for Revitalize Detroit, don't worry. I'm not gonna back out on a charity event. I just forgot that we were doing something long term." He sighed. "How long is the season again?"

"I'm sorry," Darius said, voice loud. "But who the fuck am I talking to?"

"Darius, seriously, listen—"

"No. You listen. You've spent the better part of the last two years bitching about not being able to play ball anymore. Which made sense 'cause we both agreed it was wiser to make the shops the focus, and it's worked out for the best."

"Yes," Khalil said. "Completely agreed."

"And you were all hyped about putting a team together for Revitalize Detroit and doing something for the community, while getting back to the sport you love."

"Yep, that was me."

"And now that we got this team together, and you convinced us all to keep going after the charity event, to play a season for the Hoops League, now you forgot?"

Khalil sighed. He didn't know what to say. Darius was right. He'd been thrilled to start playing again. Particularly now that the shops required less attention. But the thought of weekly practices and games . . . he just didn't have the energy.

"You're not going to say anything?" Darius asked.

"I don't know what to say!" He wanted to elaborate, but nothing he was comfortable saying had the right meaning. "I'm . . . I dunno." He shook himself. "Course I'm gonna do it. Just feels like a lot going forward."

Darius crunched some more, then sighed.

"Listen, man, I gotta go. Gotta pick my dad up from the clinic."

Khalil's heart lurched.

"Do you know when you'll get the results back?"

"Next week. Meantime the geezer's pissing us all off. He's sure nothing's wrong, but Mom's certain there's a problem."

"Give him my best?" Khalil asked.

"Will do." Darius took a deep breath. "You're sure about ball? You were all excited about it before. But we still have time to back out."

"Nah, nah, you're right. I wanna do it. Got sidetracked with focusing on the block party. That's all."

"All right. Got me wondering about you, man."

"Wondering?" He picked up the TV remote, spinning it in his free hand.

"This hesitation with a girl you're into. Never seen you not sure with a woman before. And now ball? Forgetting about an entire season? Especially since you've gone so long without doing something you love?" A sad laugh escaped him. "Maybe that's the problem."

Khalil frowned. "What?"

"Been too long for two of the things you love—basketball and women. Maybe you're getting old and rusty."

Khalil rolled his eyes. "Go get your dad, Dare. Before I have to come over there and kick your ass."

"Aight, man. Later."

Khalil hung up and placed his phone on the coffee table. His dryer beeped from the laundry room. And the dishes were still in the sink. As much as he needed things in their place, he was good on the couch, not in the mood to deal with all that right then. He leaned back, flicking on the TV, flipping mindlessly through the channels. Women and basketball. So, Darius had a point. He wasn't acting like himself. In the past, he'd have never walked a woman to her car without asking for her number. Technically he already had it in the client info file at the shop, but he wouldn't use it without her permission.

Khalil clicked through some movie options, but nothing caught his eye. He'd been young and stupid in the past, moving forward with the assumption that a girl who looked at him twice was obviously interested. Maybe this new hesitation was a sign of becoming more mature. He settled on ESPN as they went to commercial.

And the ball situation? He stretched out, ankles crossed on the armrest, arms crossed at his chest. His couch, his room, his apartment? Much more appealing.

CHAPTER TEN

Even if it was for charity, Khalil was playing for bragging rights. Getting into a locker room, the smell of hard work, the rubber of basketballs, soap and steam from the showers, and he was back in his element, back when the recruiters had been circling. And it felt damn good. He and Darius had also donated funds and free haircuts, but Khalil was going to wipe the floor with the opposing team. It had been far too long since he'd played with anyone other than friends, and after the practice sessions over the past week, he needed to see if he still had it.

Walking out of the locker room and into the gymnasium, Darius rolled his eyes at Khalil's contagious, frenetic energy. "Dude, I'm thrilled you're excited," Darius said. "But can you please remember that we're here to raise money and to make sure that the Fades look good?"

"Can you please stop nagging?" Khalil asked. "I hear you; I know. But if that's all there is to this, we shoulda written a bigger check and you could have spent your Saturday afternoon on your couch watching replays of real games. I'mma play, and I'mma win."

"'Lil. Please. Winning isn't the most important—"

"Says the losers." Khalil scooped a ball off the floor and chucked it at him.

Darius caught it and began to dribble, shaking his head.

"This is not gonna end well."

Darius was only half right. The game against the owners of a local sporting goods store ended quite well for their team: 78 to 50. Darius twisted his ankle and had to be helped off the court, but not before they'd shown off some of their college moves. Khalil's dunks drew cheers from the crowd, each one attracting more attention from the other events at the Coleman A. Young Community Center's Revitalize Detroit weekend. Once the game was over, Khalil was covered in sweat, buzzing with adrenaline, and elated with his team.

Smiling and ribbing each other, both teams shook hands and then participated in a post-game event. Accepting a towel and giving Darius an arm to lean on, Khalil helped him into a mock press area. The community center had elementary school students interested in journalism interview the players after the game. Getting Darius into a chair, Khalil was blindsided by a little girl.

"Ewww! Uncle Khalil! You're all sweaty," Madison said, jumping away before he could hug her back.

"Oh, am I?" He made a show of looking down at himself. "Hadn't noticed." Then he whipped off his shirt and mussed her hair with it.

"Oh my God!" she shrieked. "Gross!" She started laughing and Khalil joined in.

"Okay, Maddie. Maybe you're right. A little bit gross. Darius is less gross; why don't you interview him?"

"Hey, clever lady," Darius said. "Hit me with your best shot."

Smiling, Khalil stood and stepped back to let Madison get closer and start her list of questions. He felt eyes on him, so he turned and got slammed by a burst of adrenaline.

Vanessa was on the other side of the room, looking at him.

She crooked an eyebrow and waved. He waved back, extremely aware of being naked from the waist up. She began making her way toward him, her path uneven and slow as there were people milling all over the place. The game had just ended, and he hadn't showered. Madison was right—he was sweaty and probably reeked. He looked down at the balled-up shirt in his hands. It would be weird if he put it back on. But what did it matter? There were other players with their shirts off; why was he making it a thing? He glanced back up; she was almost to him. The towel was still in his hand. He draped it over his shoulders. That was less weird, right? He hoped to God that the advertising claims of his deodorant were true and that he had another twelve hours before he was no longer fit to be around people with working noses.

"Hey," he said.

"Hey." She slid one hand into the back pocket of her jeans, the other tucking a folder against her side. "Nice game."

"You watched?" He didn't give in to the urge to look her up and down, to see if she was wearing another pair of sexy heels. She was holding her head a little funny too. Like she was trying not to look *him* up and down.

"Yeah," she said. "Hadn't planned on it, but the crowd kept going wild. I wanted to see what the excitement was about."

He laughed and wiped his brow.

"So, barber by day, basketball superstar by night?" she asked.

Normally, he wouldn't have hesitated. He would have humble-bragged, complimented her, said something flirty. But Vanessa messed him up, sent out some vibe that was positive but warped his game. At the shop, he'd taken his lack of flirting as a sign that he'd gained some degree of professionalism. At the café and the block party he'd been awkward. But now, they were not at work, he was half naked, she'd just told him he'd impressed her on the court, and he had no idea what to say.

"Um." He shrugged, smiling. "I guess. We have a good team. And . . . um, it's for a good cause, right?"

WHO am I right now?

"It is a good cause," she said. And she looked. So fast, he almost missed it. Her gaze shot down his chest, over his bare stomach, then back up to his eyes. Her bottom lip tucked in a tiny bit, like she was biting the inside. She glanced at the doorway; he didn't want her to go.

"What brings you here?" he asked.

"The community center invited me. A bunch of us, actually. Women in STEM. A short presentation for the kids, then Q&A."

"That's cool," he said. "It's um . . . good to see you." She smiled and he stalled out again. He was losing his mind.

"Uncle Khalil!" Madison was next to him, pulling on his hand. "Darius sent me over to interview you. He said you need rescuing."

Khalil glared over his shoulder at Darius, who was pretending to examine something on the back of his hand. He looked up, his smile barely under control, and waved at Vanessa.

"Hey!" he said to her. "How's it going?"

"Hey, Darius," Vanessa said. "Good game."

It was beyond stupid for Khalil to be as annoyed as he was by Vanessa smiling at Darius. He took a deep breath and squeezed Madison's hand.

"Thanks, Maddie. I'd love for you to interview me. Just give me a minute or two?"

"I won't keep you," Vanessa said. "We're gonna start in a couple minutes anyway." She smiled at Madison. "Uncle Khalil is all yours."

"Thanks!" Madison said and tugged at his hand again, pulling him away from Vanessa and toward two empty chairs.

"Hold on, Maddie?" he asked. "Vanessa? See you next week?"

"Yep!" she said, turning and slipping into the passing people as she headed for the next room. He couldn't get a good angle to check her out. But she moved like she was wearing those heels again, so he imagined that she was. He sat down with Madison, focusing on her as she carefully opened her notepad and arranged her list of questions on her lap. He chanced another glance at Vanessa, willing her to look back at him before she disappeared through the doorway. He was rewarded with her shy smile as she glanced back and caught him watching her.

Bye, she mouthed.

He winked and smiled back.

Welp. My presentation is fucked.

Vanessa stepped just inside the hallway, leaned against the wall, and took a breath. It had been bad enough when she'd ducked into the gym to see what all the cheering was about. She'd finally managed to be neutral about basketball, so she hadn't planned on watching the game. But she'd never heard a crowd react for a charity game as though they were watching the Final Four. She'd climbed up the side of the risers, expecting a surprise celebrity player. Instead, she caught sight of an Adonis zooming down the court and flying in the air to dunk. She lowered her gaze to check her footing before climbing down, then recognition clicked. And in spite of herself, she was back in high school again, and Tony was leading the team to victory. But his hair was the wrong color. Shaking her head hard, she snapped back into reality at the sight of Khalil's smile. He looked so happy, so clearly in his element. She'd stored some of the most impressive moments for private review later on, until they'd been obliterated by the sight of Khalil with no shirt on, joking with a little girl.

Stop being ridiculous.

She stood straight, shoulders back, and strode down the hall, to Rec Room Four where the STEM talk would take place. After greeting the organizers, she got into game mode: seat taken on the panel, water bottle opened, first sip taken so she wouldn't spill later on. She opened her folder and reread her talking points—they were few and brief. Kids this age had a good grasp on STEM—she wasn't there to teach them anything. Just let them know what she did and make herself available for any questions.

How could Khalil have gotten more attractive?

She chided herself for straying off topic. The woman beside her developed pharmaceuticals. Vanessa knew nothing about that. She turned to introduce herself, but the woman's phone rang before Vanessa could open her mouth. The seat on her other side was still empty.

His skin was glowing. Not sweaty. Warm, and soft looking, but so damned MALE with those lean cords of muscle underneath. The other players looked like they were half dead, but not Khalil. He could have gone another couple . . . Wonder how many rounds he can go?

Her whole body flashed hot, and she cleared her throat. This was no time to lose her focus. Especially not because some hot guy turned her head. She wouldn't allow herself to give these children less than her full attention. Especially the girls. They were the most important people she'd cross paths with that day; they needed to know that. Besides, this was just physical. Just a physical attraction. And that happened all the time. He was simply blessed with a scandalously beautiful face . . . and chest . . . and abs . . . and those V-lines . . . She snatched the water off the table. She took a sip.

Don't think about his V-lines.

Another sip.

Cannot think about his V-lines. Cannot think about . . . But he was kind. And humble, even though he was clearly a well-respected member of his community. He even met most of The Basic Requirements. And while he wasn't black, he had experience dating black women. If anything happened between them, she wouldn't have to be some sort of guide to a culture he wasn't familiar with. She took another, more measured sip. Maybe he was interested. But maybe he was just a flirt. Like at the party. And at his shop. He'd been friendly and kept her laughing, but just to get her to become a repeat customer. That was all it was. If he were really into her, he would have asked for her number already.

"So, I think that's it," the organizer of the STEM talk said. "Kids, let's have a big hand for our guests today." The children applauded, and Vanessa and her fellow participants thanked them. Everyone began to leave and then someone tapped Vanessa on her shoulder.

"Hi," the familiar little girl said.

Vanessa smiled. "Hi there; you're Madison, right?"

"Yep. Uncle Khalil asked me to give you this." She handed Vanessa a folded piece of paper.

"Hmm," Vanessa said. "Do you know what it says?"

"Nope." Madison looked everywhere but at Vanessa. "He made me promise not to look at it."

"Uh-huh," Vanessa said. "And why didn't your uncle bring it to me himself?"

"He waited for a little while, but he had to go," Madison said.

"Ah." Vanessa nodded and unfolded the note.

Hey, Vanessa. Remember the client info card you filled out? Mind if I use your number for personal reasons?—Khalil

Vanessa's cheeks warmed. She looked up at Madison.

"You want to be a journalist, Madison?"

"Yep!"

"You know, sometimes journalists have to keep their information a secret, right?"

"Uncle Khalil said that too!"

Vanessa chuckled. "Did he?"

"Uh-huh. Said I can't tell you he really hopes you say it's okay." She clapped a hand over her mouth. "I wasn't supposed to say that!"

"Don't worry," Vanessa said, smiling. "Here's the thing. I'm not going to say it's okay. I'm going to give you a different message."

"Okay. What is it?" Madison flipped to a blank page in her notebook and opened her pen. "I'm ready."

Vanessa smiled. And decided to jump. "Please tell him I wondered what was taking him so long."

Madison carefully formed each letter, then read Vanessa's message back. She paused, her brow furrowing.

"What if he doesn't get it?" she asked.

"Well, you wrote the message down perfectly. If he doesn't understand, he should have asked me himself, okay?"

"Okay." Madison shrugged. "See ya!" she said, then disappeared into the crowd.

CHAPTER ELEVEN

Vanessa hung up, tossing her phone in the middle of the folded stacks of clothes on her bed. She was disappointed by the developer's reaction but not surprised. He'd failed to provide the service, yet he'd argued *Vanessa* was being unfair by switching contractors. Knowing he'd accepted and completed major projects for two of the douchiest dudebros in her field—when he was supposed to be overloaded with work for her—made it clear that he'd shifted his loyalties elsewhere. At least she'd been able to enjoy his surprise at her knowledge that he'd accepted the other jobs. Guys like that consistently doubted her connections and clout.

Her phone started buzzing again as she refilled her moisturizer in the bathroom. She didn't rush to answer, not needing any more excuses. She decided to keep packing and deal with her phone later, but she took a quick glance when she returned to her bedroom. Missed call from a number she didn't recognize. Her lips bunched to the side, she waited for the notification of a voicemail, but it never came. Then her phone buzzed again with a text from the unknown number.

Hey, Vanessa, it's Khalil. I suck at voicemail.

Excitement sparkled all through her before she could check herself. She was too old to react this way because a boy had called her. She thought of stretching out on her bed, but she wouldn't be able to relax with all the clothes for her trip right next to her. A quick glance at the clock and she decided to give herself a fifteen-minute break. She went downstairs to the living room, curling herself into her love-seat.

"Hey," Khalil said when he picked up. "Thanks for calling me back. And for being cool with me calling in the first place."

Vanessa laughed. "How much choice did you give me? Sending Madison to ask if it was okay. Was I going to say no?"

His laughter was deep and warm.

"Didn't play fair, did I?" he asked.

"Not really," she said. "But it was a cute approach. I can give you points for that."

He laughed again, and she savored a hit of her new favorite drug.

"I'll take any points I can get. So what are you up to today?"

"Packing. Conferences and meetings in Dallas, then Charleston, then Houston."

"Wow. You travel a lot. Ever get lonely?"

The red KitchenAid blender on her counter caught her eye. The one she'd been so happy to buy but rarely had the chance to use. Along with the matching refrigerator that never had more than three days' worth of food in it.

"I do." Her answer came out with a soul-weary sigh. "Sorry," she said. "Don't mean to sound all maudlin. I'm fortunate to do some-thing I enjoy, even if it comes with challenging details."

"I don't think you sound maudlin. It sounds like you get tired of your grind sometimes," he said. "In other words, you're a normal human being."

"Thanks."

"Here's an idea. How about I go with you? You can take me along, in your pocket, and text or call me whenever you get lonely. Even if it's late."

She drew her knees into her chest. There was something woven all through the kindness and warmth in his tone, the light joking in his words: a gentle crackle of vulnerability that had her bending and folding into herself like slowly melting butter.

"That's really sweet, Khalil," she said.

"But too weird?" he asked, the vulnerability nudging its way to the fore.

"Not at all. It's one of the nicest things anyone has offered to do for me in longer than I can remember. I may take you up on that."

The little rush of a laugh he let out tipped her off to the fact that he'd been holding his breath, waiting for her answer. Mr. Kind and Charming was being so cute she thought she might die.

"Good. There is one thing, though. Something you have to promise me to cement this little arrangement," he said.

"Oh? What's that?"

"No one else gets to cut your hair, okay?"

She laughed. "That's it? That's all I have to do to have you at my beck and call whenever I'm lonely in a strange city?"

"Of course. Think I'm getting the better end of the bargain," he said. "I just have to answer the phone. You have to actually come to my shop."

"Hadn't thought of it that way. But I have a counterargument. Another clause to add before we sign off on this thing."

"What's that?"

"Communication is a two-way street. If I get to call you when I'm lonely, you get to call me."

She and Lisa had agreed to disagree that a person could hear another's smile on the phone. Lisa had been willing to back down on her position a little and say that what she was hearing was the change in pitch when a person speaks with a smile, rather than the smile itself, and Vanessa had agreed. But maybe she'd been wrong. Because right then, she could tell that Khalil's grin was a mile wide, even before he spoke.

"I think that is an excellent clause," he said. "I agree wholeheartedly."

"Then we have a deal." She hoped he could tell she was smiling too.

"Deal," he said.

CHAPTER TWELVE

Watching the Charleston airport grow smaller, Vanessa rubbed her temples, hoping her next stop would live up to its reputation for diversity. If "Southern hospitality" meant that she had to assert her right to be in certain spaces, despite the fact that she was one of the featured speakers of the conference with a reservation at one of the city's five-star hotels, she'd had her fill for a lifetime. It wasn't uncommon for her to have one of those experiences during a trip, but seven times in five days was a new record. She'd heard good things about Houston; hopefully it would live up to the hype of being a place where a black woman could just go about her daily life.

In her frustration after arriving, she'd almost reached out to Khalil again. But so far, they'd shared only a couple sweet texts and a few brief calls. She didn't want to get in touch only to complain.

As the HouSTEM Expo stretched from afternoon into evening, Vanessa's irritation melted away. She took advantage of her company's stand at the Expo, spending some one-on-one time with employees she rarely got to see. One of her interns had been eager to share some new ideas that Vanessa was happy to chew on for a while.

Sam Martin, the CEO of another app developing company, had stopped by in the morning to speak with Vanessa about how the planned evolution of one of her apps could dovetail with one of his. Another CIO had reached out through LinkedIn, hoping to have a discussion about the success of one of her projects in the European market.

After taking another stroll through the Expo herself, she spoke with the LinkedIn contact, agreeing to a coffee the following afternoon. Sam had suggested dinner at an exclusive restaurant. As much as she'd have loved to try out the nationally reputed chef, Vanessa didn't do dinner meetings. Too many of her male colleagues had blurred the line between professional and personal. It had given her a reputation as being aloof, but the rest of her public demeanor would have to be sufficient to counteract that. She did hesitate a moment, wondering if she'd gotten far enough in her field to be able to relax a few of her personal rules, but caution prevailed. She countered with drinks and Sam suggested a pub next to his hotel. Vanessa sniffed through a flutter of concern.

Awfully convenient, right next to his hotel. But maybe he doesn't know anywhere else.

She opted for a feminine yet serious outfit: the pants from a navy suit that fit at the waist but were wide legged enough to only give a hint of her hips and zero idea of her ass, and a crisp blue and white pinstriped button-down. Simple, straight silver earrings for a little motion and only her top two buttons undone. She was about to step out of the bathroom of her hotel when the half-carat engagement ring with the infinity band in her jewelry case caught her eye. The just-in-case gift from Ma-Max: protection against lecherous men and economic crises.

Haven't worn it in a while. Probably don't need to. But the last time I got invited to a professional dinner I kicked myself for leaving it behind. She slid it on.

As she stepped through the door of the pub, Vanessa recognized some of the other conference attendees. Nodding brief hellos, some of her concern dissipated. The place was well lit and busy. But after taking a quick lap past the bar and glancing around the high-top tables, she saw that Sam was nowhere in sight. She flipped open her clutch, her phone already alight with a message.

> Sam: Hey, had trouble finding a spot. I'm in a booth along the back wall.

A booth?

> Vanessa: Okay

She continued farther along the bar, behind a low wall that separated the area of the pub mostly for drinking from the one with sit-down tables to eat.

I said drinks, not dinner. That's minus one point, Sam.

She plastered a professional smile on her face as soon as she saw him at the second-to-last booth in the pub. She intentionally relaxed her forehead and the muscles around her eyes, refusing to let her annoyance show right away.

"Hey, Vanessa, thanks for coming. Listen." He leaned forward as soon as she slipped into the seat across from him. "I'm sorry about the seating. The bar was packed when I got here and there was a rowdy group watching the game on the big screens." He nodded in that direction, and she noticed that the televisions were focused on the area around the bar, not in their section. "I figured if we stayed over there, we'd have to yell to be heard. Hope you don't mind sitting here," Sam said.

He made a good point. And had a good reputation. She let it slide. "You're right," she said. "I'd rather not lose my voice."

A waitress appeared and Vanessa ordered a glass of Chardonnay to Sam's local craft beer. The waitress suggested a plate of loaded potato skins, and while Vanessa refused to let things last longer than a drink or two, she didn't think drinking on an empty stomach was wise. Sam went along with her choice.

Having come up in the industry at the same time, they knew a lot about each other's work. It was easy to keep the conversation rolling. Her wariness faded, and she was enjoying the chance to talk shop with someone who got it. Sam's phone lit up with several notifications while they were talking, but each time he simply glanced at his screen, then clicked it off without hesitation. Vanessa couldn't remember the last time she'd had a discussion with anyone her age who didn't at least excuse themselves to answer.

The waitress came by again, and both Vanessa and Sam ordered another drink. Sam had taken out his tablet to get Vanessa's read on some of the challenges he and his programmers were facing. Wiping her fingers on a napkin before reaching out to touch the screen, she caught Sam's glance at her ring out of the corner of her eye. She chose to ignore it, wanting to focus on her passion. Before she knew it, the potato skins were gone, but her stomach was rumbling.

"Listen," Sam said, letting his tablet rest on the table. "I know we said just drinks, but I'm starved, and I'd rather not stop talking now. It's nice to get the chance to really talk with someone who gets the industry and shares my perspective on how it could develop. Do you mind if we eat so we can keep talking?"

"I think that's an excellent idea," Vanessa said. "Good food, good conversation; it's rare to get."

Sam smiled. "Exactly."

The waitress returned and they ordered dinner. Sam opted for another beer, but Vanessa wanted to slow things down with a sparkling water. For a millisecond, she thought she caught a trace of disappointment cross Sam's features.

By the time dessert rolled around, they'd hammered out a tentative plan for dovetailing projects they had in the works. The din of the pub had changed—lights dimmed closer to the bar, music became more apt for dancing. Vanessa glanced at her watch, surprised at how late it had gotten. Sam noticed too.

"Woah," he said. "Guess this was a good working dinner. Didn't see the time pass."

"Me either. Great suggestion on your part," she said, catching the waitress's eye to ask for the bill.

"Mind if I cover it?" Sam asked. "Could use the business expense."

"Okay," Vanessa said. "But next time it's on me." The words were barely out of her mouth before she realized her mistake.

"Next time?" Sam asked, the friendly veneer slipping from his face.

Fuck. Thought this was clear.

"Yeah," she said, voice light. "I imagine we'll need another meeting or so to work through the details. Maybe lunch in my office the next time you're in Detroit." *Please just take it as that.*

Sam nodded. "Cool." He glanced away a moment, then back at her, his attention catching again on her left hand. She shifted the ring from underneath with the tip of her thumb. She caught the glint of the diamonds, and he must have as well. "There is one other thing," he said.

"Yes?" *Keep it professional, Sam. Please let's stay in safe, professional territory.*

"I've been wondering," he said. "Actually, a lot of us have been wondering."

The "us" caught her off guard.

"Wondering?" she asked.

"Yeah," he said. He looked down at his lap, then back up at her. "You keep a tight lid on your personal life. You know, 'on the down low.'"

She really could have done without the air quotes he tossed in, and the choice of words from a white man to a black woman.

Leaning back against the booth, she wrapped her hands together, resting them in her lap.

"'On the down low,'" she repeated.

"Like, maybe there's no point in asking, 'cause there's some chatter that men aren't your thing, but I've always wondered."

She took a steadying breath, letting the expletives flow silently.

"Well," she said. "I'm not exactly sure why anyone needs to wonder anything, but if there's been enough chatter that you feel comfortable asking, why don't I let you be the one to put things to rest? Yes, in fact, men are my thing. As my fiancé can attest."

"Fiancé?" Sam asked.

Vanessa congratulated herself on not slapping the surprise off his face.

"Fiancé? Wow. Had no idea," he said.

"Really, Sam? You've got me wondering why my relationship status is subject to discussion."

"Wait, no, don't take it like that. It's nothing bad," he said. "Well, it's kinda disappointing for me but good for you."

Vanessa promised herself that no matter what, this was the very last one-on-one evening invite she'd accept from a man in her field. Or even tangentially related to it.

"Why disappointing for you, Sam?" she asked, rubbing the bridge of her nose.

"Well," he said, shrugging. "Always wondered."

She arched an eyebrow.

"You know, about being with a black woman. Getting my swirl on."

She buried the sting before it could show. The layers of wrong in his words, and his assumption that she would be available for his curiosity, smothered her. There was no room for her to take a breath, let alone speak. How many times a year did they cross paths? She and Sam bumped into each other a lot. They had multiple business connections. Up until a few minutes ago, they were making plans to begin working together.

And he had to pull this shit, make her a thing, a toy for some game he felt entitled to play. He'd put her in the impossible position of having to say that there would never be anything other than business between them, and to magically say so without offending him. If he'd participated in the gossip and guessing about her sexual orientation, there was no way of knowing what he'd say if he walked away from the pub with his fee-fees hurt. Had it been anyone else, anywhere else, Sam would have already been drenched in her water. But she had an image and a company to protect. If she let out her anger, she'd be a stereotype before sunrise. She dredged up her very best protect-the-man's-ego smile.

"Well, Sam, I can understand wondering about a new experience. But I'm not the right person to help you." She shrugged and picked up her water for a sip.

"Guess the timing wasn't right," he said, pointlessly confident smile still in place. "Gotta admit, I'm a little envious of the lucky guy—what did you say his name was?"

For a hair's breadth, she thought about not giving him a name. She shouldn't have to embellish the lie. But would Sam believe her, let her walk away with some level of respect without a name? She seized the first one that came to her.

"Khalil," she said, taking another sip.

"Khalil. Cool, yeah. Makes sense," Sam said.

Vanessa raised an eyebrow.

"You're not into the swirl either, I guess. I can get that."

Sam kept hitting her with stacks of insults she wanted to address but couldn't digest. The ones taking up the most space in her mind were why he assumed that she would accept his advances, and that Khalil was Black. Why hadn't she anticipated that a white guy would make that assumption? Then the waitress was back, and Vanessa snatched the bill out of her hand.

"Excuse me," she said. "Sorry, just realized how late it is, and I really must be going." Vanessa got her credit card out and handed everything back before the waitress could speak.

"I thought this was on me," Sam said.

"Let me. I insist."

The waitress was already gone. Vanessa didn't want to wait.

"Listen, Sam. I gotta head to the ladies' room, so I'll grab the waitress and pay at the bar. We'll probably bump into each other tomorrow, right?" She was already sliding out of the booth.

"Uh . . . yeah. Sure," he said. "See you tomorrow."

The additional flip of the lock and the clink of the security bar on her hotel room door released the last bit of self-control keeping Vanessa's anger in check. She kicked off her shoes and let it out, stomping her feet and pounding her fists against an imaginary Sam and all of the other clueless, asinine men who assumed she would be receptive to their advances.

Why? Why did it have to go there? "Get my swirl on"? Her flails turned into shadowboxing and jumping up and down. She let herself work it all out, until she plopped onto the edge of her bed to catch her breath. Words cropped up unbidden:

"'Interracial dating' isn't wise. We aren't real to white men. They barely respect white women. That old plantation mentality of any black woman being available hasn't gone anywhere."

Vanessa rubbed her forehead, willing Ma-Max's admonitions down as she fell back onto the bed. It was the twenty-first century. Vanessa wasn't so sure that white women were better off when it came to some white guys. She knew plenty of stories of plenty of women who'd been punished in some way because they said no. She switched to rubbing her temples, yawning wide to relax her jaw.

Yeah, Sam was one of many. While she was disappointed, she wasn't surprised. But she refused to let this latest example prove Ma-Max right, even though he'd managed to hit almost every detail of her criticisms about how white men saw black women. Vanessa took a deep breath and decided to get some contradictory proof. Reaching for her clutch, she dumped the contents and grabbed her phone.

> Vanessa: Hey. Just a little apology. I found myself in an uncomfortable position, and the first fake fiancé name that came to mind was Khalil. Hope you don't mind.

She reread the first text he'd sent her, saying he sucked at voice-mail. It was sweet. He was so sweet. Then the others, asking if she'd had a safe flight, wishing her a good evening after a quick chat. She couldn't remember the last time she'd responded to a first text from someone with an immediate phone call. She was still pondering when the phone buzzed in her hand, jumping her back to the present.

> Khalil: First off, I'm sorry you needed a cock-block.
> But I don't mind being one for you at all.
> Vanessa: Thanks.
> Khalil: Feel like talking about it?
> Vanessa: It's been a productive day professionally but shitty personally. Don't want to call you to complain.

She waited a moment for his reply, then put her phone on the bedside table. Relaxing onto her back, she unbuttoned and unzipped her pants, staring blankly at the ceiling. Part of her thought she should fold her pants correctly over the little valet in the corner, but she didn't want to get up. She shimmied out of them and let them slide off the bed. Then her phone buzzed and she answered the call.

"Hey," Khalil said. The gentle depth of his voice loosened the knot between her shoulder blades. "I meant what I said before. You can call or text whenever you need to talk. And it sounds like you do."

She sighed. "Yeah."

"Then I'm here," he said. "What's wrong?"

She started from the beginning with a few brief anecdotes about uncomfortable situations she'd found herself in over the years, how she'd ended up with a personal rule about not being on her own in a meeting that could shift from business to personal. Partway through relaying that evening's experience, she paused.

"I must be boring you," she said.

"Why do you say that, Vanessa?" he asked. And she wondered how he managed to make her name sound so good.

"I'm going on and on, complaining. I don't want it to sound like I have a big head or anything. It's just that—"

"Guys can be assholes."

"I'm not painting all men with the same brush," she said.

"I know you're not," he said, a smile in his voice. "It's an objective fact. Trust me, I'm an expert."

She scooted up the bed, leaning against the headboard.

"Are you now?" She didn't hold back her own smile. "That's not the impression I get."

"No? Good," he said. "Means I'm getting better at concealing my dark side."

Vanessa's laughter caught her off guard.

"I find it very, very hard to believe that you have a dark side," she said.

"That's encouraging. But I can admit that I had a period of clueless selfishness when I was younger. I used to be way too cocky."

"Personal experience has taught me that the sexiest ones usually are the cockiest." Catching fire, she clamped her mouth shut for admitting too much. She needed to say something, fast. "That's why I've never taken sexy guys too seriously." *Shit!* She face-dove into the pillow next to her. That was even worse. She could almost taste her knee she'd shoved her foot so far down her throat. Not trusting herself with another word, she waited for his reply so she could find the words for an apology.

"Good thing I'm not very sexy, then," he said.

She sat up.

"Are you . . . There's one of two ways I could read that statement," she said.

"I'm listening."

"Well, on one hand, you've just told me that you're either blind or completely oblivious to your considerable sex appeal. On the other, it sounds like it's important to you that I take you seriously."

He chuckled. "I do want you to take me seriously, Vanessa. I hope you do. And concerning sex appeal, that's in the eye of the beholder. Different people find different features attractive. I can't go around making assumptions."

She rolled her eyes, sitting up to unbutton her shirt.

"Okay, Khalil. We'll pretend you don't know that you're pretty damn sexy. Like you didn't catch Lisa's jaw hit the ground when she met you. For the record, I do take you seriously. Didn't mean to give you the impression that I don't." She paused, wriggling out of her long sleeves and tossing the shirt on the floor with the pants. "I'm very discriminating when it comes to my fake fiancés. I don't go around pretending to marry just anybody."

"What are you doing?" he asked. There was a rumble of heat in his voice that sent a shiver over her skin.

"Um . . ." She swallowed against a dry throat. "Getting ready for bed."

"Ah," he said. She heard some shifting, a grunt of effort on his end. "I don't want to be that guy, but I am wondering what you're wearing right now."

Vanessa let out a slow breath. She hadn't anticipated that turn in the conversation. She really wanted to follow it. She headed for the bathroom.

"We're at a crossroads in this phone call, then," she said, flicking on the light.

"That we are," he said.

"First, tell me where you are," she said.

"Stretched out on my bed."

She checked the clock on her phone. It had been late when she'd gotten back, and they'd been on the phone longer than she'd realized.

"You said you're an early riser. Am I keeping you from getting to sleep?" she asked.

He chuckled, short and deep.

"You usually keep me from getting to sleep right away, Vanessa. Whether we're on the phone or not."

Her "oh" slipped out like a puff of smoke. She moistened her lips. "Haven't gotten into my pajamas yet," she said.

"No?"

"I started getting undressed right before I texted you." She unsnapped her toiletry kit and rolled it open.

"Oh," he said.

"I'd just kicked off my slacks when you called."

"I see," he said.

"I was getting out of my blouse when you asked what I was doing." She fiddled with her toothbrush.

He sucked a quick breath between his teeth. His voice was low, but soothingly calm when he spoke again. "You don't have to tell me any more, Vanessa. Sorry if it was weird to ask; I was just curious."

"I like that you were curious," she said. And she got rewarded by hearing his smile again.

"You've already had to deal with one skeezy guy today. I don't want to add to the list. Though . . ."

She reached behind her and unhooked her bra, the effort shading her voice.

"Though what?" she asked.

"I can admit that I'm kind of jealous of Mr. Skeezy."

"Jealous? Why?"

"'Cause he got to eat with you, sit across from you tonight."

Vanessa's heart dropped.

"Khalil," she said. "What a sweet thing to say."

"Not weird?" he asked.

"Not at all." She ran a fingertip along the edge of the sink. "And you're the farthest from skeezy I can imagine," she said. "Promise not to judge me for what I'm about to say? Think I'm a little too forward?"

"Promise," he said.

"I don't sleep with a bra on, so I just got rid of that."

He groaned deep. "Are we inching into the 'torture Khalil' portion of this call?" he asked.

She laughed. "I have no intention of torturing you. Guess I got caught up in the moment. You make me feel comfortable enough to do that, to say things I might not say to someone else."

"Wow," he said. "Feel like I've earned something special."

She couldn't believe how warm her cheeks got. She couldn't even look at herself in the mirror.

"Makes sense," she said. "You seem like . . ." She nibbled her lip, fighting her nerves. She squeezed her eyes shut so she could jump. "You seem like a pretty special guy."

He stammered a moment, then took a slow breath. "Did I win the lottery tonight or something?"

She laughed.

"No, I'm serious," he said. "Vanessa Noble thinks I seem like a special guy, and we're fake engaged? That's it. My week is made. Can't get any better."

"Why are you so silly?" she asked.

"Because it makes you laugh. And after the past few days, it sounded like you really needed it." His tone had gotten more serious. She could imagine his face, dimples still there as his smile faded, but his eyes warm, open, and sincere.

"Thank you, Khalil," she said.

"Think you'll sleep a little better now?" he asked.

She nodded. "Yeah."

"Then I'll let you go, Vanessa. Sweet dreams. And promise to call me if you're feeling stressed or down or need a laugh, okay?"

She smiled.

"I promise. Good night, Khalil."

"Night, App Goddess."

Wrapping the bath sheet tighter around herself, Vanessa cracked the bathroom door after her shower, letting the steam out and that morning's headlines from the TV filter in. Checking her phone, she was relieved to see that she was ahead of schedule. But more important, she had a notification that made her smile.

> Khalil: Morning, Vanessa. Hope you had a good
> night's sleep. Have a great day.
> Vanessa: Morning, Khalil. Hope you have a good one
> too.

She was in her Uber, doing a read-through of the notes for her talk that morning when she got his reply. She opened it up and laughed so hard she had to excuse herself for making the driver jump. He'd sent a selfie making an insanely silly face, and another flashing that sincere and sexy smile.

> Khalil: I tried to think of a goofy response, even tried
> bending myself into letters like a cheerleader to spell
> "Go Vanessa," but I do have a little pride. Instead I
> hope the first photo made you laugh. You can use
> the second if you end up with someone who's too
> nosy and you need proof of your fake fiancé.

She tapped the second photo open and traced the line of his jaw with her fingertip. A face that gorgeous should have been selling cologne, or designer suits, or SUVs. He was so beautiful *and* so generous and kind. Smiling, she assigned the photo to his contact info. And the connection between his name and his photo brought back something Sam had said.

> Vanessa: You're too much. Thank you. You did make
> me laugh. Made me think of something. Do people
> assume you're black before they meet you? Because
> of your name? Never occurred to me, but Mr. Skeezy
> said something like that.
> Khalil: Welcome to my ENTIRE life. It's comical some-
> times. Especially with ball, or if the person knew Dar-
> ius first. I mean it's cool, I don't mind.

The driver pulled up to the convention center and Vanessa couldn't answer right away. Phone still in her hand, she ran into an acquaintance she'd been trying to connect with for several days. She asked the other woman if they could walk in together, but she needed to answer Khalil.

> Vanessa: Just got to the expo & can't talk for a while. I wanna know more if you care to share.

She slid her phone into her pocket right after hitting "send" and joined her colleague to start day two of HouSTEM.

Her fingers were itching by the time she'd finished her talk and fielded the Q&A. The moderator had been wonderful at redirecting when the questions turned into comments. Even though that was part of the territory, it got old. And she had even less patience for it that day because she was sick of being kept from Khalil's reply.

She made her polite thank-yous and slipped behind the rope of the catering area for conference presenters. Sliding her phone out of her pocket, she smiled at the notification from Khalil.

> Khalil: My mom is Berber American. Her family's from Algeria in North Africa. My dad is French American. Both my parents' families immigrated to America before they were born. It was really difficult for them at first because of the history between France & Algeria. My mom's dad threatened to disown her. But my parents didn't care. Been together since they were teenagers. Mom chose our first names. She didn't know they might "sound black," but whatever. Love my name, try to live up to its meaning. I'd never change anything.

Vanessa reread his text, sipping an iced tea. From a quick search she learned that his name meant "friend." It certainly seemed like he tried to be a good one. She didn't want to recognize the spark of hope that flickered to life at the part about his parents—that they'd faced adversity about their relationship and not caved. They'd set an example for Khalil, maybe one that he'd follow if things got interesting.

CHAPTER THIRTEEN

Khalil had a smile in place and a spring in his step. Either he was turning into a total sap, or he was making great progress. According to Dr. E, the increased irritability he had been noticing wasn't necessarily anything to worry about, and he was expecting less perfection of himself. And all his *stuff* wasn't standing in the way of getting to know Vanessa.

Checking his phone in the elevator, he was glad to see he hadn't missed any messages and still had a good hour and a half before his first afternoon client. Reaching the lobby, he was surprised by a buzz from his pocket.

> Vanessa: Hey. Know it's last minute, but are you free for lunch?

His smile hurt his cheeks.

> Khalil: Yes. But I thought you weren't back until Thursday.
> Vanessa: Decided to come home early, but need a break from the office

He jogged to his Jeep, getting it started before he'd closed the door.

> Khalil: What do you feel like?
> Vanessa: Easier for you to get something near the shop?

Khalil: I'm downtown. Got an hour or so before I get
back to work.
Vanessa: Tamaleria Nuevo Leon from Mexicantown
has a food truck in Midtown today. Too laid back?

If she wanted him to meet her at a vending machine in a gas station, he'd be there with bells on.

Khalil: Sounds great.

As soon as she sent him the address, he peeled out of his space
and headed straight there. He circled the block once, her car nowhere
in sight. Worried about being too late to offer to pay, he parked and
speed-walked. The line was long, but she wasn't there. He hesitated,
thinking he could wait for her so they could walk up together, but he
didn't know how much time she had. She might have suggested the
truck because she was in a rush. He got in line. After a few too many
glances around and confused looks from the guy behind him, he
checked his phone. Nothing yet, so he sent a message.

Khalil: I'm here. Got in line because it's kind of long.

He kept his phone in his hand. The food smelled awesome, forcing him to tense his abs to keep his rumbling stomach from catching
anyone's attention. He looked around again and made a mistake.
There was a woman several people behind him, checking him out.
He'd had a hopeful smile on his face when he'd looked back, and she
looked him up and down again, wetting her lips. He'd have to be
impolite. He turned to pretend to study the menu, his back firmly to
the woman. He moved forward with the line. Finally, his ears pricked
at the sound of heels on asphalt.
"Hey there."
He instantly relaxed. He knew that voice.
"Hey," he said, smiling down at Vanessa. Then he stalled out. She
had her hands in the pockets of a light bomber jacket, paired perfectly with her burgundy heels. Her jeans looked fitted enough for
him to wish she'd walk ahead of him so he could see how well they
followed her slim curves. He cleared his throat, telling himself to

behave. She'd returned his smile, but looked nervous too, her arms shifting oddly, like she'd thought to take her hands out of her pockets, then decided against it.

"Thanks for meeting me," she said.

"My pleasure. It's good to see you."

Her copper cheeks seemed to redden a touch and she gave him a sweeter smile.

"You too."

The man behind him cleared his throat and Khalil realized they'd missed the people moving ahead. Vanessa filled the space, too close for him to shoot a look down her body. But he got rewarded with a brief hit of lavender, and he barely hid his goofy grin.

"You eaten here before?" he asked as she studied the menu on the side of the truck. She shook her head.

"Heard great things but didn't want to come by myself. I like sharing new experiences with, um, friends."

"Cool," he said. Then he looked up at the menu, truly reading it for the first time. His nervousness subsided, leaving only a yearning to reach for her, pull her close to him, little spoon to big spoon.

They placed their order and after politely refusing to let her pay, he waited for the food while Vanessa edged her way to a fold-out table nearby. Carrying two trays loaded down with tamales, tacos, and mouthwatering salsa, he squeezed his abs again, worried she'd hear his stomach even over the street noise.

She took her tray, thanking him. He sat, trying to fold his legs under the minuscule table. Vanessa giggled.

"Not really made for you," she said, pointing to the table and chairs. "I hesitated about the larger table, but the guy at the other end is eating fish. I can't stand the smell of it. Even the sight is difficult."

He shook his head. "I'm used to squeezing in to fit. The company makes up for a little discomfort," he said, savoring her smile again.

"You are a sweetheart, aren't you?"

He shrugged. "I try, I guess. Don't really have a choice, do I?"

She scrunched her eyebrows together, working through a bite of taco.

"Well, I didn't get to be your fake fiancé by being a jerk."

She laughed, covering her mouth with one hand.

"You did help me out there. Have to say I'm confused about something, though."

He leaned closer, wishing the rest of the world away. But he lost his center of balance and the chair jerked forward, almost toppling them together. She caught his forearm, stifling a laugh.

"You okay?" she asked.

He rolled his eyes.

"Just mildly embarrassed." He repositioned his lemonade and made sure none of his lunch was close to the edge of the table if he got any clumsier.

She crinkled her cute nose, pursing her lips to the side.

"You shouldn't be. Got me feeling a little vindicated," she said.

He chanced a taste of his tamales.

"Why?"

"Always feel like the world is made for tall people," she said, eyes twinkling. "But I guess there are limits."

"Yeah," he said, trying his salsa. "There definitely are. You said you were curious about something?" The shy tipping-down of her chin made his heart race.

"You told me about school, but now . . ." She picked at her chips, opened her mouth to speak again, then closed it. She sat back and looked up at him. "How exactly is a guy like you single? Fidelity is important to me, even with my fake fiancés. I just don't get how it is that you're on the market at all."

He grinned and leaned back too. Carefully. This was a line of questioning he was more than happy to follow. But teasing her could be fun.

"Who said I was on the market?"

Her eyes widened.

"Didn't you say you were single?"

"I was. But that was before you decided we're getting married.

When's the big day, by the way? I'm free tomorrow afternoon and on Sunday, but it'll take a few days for me to check with my family. Tuesday might give everyone enough time to clear their schedules. We could head to the courthouse after I finish your hair."

She laughed, free and open and beautiful. The rest of the world melted away. He loved her laugh and promised himself to make it happen as often as possible.

"Tomorrow might be a little tight," she said, starting her lunch again. "I don't have anything to wear."

He blatantly checked her out. Her eyebrows shot up.

"I think you look great," he said, picking up one of his tacos.

She rolled her eyes.

"Thanks. The view's not so bad from here either."

They ate in silence for a while. He hoped his deep breaths weren't too noticeable, but the urge to catch another hint of her lavender overrode any concerns about being weird. She finished her food, wiping her fingers on a napkin, and leaned back, sipping her hibiscus tea.

"Okay, I'm harping on it," she said, putting her cup down. "But how are you single again? Some sort of work-driven choice? If it is, trust me, I'll be the last to criticize." She winked at him and his skin got all tingly.

"You want the abbreviated version, or the sob story?" he asked. His heart tugged at the sympathy in her eyes.

"I don't want to dredge up any pain," she said.

"I'd like to be honest with you."

Her half-smile was too cute. He caught a mild hesitation, though. Her hand was close, and she spread her fingers near his, then picked up a napkin that had been between them. Maybe he was reading too much into things.

"I'm happy to hear whatever you'd like to share," she said.

"I think . . ." He swallowed, his desire for honesty clashing with his worry that it would make her run. He took a breath. "I think the timing was wrong with my ex. She was ready for a deeper, long-term commitment. Understandably so. She had her shit together and was ready to move on to the next stage of her life. I wasn't."

Vanessa's expression hadn't changed, so he went on.

"We were together for a while—about a year. We met at a UM alumni event. She was working for Ford. Her career was really solid, but it was just as Darius and I were getting Fade Two off the ground. She had a lot of experience under her belt, and I was kind of a struggling entrepreneur. Sure, business was going as well as it could, but the first couple of years of any new venture are stressful; you get that."

"Yeah," Vanessa said.

"So things were going fine, but she was ready to settle down, start a family. I wasn't because . . . well, I didn't feel like I had much to offer. I wanted to spend more time building up my business, and we were already planning our third location. The timing just wasn't right to me. Then she got an offer in New York. She would have been crazy not to take it."

"Do you feel like she's the one who got away?" Vanessa asked.

He paused. For a while he had thought that, but looking back, with how all his *stuff* had gotten in the way, he wouldn't have been the right person to be with anyone. He pushed the feelings of inadequacy to the side.

"No," he said, smiling. "We were almost right for each other, but there was other, um, stuff."

Vanessa nodded, her gaze off to the side, as she took a little more of her tea. She looked back at him.

"You said she was black, right?" she asked.

"She was."

"Okay."

He wasn't sure about her tone. It's not like that couldn't have been the right answer; it was the truth. He hesitated, unsure of what to say next. Maybe it was time for a subject change.

"How um . . . was Darius cool about you being together?" she asked.

He cocked his head to the side, wondering why Darius's opinion about his relationship would matter, but he just decided to continue with the truth.

"Yeah, he was supportive. There for me when we broke up because I think he understood that it was a difficult decision."

"What about your family? Did they have any objections when you were together?"

"My family? No way. My mom was pushing for us to get married and have kids almost from jump. She was teasing, but I think there was some truth to it. We made a good couple, and I never got the impression that anyone thought differently. My dad used to joke that he wondered what she saw in me."

"That didn't hurt?"

"No, it wasn't like that. I know my parents are proud of me. He was just giving me a hard time."

"That's cool," she said.

He nodded, smiling, but he was surprised at the little sting that was still there. He'd been down after the breakup, but then emotionally things had gotten so much worse. It wasn't the right time to think about that. He couldn't risk getting all sad. He reminded himself there was no reason to, he was sitting across from Vanessa, and she was showing an interest in him, who he was and how he thought about things.

Vanessa shook her head. "Surprised me again," she said, folding her napkin at the edge of her tray.

"Why's that?"

"I'm used to the 'he said, she said,' 'my ex was crazy' line. Nice to see someone taking responsibility for their part in the situation."

He shrugged again. "Wouldn't be right for me to use her to make myself look better."

Vanessa nodded, then her eyes went wide.

"Oh, Khalil, forgive me," she said.

He pulled at his straw, lost. "For what?"

"I used you when I needed something. I mean yeah, you weren't there, but still."

If that was using me, don't stop. Use me all you want, Vanessa.

He shook his head, hiding his chuckle behind a smile.

"You didn't use me. You protected yourself, and I'm glad to help. Just a little disappointed that it only seems to be an out-of-town situation." He kept himself from saying another word by taking a sip through his straw. Which he realized was better—she was staring at his mouth. He rolled his lips, moistening them. She took a quick breath, then looked back at the table.

"I . . . um . . ." She folded a napkin on her tray, taking her time rearranging her trash. "As long as we're cool." She didn't look up. He waited until she did.

"Very cool."

"I'm glad you called. I think we should do this again," he said as they walked toward their cars.

"We should," she said. "In the meantime, we'll see each other this Tuesday, right?"

"Just for your haircut, or the ceremony?" he asked, winking.

She laughed. "Let's take one thing at a time. Just a haircut."

He clutched a hand to his chest, pretending to be crestfallen.

"Okay," he sighed. "I'll be patient. Can't wait to see you then."

"Have a good afternoon, Khalil," she said, head to one side, giving him that sweet smile he was getting addicted to.

"You too, Vanessa."

In the car, headed to the shop, he went over the conversation again. Maybe he'd said too much about Nia. He hoped he hadn't given Vanessa the impression that he was pining away. He didn't think he'd done or said anything weird. Hadn't let on that it had been nearly a year since the breakup, and he'd spent that time going through the scariest emotional ups and downs of his life. He adjusted himself in the seat, waiting for a light to change. When things wrapped up with Nia, he'd already been fighting the mood swings, his emotions all over the place. Thankfully, Darius had chalked up Khalil's moodiness and inability to keep from lashing out to grief over Nia. It had been easier to hide behind that than to be honest about how he'd really been feeling. But had he understood himself? He pulled into the parking lot closest to the shop. He understood that he was interested in Vanessa, wanted to get to know her better, show her that yeah, he definitely thought she was more than cute. He hopped out, clicking the fob to lock the doors as he started up the street. His game was gone, so he couldn't think of a way to tell her without coming across as a total loser. Maybe he could show her. That had been one of Nia's criticisms. Telling too much, not showing. Yeah, that's what he'd do. Show her that he was into her. The next time he got a chance.

CHAPTER FOURTEEN

Four cities in less than two weeks was a bad idea." Vanessa rubbed the back of her neck, then forced herself into better posture. The Alphastone app package was in the beta testing phase, with less than optimal results. Her body had finally settled back into Eastern Time, and she'd needed a night out with friends, but maybe tonight was too soon.

"You get all testy when I say 'I told you so,' and yet you keep creating opportunities for it to happen," Lisa said, elbowing her in the side. Vanessa rolled her eyes and elbowed back.

"All right, all right." She shot a glance over the VIP section. "Where's everyone else? We can't celebrate Dani's birthday without the birthday girl."

Lisa checked her phone. "Mitch said they're on the way. But . . ."

"But?"

"I don't know what's going on with them. They've been so disgusting lately. Like, all brand-new couple and shit, late for everything, and when they do appear—"

"Dani's hair and makeup are all messed up and Mitch has to rearrange his clothes?" Vanessa asked.

"How'd you know?"

Vanessa nodded toward the entrance to VIP. Dani and her boyfriend, Mitch, waved as they approached, Mitch buttoning the second button on his dress shirt, Dani glancing at her reflection in a mirrored column.

"Eww . . . they must have done it in the car!"

"Lisa, please," Vanessa whispered. "Let's just pretend we don't know." She stood to hug Dani. "Hey, birthday girl!"

"Hey, App Goddess. Good to see you. You home for a little bit, or off again tomorrow?"

Mitch joined them with a nod, the happy couple sliding onto one of the other couches Vanessa had reserved for the group. When she was in town, Paradigm was Vanessa's go-to club for an evening out. Vanessa had helped Cedric, the owner, with his tech, and in return she enjoyed some benefits, like the largest reserved section in VIP: three white leather couches, huge coffee table in the middle, and a dedicated waiter. Vanessa caught his eye and nodded. He nodded back and disappeared.

"I'm slowing down a little," she said. "In town for a couple weeks before heading to New York to meet with a big client, then nothing booked for a while. Been too busy to really follow what some of my programmers have been up to, and I'll probably need to crack the whip a little."

"In town a couple weeks?" Dani asked. "That is cause for celebration." She winked at Vanessa, then gasped as the waiter appeared with a platter of tapas for the group, a bottle of champagne, and glasses. After a toast and the arrival of Jen and Bibi, the group moved to the dance floor overlooking the rest of the club. Five songs later, Vanessa returned for a refill from the waiter. Her phone vibrated against the glass tabletop, lighting up with a notification.

Khalil: You're killing it in that yellow.

She giggled, only stifling her reflex to smooth her hair because of the glass in her hand. She slid onto the couch to trade the glass for her phone.

Vanessa: Am I?
Khalil: You are.

She glanced around the club, at the VIP section and down over the dance floor.

Vanessa: Where are you?
Khalil: Left end of the bar.

She stood, leaning over the railing, trailing her gaze down the bar until she saw him. Darius was beside him, talking to a man she didn't recognize. Khalil waved and her heart fluttered.

Vanessa: Wanna join us?
Khalil: Don't want to crash your party.

Fingers poised to reply, she caught him tap his index finger to his lips. He glanced up at her, then back at his phone.

Khalil: That sounded stalkerish. Sorry.

She smiled, shaking her head.

Vanessa: It's cool. Are you coming?
Khalil: Can I bring a plus two?
Vanessa: Of course.

Standing to go ask Eddie the bouncer to let them in, Vanessa wobbled on her feet when Dani surprised her with a hug from behind.

"Hey," she said over Vanessa's shoulder. "Thanks again for my b-day party."

Vanessa hugged Dani's arms still around her.

"Glad to do it," she said. "Hope you don't mind me inviting someone to join us."

"Oh? Who?" Dani let go and grabbed her champagne glass off the table.

"His name is Khalil, and he's bringing his friend Darius and another guy up here. Saw him downstairs and invited him."

"More guys? Excellent idea. Are they single? I know Jen's ready to start dating again. And Mitch and I would love to have another couple to do things with."

Vanessa was jolted by her prickly irritation at the possibility of Khalil being interested in Jen.

"Um . . . I'm not sure. Lemme go tell Eddie—"

At the doorway leading to VIP, Khalil and Eddie were stepping out of a hug, laughing with each other. Khalil gestured over his shoulder, and Eddie hugged Darius as he reached the top of the steps.

"Is that them?" Dani asked.

"Yeah. Guess they know Eddie," Vanessa said. Eddie shook the third man's hand and followed Khalil's nod to Vanessa and Dani. Vanessa waved and Eddie nodded, unhooking the velvet rope. Darius and the other man stepped through, but Khalil waited, taking out his phone and speaking to Eddie again. They shook hands, and Khalil joined his friends, leading the way to Vanessa.

There was no reason for her knees to get all weak. Or for her breath to get irregular and hard to catch. He smiled, and her pulse jumped, and her hands got tingly for no good reason.

"Girl," Dani whispered. "Forget Jen. Which one you want? 'Cause damn. Daaaaaamn."

"Shhh, Dani!" Vanessa hissed. "Hey!" she said too brightly as the men reached their corner.

"Hey, Vanessa," Khalil said. "Thanks for letting us crash."

She nodded and made the introductions, only stumbling a little over her words. Khalil caught her nod and joined her on a couch.

"What are the odds?" she asked him.

"Of what?"

"Never meeting in undergrad but bumping into each other twice in a few months."

He shrugged. "Maybe the universe conspires," he said, smiling.

The two groups gelled better than Vanessa could have hoped. Khalil's friend Reizo was chatting with Jen; Lisa and Darius seemed to be happy to have found each other again. Vanessa thought about joining them on the dance floor but accepted Khalil's invitation onto the little balcony overlooking the rest of the club.

She liked his cologne. At the shop, it was hard to distinguish between different aromas. There were always men who wore too much

cologne, the smell of the disinfectant for the combs, the fabric soft-
ener in the air from the dryers in the back. The shaving cream they
used overpowered the room, its menthol undercurrent battling for
supremacy. But there in the club, the aroma of mixed drinks didn't get
much farther than the glasses that contained them. The birthday cake
lay in ruins on the table, under a vanilla-scented cloud. This warm
fragrance she was currently enjoying—bergamot, cedarwood, a touch
of fresh-cut grass—had to be coming from him. He took a breath to
speak, and she realized how close to him she'd gotten: His watch
grazed her fingertips where their hands rested against the railing.

"I . . ." He wet his lips, glancing at hers. He cleared his throat and
looked her in the eye again. "I really enjoyed lunch the other day," he
said.

"Me too."

"What if we made it a regular—"

An explosion of breaking glass cut him off, a passing waiter's tray
crashing to the floor. Vanessa jumped like everyone else, and her foot
landed on a piece. She wavered as it crunched, and she shifted her
weight, hoping to avoid any shards catching the exposed side of her
foot.

"You okay?" Khalil cupped her elbow, steadying her.

"Yeah. Stepped on some glass, but I don't think it got into my
shoe."

He looked down. "Yuck. It's all over the place. Gimme your
drink."

She did, keeping her feet as still as possible. He put their glasses
on a nearby table and returned, stepping over the largest pieces of
broken glass. Two waiters scurried around, getting brooms, asking
patrons to be careful while they cleaned up.

"Hmm," Khalil said, assessing the floor. "This won't do."

"What?" she asked.

"No path for you to avoid the glass. Just had to wear the sexy
shoes tonight, huh?" he asked, winking.

" 'The sexy shoes'? These are hardly—"

Then she was in the air, up against his side. He'd scooped her up
and the easiest thing to do was let her arms fall around his neck as his

circled her waist and he stepped through the field of glass. That bergamot-cedarwood-fresh-grass scent was him. And the smell concentrated deliciously where his neck met his shoulder. The only logical thing to do, to help him maintain his balance, was to cling as tightly as she could to him, letting her cheek rest against his shoulder, his throat inches from her nose. She drugged herself high with another deep breath, but the popping glass snapped her back to the present.

"You're stepping on it too. What if it gets into your shoes?" she asked.

He reached the couches and wrapped his other arm around her waist, pressing her close, and then let her slide down to her feet.

"Um . . . closed shoes," he said. He cleared his throat. "I'm okay."

Neither one of them moved, and Vanessa doubted they were okay. She wanted to reply, but the heat of his biceps against her palms slammed into her awareness.

"Oh," she said, jerking her hands away and taking a step back. His grip around her waist slackened before she was ready, and she wobbled.

"Maybe we should sit," he said, catching her wrist, then releasing it as they sat on the couch.

"Good idea." Still off-kilter, she glanced down to check the soles of her shoes.

"Do you have a problem with my shoes?" she asked.

He smiled. "Not a problem. Just wonder how you can walk around in torture devices all the time, as though they don't hurt. Those shoes you wear must be painful."

"'Those shoes I wear'? Do all of my shoes offend you?" She smiled so he'd know she was teasing.

"Nothing you wear offends me, Vanessa," he said. "But you can't tell me your feet don't hurt."

She shrugged.

"Okay. Desperate measures. Wait here." He was gone before she could open her mouth. She checked the dance floor. Her friends were having a great time, Lisa in particular, with Darius. Khalil returned, putting a glass with ice, another with what looked like olive oil, and a stack of napkins on the table.

"Foot, please," he asked.

"I'm sorry?"

"I need your foot," he said. "In my lap."

She gawked at him.

"Okay," he said. He leaned over, grabbed her right ankle, and turned her leg, sitting back with her foot in his lap. She was happy she'd worn her yellow jumpsuit and not her yellow minidress.

"What are you doing?" she asked. He'd bent his head, scrutinizing the straps around her ankle.

"Trying to figure out how to take this off."

"You are not going to take off my shoe!"

"Why not?"

"Because . . . it's . . . they're my feet!" She'd had a pedicure the day before, but she'd been dancing and the leather insoles weren't exactly breathable. He leaned back, appraising as she tried not to freak out.

"You have really cute feet, Vanessa," he said. "Does it bother you if I touch them?"

"Um . . . no . . ." She glanced around. The couple on the couch closest to them were in a serious conversation. The women beside them had been making out since the waiter dropped the glasses. The lights were too dim to see anyone well. She looked back at Khalil. He was studying the straps again.

"Are you . . . into feet?" she asked.

"No," he said, still studying. "Not into . . . feet." He looked her in the eye and her heart took off.

"Um. Okay," she said. Then her sandal slid off. It was impossible to remove that quickly, unless he'd already figured out how and had been giving her a chance to back out. He placed it on the floor, then tossed a piece of ice back into the glass. *When did he pick—* All thoughts stopped and she melted into the couch. He'd placed his chilled hand on the top of her foot, where the muscles had been stretched, straining to keep her upright.

"Is that okay?" he asked.

She moistened her lips to answer.

"Uh, yeah."

"Needed that?"

She nodded.

"I can continue, if you'd like." He dipped his thumb in the olive oil, then rubbed her foot, squeezing the ball gently.

"Do you know what you're doing?" She didn't know why she was asking; no one had ever massaged her feet before. But it sure felt right.

He flashed her a sideways grin, a hair's breadth from wicked. Moistening his lips, he looked her in the eye.

"You know I got you, Vanessa," he said. He squeezed and rubbed, massaging the lubricated skin with slow, deep strokes. She should thank him. Should let him know that it felt good and she appreciated it, but her ability to form a coherent thought was gone. He cradled her foot, rotating it, and all she could do was let her eyes flutter closed as her head lolled back. He answered her sigh with a "Damn." She smiled.

"More tense than you thought?" she asked, raising her head to look at him.

"Not that," he said. His gaze intensified, not wavering at all. Her shyness kindled, but she forgot about it as he rolled a knuckle down her arch.

"You're exquisite when something makes you feel good," he said. He rubbed deep. She couldn't stifle her groan.

You think I'm happy now, you should see me in bed.

His hands froze. Her breathing did too. She opened her eyes and realized she hadn't thought that, she'd said it out loud. She flashed hot. If there was a way to back out of that sort of a confession, she had no idea what it was.

"I would imagine . . ." He looked at her foot, massaging again. He'd have a crease in his forehead one day, a line that would get deeper over time, formed from laughing, or from moments like right then when he seemed to be trying to find the right words. He looked back up at her. "I could . . ." He looked away. "I . . . um, have imagined that you are. Enchanting. When . . ." His cheeks bloomed red and he let out an awkward chuckle. "Dammit, Vanessa." He shook his head, smiling.

She swallowed, her throat thick. "What?"

"I have like, no game with you. How do you do that? You . . . you shut it down, and it's like I'm fourteen years old again." He shrugged. "Zero game."

She could have teased, acted offended that he'd try to spit game to her, rolled her eyes and told him to stop coming up with silly things to make her feel unique. But she couldn't say any of those things because of his smile. She loved it and needed to see it as much as possible.

"Thanks? I guess?" she asked, smiling back.

He nodded, glancing at her lips. Then looked at her foot again, massaging deep, with both hands.

"You're welcome," he said.

She relaxed back into the couch. The music had changed, the club lights even dimmer. Part of her was still self-conscious, surrounded by people, her foot in Khalil's lap while he "attended to her." She would stop it. She'd thank him in a moment, pull her foot back and suggest they go join the others to leave behind the spell of what was happening. Then he stopped rubbing, giving her a final caress along the top of her foot, and slid it gently out of his lap.

"Thank you so much, Khalil. That was amazing. You—"

He leaned over and caught her other foot, undoing the strap of her sandal.

"What are you doing?" she asked.

He looked up. "Starting on the other foot?"

"But why?"

"You're aware that you have two feet, right?"

"Yes, but you don't have to do that."

He sat up straight, frowning.

"I'd like to do that," he said. "Do you want me to stop? Please, be totally honest. Say the word and I won't touch the other one." He held his palms up.

She did not want him to stop. She wanted him to give her left foot the same magic that had the right one feeling better than it had in weeks.

"Please continue."

He smiled. "Gladly. But before I get started, let me share my plan. I'm gonna take care of this one, then we're gonna stay here on the couch until you're ready to leave. I'll carry you downstairs and out to your car 'cause I don't want you to undo all my hard work by putting those shoes back on." He winked and smiled when she took a breath to protest. "Then, once I'm sure you're safely behind the wheel and you've promised me you won't put them back on once you get home, I'll wish you good night."

There was a challenge in his eye. Massaging her feet, then carrying her out of the club like . . .

"You aren't my servant, Khalil. It's bad enough that I've got you rubbing my feet in public, how's it going to look if you carry me out of here?"

"You're right. I'm not your servant," he said. He leaned into the couch, draping his arm over the back. She could easily pick up his fingers, lace them through hers. Instead she laced her own together and met his gaze again.

"But I like serving you," he said. His eyes were darker. The lush curve that was his bottom lip looked pinker, warmer. The tip of his tongue flashed across it, and hers followed a similar route, running along the inside of her bottom lip. Then the buzzing, giddy tension that had been sitting in her chest and humming down her arms stilled. The sensation morphed and deepened into something slow, heavy, and molten that curled down her body to rest, warming, between her thighs. She squeezed them together.

"You do?"

"Very much," he said.

"Okay . . ." She needed a breath to calm the tremble in her voice. "But there's a hitch in your plan."

He started on the left foot, making her eyelids flutter again. "What's that?" he asked.

"I didn't drive. Rode with Lisa."

"Hmm . . . that does complicate things. Because it looks like Lisa may have a different timeline," he said. She followed his nod toward the dance floor. Lisa and Darius were locked at the hips, chest, and nearly the lips. Vanessa was happy for an instant, then she raised an eyebrow at Khalil.

"Was this some sort of arrangement?" she asked. "You two each other's wingman?"

Khalil chuckled. "I promise, Vanessa, no arrangement. No wingmen."

"Did Darius drive?" she asked.

"Nope. I did. Reizo too." He pressed his thumbs in deep, squeezing a groan out of her.

"Guess you'll just have to drive me home, then," she said.

He flashed her a wicked grin. "Guess I will."

"I can walk inside," Vanessa said, a finger hooked through her sandal straps. Khalil had opened the passenger door but turned his back to her, waiting for her to climb on again.

"Of course you can," he said over his shoulder. "But I'm not willing to risk it."

She rolled her eyes and slid forward, wrapping her arms around his neck, her legs around his waist. Indulging herself, she inhaled deep as he stood, hoping the motion would conceal the press of her chest and stomach to his back as she filled her lungs with the smell of his cologne, and of him. He closed and locked the door, and she was grateful that his attention was elsewhere so she could close her eyes and tuck her cheek to his back, pretending that he was hers for a moment.

Be ridiculous for the minute it takes to get to the door, then grow up. Do I even want him to be mine?

He took the stairs with ease and reached her landing before she was ready. He squatted, sliding her onto her doormat.

"Thank you, kind sir," she said. He stood to his full height and laughed.

"You are tiny. I knew it! The shoes are part of your brand, but they're functional too, aren't they?" His smile was way too handsome for someone giving her a hard time. She play-punched his arm.

"Seriously? Is that what this was? Some big ploy to get my shoes off so you could make fun of the short girl?" It was irritating to have to tilt her head so far back to make eye contact with him. He laughed, rubbing his arm. "Has it ever occurred to you that I am not short so much as you are ridiculously tall? You're like a giant." She opened her bag, fishing for her keys.

"How tall are you? For real. Let's look at this objectively," he said.

"I'm five five," she said, not making eye contact.

Then his fingertip was under her chin and he tilted her head until she met his gaze. He arched an eyebrow. She rolled her eyes.

"Okay, fine. Five one."

The expected tease didn't come. His smile faded and his gaze fixed on her lips. He grazed his thumb across her chin.

"You're adorable, Vanessa."

She frowned and pulled away.

"Guess no one's ever told you not to call short women 'adorable.'" She got her key into the lock. "Kids are adorable. Puppies are adorable—"

"You are sexy adorable," he said. He brushed her cheek with the back of his finger. "I'm sorry, I didn't mean to upset you." He stepped back, hands in pockets.

"It's okay," she said, missing his closeness. "Kinda defensive about it after getting teased for years." He nodded, still watching her lips. She took a breath to speak, but he beat her to it.

"Go inside, Vanessa?" he asked.

"You . . . want me to go?"

"Just want to know you're safe. Go in? Lock the door?"

"Safe from you?"

He shook his head, glancing down.

"That was awkward. Sorry. Like I said, no game." He shrugged. "You being safe is important to me. I wanna hear the lock before I leave, know that you're okay." He smiled but got the intense gaze on her lips again.

"Um . . . okay, Khalil. Thanks again for tonight," she said, opening the door.

"Thank you, Vanessa," he said.

"See you next week."

"Looking forward to it."

She grinned and stepped inside.

CHAPTER FIFTEEN

"Come again?"

Darius placed the clipper blade he was sharpening next to his waterstone. Khalil added a little more water to his own, not meeting Darius's stare. He picked up the next blade with his magnet and shrugged, before starting again.

"Didn't kiss her," he said.

"But you took her home?" Darius asked.

"Yeah, back to her place."

"And what? Did you slow down long enough for her to tuck and roll out of the car?"

Khalil rolled his eyes, mentally counting out the last four strokes before changing blades.

"Of course I walked her to her door. Well, carried her."

"What do you mean 'carried'?"

Khalil stopped sharpening and ran a hand down his face. He looked at his friend. Darius raised a hand.

"Sorry. Out of line," he said.

"Nah, it's nothing." He slumped back against the wooden dining chair, tapping his fingertips on Darius's kitchen table. "It's just, she's got me messed up, off my game." He stood, the chair grating along the low windowsill as he grabbed a soda off the island.

Darius grunted, picking up his blade again. Khalil caught the quirk of his lips, the struggle to keep his laughter to himself. For once he pretended he hadn't noticed. Popping the soda and drinking a little, he returned to his work. Counting backward, he had two strokes left on that blade when Darius spoke again.

"Maybe you don't want to kiss her." His gaze didn't stray from his own blade and stone.

Maybe north was east and when the sky got dark at night it was because the sun had been eaten by a giant snake.

Khalil grunted. Next blade.

"All I know is it's been 'Vanessa this' and 'Vanessa that' for the past few weeks," Darius said. "You get this dopey grin when she texts; you look like someone stole your puppy when you get a message that isn't from her."

"How would you know when—"

"When it's her or not? See dopey grin I just mentioned."

Khalil switched blades. Yeah, he liked it when she texted him. What was the harm in that? He focused on his blades, the slice-drag of their work filling the silence. Once the blades were done, they could sort the reserves into boxes, put the ones in use into the clippers and take them back to the shops. A sharpening service would save them time, but then they'd lose the opportunity to share a manual task while getting stuff off their chests with someone who'd never judge.

Khalil finished his last blade and folded a dishtowel to wipe down his stone. He'd wanted to kiss her, been dying to do it. But at the last moment his *stuff* had gotten in the way and his budding confidence crumbled. Then, like a nutcase, he'd told her to go inside. Standing, he grabbed his soda and stepped through the back door onto the patio. He pulled out his phone.

> Khalil: Keep wondering why I didn't kiss you last
> night.

He gulped some more soda, willing his nerves to settle while he waited for a reply. The App Goddess couldn't be far from her phone. It shouldn't take—

> Vanessa: Been asking myself the same thing. Figured
> you didn't want to.

He cursed himself as a blue jay flitted by. It landed on a branch of the tree in Darius's backyard and looked at him.

Fuck being smooth.

> Khalil: You have heart-shaped lips. Full and sexy but arched with that perfectly shaped cupid's bow. They're arresting and intimidating and beyond perfect with the shape of your face. I'm an idiot for missing an opportunity to find out how they feel, instead of this unhealthy preoccupation with how they look. I hope you'll give me the chance to make up for my mistake.

He chugged the rest of the drink to avoid looking at the phone and throwing up out of anxiety while he waited to see what she'd say. The bird hopped on the branch, looking at him out of one eye, then the other.

"What?" he asked it. Then his phone buzzed.

> Vanessa: "Sinful," "lush," "decadent." Wish I had better words to describe yours, but all I can think of right now are the ones I've been using during my own irrational obsessions. Please take the next chance that presents itself.

CHAPTER SIXTEEN

The chime above the door of the Original Fade let out an ugly off-key clank as Khalil stepped inside. Looking up, he realized one of the bells was missing. Taking in the rest of the shop, dozens of minor details caught his eye: Dust bunnies of hair gathered around two of the chairs on the right. The mirror at the last station had a small crack at the bottom. If it had been occupied, the usual products and tools would have covered up the imperfection. But that had originally been Chris's station, and now he was working on a client's beard at the middle station on the left. Khalil didn't care how his employees chose which spot to work, but he did care about the film of dust on the skin care products near the register, the magazines falling apart in the waiting area, and the fact that Rodriguez and Pax, the two most senior employees, were on the right side, and Chris and Joel, the newest, were on the left. The division in the team was laid out for all to see.

Khalil smiled and greeted each of his employees with a hand-shake and said hello to their clients. There may have been tension, but the available chairs were full, and there were two men in the waiting area, so money was coming in, even on a weekday afternoon. He asked Rod to meet him in the back room once he'd finished with his client. And he caught Chris's worried glance while Khalil was talking to his manager.

Khalil pulled the boxes of freshly sharpened razor blades out of his bag and opened the small closet in the back to put them away.

And he was rewarded with more proof that things were not going well. The supplies were cluttered all over each other. Frowning, he started reorganizing things, trying to keep his disappointment in check. He was nearly finished when Rod joined him.

"Boss man," he said. "What's up?"

"Rodriguez," he said, standing from where he'd crouched to deal with the bottom shelf. "I think I should be asking you that question."

"What do you mean?"

"Is everything good with you? Outside of work, I mean. Any stress or stuff going on? I'm not asking for personal details or anything, just want a full picture."

Rod's brow scrunched deep.

"Nah, everything's good, chief."

"What's the deal with my shop, then?" Crossing his arms, Khalil leaned against the counter beside the washer and dryer. "You said you wanted to run things, have the additional responsibility that went along with the additional pay. Even proved it when you were assistant manager. But now . . ." He looked around, shrugging. "This is not how things were before."

"Look," Rod said. "I can't do everything, so I have to delegate. And sometimes they don't do a very good job. I don't know what that little rat—"

Khalil cut him off with a raised hand.

"Are you talking about one of my employees like that, Rod?"

"Yeah, the new kid. Look, he's nice and all, but he's got an attitude. Darius told him to get it together the last time he stopped by, but the kid thinks he's too good to chip in."

Khalil let his head loll down, pinching the bridge of his nose. His skin prickled hot: from his shoulders down through his fingers. Clenching and relaxing, he fought the sharp irritation. He was generally slow to anger, but Rod was speeding him up. He spoke without lifting his head.

"Before you go down that road, you are aware that Darius and I talk, right? Every day. Especially about anything that has an impact on our business."

"Uh, yeah," Rod said, voice less blustery than it had been.

"So. Did Darius single out Chris, or was he speaking to the whole team?"

Rod shoved his hands in his pockets.

"Whole team, I guess."

Khalil nodded, arms crossed, still looking down.

"And who was supposed to set the example, Rod? Through actions, not words."

Rod didn't answer, so Khalil made eye contact with him. He raised an eyebrow.

"Yeah, all right. Me," he said.

"So why did I need to come here to see that one of the mirrors is broken and the chime over the door needs fixing? All you had to do was call me, shoot me a text so I could get that handled."

Rod nodded, attention on his shoes.

"And to be honest," Khalil said, "the way things have been going, I should promote Pax to be manager."

"What? A chick? Why?"

"You cannot be serious," Khalil said. "Plumbing's got nothing to do with ability."

Rod shook his head. "I knew it. She's been talking to you and Darius behind my back. You'd reward disloyalty with a promotion?"

Khalil blinked twice. Rod had an interesting take on loyalty considering the fact that it was Khalil's shop. He waited a long moment before replying, letting the hot tingle of irritation subside. He hadn't had to work so hard to contain his anger in months.

"Listen, Rod, I came to see how y'all were doing, if the team was getting along better than before. The last thing I expected to learn was that you think the staff of this shop has an obligation of loyalty to you. Last I checked it said Sarda and Simmons on the business license, and we're the ones writing the checks to the IRS. But if you're volunteering to chip in on that, feel free.

"I said I should promote Pax because it takes one look to see that she's got more pride in the shop than you do. Her station is spotless." He took two steps back to the closet, motioning for Rod to follow him. "Her section of the stock closet was the only one that wasn't a mess. Except for Chris's. It could have been a bit better organized, but it wasn't the pigpen yours was. And when was the last time you cleaned your mirror, or really swept under your chair?"

"That's Chris's job, not mine," Rod said, hands spread wide.

Khalil nodded. "Got it. Darius and I are gonna have a talk." He shut the closet doors. "We'll let you know what we decide." He squeezed his way past Rod on the way out.

In the car, he cursed himself for not paying attention to the time and getting stuck in traffic. He clenched his fists around the steering wheel, then let go, stretching his hands as wide as possible.

Cannot believe that asshole. He rotated his jaw to stop clenching it. *Whose fucking shop does he think it is?* Khalil couldn't wrap his mind around the situation. Rod had been an awesome employee when they'd opened the Original Fade. They'd never had to ask him to chip in. He'd taken a lot of pressure off Khalil and Darius as they got their feet under them. And now? Getting into the turning lane, Khalil shook his head against the idea that Rod had gotten an ego from being promoted to manager of one shop. It wasn't that serious.

The light turned green, and the cars ahead began to turn. Except for the one right in front of him. The light was quick, just enough time for four or five cars to get through. Khalil couldn't remember the number of times he'd had to wait through multiple light changes. The car didn't budge. He knew there were only a few seconds left.

He laid on his horn, yelling as loudly as he could at the driver. They started to accelerate, and he couldn't hold back, punching his horn again and again, as he sped up. The light was yellow by the time Khalil reached it, but he sure as hell wasn't stopping. Making it through, he sped up enough to get next to the woman who'd been ahead of him. His windows were already down, as were hers. He leaned over the passenger seat and screamed out the window.

"LEARN HOW TO FUCKING DRIVE FOR CHRISSAKE!" Then he gunned it, passing her and zooming through the next two lights as they turned yellow.

The third light was red. He stopped. His heart was racing, his breath coming fast and hard. He let go of the wheel to open and close his hands against the shaky feeling inside.

What the hell was that? He blinked, trying to free himself from a coating, a submersion in rage. He glanced in his rearview mirror, hoping to God the woman was gone, had turned somewhere else so he wouldn't have the mortification of seeing her again. He swallowed against a dry throat as he felt his face bloom red with shame.

What is wrong with me?

"Maybe you are the crazy one," Darius said through Khalil's wireless earpiece. They needed to talk, but Khalil had to have both hands free. He stopped scrubbing his shower wall.

"How am I the crazy one? Rodriguez is talking like it's his shop and the people who work there are supposed to be loyal to him, not to us. Even though I don't like this whole 'loyalty' idea at all."

"Yeah, that's not cool," Darius said. "Not to change the subject, but what are you doing?"

"Cleaning," Khalil said, squirting more of the cleaning paste on a sponge and attacking the water spots on the glass.

"Um, do you need me to go? Because you sound like you're really into it. You're like, out of breath."

Khalil stood up. "Am I? Sorry. Walking into the shop and seeing how dirty it was must have set me off. Came home and all I saw was dust and smudges everywhere. Couldn't take it."

"You've been cleaning since you got home?" Darius asked.

"Yeah, why?"

"You've been at it this intense for two hours? Your apartment isn't that big," Darius said.

Khalil stopped scrubbing again and raised an eyebrow.

"How would you know how long I've been home?"

"Rod called me right after you left, said he wasn't gonna be assistant manager to a girl."

Khalil wiped his brow with the back of his hand.

"You told him that attitude is not gonna fly, right? I didn't say I was going to promote Pax. I was saying that she clearly gave more of a damn about the shop than he does. Way to take it out of proportion."

"Yeah, I told him I seriously doubted you were gonna make a management decision like that without talking to me, and since it was the first I'd heard . . ."

"Yeah." Khalil hopped out of the shower. "Hold on, man, gotta run the water."

"Do you want me to—" Darius was cut off by the spray. Khalil guided all the cleaning product remnants down the drain, then grabbed the squeegee and eliminated every drop of water clinging to the glass. He stood, proud of his work.

"Um, 'Lil. Hot as it is listening to you huff and puff, I really think that's more of a conversation to have with Vanessa."

"Funny. I'll let you go, Dare. But we do need to figure out what we're gonna do at the Original. I don't think things can continue like this."

"You're right. You gonna call your girlfriend so she can listen to you get all hot and bothered with the cleaning?"

"Christ, Darius. Will you please stop giving me shit about Vanessa?" Khalil's throat hurt from snarling, but he didn't care. He had enough going on; he didn't need grief about a girl who threw him off all the time.

"Woah, dude. I was joking. You sure you're okay?" Darius asked.

"I'm fucking fine. I have to go." Khalil wiped his finger dry on his shirt and pressed the button to end the call. He tossed the phone on the kitchen counter as he headed for the closet to get the vacuum.

Just need everyone to leave me the fuck alone and let me get this apartment clean before I lose it.

An hour later, exhausted, but with his apartment spotless, Khalil took a long shower. He scrubbed himself as intensely as he'd scrubbed his home, wishing he could wash away this anger that kept popping up. It had been a particularly rough day. He hadn't been able to hold his irritation in check like usual. That realization stopped him mid-shampoo. He'd been stuffing down anger lately. And now he couldn't ask Dr. Edwards because he was still embarrassed at having skipped their last two sessions. He'd just have to work it out himself until next month.

If anything, he should be in a great mood: Apart from the tension at the Original, things were going well at his shops, and he was getting to know Vanessa better. The water that rinsed the suds out of his hair couldn't rinse the smile off his face at the thought of her. She wanted him to kiss her. He'd fumbled the first opportunity, but she wanted him to take the next. Absently, he gathered some suds from his chest and stomach, bringing a handful to coat his dick. He just thought of her and he was already getting hard. He smiled again. Maybe he shouldn't be kicking himself for not kissing her. The tease guided the anticipation so that it grew fuller, deeper. He'd have to learn for her, but he knew that drawing things out, edging himself, always made the first touch or kiss or orgasm that much better. He rotated his hand, tightening his grip to that point just below pain. Letting his head fall back, he panted, his other hand on the wall, bracing himself. After intentionally letting several days go by, days he'd fantasized a lot about Vanessa but had not acted on those fantasies, in no time he was close and had to choose: let go, or stop, frustrating himself in order to make the next time that much better. But then Vanessa's lips passed in front of his mind's eye, full and lush and perfect—

His sputtered groan echoed off the bathroom walls, the fingers of his free hand curling against the tile. Listing a moment, he let himself fall into the dizziness, into the rush of hormones that got him so high, feeling so good. Eyes closed, his breathing getting back to normal, his heart stopped pounding against his sternum. Smiling again, he let out a slow breath, leaning into the spray, letting it rinse him off.

Fuck. Needed that. Maybe that wasn't road rage. Maybe I've just been holding back too long.

Coasting on the last bits of his post-orgasmic high, Khalil got into an old pair of basketball shorts. Turning out of his bedroom and into the hall, he decided he needed to call Karim. They'd spoken the day before, but suddenly it couldn't wait any longer. He jogged down the hall, snatched his phone off the kitchen counter, got to the dialer, and held down "1."

The phone kept ringing. Khalil cursed when it went to voicemail. He waited for Karim's greeting and the tone.

"Hey, man, you okay?" he asked. "Call me back?"

He ended the call but couldn't bring himself to put the phone down. He started counting to thirty but only made it to twenty-one before he had to call again. Karim answered, his voice strained.

"Call you right back," he said out of breath.

"Okay—"

"I'm not finished talking to you!" His sister-in-law's screech came through loud and clear.

"I am DONE being shouted at!" Khalil heard Karim fire back before the line went dead.

Khalil put the phone down on his coffee table, crossing his arms against himself. Karim had told him about the fights, about Laila's drama, how she punctuated her disagreements with a slammed door or by throwing pillows across rooms. Khalil had never heard Karim raise his voice with her before, so things had to be worse than he'd let on. Khalil's phone rang.

"Hey," Karim said. Khalil caught the sounds of traffic, of Karim's loud breathing as he walked quickly, somewhere outside.

"What the hell was that?" Khalil asked.

Karim let out a combination sigh and laugh.

"That was Laila's Tuesday-night special: denial, deflection, and blaming." He paused for a second, his breath still heavy and fast. "Actually, it's her any-night special. But this time I was a little more prepared for it. I confronted her about cheating."

"She's cheating on you?" Khalil's blood sparked hot, ready to fight.

"I'm not certain, but there're too many signs. She's been coming home late, not being where she's supposed to. New passwords on her phone and laptop. Couple of times I stopped by her office to take her out to lunch, like we used to do all the time. But she'd be out when I got there, and if I texted her, asking what she was up to, she'd say shit like 'stuck at the office' or 'working through lunch.'"

Khalil tipped the bottom half of the phone up, so the microphone couldn't catch his curse.

"What do you want to do?" he asked Karim, phone back in place.

"I don't know. There are times when things are perfect. Then others when it's hell on earth. When I tell her I can't live like that, she gets better, but I don't know. Being married is serious. And I know it's work, but Jesus, it's like she can't go a full two months without some dramatic scene. Do you remember if her parents are like that?"

Khalil scrunched his brow, searching his memory. He hadn't spent much time with Laila's family, but their mothers had been close. Though there'd been a big rift at some point, and he couldn't remember the last time his mom had brought Laila's mother up.

"I don't, sorry." He paused, not wanting to upset Karim, but he couldn't hold his tongue. "Whether they were or not, I don't like you going through this. Have you guys considered counseling?"

"Yeah." Karim's breath was finally back to normal. The background sounds shifted from street noise to soft jazz.

"You at that jazz club down the street from your place?" Khalil asked.

"Yeah. Need to clear my head."

"I hear that," Khalil said.

He held on as Karim got settled at the bar and ordered a drink. He'd been set to lift his brother's spirits, but Karim's next question knocked him off track.

"Please tell me things are better with you. You dating yet? Isn't it time for Khalil the Player to get back in the game?"

CHAPTER SEVENTEEN

Vanessa was due for Sunday Lunch at Ma-Max's, and she should have been getting dressed to go, but she was squinting at her desktop screen, scrolling through her bank account activity for the third time. It had been over a week and there was still no second charge from Paradigm. The first was there: for the VIP section, the tapas, two bottles of champagne, and the birthday cake. But there should have been a second one for two rounds of drinks, and the third bottle of champagne. She'd expected the charge no more than forty-eight hours after the party, but it still hadn't gone through. She'd given Cedric permission to charge the remainder to her card and send her an email with a detailed receipt, but that hadn't shown up either. He'd been out of town for a week, so she'd thought to give it a little longer, but something was wrong. She had to call.

"Hey, Ness," he said after several rings.

She asked about his vacation then got to the point.

"I still owe you for Dani's birthday," she said.

"No, you don't," he said. "The bill was paid that night."

"You sure?" she asked.

"Since when am I unsure about money coming in?" he asked.

"Good point, but it didn't come out of my bank account," she said.

"I know," he singsonged.

"Who paid, Cedric?" she asked.

"Promised not to say."

"Why does this tickle you so much?" she asked.

"Because it's cute. I appreciate your concern about the bill getting paid. You're a great guest to have. Makes me happy when something nice happens for you," he said. "Now, as much as I'd like to tease you further, I have to go. A million details for an event tonight."

Vanessa politely said goodbye, irritated by Cedric's little game.

During the drive to Ma-Max's, she chewed over what he'd said. Someone else had picked up the check and he thought it was cute? Maybe Lisa and the others had chipped in behind her back. They'd taken turns paying for nights out in the past, and when anyone had offered to split or chip in, it wasn't some big secret. Cedric was being weird. Taking the exit off the freeway, she reminded herself that Cedric was generally weird, so maybe he was just messing with her head. She let it go until she pulled into Ma-Max's driveway and something from the block party came back to her. *The Khalil Sarda treatment.* Turning off the engine, she grabbed her phone and pulled up her last text with Khalil.

> Vanessa: Hey. Hope this doesn't sound weird, but did you pick up the check at the party?

"Vanessa?" Ma-Max called out as Vanessa walked through the garage and into the kitchen.

"Coming!" she answered. The phone buzzed in her hand.

> Khalil: Uh-oh. Been found out. The manager promised not to tell.

She looked up just in time to avoid plowing into her grandmother but didn't get the surprise off her face before Ma-Max caught it.

"Baby? Is everything all right?" she asked.

"Mm-hmm," Vanessa nodded, sealing her lips together.

Maxine looked her up and down, squinting.

"If you say so, baby. Come on, lunch is ready. Letta's running late."

Vanessa followed her into the dining room. The food smelled delicious as always, and the table was set beautifully, but the textured plastic of the phone in her hand took most of Vanessa's attention.

"Ma-Max," she said, sitting. "I'm sorry, but I really have to answer this message. Then I'll put the phone away for lunch, I promise."

"Okay, Vanessa. Don't like to see you so stressed," she said. She nodded for her to go ahead, while filling a glass with cucumber mint water.

> Vanessa: You didn't have to do that. I appreciate it, but it's too much. Treating us at the block party was so kind. I hope you didn't think I invited you to join us for the birthday party because you covered our meals before.
> Khalil: Know you didn't expect it. Wanted to do it.
> Vanessa: Why?

"Are you sure everything's all right, Vanessa?" Ma-Max asked, drawing her back to the table.

"Excuse me. Just a surprise that's all." She reached for the water, taking a long sip to cool the flush of heat that came from remembering Khalil's hands on her, his gentle words that turned her on but never pushed too far. She'd thanked him for paying for their meals at the block party and at the food truck. He'd brushed it off. She certainly hadn't invited him to join Dani's party out of an expectation that he'd do the same. Her phone buzzed again.

> Khalil: I meant what I said. I like serving you. Meeting your needs, covering for you financially is part of that for me.

Her cheeks caught fire and her hand shot up, covering the smile that crashed across her face.

Ma-Max cleared her throat again. Vanessa looked up.

"What's his name?" Ma-Max asked, smiling.

"Um—" Her phone buzzed again.

> Khalil: But if I've overstepped your boundaries, please let me know.

She needed to reply to Khalil, but she needed to manage Ma-Max as well. She took a deep breath.

"His name is Khalil. He's just said something very kind to me, and I'd like to call him instead of texting back. Do you mind?"

"Baby, you know I am all for voice communication. If this young man has you needing to say things directly to him, I will not be the one to stop you. Go into the guest room if you need some privacy."

"Thanks," Vanessa said, scooting her chair back and heading down the hall.

"Hey," Khalil said, answering after the first ring.

She pushed off the inside of the closed door, stopping beside the bed.

"Hey," she said softly. "I'm at my grandmother's, about to start Sunday Lunch; I can't talk long."

"Okay. Are you angry?" he asked.

"Not at all. Cedric, the manager, was all mysterious about it." She sat up straight on the edge of the bed. Talking to Khalil might relax her, but she was still at her grandmother's house and knew better than to crease the bedspread or disturb the decorative pillows. "It was really generous of you. You like meeting my needs?"

"I do. I hope that's okay."

She bit her lip, squelching a nervous squiggle of excitement.

"I guess this is a thing, huh?" she asked.

His slow inhale came through loud and clear.

"And you don't want it to be?"

She sighed, squeezing her eyes shut at the awkward. How to explain without sounding seriously judgmental?

"No, I could. It's just—"

Opening her eyes, she caught a shadow under the crack below the door. Maxine Noble would never eavesdrop, but Vanessa wasn't going to make it easy in case she was having a lapse in judgment. She rounded the bed and slid to the floor, cross-legged, facing the wall.

"Sorry," she whispered to Khalil. "My grandmother knows I'm

talking to a guy, and I think she's listening at the door. I'll have to be quiet."

"Okay," he whispered back. "But tell me what's going on with you. You've got that worried tone in your voice."

"You know my tones?" she asked.

"I'm working on learning them."

She flushed hot. *How is he this considerate?*

"It's just . . . Like anyone, I've had certain learning experiences when it comes to dating, and based on those, I have a list of basic requirements."

"And I don't make the cut?" he asked.

"You do, mostly." She drew her knees up to rest her head on them. "You're polite, driven, family seems important to you. You're attractive and have a good educational background." She sighed. "Please don't think I'm horrible, but my grandmother dated a white man after my grandfather passed away, and it got ugly and ended with her heartbroken, and Lisa's ex, Justin, was great for so long, and then he started criticizing her for making everything about race when she wasn't at all, and by the end he was calling her racist against white people and making her doubt herself. I had a really bad experience a little over a year ago. And a humiliating one when I was younger." She took a breath. She'd kept her voice down, but the hurt didn't stay down with the volume. "So, based on all these experiences around me, and the stuff we've already talked about, it seemed that the safest option was to believe that only a black guy could see me as a real person, an individual." She sighed again. "I hate the way that makes me sound."

"It sounds to me like you're a person trying to protect her heart," he said.

"You sure?"

"Yeah. I think we've all got a list of what we'd like in a person. Maybe not a formalized thing, but we all have experiences that leave us with painful lessons," he said. "Do you feel like I see you as an individual?"

She paused, evaluating how he'd been with her, how he'd been with other people. His calls, his concern when she'd been on business trips. Remembering things that had stressed her out at work and asking about them. The care he'd taken for her physically and financially at Paradigm. He and Darius couldn't have been best friends if Darius wasn't an individual in Khalil's eyes. Khalil couldn't have had a good mentoring relationship with Big Brothers Big Sisters if he saw the child as a stereotype. There had to be a real connection there. She sighed, smiling at the tingly warmth in her chest.

"I do. Thank you for choosing to look at my list that way. Maybe I've held on . . ." She closed her eyes. "All I know is that list or no list, I'm curious. About you."

She loved hearing his smile.

"I'm curious about you too," he said, voice soft.

She smiled again, then stopped short.

"Not because you paid for half of Dani's party," she said. "Or for the stuff at the block party. Or lunch. I'm not like that."

He chuckled. "I know you aren't, Vanessa."

"You can call me Ness," she said.

He chuckled. "Sounds like I've hit the lotto again. A nickname?"

She smiled. "I think you deserve it."

"Thank you."

The idea of getting back to Ma-Max stung a little, but she needed to.

"You're welcome," she said. "I'd better go."

"Don't want to keep your grandmother waiting," he said.

"Yeah."

"Shoot me a text?" he asked. "Later on, so I know you're good?"

"Will do. Bye, Khalil," she said.

"Bye, Ness."

She ended the call, resting her phone against her thighs. After a shy smile, she got up and padded to the door. Pressing her ear to it, she was surprised not to hear anything on the other side. Snapping the door open, she caught Arletta and Ma-Max in the hallway, bumping into each other as they turned in opposite directions, pretending to be walking by.

"Seriously, ladies? Eavesdropping?" Vanessa asked, following them down the hall.

"We were doing no such thing," Maxine said. "Letta wanted to take a look at the rose color I painted the hall. She's thinking of repainting her bedroom."

"You repainted years ago," Vanessa said as they returned to their seats at the table. "I'm sure Auntie Letta is familiar with the color." She looked at Arletta, getting only a shrug in reply.

The orange and yellow carrot salad was closest to her, so Vanessa served herself first, while giving her grandmother as much side-eye as she dared. Maxine didn't correct her on her manners, so Vanessa knew she'd been trying to listen in.

"Ma-Max, is there anything you'd like to ask me?"

"I think the more important question is whether you have something to share. You know how I feel about keeping secrets when it comes to relationships."

"That was a low blow, Max," Arletta said.

Vanessa huffed a breath through her nose.

"I don't mean anything by it," said Maxine. "It's just that—"

"As you already know," Vanessa said, daring to cut her grandmother off, "his name is Khalil. We are simply getting to know each other, something that has happened other times in my life that I have not told you about because nothing came of it. No secrets are being kept. I don't imagine you'd like me to tell you about every person I trade a few words with, Ma-Max. With as much as I travel and network, I'd have to spend every minute I visit telling you about other people." She shoveled in a mouthful of carrots and chomped. Arletta raised her eyebrows and sipped her cucumber water.

"You make a good point, baby," Ma-Max said. "You are grown and know how to separate the wheat from the chaff. But I must say, I've never seen you react that way to a message you've gotten on that thing." She tipped her chin at Vanessa's phone beside the silverware.

"How's that?" Arletta asked.

"She blushed," Maxine said. "Even sighed with her hand over her heart."

Vanessa's face caught fire.

"Our Ness?" Arletta asked. "Miss Cool Under All Circumstances?"

"You two are making it very difficult to respect my elders right now," Vanessa said. "Can we please talk about something else?"

"Come on, just a little detail? To tide us over until the next time we get to hear about him?" Arletta asked.

"Time that's ticking away on your biological clock, baby," Maxine said.

Vanessa and Arletta glared at her.

"Not helping, Max," Arletta said.

Vanessa's gut reaction was to stay close-lipped. She didn't owe her grandmother an update on her love life. Then again, after having been someone else's dirty little secret, she refused to do the same to him.

"His name is Khalil, Auntie Letta," she said. "He's twenty-eight. Morehouse man, MBA from UM, entrepreneur, gentlemanly, and Lisa and Bibi like him."

Arletta beamed, nodding her approval. "He sounds lovely," she said.

"He does," Maxine said. "What do you know about his people?"

That was enough. Ma-Max hadn't asked what kind of business he owned, and Vanessa didn't want to get into it, sure she'd have some remark. Detail time was over.

"Haven't gotten to all that, Ma-Max. Like I said, we've just been getting to know each other." *And he's been massaging my feet and carrying me around, paying for my meals and nights out and saying things that light my whole body on fire, but you don't need to know that.*

"Well, if things continue going well, I look forward to meeting him."

"Me too," Arletta said. "But take your time, baby. You're still in your twenties. Your biological clock isn't in nearly the rush that your grandmother is."

CHAPTER EIGHTEEN

It was heavy-hot outside. Vanessa could barely stand it. The only times she agreed with her grandmother and cursed the concrete and steel city she'd chosen to live in were on humid days, like this one. It was good reason to wear a skirt. She kept telling herself it was for the heat and that she was confident in it. She most certainly was not wearing the skirt because she was about to see Khalil.

"Hey, Vanessa." Darius's warm smile was easy to return as she crossed the threshold of the Fade. She said hello and nodded to the man in his chair. Khalil wasn't there.

"'Lil ran to the store," Darius said. "Told me to get you settled if you got here before he did."

She nodded, slipping into Khalil's chair. Darius put a cape on her and pumped the pedal a couple times to raise the seat. She raised an eyebrow at him.

"Having fun with the short girl?"

Darius smiled. "Just trying to help. And you're not so short." He winked at her reflection and stepped on another pedal, the back of the seat reclining a little. "Use this for beard work, but why don't you relax a bit before he gets back."

"Thanks." She got comfortable as Darius returned to his customer. The angle of Khalil's chair was just right to catch the reflection of a row of trophies in a new case behind her. She swiveled the chair and squinted.

"Darius, whose trophies are those?" she asked.

"Khalil's," he said.

"None of them are yours?"

He looked up. "Course not. Khalil's the one with the skills, not me."

"But I saw you play. At the charity game."

"Uhh . . . thanks, but you only saw me assist Khalil," he said.

She scooted out of the chair and went over to the case tucked behind the register. Local championships, state, regional. A framed photo on one end of the case caught her eye. A high school team, boys grinning, falling all over one another, a giant trophy in the middle of the group. "National Champions" written across the bottom. A young, but already handsome Khalil near the center of the group, an arm around one of his teammates, laughing. The tinkle of the bell above the door brought her back to the barbershop. Grown-up Khalil was at the door, a grocery bag in one hand, an apple missing a large chunk in the other.

"Hi, Vanessa," he said around the bite in his mouth. "Sorry." He covered his mouth with the hand holding the apple.

"Hey, Khalil, no worries," she said.

He raised the bag. "Just gonna . . ." He pointed toward the back room.

"It's okay, take your time." She took another look at young Khalil and his teammates, then returned to his chair.

"Did he play in college, Darius?" she asked.

He turned around, facing her, and shut off his clippers.

"You don't know?" he asked.

Uh-oh. "Should I?"

Darius blinked a couple times. "He usually finds a way to bring it up. When you guys were talking after the game, I figured he had. Okay. You know he went to Morehouse, right?"

She nodded.

"They offered him a full ride," Darius said. "Just like UNC Chapel Hill, Duke, Villanova, and UCLA." He glanced up as Khalil joined them. "But I guess you didn't hear that from me," Darius said.

"Didn't hear what?" Khalil asked. "Hey," he said to Vanessa, a gentle hand on her shoulder.

"That you really are some sort of basketball star," she said to his reflection. He shot a glare at the back of Darius's head, then shrugged at her.

"I loved to play when I was younger. Still do. Ball opened some doors for me, but I knew I wasn't going pro, so I don't talk about it as much as I used to." He tapped the pedal a couple more times, raising the seat higher. She caught the dubious look Darius gave him, and the eye roll Khalil shot in return.

"I . . . hope I haven't touched on a sensitive subject," she said.

"No." Khalil shook his head. "Not at all. So what are we doing today? Shape-up like usual?"

Darius finished with his customer and stepped into the back to make a call. Vanessa was actively working not to stare at Khalil's jaw, and that tendon down the side of his neck she wanted to lick, when Darius's voice got loud and frantic. Khalil turned off the clippers and raised his head.

"Gimme a sec," he said to Vanessa. He leaned over to put his clippers down as Darius rushed out of the back room, eyes wide.

"My dad's missing," he said to Khalil.

"Missing?"

"It's this thing—he's been getting restless, confused in the evening. My mom thought he was in the living room, but when she went in, the patio door was open, and he's gone. She called Rachel, and they're out looking, but—"

"Go," Khalil said.

Darius's gaze flitted to his chair, the previous client's hair still on the floor around it, then to the cash register. He gestured over his shoulder with his thumb.

"I can't leave you with—"

"Man, go. I can handle closing up."

"There's all the—"

Vanessa leaned forward in the chair, to make eye contact around Khalil.

"Darius," she said. "I'll stay and help Khalil. You aren't leaving him with anything."

He was looking at her, but she didn't know if he was seeing her. Khalil stepped past him, patting his arm, then jogged into the back room and out again. He handed Darius a backpack.

"Go," Khalil said. "Hit me up when you can, we got things covered here."

Darius took the bag, blinking at it, then at Khalil.

"Okay, thanks," he said, more to the floor than to either of them. Then he was gone.

The quiet he left behind was sharp and heavy. Khalil's gaze stayed out the window a moment, then he looked back at Vanessa again. He picked up the clippers and returned to his spot behind her.

"You okay?" she asked, before he turned them on.

He met her gaze in the mirror and smiled. It was almost the smile he'd given her at the club, the one she'd been dying to see again. But the sadness in his eyes made her heart fall instead of soar.

"Yeah," he said. "Thanks."

After a few quiet moments, and a lot more concentration on her hair than she thought it required, he began to explain.

"Dare's dad's been showing some early signs of what might be dementia. I think his doctor said something about strange behaviors at sundown, but I'm not really sure. Maybe that's why he wandered off."

"Maybe," Vanessa said softly. "You and Darius are really close, huh?"

Khalil smiled, his focus on her hair, but the look in his eyes was distant.

"Yeah. Thick as thieves. Since freshman year."

"That's great."

"He's like my fifth brother."

"Fifth?" Vanessa said, failing to keep the surprise out of her voice.

"Yeah," he chuckled, moving to her other side. "I have four brothers. We're really close, talk all the time, but the number always surprises people. I've got two older and two younger, but my identical twin doesn't like to admit that he's younger than me. Three minutes older is *still* older, right?"

He met her eyes in the mirror and she was happy to see some humor in his.

"Well, that would *technically* make you the middle child."

"Exactly." His smile dimmed as he returned to her hair. "So yeah, Dare is closer to me than anyone except Karim, my twin. Dare's mom even tried to get me to date his sister, Rachel. Said I'd make a good son-in-law. But that was too weird." He shuddered. "Like trying to date my own sister."

Vanessa was quiet, getting the impression that Khalil needed to talk, and reeling a little from all the information. Khalil came from a large, close-knit family. Although he hadn't told her the exact number before, it made sense that he came from love, based on the way he gave it so freely. The affection in his voice was clear: Darius and his family were Khalil's family of choice, so seeing Darius hurt naturally hurt him too. He was worried about Darius's dad, and his mother and sister. And he had a twin brother . . . that was completely unfair. There was another man walking around with those eyes and those lips? She bit the inside of her cheek. Khalil was sharing personal things with her, working through some difficult emotions, and she was sitting there lusting after him. She tried to refocus, get her mind into an appropriate, supportive space. Readjusting her hands under the cape, she rolled the beads of her bracelet between her fingers; her own silent "stay good" rosary.

He finished quickly, holding up a mirror so she could check the back. She nodded her approval and thought to focus on his shirt to thank him, not his eyes. But she hadn't noticed that the collar of his dress shirt was unbuttoned, a hint of warm-looking skin visible.

Get yourself together.

He barely had the cape off before she hopped to her feet.

"Where should I start?" she asked, looking around the shop.

Khalil didn't answer. He was staring at her legs. She followed his gaze and chuckled.

"Okay fine, I'm wearing heels again. You didn't expect me to walk around barefoot forever, did you?"

He blinked twice, then looked at her feet.

"Yeah. No, it's the skirt. I'm used to seeing you in pants," he said, folding the cape.

"Oh. Good point," she said. "I'm not really a skirt girl. Like slacks better."

"Why?" He wasn't looking at her.

She shrugged. "Better pockets?"

"Ah," he said.

"So, where should I start?"

He locked the front door and Vanessa swept while he dealt with the register. He mopped while she folded the towels that had been in the dryer, then joined her in the back room.

"Do you ever wear flat shoes?" he asked, putting the freshly washed towels in the dryer.

She laughed, leaning over the folding counter to add another towel to her stack.

"What is this obsession with my footwear? I thought you weren't into feet." When she leaned back to where she'd been folding, he was a lot closer than she'd anticipated. They didn't touch, but the heat from his body warmed the side of hers. He picked a towel out of the pile and started folding.

"I'm not," he said, voice soft. "Don't get me wrong, they look good. But they also look like they hurt. You look great. All the time, Vanessa. I'd never tell you what to wear. But even in . . . let's say, sweatpants. An old T-shirt. Just hanging out on a Sunday afternoon. I bet you're stunning."

"You've been thinking about me in sweats?"

"I've been thinking about *you*. The look—the heels, always put together, it's nice. But there's so much more to you than that."

Vanessa didn't know what to say. And even if she had, she wouldn't have been able to draw breath to say it. The back room had just gotten a lot hotter. He gave her a sultry half-smile.

"I can finish these towels," he said. "Why don't you grab a seat?" He nodded toward the small table at the other end of the room, a lone chair beside it. The grocery bag he'd had earlier was on top, another apple inside.

"Yeah, okay." She sighed, approaching the table. So it wasn't all about the outside with him. She probably should have guessed that already. But hearing it sent warm tremors all over. *Maybe he really sees me as an individual. I'm not just part of some mass of black girls for him.* She grabbed the apple in the bag and turned back to him.

"What you're saying," she said, "is that you're . . . into . . . me. For *me.* It's not all about the image for you."

He stopped folding, turning his back on the towels.

"The image grabs attention," he said. "*You,* the person inside, keeps it."

"Huh. Mind if I steal this apple?" she asked, waving it at him.

"Help yourself."

She went to the sink to wash it. She glanced at the small table, then back at the counter where he was folding the towels. There was enough space for her on the edge. He jumped when she scooted up, then chuckled as he started a new towel.

"Is this an okay seat?" she asked, taking a bite.

"Are you comfortable?"

She nodded.

"That's all that matters." His gaze fell to her lips. She swallowed, harder than she wanted, but the shiver going through her didn't leave much choice.

He let the towel in his hands slump back into the pile and brought his hand to her cheek, his gaze unmoving.

"You have . . ." He grazed his thumb under her lip, wiping away a drop of juice from the apple. His lips parted. She would have guessed that he was breathing a little faster, but she couldn't tell. Her own breath was too loud in her ears. He caressed her cheek. "You—"

"Khalil." She startled them both, and he looked into her eyes. "Next chance that—"

He cut her off, suddenly there in front of her, close, her face cradled in both his hands.

"Next chance that presents itself," he whispered, those sinful lips close enough that she could feel their heat with her own. He smiled, tilted his head, and whispered her name before bringing his lips to hers.

He was kissing her, but he wasn't. There was the heat, the electrified explosion that was the end of her yearning for his lips on hers, but there was something else. Her mind playing tricks on her, teasing her with a flash of being under him in bed, the hot, steamy press of his skin against hers from chest to thigh. One of his hands cupped her head while the other supported her back, but was it real or in her mind? He nibbled on her bottom lip, teasing her mouth open, and a sound came out, a high-pitched gasp she should have only made as she got close. But she couldn't be getting close to an orgasm, he was just kissing her, they were in the back room of his shop, not naked together in bed. He groaned, a deep, yearning sound. The vibrations coursed through her, his tongue delving, stroking gently. Too gently for her taste. She tightened her grip on his shirt, wanting him closer. But when had she run her fingers into his hair? He pulled back, hissing and licking his lips.

"I like that," he whispered.

She tugged his hair again. "That?"

He groaned. "Shit, yes."

She moaned back as their mouths met again, and any pretense of a gentle kiss was tossed aside. Tightening her legs around his waist, she wondered when she'd wrapped them around him. He smiled against her, the hand on her lower back sliding down her thigh to hook under her knee. He jerked her forward, bringing her to the edge of the counter, her body flush against his. She ground against him. He pulled back.

"Damn, Vanessa," he sighed.

"Too much?" she whispered against his lips.

"No. You feel so fucking good." He gripped her thigh, fingers digging in.

She slid hers through the open V of his dress shirt, skin against skin.

"You too." She sighed. "But how do I taste?"

He growled, coming back at her open-mouthed.

They kissed and writhed for an eternity, and for no time at all. She kept getting lost in the back and forth flashes between reality and fantasy. He found a dangerous spot on her neck, sucking then biting, and she cried out, tightening her legs around him as she fell back against the counter. He leaned over her, palms flat on either side, panting like she was.

"I want you, Khalil," she said.

He shot her the best, sexiest version of that grin.

"I want you. But not like this."

The wave of arousal that had threatened to crash over her quickly abated.

"Wait," he breathed, stroking her cheek. "Stay with me. I . . ." He looked away, annoyance skittering across his face. Then he shook his head and chuckled. "How do you do this to me? It's like I can't be cool. Words feel clumsy."

"I really like your clumsy words."

Stroking his hand up her arm, he smiled.

"I've wanted you, been burning for you since you first crossed the threshold." He met her gaze. "But not like this. I don't want our first time together to be hidden in some back room. I want to make love to you in a bed. Slowly. It has to be much more special than a frenzy on a table."

She let out a deep breath. She hadn't been set for romantic.

"Okay, Khalil," she said.

"Are you angry?" His mastery of simultaneously sexy and adorable should have been illegal.

"I'm not. Just frustrated 'cause you've already got me so wound up."

His grin slid incandescent.

"Do I?" He leaned over, his lips close. His body heat, his arms, formed a cradle of desire around her.

"Like you don't know that," she whispered.

He grunted deep, gripping her thigh.

"Can't have you frustrated," he said. He brushed his lips against hers, pulling back as she tried to deepen the kiss. She couldn't stifle a growl. He chuckled. "Nope. That won't do at all." He kissed her deep, stoking the fire, making her eyes roll back. He released her lips to work down her neck again, finding the sensitive spot on the opposite side. When she moaned and grasped his hair, he groaned, letting his weight fall against her. She pulled his hair hard enough to make him stop.

"How . . ." she panted. "How is this not frustrating me?"

He shifted over her, slowly running his fingertips up the inside of her thigh.

"You know I got you, Vanessa," he whispered as he made little circles inside her knee, up her thigh a few inches, then back to her knee again. Her unsteady breathing pressed her chest to his. He slid his cheek against hers, his lips at her ear.

"I would love to touch you right now," he whispered. "May—"

A sharp vibration cut him off, his eyebrows knitting. Vanessa held her breath. The buzzing started again, against the wooden counter-top, on the inside of her knee. Khalil straightened, sliding his hand in his pocket to retrieve his phone.

"It's Darius," he said to her, the waver in his voice closer to fear than heat.

"Answer," she said, nodding as she pushed herself up.

"Hey," he said, one hand on Vanessa's thigh. She couldn't hear what Darius was saying, but she could read the result all over Khalil. The corners of his eyes tightened, irises shifting from side to side. His lips parted, his breath quickening. Getting scared, she laid her hand over his. He looked up at her, kind recognition over his features, then looked back down again.

"Okay," he said. "No, you know better. You want me to call Mo? He—"

Vanessa gulped down a painful swallow.

"Okay, man, I'm on my way," Khalil said. "It's gonna be okay." He hung up, letting out a slow breath before he looked at her again.

"They still can't find him?" she asked.

"No," he said. "Listen, I'm sorry to just leave—"

"Don't apologize," she said, sliding off the counter and running her hands down her skirt. "Is there anything else that needs to be done?"

He glanced around, shaking his head, and grabbed a messenger bag off a shelf.

"No, we already took care of the important things."

He followed her out of the back room, flipping off the light and sliding the door shut.

"Could you use an extra set of eyes?" she asked, shifting her purse onto her shoulder.

Khalil flipped through his keys as they crossed the shop. He paused.

"It's . . . that might help, but I don't know, don't want—"

Vanessa raised a hand, shaking her head.

"It's a family matter," she said. "I don't want to intrude."

"Sorry." Khalil shrugged. "I'd say yes, but I don't know how Darius would feel."

"Khalil." She squeezed his arm, smiling. "It's okay."

She waited outside as he set the alarm and brought the security grate down.

"Let me walk you to your car," he said.

When she tried to refuse so he could get to Darius, he wouldn't hear it. "I need to know you're safe too."

Chivalrous even when he's worried about someone else. She led the way as quickly as possible. Nearly there, she unlocked the doors and turned to say good night. He walked past her and opened her door, waiting for her to sit down.

"Thank you, Khalil," she said. "Now go. Please send me a text when you find him. Just so I know everyone's okay."

He nodded, then squatted down in the open door.

"Is it weird to ask for a good night kiss right now?"

"Not at all," she said, leaning forward to cradle his cheek. It was the most emotionally jumbled kiss she'd ever had: There was the beginning of a spark there, the heat from the back room near the surface. But she could feel his worry as plainly as she could feel his lips. She pulled away before she wanted to.

"Go," she whispered.

He smiled, grazing her chin with his thumb.

"Thanks for understanding."

CHAPTER NINETEEN

Khalil parked in front of her house, unable to tell if she was inside. His eyes still ached from little sleep. Her car wasn't in the driveway, so he thought to leave the bracelet in her mailbox, but instead of opening his door, he picked up his phone.

"Hey," Vanessa answered. His body began to hum.

"Hey. I found your bracelet in the shop. Guess it must have fallen off last night." He plucked it from his cupholder. He'd wanted to put it on, but he'd been afraid to break it, her wrist being so small. "I'll leave it in your mailbox for you?"

"Oh. You can, but I'm in the garage. You can bring it back here . . . if you want."

He gulped, to keep his excitement from altering his voice.

"Sure," he said. "Be right there."

The memory of her lips, the softness of her skin, had been a blissful reprieve after the fear of not being able to find Darius's father. And when they finally had, Khalil had gone home and let those memories engulf him. Now, approaching the garage, his heart was racing. Would she let him touch her again? Should he? The happiness from what had passed between them the previous night had been tempered by his doubts that morning. A line had been crossed between them, and he was worried that he was dragging all his *stuff* right over it. Even though he'd put in the work with Dr. E, he couldn't get past the fear that Nia had been right, that a man who couldn't control his emotions wasn't really a man at all.

Rolling the beads of her bracelet between his fingers, he approached the open garage, hands in pockets. Vanessa was at a wide, high desk along the back wall, natural light from the large window in front of her, gilding her skin. And so much more of it was visible than he'd ever seen. In flip-flops, short denim shorts, and a black tank, she stole his breath. She looked up from what she was drawing and smiled.

"Hi."

He smiled back but couldn't speak, the spark from seeing her lips too strong, now that he knew how they felt.

He stayed just inside the door. She put her pencil down and swiveled her seat to face him.

"Are you okay?" she asked.

He nodded. "Rough night."

"Thanks for texting me after they found him. How's Darius?"

"Shaken up."

"Makes sense," she said, nodding.

Then he wasn't sure what to say. He shifted his hands in his pockets again, rolling the beads like his feelings.

"You look like you're worried I'm going to bite," she said.

He shook his head and joined her at her desk.

"What are you drawing?"

She shrugged. "Different things."

"Didn't know you were an artist," he said. "Thought you only drew to design apps." The top page was a detail of the large tree outside the window. Underneath, bits of other sketches peeked out.

"I'm not really an artist," she said. "It's just something that helps me relax, think through things."

He watched his thumb glide along the edge of the desk.

"Got a lot on your mind?" he asked. She didn't answer.

He looked up and got lost in her eyes. There was a wave, a bend in the air between them, and he was suddenly unsteady on his feet.

"I have a problem, Khalil," she whispered.

"What's that?"

Then she was off her stool, pushing herself onto the desk beside him. She drew him between her knees, her hands cradling his cheeks.

"I'm too short to kiss you first."

She brought his lips to hers, and he died. A blissful death. Apparently, he was lost or off-kilter all the time, because when he kissed Vanessa, when he touched her the way he wanted, he was home. He was safe and everything was right in the world. Her arms over his shoulders, hands in his hair, legs around his waist: Every part of her was right where it belonged. The insanity of thinking that about someone he hadn't known for long freaked him out, but he didn't want to go down that path. Instead he pulled her close, as tightly as he could. He broke the kiss to whisper to her.

"You are perfect, Vanessa. Absolutely perfect." He pulled back to stroke her cheek. "You let me know when and I'll bend down or scoop you up, whatever you want." She giggled and he needed to kiss her again, dying that perfect death a little more. She put a hand to his chest and pushed.

"How long are you gonna make me wait?" she asked.

"Wait?"

"For you." She paused, breathing deep. "I need you."

The air bent again, a surge sparkling hot over his skin.

"You have me," he said. He pulled her legs tight around his waist, holding her close, and picked her up off the desk.

"Where?" he rasped.

She pointed to a stairwell at the opposite wall.

"There."

He couldn't keep his lips off hers as he got them clumsily across the garage. At the doorway, her arm cast out, swatting at something to his left as he took the first step. The rumble and creak of the closing garage door registered in the back of his mind, but the forefront was all about Vanessa's lips, about her body flush against his. His foot caught on the fourth step, and she shrieked into his mouth as they bumped against the wall.

"Sorry," he said.

"It's okay," she whispered, her nails making his scalp tingle.

Then they were on the landing and he let her slide down him, taking a moment to catch his breath, mesmerized by her breathlessness and swollen lips. She reached behind her to turn the doorknob. Grabbing a handful of his shirt, she pulled him into the room.

He caught the layout in his peripheral vision: a bed to his right, an open door leading to a bathroom beyond it. She kicked off her flip-flops. He stepped out of his shoes.

"I don't understand, Khalil," she said.

"What?"

"Why do you seem afraid of me right now?"

Maybe because I'm terrified by everything I'm feeling. No one has ever messed me up as fast as you have.

"You intimidate the hell out of me," he said.

She laughed, flashing him that amazing smile, hands on her slim hips.

"How can I intimidate you? You're like a model. If anyone should be intimidated here, it's me."

"You're so perfect," he said. "How can I not be intimidated?"

She wrinkled her adorable nose.

"Was that you trying to spit game to me?"

She was right. That did sound like game. The bathroom caught his eye.

"Come here," he said, grabbing her wrist and pulling her toward it.

He needed to blink a few times once he turned the light on. Vanessa blinked too then looked up at him, an eyebrow raised. Looking straight at her made him all nervous again, so he faced the mirror.

"Look," he said, nodding at her reflection. He stepped behind her, and she chuckled.

"Are we back at the shop?" she asked.

She was right. They'd looked at each other through a mirror a bunch of times. It was familiar and steadying.

"Good point," he said. "Let me tell you what I see when I look at you."

"Okay . . ."

He stood behind her, hands gently on her shoulders, and she looked at his reflection.

"First," he said, leaning down to brush her crown with his cheek.

"Only a confident woman can rock this style. Confidence is always sexy, and you've got it in spades. But then . . ." He leaned closer, putting his hands on either side of her on the bathroom counter. He nuzzled her behind the ear, taking a deep breath, getting high on her scent. He let his eyes close as he whispered to her.

"You smell . . . amazing. There's that lavender that lingers after you leave and keeps me yearning for more, but underneath that, deeper, warmer . . ." He took another deep breath, tracing the curve of her neck with his nose. "The dark richness of your skin. You're soft, sweet, and as I was lucky enough to discover last night, delicious." Her sigh encouraged him to open his eyes. She'd let her head fall to the side, eyes half closed, lips parted. He was grateful for their difference in height. It forced him to step back to bring his head close to hers. With the space between them, she couldn't feel the erection that had already tented his pants. He ran two fingertips down her nape. She shivered.

"I can't tell you how many times I've fantasized about kissing you here. How these few inches of skin have taunted me every single time I've been behind you." He breathed across her nape, dragging his lips in an open kiss. She gasped, eyes shut, head falling forward. Her two-handed grip on the counter encouraged him on. He drew his fingers down, between her shoulder blades, bumping over her bra, down the curve of her lower back. Goosebumps and chills bloomed in his wake.

Licking his lips, he got directly behind her but maintained some space between them. He reached her waist. Crouching, he circled it with his hands.

"This," he whispered. "Your tiny waist. The way it fits in my hands. Don't want to get all caveman on you, but . . ." He grunted. "That's really hot."

She fluttered her eyes open and looked at his reflection.

"I like your hands on my waist like that," she whispered.

"Yeah?"

She licked her bottom lip and nodded.

"Yeah."

Emboldened, he slid his hands down, fighting himself not to grab her hips and thrust her back against him.

"I love your hips," he whispered. He couldn't help himself from squeezing, hoping his touch wasn't too hard. But then she gasped, and he squeezed a little harder, moving her a little, claiming just a bit. Her eyes shut, she let her head fall back against his shoulder, gasping open-mouthed. He caught the tension in her arms, her fingers bowing against the counter, and the subtle pushback of her hips into his hands. He squeezed again, breathing deep, steadying himself before he moved on. Closing his eyes, he rested his head on her shoulder.

"And this . . ." He molded his hand over the back pocket of her shorts. "This perfect, round, mouthwatering curve." He cupped it from underneath and squeezed. "Don't laugh, but now I finally understand the cheesiest of all lines."

"What's that?" she asked.

He rolled his eyes at himself but said it anyway.

"I hate to see you leave, but I love to watch you walk away."

She giggled, opening her eyes.

"Okay, cheesy. But I'll take it." She winked at him.

He held her gaze in the mirror, mouthing her shoulder as he squeezed both cheeks. Her wriggle made him shudder and he let go, before his lust took over and he bent her at the waist. Sliding his hands forward, he tucked a thumb under her tank and stroked the skin on her stomach. She shivered and smiled, eyes closing.

"You aren't going to stop there, are you?"

He smiled and inched the tank top up, until he could cup her breasts in each hand. He needed a breath, then another. It had been more than a decade since he'd lost control just from touching a woman's breasts, yet here he was, about to embarrass himself in front of her. But no way was he letting go. He brought his lips to her shoulder again.

"These are heaven," he sighed, cupping and massaging. Gently, learning how to touch her based on her sighs and little whimpers. He palmed her nipples over her bra and her eyelids squeezed tight as she sighed. He stopped, sliding his hands back down her sides to regain a little control. She opened her eyes as he let her tank settle and brought one of her arms up around his head. He smiled against her ear as she ran her fingers through his hair.

"Careful," he whispered. "That's my spot."

"Is it?" she asked, grabbing a handful and tugging hard as she arched back against him. He hissed, grabbed her wrist, and spun her to face him. They stared at each other breathlessly an instant before she ripped her tank over her head. Then her hands were under his shirt and he couldn't get it off fast enough. Biting her lip, she traced her fingertips slowly down his chest, circling his nipple, making it tighten painfully. He shuddered and she grinned.

"You know," she said, watching her fingers bump slowly over his abs, "I almost passed out that day at Revitalize Detroit."

He wasn't in the best place for words, but he got it after a second.

"The charity thing?" He managed a chuckle. "Was I too ripe?"

"God, no," she whispered. "You were a demigod. You are one. Seeing you like this? I couldn't think straight. Forgot half my presentation." Then, palm flat against his stomach, she leaned forward and circled his nipple with her tongue before sucking it between her lips. He cried out, bracing himself with a hand on the wall. She looked up, a smile in her eyes as she plucked at his nipple with her teeth.

"Vanessa," he growled.

She sucked hard again, trailing her fingers down to the waist of his pants. She grabbed at his belt with both hands and released his nipple, blowing cool air across it.

He groaned through clenched teeth.

"Still afraid of me?" she asked.

"Hell no," he said, crouching to devour her mouth. He had the presence of mind to cup her head gently, but not enough control to keep from pulling her hard against him with a hand across her lower back. The only idea in his head was *more*. She whimpered and moaned against him then pushed away and pointed to the drawers under the sink. "Second from the top," she said. Then she was backing away toward the bed, smiling, unbuttoning her shorts.

He opened the drawer and grinned, grabbing a box of condoms and following her. He fought between his rising want and his nerves about overwhelming her. Her shorts hit the floor and he gasped at the sight of her like that, in her lacy black bra and panties. He blinked again, not trusting his eyes. He stalked toward her, tossing worry aside.

"Stop," she said, a hand raised.

Heart seizing, he froze.

She smiled at him. "Close your eyes."

Cocking an eyebrow, he did as she asked. He tilted his head as he strained to listen. Fabric rustled, maybe curtains closing. She passed close and he turned to follow. She stroked his arm, leaving a trail of sparks.

"You're doing great, handsome. Just indulge me a couple more seconds," she said.

"Yes, ma'am," he said, smiling.

"Cute." She was somewhere behind him, a drawer opening, a little shuffling. She passed again on his other side; there was a faint click, maybe the sound of a light being turned on.

"Are you going to blindfold me?" he asked.

"Would you like me to?" The pitch of her voice changed, like she was exerting herself a little.

"Could be fun." He shrugged. "But let's not get ahead of ourselves. Won't unveil all my kinks right off the bat."

She laughed. "Kinks? Sounds intriguing."

Her voice was muffled, her back to him, he guessed. Then a scraping sound, and the powdery burn of a lit match tickled his nose.

"What are you up to, Vanessa?" he asked.

"Almost done," she said. She passed him again and lit another match. "Don't worry. No danger, unless we get careless."

He raised an eyebrow in her direction. Then all was silent.

"Okay," she said. "You can open your eyes."

The room was bathed in a soft, warm glow. She'd drawn the curtains as he'd guessed, but he'd missed the string of fairy lights over the headboard when they'd come upstairs. There were tea lights all over, taller white candles on the dresser and the nightstands. He was surprised by his reaction: It was the first time in years he'd felt shy about a woman inviting him into her bed.

"You said you wanted our first time to be special. Not some hurried frenzy," she said, shrugging and gazing to the side. "This is the best I could do in a pinch."

He tossed the condoms on the bed and walked over to her. Miss All-Put-Together actually looked bashful. His heart swelled.

He cupped her face in his hands.

"This is absolutely perfect," he whispered. "Not a surprise, though. Perfection comes from perfection." He stroked her cheeks with his thumbs. She smiled.

"Kiss me," she said.

He hurried to obey.

Vanessa's imagination was good, but the reality of Khalil was so much better than any fantasy she could dream up.

She'd memorized the softness of his lips, the silk of his hair between her fingers. His groans vibrated through her, washing away her nerves. She discovered she loved kissing him while he smiled. She wanted to get on the bed. Then they were moving, but she wasn't sure if she was leading them there, or if he was leading her. And she grinned because it didn't matter.

Her legs bumped up against the edge as she ran her fingertips down his chest again. Grabbing at his belt, she broke the kiss.

"I want these off," she said, tugging at his pants.

She needed to reevaluate her favorite sounds. His hungry growl gave her an even better hit than his laugh.

"Yes, ma'am," he said, unbuckling and unzipping.

Giggling, she pushed herself up onto the bed but didn't take her eyes off him, refused to miss a second of the show. He shoved his pants down and she caught fire, unable to keep herself from staring, gasping as his erection bobbed, arcing his boxer briefs forward. He stroked a hand over it, his grin wicked.

"Vanessa," he said. "You keep looking at me like that and I'm gonna come on the spot." He grabbed the base of his cock over his shorts and she was seconds away from a heart attack. She looked into his eyes.

"Sorry," she panted.

"For what?"

"I'm usually much more in control." She licked her lips and shot forward.

"What—"

Later, when she replayed this particularly good day, she'd take time to savor his surprise, smile at his shock when he realized what she was about to do. But right then, she was single-minded.

At the edge of the bed, she ripped his briefs down and grinned as he slipped free. A thought to be gentle flitted across her mind but didn't stick. She was focused, tuned in to his sounds, his breathing, to keep herself in check. Grabbing the base of his cock and glancing up to meet his shocked gaze, she sucked the head into her mouth.

He groaned deep, jaw clenched, unchecked yearning darkening his face. His hand stuttered at her shoulder, gripping to steady himself or her, she couldn't guess. And she didn't care. She twisted, pulling him in a deep drag as she let her eyes flutter shut, listening to him, learning what he liked.

He choked out her name, his voice far away. She glanced up to find his head tilted back as he panted. Smiling, she moaned around him and savored his choked groan. She wriggled onto her side, not letting go, and got a hand free to slide between his legs. He sucked in a sharp breath and his hips rocked forward once, then stilled.

"Stop," he rasped.

She looked up at him but didn't let go. He looked at her, then quickly away, groaning deep again. He pulled back hard, freeing himself.

"Stop," he panted. "Stop now . . . I can't take it."

"Did I hurt you?"

"God, no. I'm about two seconds away from losing it, and that's not okay." His face got even darker, needier. She'd have been scared if it hadn't turned her on so much. "You come first," he growled. "Panties off."

She moistened her lips as she rolled her underwear down, watching him get out of his and climb up onto the bed. She scrambled back, intending to get up to the headboard, but he caught her, pulling her flat onto her back, his hands under her knees, kneeling between her legs. He froze, staring. A hiccup of nerves passed through her until he pulled in a ragged breath.

"Goddamn. You are beautiful here." He looked into her eyes, unadulterated wickedness in his gaze. "Let's see how you taste."

Then he was down, mouth open wide, licking her long and slow and lewd, up her slit, between her lips, finishing with a sinuous, burning lash across her clit. She shouted, her back arching.

"That's it, Ness," he said, grinning. He did it again. Over and over. She was trying not to push back, trying not to be greedy, but she broke. She threaded a hand in his hair and he nodded, his moan vibrating through her. His lips, his tongue, even his chin and cheeks massaging her, caressing her, driving her outside of herself.

How is it possible to be this turned on?

Eyes locked on hers, he angled his head, lips forming a gentle suction around her clit. She cried out, bucking against him, and he winked. He let go of one of her thighs, then she felt his finger glide along her opening. He paused, still sucking gently, but he raised an eyebrow as he touched a fingertip inside her. She nodded, mouth open.

He penetrated her, increasing the suction, and she cried out again.

"My God, Khalil, yes." She shuddered.

He stroked, sucking a little harder.

"Shit yes, like that." She sighed.

He groaned and sucked harder, moved his finger faster.

"Another," she gasped.

He obeyed, groaning with her, crooking his fingers as they moved in and out. She gave in, grinding against his face, hand tight in his hair. He pulled his free hand up, pressing his palm against the base of her abdomen, his fingers inside moving fast, stroking a spot that took away the meaning of words.

She wanted to encourage him, tried to tell him yes, she was getting close. But words turned to gibberish, to grunts, her head bending sharp to one side as she squeezed her breast hard over her bra. He groaned deep against her and folded her up a bit, his hand moving faster, the suction getting impossible to bear as he rotated his lips, tugging her clit in a tight little circle.

She looked into his eyes and the orgasm came, wrenching her out of herself. Every molecule of skin exploded, her muscles clenching hard, forcing her up off the bed and into an alternate plane where she floated, high for a blissful eternity.

Coming back down was easy. The cloud of endorphins that awaited her made a soothing transition back to earth. Khalil was there, still between her thighs, lapping her gently, kissing her skin. He smiled at her when she looked down at him.

"Hey," he whispered.

Reaching for him, she cradled his face when he got close.

"What did you do to me?" she asked. Her voice hadn't fully come back.

He smiled, blushing.

"I hope I made you come," he said.

She shook her head. "You killed me." She swallowed as she stroked his cheekbones. "You killed me and brought me back to life."

He chuckled. "If it felt good, I'll take that as a compliment."

She nodded then pulled him down to kiss her, consuming him, the taste of her bright and strong on his skin. But that was just fine. She needed to mix with him, wanted to taste herself on him, as he'd eagerly, happily feasted on her. And the way he kissed her back told her he was hungry for more.

The kiss was a necessary break. Concentrating on her helped him back away from the edge, and knowing he'd satisfied her encouraged him to follow his intuition. She read his need as well, shooting that arousing pain down his back as she gripped his hair, devoured his mouth. She caught his tongue, sucking on the tip. He felt her smile, and he opened his eyes, reading the tease in hers.

"Why do I get the feeling you're a little orally fixated, App Goddess?" he asked.

She smiled again, and he discovered it was possible for her to look wanton and shy at the same time.

"Naughty," she whispered. "Reading my secrets. What can I say? You taste really good."

He grunted and kissed her again. She pushed him back and looked down his body, at the bed, at the edge, and frowned.

"What's wrong?"

"You are tall," she said. "And, technically, I am a little short."

He glanced down too.

"Ah," he said. "We have a logistical challenge here."

She shuffled up, her head on a pillow.

"Come closer," she whispered.

Smiling, he did, eagerly accepting the invitation to cradle himself between her legs. A spark of want rolled through him as he ground his length between her labia. Her breath caught in the best way possible, and she ground back up against him. Her sigh made him lick his lips, but her sudden chuckle stopped him in his tracks.

"You're going to bang your head," she said.

He looked up, and she was right. The headboard was so close it was blurry. He laughed.

"Okay, that won't work." He couldn't ignore his instinct to grind against her again. She rewarded him with a higher-pitched gasp then shot him a warning look.

"As much as I love that, I'm gonna need for you to focus for a minute." She skirted a hand down and dragged her fingernails up his lower back. A deep shiver jerked him to the side, taking his breath away.

"I'm not staying focused?" he asked. He rotated his hips hard against her, savoring her sharp breath, the sudden dilation of her pupils.

"You're too naughty." She pushed one shoulder hard, pulling the other, and he followed the motion, rolling onto his back as she slid on top of him. Biting his lip, he circled her waist again, a groan scraping his throat.

"If this is my reward for being naughty, I hope you'll forgive me if I misbehave all the time," he said, rolling his hips. She sighed his name, eyes fluttering, lips open. That expression was going to haunt him the next time he was in the shower. A burst of moisture kissing the base of his cock forced the breath out of him.

"Shit, Ness." He gripped her hips, rolling against her again.

Her palms flat against his abdomen, she stuttered a grind of her own, eyes hooded.

"Condom," she breathed.

Glancing around, he realized he'd lost track of the box. But she hadn't. She looked over her shoulder, then bent back to snatch it from the edge of the bed. He loved the way she ripped it open, like she was starved.

"Does Miss All-Put-Together always have candles and condoms at hand?"

She laughed, pulling some out.

"For guests. Candles to make the place cozy and condoms just in case," she said. "I see you opted for the larger size." She raised an eyebrow, teasing him back.

"Was I wrong to?"

Tossing one to him, she shuffled down his legs and grabbed his cock, a tighter grip than she'd had before, twisting hard. He groaned, eyes rolling back.

"Doesn't seem that way to me," she said, licking her lips and stroking him some more.

A warning growl forced its way out and he glared at her.

"Keep it up and we're not going to need the condom," he said.

She raised her hands in surrender, then reached back to unhook her bra. He tore the package open and tossed it aside, staring as her last bit of clothing fell away.

He forced himself to look at the condom to get the stupid thing on correctly, then grabbed her with a palm flat on her back and pulled, leaning up to catch her nipple in his mouth. His brain shut off. He was done teasing for the near future. The last orderly thought he had was to not get too excited and hurt her. Then it was gone, the sweet nub of her hardened skin goading him into worshiping her breast, cupping the other. Her moan tumbled down his spine, lighting him up, but all he could register was her taste and the lavender cloud surrounding him.

"Khalil." She gasped, pulling back so she could look down at him. "I need you inside me, now."

He nodded, panting, and she raised herself up, caught him at the base, and guided him home.

His back arched and his eyes shut against the work of not coming immediately. Particularly as echoes of "home" passed through his consciousness, confusing him, throwing him off. Her sigh of satisfaction pulled his eyes open and worry collapsed as need took over, locking their gazes together. She set a rhythm and he followed, touching her, caressing, grabbing, stroking. He couldn't have said where. He only knew he lived in a mounting madness to feel her everywhere at once.

She keened, accelerating, tipping back. Panting already, he bent his knees and she smiled, leaning into them to brace herself as she rode harder, faster. Gritting his teeth, he caught a signal of hope, her skin deepening, her chest getting darker. He was close, but she was going to finish first. His pride wanted her to come twice. Digging his fingers into her hips, he growled hard enough to burn his throat, then he focused on that pain to pull himself back. She was increasing the rhythm, the tight, slick friction around him growing almost too intense to bear.

"Khalil," she moaned, head thrown back, skin glowing. He took a risk. Supporting her lower back, he sat up, altering their angle, getting himself in position to catch the rhythm again, a hand behind him for balance. Her eyes shot open, locked on his, and a steadying hand went to his shoulder. He sped up, she met him, mouth falling open as she panted.

"Khalil!" she gasped again, the pitch of her voice tightening his balls. He nodded.

"Yeah, that's it, babygirl." He panicked at the slip, and she caught his worry.

"What's wrong?"

He struggled to speak. "Maybe weird."

She shook her head, a half-smile bending her lips, her thrusts taking him deeper as she leaned in close. He couldn't breathe.

"No . . . love it." She glanced down at his lips, hesitating. Then she looked back up into his eyes. "Your babygirl."

He felt silly for the wave of giddiness that exploded out of his heart, but he couldn't care.

"My babygirl," he panted against her lips before taking them, claiming her mouth with the same need she was claiming his body. Then she came, her orgasm undulating her body around him. Her hips jerked out of rhythm, pressing her body against his as her head tilted back, a groan wrenching from her lips. He stopped fighting himself, the wave crested and crashed, and he died happily in her arms.

They crumpled together, into the bed. He had enough presence of mind not to crush her, getting them onto their sides, pulling her close to cradle her into his chest. He adored her snuggling into him, her legs intertwining with his, the tickle of her slowing breath against his skin. He wanted to stay put, never move again, but the condom had to come off. He kissed the top of her head.

"I'll be right back, Ness."

"Thought it was 'babygirl.'" She sighed, eyes hooded.

He gleefully kicked the rational argument that it was too soon right out of his head.

"It is," he whispered.

She was in the middle of a feline stretch when he returned, and of all the beautiful bits of her laid out before him, her stomach caught his eye. He slid back onto the bed and kissed her, just below her navel.

"What are you doing?" she asked.

He couldn't answer. Just stroked his cheek against her, moving his open lips across the little rise of soft skin. He leaned back a few inches to run his fingers over the silky curve of her.

"I love this part," he said, stroking again, covering it with his hand. He planted an arc of kisses between her hip bones, across the roundest part. "Can't see it with your clothes on. I'm enthralled."

She laughed. "You're enthralled by my pooch?"

"You do not have a pooch," he said, side-eyeing her. "You have a sexy, delicious curve leading from your navel to the promised land."

She laughed again. "Come here," she said. "Snuggle with me a little while longer."

He looked into her eyes and grinned.

"Your wish is my command, babygirl."

Then he found himself right where he wanted to be, where he wanted to believe he belonged. She wasn't in the right spot to tuck her head under his chin again, but he needed that closeness, so he pulled, wrapping them together, arms and legs. He caressed her head, the tiny soft curls that had brought them into each other's lives. She looked up at him, and his heart stilled. He liked this pleasant surprise, that he could be soothed by the same eyes that made his heart pound and breath race. He smiled at her; she gave him one back. Her perfect, dainty hand appeared, and she ran her fingertips down his face, as though she were drawing his eyebrows, sculpting his nose, blessing his cheekbones. He let his eyes close.

"What are you doing?" he whispered.

"Memorizing your gorgeous face," she said.

"Had no idea it was worth memorizing." Her fingers stilled. He opened his eyes and met hers.

"I think it is."

He got lost again, falling into the deep pools, feeling cherished but confused. The logical part of his mind couldn't let go of the idea that it was too soon for everything he was feeling. He was curious to know if she was as surprised as he was. But that seemed silly, couldn't be—

"What is it?" she asked.

He smiled.

"Caught me." He grazed his fingers over her shoulder, down her side, to the gentle swell of her hip. He shrugged. "Don't really know. It just seems—"

"Strange? Too soon for things to feel this intense?" she asked.

He met her gaze again. She seemed cautious, not afraid.

"Yeah," he said. "Not that I'm complaining."

"Me either."

"I want to be rational," he said.

"But it's not working," she said.

"Exactly."

She cradled his cheek, swept her fingertips along his jawline. He kissed her thumb as she stroked his lips.

"This ever happened to you before?" she asked.

"Not even close. That's what was wrong before. I'm lost in strange territory here."

She snuggled a hand into his, bringing it to her lips to kiss.

"Then let's get lost together."

CHAPTER TWENTY
September

Well, well," Darius said, the bell over the door jingling through his laughter. "Shop open early, fresh coffee brewed, tunes pumping, and my business partner practically dancing as he polishes the mirrors."

Khalil laughed, tearing off another paper towel. "Aight, man, have your fun."

Darius tossed his backpack onto his chair. "Can I assume that things are going well with you and Vanessa?" he asked.

Khalil would normally have been embarrassed by his blushing, but he was so happy he didn't give a damn.

"If you're asking me about Vanessa, the woman I'm dating, I would say yes, things are going very well."

Darius laughed and offered Khalil a fist bump.

"Dating? Good. Guess y'all wasted enough time circling each other."

Khalil smiled but was stuck between wanting to share because he was happy and his desire to keep some of his budding relationship to himself. Darius took the tools he'd need out of his bag and walked around Khalil toward the back room. "Glad for you, man. What did Karim have to say?"

Leaning against his chair, Khalil shrugged. "Haven't said much to him yet."

Darius stopped in his tracks. "You haven't told him about Vanessa?"

"I have. Didn't tell him things have been getting interesting the past few weeks. He's been in this rough patch with Laila for a while." Unease about sharing anything with his twin was almost as uncharted territory as the intensity of his feelings for Vanessa. He'd been second-guessing himself a lot of late, and it wasn't a sensation he liked.

Darius nodded. "I get it. Good looking out for him. But I'm sure he'd be happy for you. Don't wait too long to let him know, huh?"

Khalil nodded. "How's your dad?"

"Better," Darius said. "Thanks."

"And your mom?"

Darius shrugged, his usual gentle smile gone.

"It's just a lot for her to manage," he said.

Khalil took the couple steps to his friend.

"I get it," he said, squeezing Darius's shoulder. Then he looked up and smiled as his first client of the day walked through the door.

Fridays were always busy at the shops, but Khalil and Darius had their hands especially full making sure that heading into Labor Day weekend, their clients were sharp. He managed to text back and forth a little with Vanessa, making sure she'd slept well and her day started off right. The texts flowed with an ease he hadn't expected after this shift in their relationship. Things had clicked, but he still found himself unsure when it came to her. Stuff that had come easily in the past—complimenting, flirting, feeling out whether or not she might be receptive to doing something that evening before asking her directly—were a challenge with Vanessa. In spite of what they'd shared up to that point, he was still crazy shy, still felt fourteen again.

Undoing the cape from his client's neck and shaking out the hair, Khalil wondered if he *had* been a player in the past. When it came to women, the beginnings had always been easy; he'd barely had to think. But now? It was like he didn't know who he was anymore. Maybe his *stuff* was a bigger deal than he hoped it was. After escorting his client to the register and scheduling his next appointment, Khalil checked his phone as he headed to the back for lunch.

Vanessa: Hey, hottie. Wanna do something tonight?
Khalil: Love to. Got anything in mind?
Vanessa: Lisa's having a get-together to kick off the long weekend. I was supposed to go, but this Alphastone project isn't going well. Don't know if I'll be up to playing nice with others by the end of the day.

He licked his lips, hesitating. She'd set him up to offer her just the kind of evening he wanted: at home, no one else around. But what if she thought he only wanted sex all the time? Then again, she'd said she was tired. He put the phone down on the counter, shaking his head at himself. *What is with this second-guessing? It's like my mind isn't my own anymore.*

Khalil: Darius and I talked about hitting up Paradigm tomorrow. Wanna make that your night out and tonight a night in?
Vanessa: Sounds great. Your place or mine?

He smiled through the bite of his sub. If she was offering to come over to his place, he'd make it worth her while.

Khalil: Mine. Sure you don't mind staying in? I'm more than happy to shut out the rest of the world with you, but I don't want to smother you either.
Vanessa: Lemme think. Locked away for the evening with an Adonis, or being "on" for a party. Hmmm . . . decisions, decisions.

Grinning, he finished the last bite and pulled up the schedule. They closed at seven, and his last appointment was at six forty-five. He wouldn't be free until eight. Darius didn't have anything after five-thirty. He'd been happy for Khalil; maybe he'd be amenable to getting him home and with Vanessa as early as possible.

At six-thirty, Khalil was changing clipper heads for his client while Darius continued the early cleanup. The bell over the door rang out, and Khalil stopped short as Chris walked in. A backpack hung from one shoulder, and he readjusted the duffel in his opposite hand.

"Yo, I'm done, man," he said to Khalil.

Khalil asked his client to give him a second. He gestured for Chris to come closer.

"What's going on?" he asked.

"I'm sorry, Khalil; y'all are cool." He nodded at Darius stepping out of the back. "Great guys to work for. But I cannot with Rodriguez. I'm new, but I'm not stupid. I already did my grunt work. I'm a barber, not Rod's whipping boy."

"Okay," Khalil said. "We want to help, wanna hear more about what's going on. I can't right now because I need to stay on schedule, but can you go in the back with Darius? Talk it out? You're a good barber, and we'd rather not lose you."

Chris nodded but kept his gaze on the floor. Darius offered a hand to take his duffel bag and squeezed Chris's shoulder as he guided him to the back of the shop. Khalil apologized to his client and got back to work, moving as quickly as possible. He frowned, torn between letting Vanessa know that he might be late, and hoping they could get the situation resolved in time for him to get home as planned. Between accompanying one client out and ushering the next one in, he sent a quick text to Pax, asking what had happened. She was more a head-down, get-the-work-done kind of person. She reminded him a lot of Mo, which was why he knew she'd give it to him straight. He received her reply before his client got situated.

> Pax: Rod wants Chris gone. Good kid, great barber. I told Rod to back off, but no. Said, "Rod's shop, Rod's rules."

Khalil took a deep breath, releasing it slowly to keep the anger out of his face. He sent Pax a quick thanks and smiled at his client, focused on the task at hand.

By the time Khalil had finished and locked the front door, Darius had convinced Chris not to quit, and the two of them had completed the closing procedures. Khalil grabbed a broom to clean up around his chair, calling Chris over.

He gave Khalil a quick rundown, explaining that for whatever reason, he was Rod's favorite target. And while he really wanted the job and liked the other employees, he couldn't continue like this.

"Listen, Chris," Darius said, "we're happy you're part of the team. Khalil and I will have a sit-down with Rodriguez to see if we can get to the bottom of what's going on with him." He glanced at Khalil then nodded toward the empty station on the other side of his. Khalil nodded back.

"I don't know how your commute would be, but we've got space here, and you're welcome to it."

"Really?" Chris asked.

"Of course," Khalil said. "There may be a transition period if the clients you've built up aren't willing to come here. But even if you lose some, it's getting to the point that Darius and I have our schedules pretty full each day. We could use another set of hands."

"Cool, I appreciate it. Figured you'd be over the drama and just want things back the way they were before I started," Chris said.

"We don't want any drama," said Khalil. "But sometimes it's necessary to bring problems to the surface so they can be addressed. Why don't you take the station next to mine? Darius and I need a minute in the back."

Chris nodded, getting his bags from the back room and settling in.

Khalil followed Darius to the back, leaving the door open a sliver and walking to the farthest end of the room.

"Rod's gotta go," Khalil said.

Darius rubbed the back of his neck.

"Dude. I get it, but—"

"But?" Khalil took out his phone and let Darius read the conversation between him and Pax. He also reminded him of the face-to-face he'd had with Rod a week earlier.

"He's not taking care of the shop, and he's strutting around like it's his?" Khalil asked. "Seriously. You've talked to him. I've talked to him. Now he's chasing away good talent? And ten bucks says he hasn't gotten in touch with Chris's clients for tomorrow to let them know that Chris won't be in. The app can do exactly that at the touch of a couple buttons. Chris must have left the Original an hour ago, it should be taken care of."

Darius slid his phone out of his pocket and opened the app. He checked the schedule for the Original Fade and Chris's appointments were still there, his clients unaware that he would not be in the next day.

Khalil leaned back.

"The Saturday of Labor Day weekend. When everyone is tryna look fresh, and right there are nine negative reviews waiting to happen," he said.

Darius blew out a sigh, head tilted back, looking at the ceiling.

"He's family," he said finally.

"He's your second cousin's stepbrother's kid," Khalil said. "We were more than clear on our expectations from the outset. Remember, in the very beginning he even volunteered to have his hours cut when things were tight. He said family is supposed to help you grow, not slow you down."

"I do not want to have to deal with my aunt over this," Darius said, looking at Khalil again.

"I'm fairly confident your mom can handle her sister. Especially once she understands that Rod is messing with your livelihood."

He took two steps closer to put his hands on Darius's shoulders.

"You know I am the last one to push even distant family away," he said. "But can you think of a better way to handle this?"

Darius shook his head. "Let me deal with these clients," he said, returning to his phone. "What do you think? Fifty percent off if they come up here for their appointment?"

"Sounds good to me," Khalil said, turning to the dryer to take out the last load and start folding.

"I can handle that too," Darius said. "Hurry up and get home to your woman."

Khalil really needed to get a handle on this blushing nonsense.

"Thanks, man," he said. "Wanna hit me up later on? We can hash it out some more. Can't fire him this weekend, but we should probably go in together and do it next week."

Darius chuckled. "I am not calling you tonight. Not gonna interrupt your 'sexy times.'" His air quotes and shudder made Khalil shake his head. He shouldered his bag, backing toward the door.

"What can I say, man?" he said, hands spread wide. "You wanted to know when Khalil the Player was gonna get back into the game."

He smirked at Darius's shaking head and waved to Chris as he left.

Out the door, headed to his car, his heart started beating a mile a minute. He had to face facts: He *was* Khalil the Nervous when it came to Vanessa. Part of him wanted to understand why that was, but another part just wanted to enjoy the ride.

"That's the grand tour," Khalil said, leading Vanessa back into his living room. Her bag caught his eye again. Snug in the corner of his loveseat, it was the largest he'd ever seen her carry and made him hope that she planned to stay the night.

"I like your place, Khalil. It's homey but still a little bachelor pad. And I love the old radios." She wandered back over to the low bookshelf behind his couch, leaning in, appraising again. He was proud of his collection, of tinkering with something that didn't work and bringing it back to life with his hands. Most of the women he'd dated hadn't been a fan of the retro styles. He loved that Vanessa was into it.

"Thanks." He smiled, then got stuck. She tucked her hands into the pockets of her jeans and turned to face him, like she was waiting for him to say something. He stretched his neck, hoping the shyness creeping up wasn't bringing a little color there. He'd had just enough time to race around, tidy up, and hide his meds before hopping in for a lightning-flash shower. Of course, that shower had included a little personal work to get his lust for her under control, and he was pretty sure he could maintain his role as host without pressuring her into anything before she was ready. He cleared his throat.

"You said you had a tough day. Wanna tell me about it over a glass of wine?" he asked, taking the few steps into the kitchen.

She followed him, shrugging.

"Wine sounds good, but I don't wanna talk about it right now," she said.

"I get it," he said, pulling a bottle of white wine out of the fridge and two glasses out of his cabinet. "A mellow evening to end a stressful week. What do you feel like doing?"

"Honestly?" she asked, looking a lot more serious than he liked. Maybe she'd changed her mind.

He nodded.

"I feel like climbing you like a tree and riding you until you make me forget my name."

She didn't smile. He didn't either. But the wave of heat that shot up his body blasted away his nerves.

"Is that a fact?" he asked softly, coming around the bar that opened out onto the living room, glasses and bottle forgotten.

"It is," she said with a determination that made his confidence skyrocket.

"Well." He stopped hiding his greed. "I like that idea, but there's just one problem." He took a step forward. She surprised him by taking a step back. But that was good, great even. Maybe if he let her see the hungrier side of him, she'd let him walk her straight back into his bedroom.

"What's that?" she asked, taking another step backward.

"I'm hungry," he said, stalking closer.

"Oh." She broke eye contact, looking over his shoulder at the kitchen. "Did you want to make something? Or we could order in?"

He shook his head, licking his lips. "No." He took a couple more steps, guiding them into the hallway, closer to his room.

"I'm starved," he said. "Haven't eaten in days. Five days, to be exact."

Her adorable confusion nearly made him smile. She was trying hard to get what he was talking about, and if he focused on how cute she was, he'd crack. Instead, he allowed himself to fall deeper into a predatory role.

"You haven't eaten in five days?" she asked, backing past his office, getting ever closer to his goal. "How is that possible? How have you gone since Sun—"

Her eyes went wide and he grinned. He looked her up and down and bit his lip as they crossed the threshold into his bedroom.

"Starved, Vanessa," he said. "Absolutely famished."

"Well," she said, pert breasts heaving. "No sense in starving yourself, Khalil." She looked him up and down, a grin curling her lips. Her hands went up to the waist of her jeans and she unbuttoned, beginning to unzip.

He was in front of her in a flash, hand over hers.

"If you don't mind," he whispered, "I'd like to do the unwrapping myself."

She smiled, nearly as wicked as he felt, and raised her hands.

"Be my guest."

He dropped to his knees, running his hands up the backs of her thighs. She was so petite that even kneeling, he was only face-to-face with her stomach. He smiled and bent a little, lifting her shirt to brush his lips across the little swell under her navel. She laughed.

"There you go again with my pooch," she said, running her fingers into his hair.

He took a deep breath, getting high off her scent.

"Not a pooch," he said into her skin. "Delicious little curve." He looked into her eyes as he began slowly kissing his way down from her navel. "Perfect appetizer before I get to feast on you."

Grinning at the ceiling, Khalil took a moment to savor what he'd learned: Vanessa had zero qualms about telling him what she wanted sexually. Once the initial blush of nerves had passed, she taught him how to make her writhe with his tongue, build her whimpers into cries with his fingers, and to profit from her short refractory period, getting her orgasms to build close and fast enough that they almost slammed into one another.

He'd also discovered that his chest of drawers was the perfect height to prop her up on, his hands under her knees to spread her legs wide and drive his cock into her with slow, deep strokes. And that she loved it. He was pretty sure she'd ripped off the top layer of skin on his shoulders, but it was more than worth it, having watched and felt her go wild.

"You okay?" he asked, turning to her beside him on the bed.

She rolled onto her side, facing him.

"I am beyond awesome." She sighed, running her fingers down his arm. "That was amazing."

He grinned again, his ego shooting through the roof.

"You hungry?" he asked.

She shook her head, eyes closed. "No. Feeling a little buzzed right now. Wanna ride it out for a while." She stretched again, exquisitely feline, and relaxed onto her back.

"Excellent idea," he said. He kissed her softly and got up to ditch the condom. He was on cloud nine and wanted to get back into bed with her, but he hadn't checked his phone for a little bit, and suddenly it was nagging at him. Squatting next to her side of the bed, he caressed her shoulder. She opened her eyes and smiled.

"Just gonna grab my phone," he said. "Want to get under the covers? Don't want you to get chilly."

She nodded and slipped under as he pulled them down for her.

"Can you bring my bag?" she asked.

"I was wondering—is it an overnight bag?"

She smiled, crooking a brow.

"Do you want it to be?" she asked.

He nodded. She reached out and cupped his cheek.

"Then it is," she said.

He kissed her palm and grabbed his boxer briefs from where they'd landed on the floor.

"Do you have to get dressed?" she asked.

He couldn't keep his grin away from wicked.

"Do you plan on keeping me naked?"

She shrugged, shimmying so that her head was in the middle of the pillow, the sheet barely covering her nipples.

"I thought we might have some clothing optional time, but I don't want to make you uncomfortable."

He smiled again and crawled up the bed, closing her in with his arms and legs. The sheet slipped, and one of her nipples popped free. He bent his head to lick it again, slow and careful, bathing it with his tongue. Her breath caught, taking his away.

"Naughty," she whispered.

"I think 'clothing optional' is a great idea," he said, nuzzling her collarbone. "I'll just throw something on to greet the delivery man."

"Oh? We're getting delivery?"

"Seems like the wisest option," he said. "If we're going to maximize the naked time." He slid two fingertips lightly down the side of her neck, across her chest, grazing the edge of her exposed areola.

"Sounds perfect to me." She sighed.

Coming back down the hall with her bag and his phone, he unlocked it to open a delivery app but was stopped in his tracks by four missed calls. All from Rod. He'd left only one voicemail.

"Uh-oh," Vanessa said. She pulled herself up, a pillow supporting her back against the headboard, and the sheet tucked under her arms. "Don't like that look."

He tried to smile, but his irritation had already developed too far to succeed.

"Challenging day at work with a staff member. Looks like he's decided to stretch the disagreement into the evening. Mind if I handle this?"

"'Course not," she said, waving her own phone at him. "Just got an email from my Alphastone contact. He's giving me a lot of pushback on one of the most significant features, and it could make the whole deal fall through." She sighed, shoulders slumping.

He sat beside her on the bed, stroking the back of his hand down her arm.

"You gonna be okay?" he asked.

"Yeah, sorry. Don't mean to be a downer. Take your time with your call. I need to follow up with a bunch of people on this."

"Okay," he said. "Gonna manage it in my office. Gimme a holler if you need anything." He stroked her bare shoulder, the softness of her skin tickling his fingers. "Stay here or feel free to wander around as you are. I like the idea of you naked all over my apartment."

She grinned, making a show of looking him up and down.

"The feeling is most definitely mutual," she said.

Khalil shut himself in his office and checked his voicemail.

"Yo, K, it's Rod." His voice was a little punchy, like he was walking fast. The background street noise made it tough to understand. "Hope you're not answering 'cause you're busy and not 'cause you're mad. Look, Chris just packed up his stuff and quit today. No warning, no notice. Totally unprofessional. We're booked solid tomorrow, and I have no idea how we can cover it all. Hit me up when you can? Lemme know if you can help. Later."

Hopes I'm not answering 'cause I'm busy? At least he's got enough sense to realize that I have good reason to be mad. Leaning against his desk, he deleted the message then called Darius.

"Why are you calling me, K?" Darius asked after the second ring. "You're supposed to be *indisposed*."

Khalil snorted. "Technically I am, but I just picked up my phone and had four missed calls plus a voicemail—"

"From Rodriguez," Darius said.

"Exactly."

"Already talked to him. Told him not to call you."

"Well," Khalil said. "It's not like he remembers how to follow instructions or anything."

"All right, all right. We talked for a while, and I don't know if firing him is the wisest thing to do."

Khalil rubbed his temple, holding himself back from shouting. More and more frequently, he was fighting against a current of rage. He had to keep it from crashing over his best friend.

"What the fuck else are we supposed to do?" Khalil asked, as metered as possible.

"Listen, I know it's asking a lot. But I already talked to my aunt, and things are difficult for Rod financially right now, and if we let him go—"

"He can find another damn job." Khalil checked himself, un-clenching his teeth.

"You're right, he can. But things are really bad for him. Like, he feels like everything else is out of control in his life. That's why he's become controlling at work."

Khalil gave precisely zero fucks. But he couldn't say that. He took a slow deep breath, tensing the muscles in his arms, then relaxing them.

"His personal issues are having an impact on our bottom line. This stuff has been going on for a while?"

"I think so."

Khalil wanted to keep things chill. Everyone goes through diffi-cult times; he could get that. Then the "Rod's shop, Rod's rules" from Pax's message came back to him.

"Then maybe this will be a learning experience. I want to be sup-portive. But even after I confronted him about wanting the title and not maintaining the responsibility, he continued to talk about the Original like it was his own. That's our shop, Dare. If it sinks, we're the ones who lose the most. Not Rod."

"That's true. But he needs another shot. Why don't we transfer him to Fade Two?"

Khalil scratched at his chin, the silence stretching between them.

"And shake up management there? Reizo's been doing an excel-lent job running things. Why should he have to share the role with Rod? Plus Chris just moved, I don't want to shuffle any more staff around. It makes more sense for Rod to stay in place, but we gotta demote him," he said.

"What?"

"If it's that serious, he can keep the job, but he won't be manager anymore," Khalil said.

"He'll never accept that. His pride won't let him work under Pax."

"Then it's his pride interfering with his livelihood. I'd have never promoted him to manager if I'd known he was like that. You could have given me a heads-up."

"Whoa, don't put this on me," Darius said.

"I'm not. I'm just saying that we didn't have a single problem with

him when we were there, when he and Pax had the same responsibilities. But like you said, he's family: If you'd had any idea that he
was like this about working under a woman, I'd have wanted to know.
No way I'd have agreed to promote him." Khalil scuffed his heel back
and forth across a spot of carpet. "Come to think of it, is there anything else you think we should both know? Like, he's strapped for
cash right now. Could he decide that we have a little too much lying
around and help himself to it?"

"Dude. Are you serious right now?" Darius asked.

Khalil shrugged. "I'm just saying. Everything was cool when we
first started. But now he's got it in his head that it's his shop. What's
to stop him from helping himself to anything there?"

"You're calling my cousin a thief?" Khalil didn't know if he'd ever
heard Darius's voice hit that pitch.

"No," Khalil said. "If he's too broke to fire, maybe he's too broke
not to find other ways of making ends meet. He nearly cost us a great
team member; who knows what else he's willing to cost us?"

Darius didn't say anything, but his breath came through loud and
clear. His anger was as palpable as Khalil's.

"I think you should get back to your girlfriend," he said.

"Aight," Khalil said. "We can figure this out later."

"Hope so. Unless you're getting how you get again."

"What the fuck is that supposed to mean, Darius?" He was off the
desk and on his feet, drenched in rage.

"How you get, dude. This isn't news. We're getting to the end of the
summer. Like every fall I have to convince you not to make drastic
changes. Think about it: Even your breakups are always around now."

"What are you talking about?"

"Shit goes down for you in the fall. I don't know, man. It's just—
let's not do anything hasty, okay?"

I'm not being hasty about a good goddamned thing.

"I don't need this shit, Darius."

"Wait, listen. I am not criticizing you. You know that, right?"

Khalil pulled the phone away from his ear, looking at it.

*Why the hell am I wasting time on this bullshit when Vanessa is naked in my
house?*

"Whatever, Dare," he said, phone back at his ear. "I gotta go. Indisposed, as you said."

"Yeah, okay, man—"

Khalil hung up. A wriggle of concern about being rude passed through his consciousness, but he ignored it. He didn't need that shit, and Darius was way out of line about his relationships. Yeah, he'd had a couple summer flings over the years that kind of sputtered out in the fall, but that was normal. Whole reason it was called a summer fling. Leaving his office, he grinned as he found the proof of how wrong Darius was still curled up in his bed.

"Hey, babygirl," he said, crossing the threshold. "What do you feel like for dinner?"

Khalil blinked in surprise, reaching the Fade. Chris was there, as expected, thanking a client for coming to that location instead of the Original. But he hadn't expected to see Pax, and at Darius's station. He put his things in the back, then walked over to greet her.

"Hey. This is a surprise," he said. "You were supposed to be off this morning."

She shrugged, focused on the part she was giving one of Darius's clients.

"D called me late," she said. "Had to take his dad to the emergency room. Was worried about making it in. Told him I'd cover. We met up for keys." She smacked her gum, gaze still intent on the client while the floor fell out from under Khalil.

"Thanks for coming in," he said, tail tucked between his legs as he went to his station. He'd been so busy being mad at Darius, he hadn't been there for him when he should have. He wanted to at least send him a text but hesitated about what to say. His first client arrived, and Khalil got him settled in, telling himself he'd get in touch with Darius just after.

Lunch came and went, the clients flowing all day. They juggled the regulars and walk-ins, grabbing a bite to eat here and there as they could. Khalil kept meaning to call or text Darius, but as the day went on, he was more and more embarrassed and uncertain what to say. A couple of texts from Vanessa boosted his spirits and reminded him that they'd see each other that night at Paradigm as planned. Actually, it had been Darius's plan, but now Khalil wasn't sure Darius would be able to go, even if he wasn't angry enough to cancel it altogether.

As the afternoon turned into evening, he took the coward's way out, texting Darius's sister from the back room when he went to get some dye. The buzz of the reply came quicker than he was ready for.

> Rachel: Dad's okay. Got home real late. And you and
> D are worse than an old married couple. He'll be
> there. A night out would be good for him.

Khalil needed to stop using the word "love" when it came to Vanessa. They'd taken up residence on the couches of the VIP room at Paradigm. She and Bibi were talking and, casually, as if it was the most normal thing in the world, she'd snuggled up to his side, her back tucked against him so she could face her friend. Then she wove the fingers of her right hand with his and brought his arm down over her, letting him protect her and show off that she was his as she stroked his forearm. And he absolutely loved it. He loved that she wanted to be close to him, wanted any and everyone to see that they were together. She'd done it in such a nonchalant way that Bibi had raised her eyebrows for only a moment then smiled and relaxed into the couch herself, approval mixing with the mellow vibe she seemed to always give out. And while it was exactly what he wanted, he knew it would be wisest to slow down, reign in what he felt, because things were going faster than he'd ever imagined. But God, if he didn't want to just fall in. Get lost together, like she'd said.

He shifted his wrist, sliding the bracelets back into place as he watched the doorway, waiting for Darius to appear. He'd been an ass, way too hasty, just as Darius had said. Vanessa rested her head on his shoulder, and he turned to press a kiss to her crown. Naturally. As if they'd been together, showing each other affection for years. He glanced back at the doorway, relaxing then tensing up. Vanessa looked up at him, then at Darius as he shook Eddie the doorman's hand. She let go of Khalil's.

"Go on, baby," she said. And again, it felt right.

"Kay," he said, slipping away.

Darius headed straight for him, hand out to shake his, and Khalil rocked back a little at his relief. The handshake turned into a hug, and Darius nodded to the bar.

"Ness got us another waiter," Khalil said.

"Cool."

Darius followed him back to the couches, greeting Vanessa and Bibi. Khalil sat on the edge so he could focus on Darius. The waiter took his order and left.

"I'm sorry," Khalil said. "I was out of line."

"Nah, it's okay. I get why you were upset." He rubbed the back of his head. "Just a full day today."

"The stuff with your dad?"

Darius shook his head. "I don't know. He won't accept that something's up. When it clearly is." The waiter returned and Darius drank a little rum and Coke. "I just want to forget about it for a while."

"Whatever you want, man," Khalil said. Vanessa slid the back of her hand down his thigh. He reached back and took it, winding their fingers together while she leaned away, continuing her conversation with Bibi. The impression that she knew he needed a little support passed through his mind, but he didn't hold on to it, doubting it would be so easy, that he'd found himself with this pixie of a woman who knew what he needed before he'd had the thought. Darius smirked, shaking his head.

"Why do I get the feeling that y'all are gonna make me sick?"

Khalil shrugged.

"I would say I'm sorry, but I'm not," he said.

"Good."

The thing nagging at him wouldn't go away. He squeezed Vanessa's hand a little tighter. She squeezed back.

"You said . . . you talked about how I get," Khalil said, watching the ice cubes in his own glass as he swiveled it. "I . . . are things problematic?" he asked.

Darius shook his head. "Maybe I was a little rough. But I've had time, watching you. Around this time of year, things get weird. You get angry real easy. I lose my man Khalil. Past few years there's been stuff at work. The water damage last year, trying to keep clients for the second shop after all that drama. And getting started the year before. We were both stressed, so maybe it was that. Think about it—it was an October when you broke up with Nia, decided to stop dating, to stop playing ball the September before last. I don't know man." He shrugged. "Maybe 'cause I'm looking so hard for patterns with my dad right now, I'm seeing them everywhere."

Khalil gulped against a sandpaper throat. There'd been a pattern before. Getting snappy, fed up with everything. Then the seeping darkness. But he wouldn't let himself head down that path again. He couldn't.

CHAPTER TWENTY-ONE

November

As the last gleaming rays of the sun dipped below the horizon, Vanessa tapped back into her messages to reread the last text from Khalil.

> Khalil: Hey, babygirl. Stuck at the shop a little late with Darius. Gonna swing by my house, then I'll be at yours.

She looked back through the window of the Grey Ghost on Watson. Darius was at the table with Reizo. They were laughing with each other as they shared a meal. A horn behind her drew her attention to the green light, and she started driving again. Khalil's message had appeared after she'd gotten in the car a few minutes earlier. How could he have been at the shop with Darius if Darius was with Reizo across town?

Twenty minutes later, pulling into her driveway, the doubt vanished. Khalil's black Jeep was parked in front of her garage. She pulled in behind him and flashed her lights, the little thrill she always got when they didn't have to be apart bouncing her out of the car. But his door didn't open. She checked her porch, he wasn't there. Taking another look around, she approached his door. The floodlight at the end of the driveway illuminated the front seat. Khalil was hunched over, forehead resting on the wheel. She raised her hand to knock on the window, but a tremor fluttered through his shoulders and he raised his head before she touched the glass. Something cold, damp, and heavy stole her breath. He raised his head and looked at her, flashing a half-smile.

"There you are, babygirl," he said, opening his door.

"Hey." She stepped back, giving him space to get out. She took a breath to ask if everything was okay, but he pulled her close, tucking her head against his chest. Knowing something was wrong, but getting that she shouldn't ask, she wrapped her arms around him tight. In the space of a breath, she felt him sag against her, not physically, but a wave of something that stopped her heart. Then he was standing straight, kissing her head and smiling.

"Hey. Missed you," he said.

She searched his eyes. Something was off. She smiled back, hoping to chase it away.

"I missed you. Wanna go inside?"

"Yeah."

She tiptoed up, and he leaned down so she could give him a kiss on the cheek. Then he caught her hand and wove their fingers together. She squeezed and led the way into her house.

Nudging his shoes off by the door, he surprised her with another peck on her shoulder before heading into the living room and stretching out on the couch. She'd finally stopped giggling at the way his feet dangled over the armrest. Her furniture had been purchased with five foot one in mind. Nothing in her house, except the California King bed, was large enough for six foot four. He held out his arms, and even though she'd been on her way to the kitchen, she joined him, snuggling in close as he made as much room for her as he could.

"Why do you always feel so good in my arms?" he asked.

She smiled against his chest.

"Could ask you the same thing," she said.

"Is it lazy that I don't want to move?" he asked, stroking his hand down her head. "We gotta eat, and of course, I have something in mind for dessert. But I just want to stay right here."

"This is perfect, baby," she said.

The silence, punctuated only by the sound of them breathing in sync, had Vanessa molding to him, drowning in his scent. She took another deep breath then tilted her head up, with the thought to steal a kiss. His eyes were closed, but he wasn't at peace. His forehead was creased, his lips smaller. His jaw looked tight.

"Khalil," she whispered.

Those gorgeous green eyes settled on hers and his lips softened, his brow relaxed.

"What's wrong?" she asked.

"What makes you think something's wrong, babygirl?" He traced the curve of her ear with his thumb.

She just felt it, knew there was something. Maybe they'd rushed things. She told the scared part of herself it would be better to find out as soon as possible.

"You seem like something's nagging at you," she said. "Are you afraid that we've rushed things?"

He shifted, so they were as eye to eye as possible. He opened his mouth, then closed it. He took a deep breath.

"I don't know, Ness," he said. "You're right, I'm not . . . It isn't you. Stuff's been tense at work, you know? I told you about Rod, Darius's cousin."

She nodded, running a fingertip along his cheek.

"And it's not easy to manage. I keep . . . Darius and I had another disagreement about it, and I hate not being on the same page with him." His face got tight again, the crease in his forehead as deep as she'd seen it. He took an even deeper breath, blowing it out through pursed lips.

"Was that when you texted me?" she asked. "Said you were stuck late."

He nodded. "I'd just left. I lost my temper. Again. I'm not proud of that." He closed his eyes, rubbing his temples.

"Darius loves you, and you love him," she said. "I don't think you're going to lose each other over a disagreement."

"Yeah. But it keeps happening. I don't understand. Sometimes . . ." He shook his head, looking up at the ceiling. She gulped at the shimmer in his eyes. "Sometimes I feel like I'm not me."

She had no idea how to respond. She didn't want to be quick to reassure him with overly simple words. But something needed to be said. Or done. She cupped his face, tracing his cheekbone with her thumb. He looked down at her and smiled.

"If there's anything, about us," he said, "I'm afraid that I'm pushing too hard, too fast. It all seems too good to be true."

She took another deep breath, schooling her worry.

"Do you want to slow things down?" she asked.

"No," he said solemnly. "I want to keep getting lost together, just like you said our first time."

She smiled, her heart beating again.

"I love that you hold on to our first time together as such a good memory," she said.

He smiled, shifting his hands on her back, pulling her face closer to his. "I love that you love that."

Sometimes I feel like I'm not me.

Vanessa rubbed her hands together, moisturizing after washing her face. Khalil was still asleep, and it was after nine. Granted, it was Sunday, a day he could sleep in, but she couldn't remember a single morning they'd spent together when he wasn't awake before eight. And his words from the previous night wouldn't let her go.

She opened the bathroom door slowly, crept around the bed and out of the room. In the kitchen, she started the coffee, still rolling his words over in her mind. They'd only been exclusive for seven or eight weeks. They'd only known each other for a little over six months. Could she really say that she knew him well enough to be sure something was off? She picked up her phone, checking off notifications. But the Khalil question kept her attention. Just like she had felt that it was right, ditching a key point on her list, like race, to be with him, she could feel that he was sad about something. Was having a relationship with her making his with Darius suffer?

Shaking her head, she went into the living room, curling into the loveseat with her mug. Khalil wasn't exchanging one person for another. He was loving and gregarious. There was room for both her and Darius. Skimming two emails from her assistant, she frowned and put her mug on the coffee table to handle it. The Alphastone project just kept getting muddier. While she'd succeeded in making them understand the core requirements, one of the tests in the final phase had failed. It would mean a significant rehaul of a lot of the work. And if that wasn't enough, there were still two people she needed to replace on her staff, and each seemed to be gunning to be the first person she let go. It almost made her look up Michigan's labor laws just to check what she could do. She traded her phone for her mug.

Look at me, I'm pissed and ready to fight someone about my employees. Why is Khalil upset with himself for feeling the same? On cue, she caught the creak of the top stair. Khalil made his way down slowly, ducking his head before the last few steps. She couldn't stifle a giggle and he turned at the sound.

"What?" he asked, smiling as he approached.

"You," she said. "I simply cannot handle you with bed head and your glasses on. There needs to be a word for devastatingly sexy-cute."

"I know one." He put a hand on each armrest of the loveseat, blocking her in. "Vanessa," he whispered, kissing her on the cheek.

"Aww. You sleep good? Ready to 'seize the day' as you like to?" He squatted in front of her and she ran a hand through his hair. He shivered at her nails on his scalp.

"Sometimes I can be a real pain in the ass." He grinned, sliding his hands up her thighs and squeezing. "The only thing I want to seize today is you."

"I'm down for that," she said. "But we probably should try to get a little outside time."

He gently took her mug out of her hands, placing it on the table.

"You're absolutely right. We should get some outside time." Then he slid his arms around her and leaned in, bending her at the waist. She yelped as he stood. "Later. Right now I need some naked-in-bed time with my babygirl."

He turned back to the stairs, Vanessa over his shoulder. She couldn't contain her laughter.

"Thought you were trying not to get all caveman on me," she said.

He grunted deep.

"Too hard. Must have little woman." He squeezed her ass, setting off a series of squirmy giggles as he mounted the stairs.

Vanessa stretched, luxuriating in waking up for the second time that day. She snuggled back into Khalil, dozing around her, his arm draped across her stomach, legs curled against hers. She looked up at him and giggled. His hair was in even greater disarray than it had been earlier, though his glasses had made it safely to the nightstand. She turned in his arms for a better look, running a fingertip down his prickly jaw. Eyes still closed, he smiled.

"When do I get to meet Ma-Max?" he asked.

Vanessa blinked, her daydreaming stopped dead.

"I mean it," he said, his eyes still closed. "When could you introduce *me* to *her*?"

She appreciated the repetition, to be sure she'd heard him correctly, but her mind wasn't quite ready to wrap itself around the content of the question. He opened one eye and chuckled.

"Are you okay, Ness? You look like I asked you to run out and grab me a yeti." He opened the other eye, blinking a couple times.

"You're ready to meet her?" she asked.

He nodded. "Well, I'd like to meet your parents when they get back, but it won't be for a while, right?"

She shook her head.

"They have another year on this mission."

He laced his fingers with hers.

"And what do you think? Will they be okay with us being together?"

"No doubt," she said.

"For Ma-Max, I have the impression that it's going to take time, and probably some work on my part, for her to be comfortable with us being together. And I know her opinion is important to you, so I'd like to get that process started as soon as possible."

"Process?" she asked.

"The process of convincing her to trust me with her granddaughter," he said. "Ultimately, I'd like her to be happy that we're together.

But I know she probably won't be until she understands how serious I am about you."

"How serious you are?"

"Hmmm," he said, searching her eyes.

"What?" she asked.

"You don't know, do you?"

Her eyes hurt from gaping, so she blinked them back down a couple times.

"Don't know what?" she asked.

He scooted down the bed, so they were eye to eye.

"I probably shouldn't tell you this," he whispered, glancing around as though there would be listening ears in her bedroom. "Just keep it between us?"

"Okay."

"Darius calls you Vanessa Sarda when you aren't around." He'd kept his face serious, but she caught the smile playing at his eyes. She loved the idea of playing along. She raised her eyebrows comically high.

"He does?" she whispered back.

Khalil nodded.

"And you don't correct him?"

He shook his head.

"I see." She tapped her finger against her lips, mock thinking. "Guess we have to be careful, then," she said.

"Why?"

"Because Bibi pretty much called you the perfect man for me after the block party. Lisa said you checked all the boxes on the Basic Requirements list before she'd met you."

"Did they?" he asked, losing the serious battle for an instant.

"Yep."

"We have a predicament then, don't we?" he asked.

"We do. Can't have all these people thinking they were right all along."

"Nope," he said. "They'd become insufferable."

She thought a moment.

"Then we'd have to be sure to keep it a secret," she said.

"What?"

"When you come with me to Ma-Max's for Sunday Lunch next month. She's out of town for a couple weeks. Think the second Sunday would be okay?"

"I'll be there," he said. "And we'll keep it top secret." He pulled her closer, tucking her head under his chin. "Should we take separate cars? Different directions?"

"I think we can manage with just one. Might be wiser for us to meet here and take yours. No one will think I went to Ma-Max's if my car is here." She hugged him tight.

"An excellent plan, beautiful."

CHAPTER TWENTY-TWO

Without opening his eyes, Khalil rolled over and grabbed his phone, wicked grin sliding into place.

"Back for more, babygirl?" he groaned. "Love that it keeps you up even when we're apart."

"She's missing, dude."

"Karim?" Khalil checked the clock, squinting to be sure it said one-thirty.

"Yeah." His brother sniffed, clearly through tears, and Khalil's heart stopped beating.

"Laila's missing? What?" He got the light on and shoved his glasses onto his face.

"I don't know. I came home, and she's not here and she's not answering her phone, and the police won't do anything and I don't know what to do."

Karim sobbed and Khalil fought back his own tears. He threw the sheet off, landing awkwardly on his feet. He started for his hall closet before his legs were ready.

"She didn't—wait, the police?" Khalil snatched the closet light on and fell to his knees, pushing the hanging clothes out of the way so he could grab his duffel bag.

"Yeah," Karim said. "I called her sister, her parents, her friends. No one knows where she is. I can think of a thousand reasons why she wouldn't answer. Why she can't." He sobbed again, and Khalil had to cling the bag to his chest and stop to breathe.

"Has she ever disappeared before?" He stood, headed back to his room with stronger steps.

"Once. She got really mad, for I don't even remember what, and she took off to her sister's for a few days. But Raniya told me she was there. Now she's panicking 'cause she doesn't know where Laila is. Even told the cops we fight all the time."

Khalil froze, the handful of socks he'd grabbed falling to the floor beside the bag.

"She told the cops she thinks you did something to Laila?"

"She implied it. And if Laila doesn't turn up, who else are they gonna look at?"

The idea of his brother being investigated, even being suspected of having done something to his wife—

"I'm on my way," Khalil said, back to stuffing clothes into his bag.

"I didn't—" Karim choked back another sob. Khalil's eyes watered, his attempt at packing getting blurry. "I didn't call for you to—"

"I said I'm on my way. You're not going to deal with this alone. Have you called Dad yet?"

"No. Didn't want to upset him if it turns out to be nothing."

An entire world of emotions fought for purchase in Khalil's mind, through every muscle, buzzing over his skin. It was already well beyond nothing. If Laila was really missing, of course the police would look at her husband.

"I'm coming," Khalil said, throwing himself into his bathroom, grabbing at his toothbrush, toppling his aftershave.

"Not now," Karim said. "It's a seven-hour drive and you'll fall asleep."

"I'm way too wound up to fall asleep," Khalil said. "I can't leave you like this."

Karim took a deep breath. "'Lil. Do not come now. I can hear you barely making it around your apartment. I shouldn't have called."

"Yes, you should have," Khalil said. He sat on the edge of his bed and recognized that Karim was right. Khalil was no good in the middle of the night. He'd knocked over everything on his bathroom countertop, there were more socks and underwear on the floor next to his bag than in it. There was no way he could drive to Harrisburg. He yanked off his glasses to run a hand down his face.

"Tomorrow morning," he said. "There's gotta be a flight. I can't drive right now."

"I'm sorry," Karim said. He sniffed hard. "I should have waited to call you."

"Nah, man, you know better." Khalil let himself fall back on the bed. "Tell me," he said. "Tell me whatever you need to get off your chest. I'm here."

Khalil readjusted himself in the seat of the Uber, headed to the airport. He kept nodding off, his head rolling to the side with each turn. He'd listened as Karim told him everything, all the horrible shit Laila had been putting him through, all the hoops, the challenges, the "tests" of his love. It was downright abusive, and he was part angry with Karim for putting up with it, part mad at himself for never reading between the lines. His brother had been suffering for years, and Khalil had been oblivious.

"We're here," the driver said.

Khalil snapped awake and got out, rubbing at his unshaven chin, checking he hadn't drooled. He hefted his duffel on his shoulder and walked into the darkened airport, cleaning staff busy, a few ground agents walking by. He'd fumbled the online check-in, so he stopped at a self-service terminal, got his boarding pass, and made his way through security. The few stores he passed were closed, bars down, lights off. He desperately needed a cup of coffee, but nothing was open.

"I'm fucked," he muttered. At the gate, there were plenty of seats available, but that way lay danger. He walked over to a wall and dropped his bag, kicking it flush against the support. Then he leaned back against it and yawned. He just needed to stay on his feet, stay awake until he got on the plane. He could squeeze in a nap to D.C., then another one on the way to Harrisburg, so he could be somewhat helpful to Karim when he got there. His eyes fluttered half shut, and he caught the date and time on the departures screen as it lit up. Sunday morning. He'd be with his brother before lunch rolled around. Something ticked in his head. Something about Sunday Lunch. Karim was upset and probably hadn't eaten. Lunch would be a good start. He let his eyes close, dozing on his feet, and waited for the airport to come to life.

Readjusting his bag on his shoulder and following his fellow passengers, Khalil rubbed the sleep out of his eyes and slid his glasses back on. He'd been lucky. There'd been some bad weather around Harrisburg, so they'd circled for nearly thirty minutes. Gave him extra sleep. He still wouldn't be himself for several hours, but he'd be with his brother. The rest would come together.

He reached into his pocket for his phone, turning it back on one-handed. When it powered up, it chirped, a notification about the rescheduled team meeting the following day, apps updating themselves, and his reminder about Sunday Lunch with Vanessa and her grandmother. He yawned and went to swipe it with his thumb. Then he stopped dead, eyes wide open.

Holy fucking shit! He was supposed to pick up Vanessa and drive to her grandmother's in less than three hours and he was nearly five hundred miles away. He turned around the way he'd come, to get back on the plane. Two people bumped past him, bringing him back to reality. He turned again, rejoining the flow as, attention back on his phone, he scooted his thumb down to call. The phone slipped, he caught it on one end, tried getting it back into position with the hand that wasn't pinned under the strap of his bag, but he overcorrected and it slipped out of his grip. He tried to catch it but ended up launching it into the air and over the railing of the walkway.

In slow motion, it arced, the ceiling spotlights reflecting off the screen, and began its descent. It flipped, curved, and landed twenty feet below him, exploding in the middle of a giant star in the marble floor, welcoming patrons to the Harrisburg airport. Khalil stifled a scream as it broke into more pieces than he could count.

He shoved his way through the people ahead of him, down the escalator and to the eight-pointed star. Funnily enough, not one of

the myriad pieces ended up outside the velvet rope keeping foot-
prints off of it. He counted the points again because he couldn't
count the pieces of his phone.

Apart from a distant, eerie laugh, Khalil had no thoughts. His
mind went as arid as a desert.

"Damn," a voice said beside him. He looked down at a man in a
gray uniform, wheeled cleaning cart beside him. "Think it's toast,
homie."

Khalil tried to reply, but first he needed to remember to breathe,
and then all that came out was a squeak.

The man stepped over the rope and grabbed a large chunk, flipping it in his hands. He shook his head.

"Even the SIM card's busted."

Slack-jawed, Khalil turned on his heel, getting himself to the exit
on legs that weren't holding him up well. Outside, he realized he
couldn't even call Karim to tell him where he was so he could pick
him up. Squeezing his eyes tight, he let his head fall back.

Please dude, just find me.

The minimal traffic was moving to the right, so he took a few
steps that way and gasped in a quick shot of air because he kept forgetting to breathe. There was a honk behind him, and Karim pulled
up to the curb. Khalil sprinted toward him, ripping the passenger
door open and jamming himself and his duffel inside. Karim's red
eyes stopped him short and he reached out, grabbing his twin and
squeezing tight.

"Thanks, man. Thank you for coming," Karim said.

Khalil pulled back and grabbed Karim's face.

"Dude. I'm here. But I fucked up. I need your phone."

"What's wrong?" Karim pulled his phone out of the center console and handed it over. He put the car in gear and started to merge
with the traffic.

"I fucked up, fucked up, fucked up," Khalil said, getting to the
dialer. "Supposed to meet Ness's grandmother today. I mixed up my
days. And destroyed my phone."

"Shit," Karim said. "Get back on a plane!"

"I thought about it. But it's not a bus, is it?" His laugh creeped him out a little. But the task at hand took his attention. "FUCK! What is her number?" The dialer sat there, as blank as his mind. Was her area code 313? Or 248? He couldn't even remember.

"I shouldn't have called you," Karim said, circling back to the departures drop-off. "Seriously, get back on a plane. Go."

Khalil shook his head, still staring at the phone. He grabbed his brother's thigh.

"Take me home with you. Even if I got on a plane now, even if I could, it would be too late. And I can't leave you right now." He took a fast breath. "Christ, WHAT is her number? How can I not—" He froze, remembering the client database. Thank God they hadn't completely ditched their website for the app.

He closed the dialer and got a browser open as Karim drove them toward downtown Harrisburg.

"It's gonna be okay, 'Lil," he said, glancing between Khalil and the road.

"She's not down with interracial relationships," he said, shaking his head, fumbling to get the website typed in, scrolling to the bottom for the employee log-in. "Her grandmother had a really bad experience. And so did Ness. She's not—her grandmother . . . She only thinks black guys could be serious. And how fucking unserious does this look? Flaking on this lunch? Fuck me!"

He got his username typed in, then got stuck. His password wouldn't come to him.

"Dude, I need you to breathe," Karim said. "You're catastrophizing. You gotta relax. Vanessa cares about you, right?"

Khalil shrugged but nodded as he typed in his password. "I hope so."

"I'm pretty sure she does, if she was gonna take you to meet her grandmother knowing how she feels. Means Vanessa thinks you're worth standing up to family." He squeezed Khalil's shoulder. "Like Mom."

Khalil's heart tugged and things got blurry for a second. Then the log-in error popped up. He tried again, new error message. He suppressed another scream, tried again. Third time was not a charm. It was still the wrong password and he was out of tries.

"Oh my God! I locked myself out." He went headfirst into the dash, Karim's phone in his lap in both hands.

"What?"

"Three wrong passwords and I'm locked out for twenty-four hours." The laugh that slipped out was high-pitched and foreign but fit the panicked madness of his situation. "I flaked on my girlfriend, killed my phone, and locked myself out of the only way to get her number a couple of hours and five *hundred fucking* miles away from when I'm supposed to meet her family." The laugh was back louder, stronger. His glasses slipped down his nose, tapping against the dash.

"Darius," Karim said.

"What?" Khalil looked at him, eyes aching.

"Darius. Does he have her number?"

Khalil sat up. "Darius. Yes. Great idea." He held up Karim's phone again, back to the dialer. He cackled. "I don't know Dare's number, either!" He looked at Karim, tears welling up. "I am legit useless right now."

"It's in my contacts," Karim said, one hand on the wheel, the other on Khalil's arm. "You're gonna call him. In a minute. Right now, I need you to stop and breathe. You are freaking out and only making things harder on yourself. You know how it is when your sleep gets fucked up. Things seem worse than they are. Give yourself a second."

Karim let go to change lanes. Khalil closed his eyes, taking a deep breath.

"Good," Karim said. "Do it again."

Khalil did, getting his breathing under control. The panic lessened, enough for him to see the reversal of the situation.

"I'm so sorry," he said. "I'm supposed to be here to calm you down and you're helping me. Shoe's supposed to be on the other foot."

Karim shook his head. "You know that doesn't matter."

Khalil looked out the window, world blurring.

"I just—" He took a breath to stop his voice from cracking. "I wanted to do this right. Don't want Ness to have to justify my absence . . . I don't want that burden on her."

Karim squeezed his shoulder again.

"I know, man. I know. It's gonna work out."

Khalil nodded, looking back down at the phone. He took a deep breath.

"Darius," he said.

Darius didn't answer, but as Khalil was leaving a message, the phone beeped against his ear. Darius texting back asking Karim if everything was okay. Then Khalil remembered another detail about that Sunday. Darius had promised to go to church with his parents and sister; no wonder he couldn't talk. But that also meant he couldn't call Vanessa on Khalil's behalf until well after lunch. Khalil typed back to explain. After a couple minutes, Darius texted him Vanessa's contact info and told him not to worry about work that week if he needed to stay with Karim.

> Khalil: Thank you so much. Love you, man.
> Darius: Love you too. And don't worry. Vanessa Sardda's gonna stick up for her man.

Khalil's eyes blurred again, and he took another breath. He swallowed, getting his emotions under control so he could explain to her what had happened. They were almost at Karim's, passing through the quaint downtown punctuated with a mix of modern buildings. It was overcast and drizzling, weather that went with Khalil's mood.

The phone rang several times, then there was a brief silence.

"Hey, Ness, it's—" Another ring came through, slightly garbled, then her message followed by the tone.

"It's me, baby. Listen, I am so sorry, but . . ." That wasn't the way he meant to start. He took a breath and tried again. "My brother's wife is missing. Karim, my twin. He called last night and I panicked. He'd already talked to the police and he was freaking out, so I got on a plane. I'm in Harrisburg with him. I fucked up, mixed up my days. Call me back? This is his number. I also destroyed my phone, so I can't answer it. I'm sorry." He hung up and looked at Karim. "Did that even make sense?"

"I think it did. Give her time to listen and she'll call back; you guys can figure something out."

Khalil leaned back against the headrest as Karim pulled into the parking garage under his building. Khalil rubbed his eyes, a couple of tears wetting his fingers.

"Fucked up so bad. And I'm so tired. I slept on the plane, but—"

"You just had another massive surge of adrenaline," Karim said. He sighed. "It's not a good weekend for the Sarda twins."

Khalil squeezed Karim's shoulder.

"Yeah." After two more deep breaths, he thought of calling Dr. Edwards. His psychiatrist could talk him down. Instead, he sighed and looked at his brother. "I just gotta lie down. Is that okay? Are you good for a little bit?"

"No worries. Let's get inside, you can stretch out in the guest room and I'll start checking in with Laila's friends again." His voice wavered. "If something's happened to her—"

"We'll cross that bridge if we get to it," Khalil said.

Karim parked and they got out, beleaguered.

An hour later, Khalil woke up, blinking at a ceiling he didn't recognize. Sitting up, he reached for his glasses on the nightstand. He blinked again at the view of the Susquehanna out the sliding glass doors along one wall of the room. He was at Karim's. Remembering why, and all the assorted drama and stress, he got out of the room, finding his brother on the couch, head in his hands.

"Apparently," Karim said, not moving, "she left a bar with a guy last night around two."

Khalil rocked on his feet.

"You called me at one-something," he said. "After you'd been trying to reach her. She just ignored your calls?"

Karim nodded. Khalil sat beside him, clenching and unclenching his fists. Laila was Karim's wife, and what Karim decided to do about his marriage was his choice. If Khalil had a degree of certainty that Karim would leave her, he'd have spoken freely. Instead he took a deep breath and was careful with his voice.

"I'm sorry I fell asleep like that," Khalil said. "I shouldn't have left you."

Karim rubbed his eyes, his head still cupped in his palms.

"You can't be perfect for everyone all the time, 'Lil."

Sounds just like Dr. E.

Khalil cleared his throat.

"How did you find out? That she . . . um . . ."

Karim ran a hand down his face.

"One of her friends was with her. One that I'd called. She lied to me last night, but I guess she was feeling guilty this morning and called me back."

Khalil exhaled slowly, keeping his temper. At least one of her friends had a conscience.

"What do you want to do?" he asked.

Karim shrugged, gazing into the middle distance. Only then did Khalil really see his twin: unshaven, hair a mess, skin sallow. He started to say something about it, then realized he probably looked the same.

"Vanessa hasn't called back," Karim said, looking at him.

Khalil swallowed against a dry throat.

"What do you think that means?" he asked.

Karim shrugged again. "Do not ask me, man. I clearly have no idea how women work."

"Sorry," Khalil said.

Karim handed him his phone.

"Don't be."

Khalil took the phone back into the guest room, closing the door behind him. He glanced at the clock. He should have been leaving to pick Vanessa up in fifteen minutes. He took a fortifying breath and dialed her number again. It rang and rang until her voicemail picked up. He didn't feel comfortable enough to leave a message. She had to be beyond pissed if she hadn't called back and wasn't answering his calls. He put the phone down on the dresser and stood looking at the river, running his hands up the back of his head. After more rest, he felt human again. But with the way he'd messed up, and how Vanessa's grandmother might see him afterward . . . he'd just set the stage to make their relationship much more difficult. If she even wanted to continue a relationship. Vanessa was compassionate; he couldn't see her breaking up with him over a family crisis. But pressure from her family might be a different story. He picked up the phone again.

> Khalil: Ness, it's Khalil. Please call me back so I can explain?

He flipped the phone case closed, taking a resolute breath, and turned to get back to Karim. Then it was buzzing in his hand.

"Explain what?" she asked, voice light.

"You . . . sound happy," he said.

"I'm always happy when I get to talk to you, baby, but where are you calling from?"

"My message didn't go through?" he asked.

"Oh, that was you? I got a weird garbled-up voicemail earlier from this number, couldn't understand anything. I figured it was a misdial or something. What's wrong?"

He sagged against the dresser, relieved that she didn't hate him, then tensed up again, recognizing that she still had the chance. He shut his eyes.

"I'm in Harrisburg," he said. "Pennsylvania."

"Why are you . . . Are you joking?"

"No, babe, I'm not," he said. He explained everything: the call in the middle of the night, the confusion, the police, Karim's distress, Khalil's panicked need to get to his brother.

"Ness, I am so, so sorry. The last thing I want is for your grandmother to think I'm not serious about you, that I wouldn't put your needs first. But that's exactly how I've made it look, and I know there's no way for me to fix it right away. I'm a colossal ass."

"You're a colossal ass for being there for your brother when he needed you?" she asked.

"Well . . ."

"You're irresponsible because someone you love was in distress and you didn't let him down? I know how you get at night. You can wake up enough for certain activities, but you are not in your right mind. I can easily see you panicking and getting confused."

"You aren't angry?" he asked.

"Not at all, baby," she said. "I'm kind of proud of you. Proud that my man takes good care of the people he loves, even when it's difficult for him."

"But I haven't taken very good care of you today," he said.

Vanessa was silent. Then he backtracked and caught the implication of what he'd said. The voice that usually told him to slow down, reign it in, was silent. So he went with it.

"Are you . . ." Her voice was barely strong enough for the microphone to pick up.

"Saying that I love you?" he asked.

"Um . . . I didn't mean to put words—"

"I love you, Vanessa," he said. "Think I have for a while. But this morning, when I realized what I'd done, how I'd messed up and what kind of stress that was going to put on you, it became pretty obvious that I am really far gone when it comes to you."

"I don't know—"

"You don't have to say it back," he said. "There's no—"

"But what if it's true?" she asked.

His heart did a sharp tensing thing that burned and made him shaky.

"What if what's true?" he asked.

She was silent a moment, and his heart did the thing again and he began to wonder if he was going to make it through that day.

"Why do we keep putting ourselves on someone else's timeline?" she asked.

He smiled. "You've been doing that too? Worrying that things are going too fast?"

"Yeah," she said. "I'm kind of over that, aren't you?"

"Ready to ditch it at any time."

"I love you, Khalil," she said. "I don't know since when, but I do."

His heart did a much better thing, sending a wave of warmth and security all through him.

"You do?" he said.

"Yeah. I love you. And I'm glad you love me. Now that that's out of the way, I can stop fighting myself about it."

He grinned. "Me too," he said.

"I can handle Ma-Max," she said.

"I'm sure you can, but this is my mistake, my job to fix it. Do you think she'd be willing to talk to me? So I can apologize?"

"She's a pain about the phone. She's kind of okay talking on one, but she's all about face-to-face communication."

"Can we do a video call?" he asked. "I really want to explain myself today."

She made a little noise, and he closed his eyes, seeing the face she made when she was thinking through something. He smiled automatically.

"We can try," she said. "I think she'll hear you out, but even if she doesn't, I'm not going anywhere, okay?"

He took a deep breath, and it felt like the first one he'd had all day.

"Thank you, babygirl," he said.

"No reason to thank me. Now get back to Karim. I'm worried about him. Will you keep me posted?"

"I will," he said. "I love you, Ness."

"I love you too, baby."

CHAPTER TWENTY-THREE

Chest out, shoulders back, Vanessa walked down the hall from Ma-Max's garage into the house. Her laptop bumped sharply against her hip with each step.

"Hi, Ma-Max," she called out, turning the corner into the kitchen.

"We're in the living room, baby."

Hearing the "we" was good. Meant Arletta was already there. Vanessa was sure she could count on Auntie Letta if Ma-Max got testy. She crossed the threshold, head held high. Arletta was by the window, Ma-Max in an armchair across from the couch. The one she always sat in to greet guests, looking polite and at ease, but in the best position to hold court. She'd had Kathryn set out tea and hors d'oeuvres. Vanessa barely concealed a smirk.

She's gone all out.

Both Maxine and Arletta's faces fell as Vanessa joined them. They looked over her shoulder, then back at her.

"Baby? You're alone?" Ma-Max asked.

"Yes," she said as she sat. She opened her laptop and typed in her password.

"I thought we were going to meet your young man today," Maxine said.

"You still can."

Maxine looked around again, and Arletta took the armchair beside her.

"Where is he?"

"Harrisburg, Pennsylvania," Vanessa said. She put the laptop next to her on the couch. "He had to go help his twin, Karim."

"He just happened to go out of town this weekend? You asked me about this two weeks ago."

"I know, Ma-Max. But it was a family emergency."

Maxine exchanged a glance with Arletta.

"Well," Maxine said. "I like to give people the benefit of the doubt, but the timing is questionable. Are you sure he isn't avoiding us? And what's that about?" She nodded at Vanessa's computer.

"Khalil's upset with himself for not keeping his word to meet you today. He asked if we could do a video call so he can apologize."

Arletta raised her eyebrows, grinning.

"He's upset with himself for not keeping his word, Max," she said. "Maybe he isn't an asshole."

Maxine rolled her eyes.

"At no point did I say that he was an asshole, Letta. I just had my reservations. Nothing to do with him specifically." She looked at Vanessa. "I promise I was coming into this with an open mind, baby."

Vanessa checked with Arletta, who nodded.

"Are you willing to do the video call?" Vanessa asked.

"We can speak in person when he gets back," Maxine said.

"I understand that, but it's important to him. He'd like to look you in the eye, as much as technology will allow, and apologize today."

Maxine and Arletta exchanged another glance.

"Of course, it can wait," Vanessa said. "But I know he'll be certain you disapprove until he speaks with you."

Maxine narrowed her eyes.

"Did you tell him I disapprove?"

"I told him the truth," Vanessa said, shrugging. "That you'd had a very negative experience, as have I, and you have reservations about interracial relationships." *And Khalil has proven both you and me wrong.*

"Talk to him, Max," Arletta said. "Sounds like good people. He's going the extra mile to be respectful."

"Okay," Ma-Max said. She scooted to the edge of her seat, picking up her glasses off the end table to look at Vanessa's laptop. "How does this work exactly?"

Vanessa swallowed a chuckle.

"It's like a regular phone call, but you can see each other, Ma-Max. Nothing too complicated." She shifted it to her lap. "I'll start and you can join in when you're ready. Auntie Letta, I told him you'd be here too, so he wants to speak with you as well."

Arletta shrugged. "Boy doesn't have to convince me. I'm very happy with what I've heard so far." She winked at Vanessa and smiled.

Vanessa repositioned herself in the middle of the couch and started the call. Khalil answered immediately.

"Hey," she said, then bit her tongue. Knowing he loved her made her a little giddy, and she didn't want to let that show in front of her grandmother. But he looked so adorably worried she wanted to kiss the screen to make it all better.

"Hey," he said. "Are you all right?"

"I'm fine. I'm here with Ma-Max and Arletta. They'd like to hear what you have to say."

"Okay," he said. Then he winked and her heart fluttered, and she was sure her grandmother would say something if she blushed. He mouthed *I love you,* and she could only smile and nod. She looked up at Ma-Max and Arletta. "Want to join me, ladies?"

They joined her on the couch, one woman on each side. Vanessa held in her smirk as Ma-Max adjusted her glasses and leaned toward the screen.

"Hello, Mrs. Noble," Khalil said. "Thank you so much for agreeing to talk to me."

"Hello, Khalil," Ma-Max said loudly. "I was looking forward to meeting you today!"

"Ma-Max," Vanessa whispered, a hand on her arm. "You don't have to shout; he can hear you just fine."

"Oh," she said, squinting back at the screen.

"I hope you can forgive me for not being there today as planned," Khalil said. "There's no excuse; I really wanted to be there. But I had a family emergency and made a mistake."

Maxine nodded, waving a hand.

"These things happen. I understand that you didn't do it on purpose," she said.

"I appreciate that. And are you Ms. Jenkins?" he asked, his attention shifting to Arletta at Vanessa's right.

"I am," she said. "Nice to meet you."

"You too, ma'am. Vanessa speaks very highly of you both."

"So tell me about yourself, young man," Maxine said. "I'd like to get to know you a little."

Vanessa relaxed back into the couch cushions, as Khalil shared some information about his background. She was relieved at how interested Ma-Max was. Her grandmother peppered him with questions, and he answered each one, politely and concisely. If he hadn't already told her that he was nervous, she wouldn't have guessed. Ma-Max scooted closer to the computer, to see or be seen, Vanessa couldn't tell. All she cared about was what Ma-Max's final analysis would be. She hoped her grandmother could get on board, because she wasn't about to stop seeing Khalil.

"Well, young man, I like what I've heard so far," Ma-Max said. "But we haven't discussed the most important part. Interracial relationships aren't easy. You'll have to deal with strangers making you all uncomfortable. Outside pressures can harm a relationship."

"I understand that, ma'am, but Vanessa is more than worth it," Khalil said.

Vanessa touched Ma-Max's forearm.

"Khalil has dated black women in the past. He's familiar with the challenges of interracial dating," Vanessa said. "Right, Khalil?" she asked the screen.

"That's true, Mrs. Noble," he said.

Maxine leaned back, letting out a small huff, but she nodded.

"And your parents?" she asked. "Were they accepting of your relationships?"

Khalil nodded. "It would have been a bit hypocritical if they hadn't been. They have an interracial marriage. Been together over thirty years."

"So you really understand the challenges," Maxine said.

"I'd like to think I do."

Maxine leaned all the way back, relaxing into the couch, folding her hands in her lap. Vanessa took it as approval but didn't allow herself to declare victory just yet. She noticed that Khalil still looked nervous, though.

"I hope this doesn't come off as too fresh or direct, Mrs. Noble," Khalil said. "But I'm having a hard time believing that you're Vanessa's grandmother. I'd believe her aunt, maybe. I guess beauty runs in the family."

Arletta laughed, clapping her hands. Maxine giggled then caught herself.

"Aren't you the charmer, Khalil?" she asked.

He shrugged, his smile looking more relaxed.

"What else can I share with you? Ms. Jenkins, is there anything you'd like to ask me?"

"Hmm," she said. "I'm happy with what I've heard so far."

"Mrs. Noble?" Khalil asked.

Maxine shook her head, placing her glasses on the coffee table.

"Not that I can think of right now. We'll let you get back to your brother. I will be expecting a visit when you get back to Detroit," she said.

"Whenever you'd like, ma'am," he said.

Vanessa smiled, running her palms together.

"I guess that's it, then," she said. "Keep me up to date with Karim?"

"Of course," he said. "I'll call you later today?"

"Sure."

After putting her laptop on the kitchen counter, Vanessa joined Maxine and Arletta at the dinner table. She was relieved to hear Ma-Max going on about how polite Khalil was and how much she was looking forward to meeting him in person.

"You could have warned us," Arletta said to Vanessa.

"About what?"

"We had no idea he was that handsome," Ma-Max said. "I'm glad I got to see him through a screen first. Might have made a fool of myself otherwise."

"You?" Vanessa asked.

"Me too," Arletta said, winking at Vanessa.

Maxine sipped her wine, thoughtful.

"June is a lovely month for a wedding," she said, posing her glass on the table. "And with your lips and skin tone, and his bone structure, your children couldn't help but be beautiful. Shame his eye color is probably recessive."

"So . . . that's it? You aren't against the idea anymore?" Vanessa asked.

"Against?" Ma-Max asked.

"Max," Arletta said. "An hour ago, you were suspicious and now you're talking weddings and babies?"

Maxine glared at Arletta. "Suspicious is strong. I was concerned. We had a good discussion when Vanessa called to ask if he could come. He has a suitable educational and career background. The right social standing. On paper he's impressive, and as the two of you have been reminding me, Vanessa wouldn't bring home just anyone. Plus, he's clearly got home training. That's the most important thing. At no time did I say that he had to be black."

"Maxine Noble," Arletta said as Vanessa's jaw dropped. "Have you had a stroke?"

"Ma-Max," Vanessa said, "you've been pretty clear. You're really okay with interracial relationships now?"

"I never said that." Maxine picked up her glass again. "I am okay with you seeing *this* young man."

Vanessa glanced at Arletta, careful not to roll her eyes. Arletta smoothed her napkin across her lap.

"Fine," she said. "But she's known him for five minutes, Max. Marriage and babies in due time."

Vanessa nodded at Arletta but kept her mouth shut. The name "Vanessa Noble-Sarda" already appealed to her more than she was ready to admit.

CHAPTER TWENTY-FOUR

Thursday evening, Vanessa took another look at the arrivals screen, stepping back from a family with balloons and signs. Karim had put Khalil on a flight home that afternoon, and she saw no reason to wait longer than necessary to get her hands on him.

She took a couple more steps back, worried he'd head straight out for an Uber. His flight had landed, so she could only wait, running her clammy palms down her jeans. Was she nervous? Or excited? Too many feelings all jumbled—she caught sight of him, and her heart lurched. She made a beeline, working to make up the difference between his long legs and her short ones.

"Baby!" she said, reaching out and catching his wrist.

He turned, grinned, and let his bag thump to the floor as he scooped her up and kissed her. He held her close, one arm around her waist, the other up her back, cupping her head as he consumed her. Her jumbled nerves washed away in a tide of relief, which ebbed, then returned with something richer and heavier. He pulled away, taking in a fast breath, and grinned, shivering when she tugged his hair.

"Babygirl," he groaned. "I missed you so much."

"I missed you," she said. "I couldn't wait; I had to pick you up. Are you surprised?"

"Very. But I have a problem."

"What's that?"

"Don't want to stop kissing you, don't want to put you down. But I don't wanna get arrested for public indecency, either."

"Kissing me is indecent?"

"The way I want to kiss you is," he whispered, close, a wicked gleam in his eye. "Where I want to."

She stifled a giggle.

"I guess we'd better get home, then," she whispered.

He grinned again, then his face softened.

"Do you know I love you, Vanessa?"

"Do you know I love you?" she asked.

He nodded, carefully putting her down. He held on to her hand.

"I'm so glad you do," he said, kissing the back of it.

Boneless, Vanessa collapsed against Khalil, resting her cheek on his chest as they caught their breath. He pulled the sheet around them, wrapping his arms around her. She snuggled in deep, reveling in his smell.

"Wanna take the day off with me tomorrow?" he asked. "I'd like to say that I have other things in mind, but I'm down with just doing this over and over."

She smiled against his skin.

"We can definitely do that. I have a video conference about the Alphastone project and one with my HR manager about an employee, but I don't have to get started until two."

He sighed. "Reminds me. Gotta talk to Darius about Rod. I just . . . After watching this shit with Karim, I have no bandwidth left for drama."

She traced the crease between his deltoid and biceps. "You didn't tell me what ultimately happened. And I didn't want to ask when he sent me your flight info."

Tension flipped through his muscles. She saw it on his arm, felt it flutter through his body. She thought to apologize, change the subject, but then he was talking.

"According to her sister, she's found someone else," he said.

"Laila wouldn't talk to Karim or to me. She's got her family believing that Karim was cold to her, didn't pay her enough attention, but that's a lie. A quick look at their bank accounts makes it pretty fucking obvious—vacations, lavish gifts, dinners out. Karim's been doing his best to keep the romance alive. I told him to let her go. What she put him through—" He stopped, breath harsh and fast, his heart pounding under Vanessa's ear. "What she's been putting him through is more than enough reason to call it quits. But she is his wife. Marriage vows are sacred. He wants to go to counseling, start fresh."

Vanessa was almost afraid to lift her head and look Khalil in the eye. She'd never felt that level of anger from him; she didn't want to know what it looked like. Then his chest shuddered, and her heart broke.

"And I didn't know," he said, his voice cracking. "He's been suffering, and I had no idea."

She went to lift her head, but then his hand was there, holding her to his chest. The other went up fast to his face, and tears welled in her eyes.

"How could you have known?" she asked, wrapping her arms around him tighter.

He shrugged. "I should have sensed it. Sometimes I'd ask how things were and he'd change the subject, fast. I should have pushed, shouldn't have let—"

She pulled up hard so they were eye to eye and cupped his face.

"Maybe he was protecting you. He knew you'd be upset and he didn't want that for you. You aren't the only one willing to sacrifice for the people you love, you know."

He kept his gaze downcast, shrugging again, moisture sparkling on his eyelashes. She wanted to find other words to take his pain away, but none came. Instead she leaned in, kissed him softly, then snuggled back into his arms.

"You're a good man, Khalil," she whispered. "A good brother."

He kissed her, hugging her close again.

"Thank you, babygirl."

CHAPTER TWENTY-FIVE

What's your read?" Vanessa asked, picking up her mug from beside her monitor.

"Everything looks clear. The developers have reached all of the targets, our contacts at Alphastone are happy. All that's left is for their IT to integrate the changes."

"You know how much I appreciate good news in the morning. Where are we on the new hire?"

"I like him," her assistant, Mae, said. "He's done good work, has impressive recs, think he'd be a nice addition to the team."

Vanessa nodded, wiping the lipstick off her cup with her thumb.

"Good. See what you can find out about him beyond what he's shared. If it looks good, I'll let you handle the offer, okay?"

Mae raised her eyebrows. "You don't want to hire him yourself?"

Vanessa shook her head. "You'll be working with him the most; you're the one who has to be satisfied. I trust your judgment."

"Well, thanks, boss," Mae said.

Vanessa's phone buzzed on the desk, a message from Khalil. Reaching for it, she was cut off by Mae's chuckle.

"I'll let you go," she said. "Looks like you've got more interesting things to handle."

Vanessa raised an eyebrow, looking directly into the camera.

"What's that supposed to mean?"

Mae shook her head. "Nothing boss. Can just tell that you've switched from business to pleasure. And that's a good thing. I'll keep you posted about the new guy." She winked and ended the call.

Vanessa smirked. Everyone was giving her a hard time, but she didn't care. Khalil made her very happy, that was that.

> Khalil: Hey, babygirl. Dinner out tonight?

It was the middle of the week and he'd said he needed to work a little late. But she certainly wasn't going to pass up time with her man.

> Vanessa: I'd love that. But I thought you had to work late.
> Khalil: Slow day. Darius is leaving early and Pax wanted to work out of this location today. Not enough clients for me and Chris too.
> Vanessa: Okay. Pick me up at 7?
> Khalil: Perfect.

Vanessa took another slow breath, trying to relax the muscles around her eyes as she looked out the window of Khalil's Jeep. She was not a fan of Madison Heights, but Telway burgers would make it worth the trip.

"You good?" he asked, glancing at her at a red light.

"Guess not at hiding my bougie side," she said.

He chuckled. "You aren't bougie." He picked her hand up off her lap, kissing the back. "You're a princess."

The light changed as her jaw dropped. She snatched her hand back.

"Am not," she said, looking out her window again.

"Are too," he said. "But that's a very good thing."

She huffed.

"Means I get to be your knight in shining armor," he said, pulling into the parking lot of a strip mall.

"Mmm. So you get to act out some sort of fantasy," she said.

He parked. "My lady," he said, hand over his heart. "Every moment in your presence is better than any fantasy I could ever dream."

She side-eyed him and laughed. He gave her a peck on the cheek and hopped out of the car. Opening her door, he bowed deeply before offering his hand.

"Cut it out, silly," she said.

"Only if you promise you're my princess."

She rolled her eyes. "Okay, handsome."

Grinning, he tucked her hand in his elbow and led the way to the restaurant, the aroma of grilled meat drawing them in. A car passed too quickly, and they stopped short. Vanessa's attention landed on a little shop, across the way from the burger joint.

"Babe," she said, tugging on Khalil's arm. "Hold on a second."

He followed her to the record store, already closed for the evening. Front and center in the window, a vintage turntable was bathed in the glow of a spotlight. Vanessa gasped.

"Khalil! My parents used to have a turntable exactly like this." She got close, restraining herself from pressing her palms to the glass. There was a record on the turntable, the arm poised in the air as if ready to start playing. The record jacket was propped up behind. Memories came rushing back. Sunday afternoons when her parents put records on after dinner and danced with Ma-Max and Papa Joe. Then the turntable got blurry, and she laughed at herself for getting so close her breath fogged the window.

"They don't have it anymore?" Khalil asked.

"No." Vanessa took another step back, checking the operating hours of the store. "There was a big snowstorm. When I was maybe, eight?" She stepped farther back, sliding her phone out of her pocket so she could pull up the store's website. "We had this enormous tree in the backyard. Like a quarter of it broke off and crashed through the ceiling. There'd been a built-in wall shelf on that side of the house and everything was destroyed." She frowned at her phone. The store had almost no web presence. She rejoined Khalil, his hands in his pockets as he admired the other objects on display. "They managed to find copies of most of the records, but my dad had had the turntable since college. They couldn't find one anywhere."

"Looks like it's part of the decor," Khalil said.

Vanessa nodded.

"Guess I'll call tomorrow. See if I can convince the owner to sell it to me. That would make an awesome surprise for my dad. Come on, handsome." She tucked her hand back into his elbow. "I'm starved."

Hours later, having fallen asleep after being sated in more ways than one, Vanessa woke up a little chilly. She wriggled back, looking for Khalil's warmth behind her. She cracked an eye open, realizing that she'd scooted past the halfway point of the bed and hadn't bumped into him. Rolling over and casting an arm out, she confirmed that she was alone. The light in the bathroom was off, the door open. So she slid out of the sheets, put on the shirt he'd tossed to the floor when they'd made their way to bed, and headed down the hallway.

The lamp on the end table beside his couch was on. He was sitting on the floor, head back on the leather seat, arms resting on bent knees, eyes shut. His stillness froze Vanessa to the spot. Something deep inside sent out an alarm. That cold, wet feeling from the day in front of her house was back, deep in her chest. She forced a breath in to speak, but Khalil moved first. His hand went up to his face, thumb and middle finger to each eye. Wiping away tears. He shuddered and sniffled, and Vanessa's heart dropped. She didn't know if he'd be okay with her seeing him like that. He'd left the bedroom. If he'd wanted her to console him, he could have stayed in the bed, hidden in her arms if he needed to. She took a silent breath and backed out of the living room and down the hall.

She sat on the edge of the bed, tears brimming in her own eyes. Maybe he was upset about Karim. They'd talked about the situation again, Vanessa thinking that Khalil had stopped beating himself up. Earlier that evening, he'd been in such a great mood. As excited as she'd been about getting the turntable for her dad, enjoying the burgers, and being with each other. He knew she loved him. So what was wrong? Why did he need to hide?

Her ears perked up at the creak of the couch. The light flicked off.

It sounded like he was coming back to bed. She jumped to her feet. No way to get the shirt off and back under the covers in time. She started walking down the hall toward him, rubbing her eyes.

"Babygirl?" he whispered. "What are you doing up?"

"You weren't in the bed," she said, letting her arms fall to her sides. "Came looking for you."

He kissed the top of her head, leaning in to hug her tight.

"I couldn't sleep. Didn't want to disturb you," he said.

She hugged back and tried to nudge herself to say something about what she'd seen, but faltered.

"Come back to bed? I don't mind if you're awake, I just need you near me, okay?"

"Sure thing," he said, letting her take his hand and lead him back to his bedroom.

It happened again on Friday night. She woke up alone, but he returned quickly. Then on Saturday. They'd gone out dancing with Lisa and Darius, Bibi and Reizo. Khalil had been present, attentive to Vanessa as always. But something was off. He smiled, he joked, but his laughter didn't reach his eyes. Vanessa tried harder, stayed closer, showed her affection. And that seemed to work, a little bit. She'd lean in and brush his cheek with hers or plant a kiss on his earlobe and he'd grin, gaze breaking from wherever it had been to lock with hers. He'd squeeze her fingers tight, whisper that he loved her, and for a flash, he was there, everything was right. But then he'd turn away and the light would go out of his eyes, even though he remained present for the people he was with. When he'd ordered a Negroni after two whiskey sours, she'd kept the surprise off her face. It was the first time she'd seen him drink that much, and he'd told her that even a little hard alcohol always left him with regrets the following morning. Darius had paused as well, but he smiled and made a joke. Vanessa had tried to catch his attention, to ask without words. But he'd avoided eye contact.

They'd gotten back late. So late that Khalil had fallen asleep in the passenger seat, after telling her again and again how much he loved her, how perfect and amazing and sexy she was. And while the compliments were nice, she figured the repetitiveness was thanks to too much alcohol. She managed to rouse him enough to get him inside and to his bedroom. But he was out cold before she could get his jeans off.

Washing her face, she'd chided herself for worrying. Everyone gets a little too tipsy, parties a little too hard sometimes. And it wasn't as though he was mean or difficult. She snuggled under the sheets and drifted off.

Until about four. A choked sound jolted her awake. The bed was cold, and she caught the sound again. Almost like a muffled dog's yelp. Confused, she sat up and slid out of bed.

The bathroom was empty, his living room too. She shook her head, trying to clear it. The group hadn't eaten much, and she'd had enough wine to make it hard to focus. The hallway listed and she took an extra step to catch her balance, right beside the office door. Then there was another muffled sound, long, slightly higher pitched. She pushed the door open.

He was sitting on the floor again, arms around bent knees, a hand clamped over his mouth, his shoulders racking as he cried. Before she could think better of it, she fell to the floor and wrapped her arms around him from behind. He sucked in a gasp and turned.

"Sorry," he said, dragging his hand across his face. "I woke you up."

The moonlight slatting through the blinds was enough for her to see that his lashes were sparkling with tears.

"What's wrong?" she asked. She shifted around him, staying close, legs clunking against his, her hands on his forearms.

"I'm sorry." He turned away hard, hiding. "You shouldn't see me like—"

"Please don't," she said.

He looked back at her, caught somewhere between the Khalil she knew and a scared animal.

"Don't what?" he asked.

"Don't run away. I know something's wrong," she said. "Something's been wrong. Please let me help?" A whimper escaped her, along with fat, hot tears streaming down her cheeks.

Shaking his head, he sucked in another hard breath and pulled her into his arms, her head tucked under his chin.

"Please don't cry, Ness," he whispered, rocking her a little. "Please don't."

She slid her palm flat against his chest and felt his heart thudding hard.

"Why don't you want me to cry?" she asked.

"I never want you to be sad." He kissed her temple. "It hurts to see you like that, makes me want to take the pain away."

She jerked up fast.

"So why would you think I don't feel that way about you?"

She searched his eyes, grateful that he was at least looking at her; he wasn't running away. Then his shoulders shook and something broke.

"I'm supposed to take care of you. I'm hardly—" A sob cut him off, and she pressed her lips together to keep herself from sobbing too. He gulped, then his gaze fell to the floor. "I'm hardly a man if I can't even keep my emotions—"

"Hey, stop that." Fear made her harsh. "That's not true." She squinted, studying his face. "Those aren't your words, are they?"

His red-tinged eyes snapped back at her, assessing. He swallowed hard and shook his head before looking at the floor again.

"My ex. That's what she said the only time she saw me cry. Said I should be taking care of her, not the other way around."

"We're supposed to take care of each other," she said. "I'll never turn my back on you for having feelings, Khalil. Anyone who would do that or say something like that doesn't love you. And I do."

She held her breath, still holding him, arms and legs intertwined. She wanted to pull him close, rock him as he'd tried to rock her. But she didn't want to force him. She needed him to come to her. Then he took a breath, deep and long, like he needed all of the oxygen in the room, and collapsed against her. She stroked the back of his head.

"I love you," she whispered over and over as he began to cry again.

CHAPTER TWENTY-SIX

Khalil had a moment to realize he was waking up before a migraine slammed into his consciousness. He groaned, and that made things worse. A pitch of nausea crashed over him as well. Grabbing the blanket, he pulled it over his head as he curled into the fetal position. He hadn't picked up on any light in the room, but there was no harm in protecting himself. The world stopped spinning, and he sighed a moment's relief. Then a new, splintering pain blasted through his eyes. They were on fire, his lids gummy and stuck together.

How much did I—

Then it all came rushing back. He had drunk too much, but that wasn't the worst part. Vanessa had seen him. Really seen him, crying like a baby. Mortified, he curled up tighter, bringing his thighs against his stomach, which protested with another wave. He was going to die. If the hangover didn't kill him, the humiliation would. He stilled. His breathing, his thoughts, everything so he could focus on whether Vanessa was behind him, asleep on her side. The room was silent. The blanket didn't shift with someone else's breathing, nor had there been any resistance when he'd tugged it over himself.

Of course she's not here, loser.

Shame bloomed, outpacing the nausea and the migraine. How had he let it happen? He'd sworn to himself never to do that again, never let a woman know that he couldn't keep himself together. He sniffled, amazed as a burning tear pressed its way out of his swollen eyelids, another escaping from his nose. How did he have any tears left? Then the fact that Vanessa was gone and he'd fucked up again ricocheted through him. He almost laughed at his ability to be an even bigger baby as more tears threatened, but a sound stopped him dead: his bedroom door creaking open. His ears pricked up as he absorbed everything he could. Vanessa's feet soft on the carpet. The shift in the air as she walked up the side of his bed. He held his breath, the edge of the blanket tight in his fingers. Maybe if he didn't move, if he stayed hidden in his little tent, she'd think he was still asleep.

Something settled on his nightstand. Small things being pushed back—maybe his glasses or watch up against his old-school alarm clock. He still refused to inhale.

"Baby?" Vanessa whispered, her hand gentle on his shoulder. She slid it down, caressing his upper arm. "Sweetheart, I know you're awake, and your head has to be killing you. Please come out so I can help?"

He didn't want to come out. He didn't want her to see his swollen eyes, didn't want to see the pity in hers. She leaned closer, fingers light over the blanket covering the back of his head, her cheek on his through the fabric.

"Please?" she whispered.

It was bad enough he'd been weak; he couldn't be cruel too. He relaxed his fingers a little, allowing himself to breathe. She didn't tug at the blanket, just stroked the back of his head and his arm again.

"I don't want to push if you don't want to," she whispered. "But it would make me so happy if you'd let me in. And don't worry. I turned off all the lights, left the curtains closed. I bet you've got one hell of a headache."

He sniffed and wiped at his cheeks, in case there were tears that hadn't made it to the pillow. Then with a deep breath, he pulled the blanket down so he could face her.

"There you are, handsome," she whispered, her smile open and sweet.

"Hey," he croaked back. In spite of the darkness of the room, he couldn't get his eyes as open as he wanted. She pressed her lips together, looking far more serious than he was ready for.

"First things first," she said softly. "Water."

She picked up a glass off a tray on his nightstand. He shifted so he could get into a sitting position, but then her hand was on his chest.

"Don't know that it's wise for you to sit up," she said. "Does your head hurt?"

"Yeah," he whispered. The nod he'd begun hurt way too much to complete. She grabbed a straw off the tray and popped it into the glass. Bending it, she held the glass close. He drank a little then paused, glancing up at her. She nodded for him to continue and he downed most of the water. She smiled.

"You feel up to some Tylenol?" she asked.

"Yes, please."

She popped two out of a blister pack, held them over his mouth until he opened up, then brought the glass back so he could finish it. He was lost. The last time anyone had treated him with such care was . . . when he was a kid. He searched her face for the annoyance, the pity that should have been there. She winked at him as he finished the water.

"Ness, I—"

"Shhh . . . Don't think you should talk too much right now," she whispered. "You've got to be super dehydrated and that Tylenol needs time to work. Lean back."

He obeyed, relaxing into the pillow.

"Feel like you might throw up? Should I grab a bucket?"

"No," he whispered. "I'm okay."

"Good. Close your eyes."

He hesitated but did as she asked. Then she stretched a cold, damp cloth across his forehead, and an even colder one over his eyes. He sighed, the pain abating a little.

"Too cold?" she asked.

"No."

"Good. I'll be right back."

Robbed of his sight and with the pain less present, he found it much easier to track what she was doing. The glass went back on the tray, the empty medicine packet crunched together. She stood, then left the room. He needed to relax, to just be still like she'd said. And physically he could, but mentally he was all over the place. There'd been no disappointment or disgust in her eyes. She'd given him the same lighthearted smile she always did when she looked at him in the morning, or when they got together after time apart. He caught himself smiling a bit. She didn't seem different. Even though she'd seen him differently. Her footsteps came padding back, there was a small flick of papers, the slick shift of one of his curtains being pulled back and something hard touching the opposite nightstand. The mattress shifted as she got back in with him.

"I'll try not to jostle you," she whispered.

"It's okay." He smiled in her direction. And it didn't hurt.

She scooted under the covers, her slim hip bumping his shoulder. She grabbed his hand and curved it around her thigh. He squeezed.

"I cracked the curtain so I can read my magazine, but if it's too much light, please say so."

"Didn't notice," he said.

"Good. I've got some more cold compresses. Let me know when you need one."

He moistened his dry lips.

"Thank you, Ness," he said. "You don't have to stay, you know. I can handle it myself."

"I want to stay, baby," she said, running gentle fingers through his hair. "Why don't you rest? We've got a lazy day today. Give yourself some time to feel better."

He was getting sick of himself, with the damn tears threatening again. But he couldn't stay quiet.

"But last night . . . I understand if you don't want—"

Her finger up against his lips stopped him short.

"Rest, baby. We can talk about it later." She paused, the sound of fluttering pages pricking at his ears. Then she was close, her nose nuzzling his jaw. "I'm not going anywhere, remember?" she whispered.

He leaned into the kiss she pressed against his cheek.

———

"So sometimes, it's just like that," Khalil said, more to his and Vanessa's hands than to her. His could have easily dwarfed hers, but she'd laced their fingers together while he was explaining his pain, the waves that broke him. He clung to the comfort of each soft bit of skin nestled against his fingers. He hadn't used the word "depression." Maybe he wouldn't have to. Telling her about Dr. Edwards had crossed his mind. But he'd flaked on his therapist so much, he doubted he still had one. Plus, getting to Dr. E would mean talking about why he'd gone in the first place. There was no way he could share all that. She shifted a little, and he glanced at her.

"It sounds horrible, baby. I'm so sorry you're hurting like that." She squeezed his fingers tight, sad smile bending her lips.

He shrugged, then prepared himself for the next part, the inevitable turning away. But her brows had crunched together and she was looking off to the side.

"It's not always like that, though," she said, looking up at him again.

"Yeah, I can usually keep it in, but . . ."

"You said that Darius mentioned something to you, at Paradigm. Something about patterns?"

Khalil nodded and focused on the softness of the backs of her hands as he stroked them with his thumbs. She was too clever, would probably backtrack a pattern and figure it all out.

"You were excited about the Hoops League earlier in the year, right?"

He nodded again. "Had a blast at the charity thing, but ever since, it's been harder and harder to do."

Her bottom lip tucked in a bit as she worried it.

"How does your head feel now?" she asked.

"Fine."

"Is it okay if I open the curtains to let in some light?"

He relaxed his hold on her hands. "That's cool with me."

He caught himself smiling at her silhouette in front of the window. He'd told her how sexy she was without makeup, in casual little tanks and shorts, and that's all she ever seemed to wear when they were relaxing at home. He liked to think she did it for him. At the last window, she stood, looking out, hands on hips.

"Has it ever been this bad before?" she asked over her shoulder.

He needed a breath and a swallow before he was ready to speak. He readjusted himself on the bed, one knee bent so he could rest his chin on it.

"Uh . . ." He ached to be honest, but his throat sealed up.

She turned around to face him and his heartbeat of a prayer was answered—she didn't seem to have noticed his hesitation.

"Or maybe when it was almost as bad?"

He tilted his head back, as though the ceiling might have an answer he was comfortable sharing. "Um . . . Dare almost kicked my ass once." He chuckled at her gasp.

"Darius? You and Darius got into it?"

He nodded. The memory had faded enough to be funny.

"Yeah. I was kinda asking for it. We were super stressed, getting to the one-year mark at the Original. Looking back, it's a wonder he didn't dissolve our partnership. I was the King of Assholes."

She pursed her lips, sauntering back to the bed.

"Why do I find that very difficult to believe?" she asked.

He grinned. "Trust me, if I'm willing to paint myself in a bad light, it's because it was the truth. Every little thing set me off. I was a jerk to my girlfriend, impatient with staff, lost two good barbers because I couldn't control my temper. I was shit to be around."

She'd raised an eyebrow at the word "girlfriend" then pursed her lips.

"What time of year was it?" she asked.

"Huh," he said, after a moment's thought. "Fall, moving into winter. Around now."

"Interesting," she said. "Well, this year you haven't been a jerk to your girlfriend, and you've managed to keep a barber who wanted to quit."

"I've been an ass to Darius again."

She shrugged.

"You've also had a huge emotional crisis with Karim. That's part of your underlying stress right now. And if this time of year your emotions are more volatile . . ." She tilted her head to the side, smiling at him. "Sounds like a perfect storm."

"I guess," he said.

She leaned forward, giving him a peck on the cheek. "Come on, babe. I'm starved." She held her hands out to him. "Feel up to eating a late lunch?"

CHAPTER TWENTY-SEVEN

It wasn't like her schedule was going to change if she stared at it long enough. Two conferences and the meeting in New York to try to save the Alphastone deal in the coming weeks, plus the projects in beta phases; her calendar was filled to the brim. Exactly what she'd been concerned about as she'd left Khalil's the day before. Her phone chirped with a notification, but she only glanced briefly to confirm that it could be ignored for a few minutes. She was so relieved that Khalil had shared, had let her in. She hadn't researched depression yet, and he hadn't named it, but it seemed like a safe guess for the moment. The ping of a chat window drew her attention back to her desktop. She opened it, but the words made no sense, her mind still on Khalil and how much pain he'd been in. Apparently was still in, but working to keep it hidden. So she'd remain discreet too. As much as she could have used Lisa's or Bibi's perspectives, she'd keep her thoughts to herself. But she couldn't clear her agenda, and she really did not want to leave Khalil on his own in the coming weeks.

Lemme deal with this chat and get some notes down for my talk. Taking a break might bring some ideas.

Pulling into her driveway that evening, Vanessa sighed. She'd given herself hours and only managed to fill her schedule up more. A contact in California would be attending the conference she was headed to in Denver. And she'd invited Vanessa to visit her corporate offices in San Francisco. The opportunity was too good to pass up, which meant that even the three free days she'd had back home had been eaten up. She groaned, stepping out of the car, and headed into the house.

A quick shower later, her doorbell was ringing. Disappointed to see the delivery man through the peephole, she opened it, then got her reward.

"Thanks, man," Khalil said as he collected their dinner.

Vanessa nodded to the man, and he left as Khalil stepped through the door.

"Right on time," she said, going up on tiptoe as he bent down for a kiss. He shot her a shy smile as he stood straight.

"Thirty minutes late," he said.

She took the bags from him as he toed off his shoes.

"Just in time for dinner," she said over her shoulder as she went into the kitchen.

To her relief, he made quick work of the hearty lasagna she'd ordered for him and accepted several bites of her ravioli. His appetite had seemed light lately. At least he looked content right then.

"Any room for dessert?" he asked from the fridge.

She shook her head. "Not one bit. But tiramisu keeps, right?"

He came back to the table, delivery box and a bowl in his hand.

"Who said I was leaving leftovers?" He winked at her as he served himself.

She nudged him under the table.

"Greedy. But if you're still hungry, go ahead. I'll get some another time."

"Just kidding. Glad you had a productive day, App Goddess."

She wanted to joke with him about that nickname but wasn't in the mood.

"Hmm . . ." he said, finishing a spoonful.

"What?" she asked.

"What's wrong?"

"What makes you think something's wrong?"

He put the spoon down. "It would make me happy if you accepted the goddess title that you deserve, but usually when I say it, you look embarrassed, not nervous."

Lying to him wasn't in the cards, especially because putting off her concerns couldn't last long. She put her utensils on her plate and stood, wrinkling her nose and shaking her head.

"You know that's just my industry nickname. And speaking of, I have a heavy agenda for the coming weeks and won't be around much," she said, trying to keep the worry out of her voice. "After California and New York, I'll have to work closely with my developers to try to save the Alphastone project. If it can be saved at all."

"Oh," Khalil said, watching her as she went to the sink.

She turned on the water, rinsing quickly, then grabbed the drain plug.

"I think maybe all that travel isn't such a good idea," she said.

He swallowed. "Why not?"

She let the water run until it warmed, focusing on plugging the drain as if she didn't know exactly where it was, and added dish soap.

"Ness?"

She looked up, took a breath, and smiled.

"Is it really the best time for me to not be here? For you?" she asked.

He rumpled his brow, scooping the last spoonful of cream out of the bowl.

"Why would it be a bad time for . . ." His forehead rumpled deeper. "For you to not be here? Or to be busy?" He popped the last bite in his mouth.

"Sorry, I'm not being clear. I mean, is it wise for me to leave you alone? You're going through a rough patch."

"And you have a business to run." He got up from the table with his dishes and joined her at the sink. "You can't cancel your plans for my sake."

His tone was a touch too abrupt for her taste.

"Are you telling me what to do?" she asked.

"No." He put his dishes in the sink, grabbed a dishtowel and started drying the ones she'd finished. "I'm trying to understand what's going on right now."

"I feel weird. I'm not sure if what I'm trying to say is right, but it's how I feel. You were so upset the other day. And like you said before, it's been several days that things have been tough for you. Weeks, actually. I don't like the idea of not being here to support you if you're in so much pain." He took a breath, but she rushed ahead. "I know you've got Darius, and of course Karim, but still. You said they don't know how bad it gets, right?"

He cleared his throat, wiping an already dry dish as he stared at it.

"My . . . *stuff* isn't reason for you to do something different," he said. There was the shadow of an edge to his voice, enough to make her button her lip and pay attention to each word. "You can't . . . I won't let you—"

"Let me?"

He sighed, deep crease in his brow.

"Can we not talk about this for a minute?" he asked.

"Okay, but I think—"

He left the kitchen and was out her front door. She stood there, mute, hands in the chilling water. Had they just had a fight? He hadn't stormed out. He'd been determined but calm. Vanessa turned her attention to the water, shifting around until she caught the plug and tugged it out. Watching the water drain gave her something to do while she reviewed. A sharp pain in her lip clued her in to the fact that she was biting it. She let go and reached for the dishtowel to dry her hands off just as the door opened.

"I'm sorry," he said.

"No, I am. I didn't mean to upset you."

He joined her in the kitchen, arms outstretched. She buried herself against his chest, latching her arms around him.

"I know," he said, squeezing her tight, sliding one hand up to cup the back of her head. After kissing her crown, he let his lips rest there as he took a deep breath. "I will never tell you what to do, babygirl. It's not my place. I meant to be encouraging, not demanding."

"I get that, handsome," she said.

He leaned away, arms still loose around her. She met his gaze.

"However," he said. "Your career, your life was on a great trajectory before you met me. I have no business derailing that."

She sat with that thought a moment, resting her chin on his chest.

"You aren't derailing anything. I'm a big girl. If I want to change my plans, that's my choice."

He nodded, stroking the back of two fingers down her cheek.

"I don't want you to feel obligated," he said.

"Big difference between feeling obligated and wanting to."

He swallowed hard, nodding again. Just as he broke eye contact to look up, she was pretty sure she caught a shimmer in his eyes. He pulled her close, and she rested her cheek on his chest, tightening her hug.

Returning to the table, Vanessa outlined her schedule for the coming weeks, along with her concerns. Khalil listened, a hand over hers. She was nervous and worried, but annoyance began to prick up as he kept tucking in smiles or looking away from her with the corners of his eyes crinkling.

"What?" she asked, once she'd finished explaining.

"You do love me," he said.

"Of course I do."

"But you know you aren't responsible for me, right?" he asked.

She nodded, surprised that he saw things that way. He squeezed her hand, then let go as he sat back in his chair.

"Your schedule doesn't seem disproportionate," he said. "Especially compared to when we first met. You traveled just as much."

"Sort of. But I had more days at home, less on my plate."

"True. Though, the most difficult time to start a relationship is when one of the parties isn't always available, right?"

He had a good point.

"If we were able to get to know each other when you weren't here on a regular basis, why wouldn't we be able to maintain what we've already got? We've done this before, babygirl."

"But you weren't hurting like this a couple months ago," she said.

The deep breath, his glance toward the living room, and his hands running quickly down his thighs made her wonder if he was planning an escape. Too bad for her, she didn't have the words to fight it just then.

"It'll be okay, Ness," he said. "We'll talk as much as we do now. You can check on me whenever you want. I'll miss you, but it's not like you're gonna be gone forever. I'm starting to wonder if I shouldn't have told you anything."

"Why not?" She flinched at the pitch of her voice. "Sorry," she said. "I really appreciate that you trusted me. I don't want you to regret it."

He leaned forward to squeeze her hand again then got closer to kiss her cheek.

"It's gonna be all right, Ness," he said. "Don't change anything with work, please."

"Okay . . ." she said. "As long as you're sure."

. . . .

Guilt and irritation were the keywords for the day. Ignoring the squeak of the chair at his kitchen table, Khalil readjusted to get more light on the frustratingly small pieces of the hair clipper he was fixing. Shaven hairs tickled his nose as they snapped up from the spring he was trying to coerce back into position. He brushed them away then noticed that he hadn't bumped his glasses. Which weren't on his face, for some reason. He glanced around, annoyed, then found them on his forehead. Grunting in frustration at himself, he let them fall into place, and the clipper pieces weren't so small after all.

Nice job, genius. No wonder you can't get any work done.

The guilt of lying to Vanessa had pushed him into fixing the clippers that had been sitting on his table for two weeks. While he couldn't fix the lie, he could fix the clippers. But something that usually gave him joy felt insurmountable. And taking so long had been tempting fate: With two clippers out of commission, he and Darius were one problem away from letting a client down. Their backups had been chilling at Khalil's while he hadn't been able to get himself together enough to fix them.

First one fixed, he grabbed a cloth to clean it and his mind slipped right back into the broken record of criticism he'd been dealing with since he'd dropped Vanessa off at the airport early that morning. In the past, she'd refused his offers to take her, as he could have done with two more hours of sleep. But today she'd come back to the bed as he was sitting up and turning off his alarm. Wrapped in a towel, little beads of moisture from the shower glistening on her shoulders, she kissed his forehead, putting a smile on his face as her lavender cloud wove its way around him.

"Promise to text me every day," she'd said, as they stood at the entrance to the security line. He'd smiled, squeezing her hand in his.

"Since when do we not text each other every day? Multiple times a day?"

"That's true," she said, tapping the corner of her phone on her chin, the boarding pass filling the screen.

"Will you call me whenever you can?" she asked. "Just so I can hear your voice. I don't even care if it's to tell me that the lunch you had was crappy and we have to be sure not to go back to that food truck or whatever anymore."

Her nervousness, her worry about him warmed his heart.

"Will do, App Goddess. Don't worry, I'm fine. Now go ahead; don't want you to have to rush to your gate." He winked at her and bent down to kiss the top of her head. She hugged him and he reciprocated, careful not to squeeze the breath out of her.

"Okay, baby. I love you," she said, accepting her carry-on from him.

"I love you too," he said, his hands in his pockets as she stepped up to a boarding pass reader and flashed her phone. The red light switched green and she walked through the opened doors. He waited in his spot, the smile coming easily as she looked back at him from the priority boarding lane. Just before she turned the corner where a frosted glass wall would keep her from seeing him again, she blew him a kiss and mouthed *I love you*. He grinned and did the same.

Returning to his car in the parking garage, the warmth faded with each step. By the time he'd sat down and turned the key, the sound of the engine coming to life barely registered. Fifties were in the forecast, but cold filled his chest and made his arms heavy. The internal chill he'd been pushing to the side for days finally bloomed and sent goosebumps over his skin. The spark, the warmth, and the intellectual stimulation that was ever-present when he was with Vanessa were gone.

He'd told her that he was fine. He was a damned liar.

Job half done on the second set of clippers, he stopped, tossing his glasses on the table to rub his eyes. The fix was easy, something he normally could've done in his sleep. But right then, everything he did was wrong. His fingers were too clumsy to fit the small pieces together. The spring kept snapping out because he couldn't focus enough to hold it in place for more than a few seconds. He sat back and crossed his arms, ignoring the thought to keep grease off his shirt. If he didn't and it was permanently stained, it would serve him right for being an idiot and wearing something he liked while doing repairs.

He got up from the table, to get away from himself. At the sink, he stopped short before picking up the dish detergent to wash his hands, remembering the charcoal soap Mo had given him for dirty jobs. Using his elbow to open the door, he got it out from under the cabinet and spent more time than was probably necessary getting each bit of grease off each bit of skin. His brother was right, it was some good soap. Khalil would make it a point not to tell him, though. Mo was always right about everything and that shit got old.

His smirk bent into a full-blown smile when he grabbed his phone off the counter and caught the flashing red light indicating a message. Then, as he flopped onto the couch, so did his mood. It was from Dr. Edwards, checking in as Khalil had missed yet another appointment. Embarrassed, he grabbed the remote and turned on the television to think of other things.

But he didn't know what he was watching, couldn't follow. The shame was back, proud and strong. He'd lied to his girlfriend, couldn't fix something that was practically child's play, and he couldn't face his therapist. He knew he probably needed to, but that knowledge changed absolutely nothing about what he was capable of doing. It disgusted him. His thumb found the channel up button and clicked again and again, while he stared through the TV. A commercial for an all-day breakfast restaurant appeared and it occurred to him that he'd skipped breakfast. He glanced at the clock, and surprise, it was almost two. So he hadn't had lunch, either. He tilted his head, looking in the direction of the fridge. Then had to look away again. There was the pile of unopened mail on the bar beside his keys and wallet. He knew that there was something from his landlord, something from the small business association. And his empty meds bottle that had needed a refill two weeks ago. Stuff that would take less than half an hour to deal with, but right then . . . every single task was just too much. It felt like scaling a mountain, and he didn't know how to do that. Something clicked, deep inside. A memory of something Dr. E had said about frustrations, how his mind could play tricks on him about the difficulty of small tasks. It might have been a comforting thought, but at the moment, it only felt like a coward's excuse for his innate failure to handle his shit. He looked back at the screen and it was blurry, in spite of his glasses. He squeezed his eyes tight, then wiped away a lazy tear that spilled out.

·   ·   ·

Briskly following the signs to the exit, Vanessa enjoyed the light, familiar charge she got when she arrived in a new city, ready for a new conference, a new chance to share her passion with like-minded people. After some quiet digging, she knew that Sam wouldn't be there—a welcome relief. In the car that the conference had sent for her, she had yet another reason to smile, reading a text from Khalil, making sure she'd arrived safely. Checking her watch, she guessed he'd be at work, so she refrained from calling him.

Vanessa: Hey, baby. Had a good flight. How's work?

She returned her phone to its spot in her purse and was looking up to glance out the window when it beeped.

Khalil: Glad to hear it. Took today off.

She was certain that he'd mentioned having a busy day. But that had been over the weekend, maybe things had changed.

Vanessa: Wise to take it easy sometimes. Can I call
you once I get settled in my hotel?
Khalil: Whatever's fine.

Phone in her lap, she told herself she was being silly. That had been a normal response. Even though she couldn't remember him ever using the word "whatever," unless he and Darius had been joking and meant to be dismissive. Trying to content herself that nothing was wrong, she looked out the window, determined not to ask if he was okay.

"Did it all work out in the end?" Vanessa asked, stretched diagonally across the hotel room bed as evening shifted to night.

"It did," Khalil said, voice soft. "Both sets of clippers are ready to go back to work tomorrow."

"And how about you?"

"I guess," he said. "Not like there's any choice unless I want to get into it with Darius again."

"Again?"

A rush of air scratched across the speaker of the phone, and Khalil cleared his throat.

"From the other day, remember?" he asked. "About Rod. But can we not talk about that? I'd rather focus on you, babygirl."

"Mmkay," she said. "I wish you'd been here for the catered lunch. It was a ballroom full of mini food trucks. I wanted to try a little bit of everything, but you weren't with me to share."

She caught his light chuckle and smiled with relief.

"Sounds like I did miss out," he said. "But I wasn't really that hungry today. Forgot about breakfast. And lunch."

"You forgot?"

"Yeah. I was so focused on the clippers, I didn't notice until super late. Just had a frozen meal thing for dinner." He yawned. "'Scuse me, baby."

Not eating was not normal for Khalil. But getting caught up in a project was. Maybe she was just looking for things to worry about.

"Was that enough to eat?" she asked. "Sometimes they're barely enough for me, even after breakfast and lunch."

"It was okay. I'm not hungry anymore, so it did its job, right?" he asked.

"Guess so." She checked the time. "I better let you go, huh?"

"Am I that obvious?" he asked, smile in his voice.

"You're allowed to yawn, handsome. You got up super early today, and even if you didn't go to work, you still need your rest. We'll talk tomorrow, okay?"

"Sure thing. Night, babygirl."

"Night, handsome."

. . . .

Six days without touching Vanessa sucked. He'd been truthful when he'd said he could manage, but the reality was starting to get on his nerves. He'd felt like he was being melodramatic until he'd actually counted the days on the calendar in the back of the shop while eating his lunchtime sub. The chime over the door sounded and Khalil checked his watch: another thirty minutes before his next client and Darius was with someone. A walk-in was welcome. His face fell as he stepped out of the back and saw Rodriguez.

"Came to bring your keys, man," he said to Darius.

Darius had stopped short, clippers still buzzing. He was silent, but Khalil's irritation was ready to go.

"What do you mean, Rod?" he asked.

"What do you think I mean? I quit. Found something better." He looked straight at Darius. "Where family means something."

Darius turned off his clippers, placed a hand on his client's shoulder, and bent to say something to him. Khalil enjoyed the few slow steps he took toward Rod, arms folded like he didn't care, but gaze tracking him hard. Rod looked at Darius, then back at Khalil.

"That was messed up," Khalil said.

Rod tipped his chin up, pulling the strap of his backpack higher up on his shoulder. "And?"

"Just give me the keys," said Darius. "This is not the time or place to settle anything."

"What's in the bag, Rod?" Khalil asked.

Darius raised an eyebrow.

"The hell is that supposed to mean?" Rod asked, pulling it up tighter against his body.

"What do you think it means?" Khalil was impressed with how evenly he spoke, in spite of the rage coating his muscles.

"Maybe," Darius said, tone between polite and what-the-fuck-are-you-doing-homie-there-are-witnesses, "that's something we can settle later on."

Khalil cut his eyes at his friend.

"I'm not waiting for shit," he said. "Open the bag, Rod." Facing him again, Khalil caught how flushed he was, how fidgety while trying to stand up straighter, make himself taller. He might have even been trying to puff his chest out. Khalil couldn't restrain his snicker.

"Or, don't show me what's in the bag. Grab a seat." He gestured toward the waiting area and took his phone out of his pocket.

"What are you doing?" Darius asked.

"Gonna ask Pax to take a quick look around, see if anything's missing," Khalil said.

"Christ, your ego. I've got my own damn tools. You wanna check?" Rod jerked his bag open, eyes narrowed at Khalil. "You are fucking that bitch, aren't you? Her and your bougie whore girlfriend. Do they know about—"

Actions and their consequences were things Khalil always tried to keep in mind. In general, he'd have been upset with himself for the cost-benefit analysis he'd made. Violence wasn't a part of who he wanted to be. However, the scale was already bending toward hitting Rod before he'd called Pax a bitch. His choice of words about Vanessa tipped the whole thing over, and before he knew what he was doing, Rod was on the floor, holding his bleeding nose.

Grabbing the towel draped over the back of his chair, Khalil dabbed at his knuckles, checking for damage. He looked at Darius's client's reflection.

"Your haircut's on me today," he said. "Next time too. I'm sorry you had to see that."

The other man shook his head.

"Nah, dawg. Talking trash about your girl like that? He had it coming."

"Thanks," Khalil said.

"Sorry," Khalil said to Darius. He hadn't moved from the moment Khalil started to call Pax. Darius blinked a few times, looked at Rod still sitting on the floor holding his nose, then back at Khalil.

"What the fuck, 'Lil?" he asked.

Khalil shrugged.

"No, seriously, man," Darius said, facing Khalil. "Go cool off in the back."

Khalil glanced at his friend. He caught his surprise but also his anger. Khalil wasn't in the mood to fight with anyone else.

"Aight," he said, heading to the back. Cursing, Rod pushed himself away, closer to Khalil's empty chair.

"Give Dare the keys, Rodriguez. Then get the fuck out," Khalil spat, before stepping through the threshold and sliding the back room door closed.

With time to settle his nerves and allow the full blossom of pain in his knuckles, Khalil vacillated between embarrassment about hitting Rod, frustration about letting things get tense with Darius again, and his need to talk to Vanessa. She was the headline speaker of her conference, giving her talk the next afternoon, so as much as he wanted to hear her voice and unload, Khalil didn't want to distract her with his drama. Plus, he was exhausted, surprisingly so. It would be easy to just crawl under the covers once he got out of the shower.

The water was getting cool, but he couldn't be bothered to care. Instead, he kept getting stuck on the pattern of stripes on his shower curtain, the lines shifting from crisp to blurry as he let his eyes focus and unfocus over and over. The curtain was there, but at the same time it wasn't, like his breath. Every few moments it felt like maybe he needed one, but the work to pull it in was nearly too much. Eyes unfocused again, he pushed himself off the wall, turning his head to let the water puddle and glide through his hair. Had he washed it? He couldn't remember. Squinting his eyes open, there were no suds running down his chest or legs. The temperature shifted down a few more degrees, and he had no idea how long he'd been in there, or if he'd even used soap.

Stepping out of the shower, he wrapped the towel around himself, vaguely aware of the water dripping from his skin but unsure what to do about it. He needed to sit. The toilet wasn't low enough. He lay down on the floor, calves resting on the edge of the tub. The floor felt safer. The cold chill of the tiles didn't get into his back and shoulders, the bathmat and towel a soft barrier. His head was wet, though. Somewhere in the back of his mind was a wisp of a thought about getting clean then lying on the floor, plus the knowledge that he was going to leave a puddle on the tile. Both logical observations, but he couldn't bring himself to care enough about either to get up. He reminded himself to breathe.

Save for the overhead light, the ceiling was blessedly bare. He stared through it. No patterns to notice, nothing to force him to think. Until the inside of his left wrist itched. The tingle coming to the fore, even more than the dull ache still present in his right knuckles. The next breath he took crept in. His heart, slow and heavy in his chest. Lying on the floor was unwise. He closed his eyes. All the pain came back, the knotted jumble of desperation that had been waiting there for him from before, from when he'd made the mistake, gone too far. Burning tears threatened behind his eyelids. He felt the slice, the sharp kiss of the knife vertically along the inside of his wrist. Then sticky, liquid heat was streaming against his abdomen. He raised his hand, opening his eyes. His skin was intact. But phantom memories were more powerful than he'd have imagined.

I can't be this person. Not again.

·   ·   ·

Sleep still wrapped around her, Vanessa pushed herself up, resting against her pillow. Rubbing her eyes, she picked up her phone on reflex, looking forward to Khalil's morning hello. But it wasn't there. She blinked a couple times, scrolling all the other notifications out of the way. There wasn't a single word from him. Her night had been short, and she only had an hour to get ready for the conference, so she got out of bed and into the bathroom as she went straight to their chat. The last message he'd sent was "good night, love you, miss you." Which wasn't anything to shake her head at. But it was seven for her, so nine A.M. for him. He was definitely awake.

It's not like he always has to text you first.

She typed out a morning greeting of her own, wishing him a good day and reminding him how she felt about him; then she got into the shower.

The morning was a whirlwind, and by the time she was rereading her notes for her post-lunch talk, she hadn't had much time to think about Khalil's silence. Her phone buzzed, and she gladly put down her note cards to scoop it up. Then she got confused by a string of emojis from Khalil. Cute ones, lots of hearts and kissy faces. But that wasn't his style. Though she'd make the most of it. Playing along, she sent back a string of her own.

> Khalil: Hope you're having a good day, babygirl.
> Vanessa: Thanks. You too?
> Khalil: It's cool. Almost time for your talk, right?
> Vanessa: Yep.
> Khalil: You'll be great. Like always.

She smiled, asking herself why she'd been making a thing out of this. Then she was being called to the stage, and she switched to game mode.

Hours later, Vanessa dragged herself back to her hotel room. The talk had gone very well, and she'd been stormed by industry colleagues as soon as she'd stepped off the stage. From there it had been more networking, then dinner, then an after-party. She'd managed to text back and forth with Lisa a little, but all her messages to Khalil had gone unanswered. Now, in a quiet place, she could breathe and her concerns about Alphastone and Khalil came flooding back. The deal was getting shakier by the day, and it felt like Khalil was distancing himself. He'd promised to stay in contact like they always did, but he wasn't doing it. Was he hiding like he'd been hiding under his blanket that morning? They'd had a good talk; he'd been adamant about her maintaining her schedule. What if his distance wasn't about his mental health? Was this break a welcome one for him?

After washing her face for a second time, she asked herself what her problem was. She knew he didn't expect her to make her entire life about him, and she certainly didn't expect that of him. He was close to his family, his friends. Double-checking the day on her phone, she realized she'd been silly. It was Thursday, and Khalil had basketball practice this afternoon. The quarterfinals for the Hoops League were next Saturday. And as competitive as he was, she knew he'd be intense about practice. If he hadn't called or sent a message, it was probably because he was still just plain beat. Memories of Khalil ribbing with the other players at Revitalize Detroit and the smile on his face brought a smile to her own. He was probably exhausted from the hard work and good times with people he cared about. She shot him a good night text and crawled under the covers, reminding herself that she was also one of those people.

. . .

Calling Dr. Edwards would be smart. The phone was right there, well, somewhere close between the bend in his couch and the loose knot of unfolded clothes beside him. Looking around his apartment—the clothes, the three beer bottles from the previous night, the dust on everything—made him think of something Dr. E had said about symptoms of a slide downward. Based on the way his place looked, he couldn't have been right on the inside. As though he needed external confirmation of that. Maybe Dr. E would have some wise words.

He'd certainly have questions about whether Khalil was still taking his medication as prescribed. Questions he didn't want to answer. All he had to do was pick up his phone, punch in a couple numbers, and speak. And he just couldn't do it. He was letting his doctor down, his girlfriend down, and now his friends down. Calling in sick for practice went hand in hand with having called in sick at work that day and the one before. But his couch felt so good, and his body so heavy, even the kitchen felt too far away for him to go get anything to eat. He didn't have the energy to walk out the front door, actually drive his car, go into a gymnasium, and play ball. The team was strong. They would make it through the quarterfinals without him. Then his phone started ringing.

"Hey," Karim said, voice scratchy.

Khalil cleared his throat to keep his voice lighthearted.

"'Sup?" he asked.

Karim apologized, then unloaded. Laila still wouldn't talk to him, had sent one of her friends to get her stuff. Karim was miserable, couldn't understand why his life was falling apart and needed to talk. So Khalil listened. Even though it meant stretching out on the couch, his dirty sock-covered feet sinking into the clean clothes as he tried to get into a position where he could make supportive sounds, keeping his own distress to himself. Listening to Karim just piled it on heavier and heavier. His brother was in so much pain, it forged Khalil's into a spiked mace, bludgeoning him over and over, leaving empty, hollowed-out gashes in his heart. He just stilled and let it happen, wiping the tears as they came but never sniffing. He wouldn't let Karim think that he couldn't call to get things off his chest.

. . . .

Vanessa left the meeting with Alphastone with a bad taste in her mouth. She'd hoped a walk around the September 11 memorial would put her problems in perspective, but she was still as flustered as she'd been when she left Alphastone's Financial District offices. Safely ensconced in her hotel room, she picked up her phone.

"Hey, babe," she said after Khalil's message ended. "I know you don't do voicemail, but I wanted to hear your voice—have I mentioned how sexy it is?—and telling you about everything would take too many texts." She gave him a rundown, then reminded him of the best fact of that day. "I'll be home to see you in three days. Can't wait. I'm counting down the minutes. Love you."

She hung up and grabbed her sketch pad, to begin mapping out some of her ideas to respond to Alphastone's concerns. When she looked up, an hour and a half had passed. Her phone beeped and she scooped it up to answer a question from a project manager while pulling out her laptop to check her schedules over the coming nine months. Then a notification for an email popped up and her heart skipped a beat.

> Kh.Sarda: Hey, babygirl. Sorry I've been tough to get a hold of. Been sick, enough that Rachel—Darius's sister—sent him over with chicken soup. He didn't spoon-feed it to me, though he had fun laughing at me. Don't worry, nothing major. Still holed up at home, too weak to do anything. I'll be fine in a couple days.
>
> There's some bad news. I won't be here when you get home. I'm going to PA with my mom to check on Karim. He's having a really rough time. We're going to try to convince him to move back home. I'll be there for four days (so sorry) then I'll be right back and we can catch up. Hope that's okay with your schedule. Can't tell you how much I miss you. Love you, babygirl.

Vanessa slumped back against the little couch in the sitting area of her suite. She'd be home in three days; he wouldn't be there. When he did get back, she'd be packing to leave the day after. She sighed, rubbing a hand over her hair. That needed cutting. If she intended to keep her promise about it, she'd have to schedule an appointment with him the very day he got back. She got the Fade app open and reserved a spot. Her hormones would just have to keep themselves under control if the first time she got to see him they were surrounded by other people.

"I need you to tell me I'm being ridiculous," Vanessa said.

"What do you mean?" Bibi asked.

Vanessa switched the phone to the other ear and returned to the couch.

"Dunno. Khalil's hard to get in touch with. Almost seems like he's pulling away. But then again, he's been sick. Maybe I just miss him and I'm imagining things."

Bibi was quiet at first, then cleared her throat.

"I ran into him the other day," she said. "Went to the other side of town for some incense. Are you sure he's sick?"

"That's what he said in his email. That he's been stuck at home. And an email was weird anyway, he almost always calls or texts."

"He seemed okay," Bibi said. "Maybe a little tired."

Did he lie about being sick?

"Probably just pushed himself to go out if he had to," Bibi continued. "If he's not himself that's probably what you're picking up on. And I'm sure he's missing you like you're missing him. Maybe he doesn't want to pressure you about coming home."

Vanessa rolled her pen between her fingers, stuck between respecting Khalil's privacy and wanting to tell Bibi how adamant he'd been about her traveling in spite of his emotional state.

"No matter what, let's look at the big picture. He loves you, right?"

"I guess."

"Didn't he say it unprompted?"

"He did."

"You're sensing that he's not himself while you're away. I see that as a good thing. Don't let yourself stress until you have a concrete reason to."

"Hmm," Vanessa said.

"You've both got a lot on your plates right now. Accept the temporary discomfort. Because he seems like he's worth trusting."

The familiar chimes announcing her arrival put an instant smile on Vanessa's face, which crumbled before her next breath. There was a woman at Khalil's station: long, dark hair pulled up in a messy bun, bared white arms a symphony of tattooed flowers, birds, and bees. Her focus was intense on the head of the client she was working on. She flashed her eyes to check Vanessa's reflection in the mirror then looked back at her client before speaking.

"Hey," she said. "You're Vanessa?"

Vanessa took several steps closer, nodding at the young man working at Darius's station. It took her a second to place him as the one who'd stopped to speak with Khalil at the block party.

"I am," she said to the woman.

"Cool. Pax. Covering for Khalil. With you in a few."

"Thanks," Vanessa said, nodding. She turned toward the waiting area, hands in her jacket pockets, and sat at the edge of a chair. She needed another look around. It was definitely the Fade. Definitely the location she'd been to many times. But she didn't know either of the barbers. The lack of both Khalil and Darius was a shock.

As she settled into Khalil's chair, Vanessa watched Pax's reflection. She was attractive but not a smiler. Fastening the cape, she studied Vanessa's head. She smacked her gum once and looked up.

"The usual?" she asked.

"Um . . . you're familiar with my usual?"

Pax nodded once.

"Khalil sent me a couple photos. Said you like the low perception fade, no hard part. Does that work?"

Impressed with Pax but disappointed that Khalil had taken time to prep her and not even reach out to Vanessa, she nodded. Pax gave her another full assessment, quick.

"Okay." She winked and smacked her gum again. "Let's go."

Vanessa smiled back. She didn't know this woman, but she could respect the value she clearly placed on doing good work. It was obvious Khalil had left her in capable hands. But they weren't his. As Pax tipped her head downward, Vanessa struggled with asking outright where Khalil was. They had one day to cross paths, but she hadn't heard much from him the past two. Only quick messages about how bad off Karim was. She knew it had to be breaking Khalil. Pax tipped Vanessa's head to the side and Vanessa looked up. The section of wall between Khalil's and Darius's mirrors was blank. No more photos tucked into the side. Pax was using an electric blue clipper, one Vanessa had never seen before, though she could imagine that each barber was accustomed to working with their own tools. But if Pax was only covering for Khalil that day, why had his station changed? Vanessa wanted to respect Khalil's privacy, but she also needed answers.

"Huh," she said. "That's funny. The pictures are gone." Pax didn't look up.

"Yeah. Team shuffled around some. Khalil's kind of nomading, though."

"Nomading?" Vanessa asked.

"Yeah. Can't figure out where he wants to work. Great boss, though." She shrugged. "Taking a step back, I think."

"Oh," Vanessa said.

"Dare was worried, but he's got stuff too. Like all of us." She shrugged again.

"Oh, that's right," Vanessa said. "Is Darius's father doing better?"

Pax pinned Vanessa's reflection in the mirror and smiled, fast.

"Yeah," she said. "Cool of you to ask."

Very satisfied with the cut, Vanessa gave a hefty tip at the register. Pax tried to refuse, but Vanessa wasn't having it.

"Gender pay gap is real," she said. "Even if your bosses are paying you right—and they better be—I bet the clients don't always tip like they should."

Pax gave her a broader smile.

"Thanks for looking out," she said. "Tell Khalil I said what's up?" she asked.

"You don't talk to him?"

"Been hard to get a hold of lately. For everyone. Figured you might have more luck."

Vanessa nodded, hiding her disappointment.

"Will do," she said. "Thanks again."

She didn't start the car right away. Tapping the steering wheel with her palms, Vanessa recognized the calculation that her subconscious had been making: Khalil wasn't where he'd told her he'd be. That was the only day for them to cross paths, and he was "nomading." He hadn't returned her call. Or her texts. Apparently, he couldn't decide where to work, even though there was only one place his girlfriend was going to be. . . . *was a jerk to my girlfriend.* He'd admitted that he had been before. His words certainly weren't in line with being a jerk, but his actions were leaving everything to be desired.

Turning into traffic, the tension between being an understanding girlfriend and one with self-respect stretched taut. Maybe this ridiculously beautiful man had been single when they met because he got bored once things reached a certain point. Maybe he wasn't even aware of it. But that was not a pattern Vanessa had any interest in being a part of.

· · ·

Frustrated and empty, Khalil settled into the seat on his Detroit-bound flight. His mom had all but shoved him onto the plane. He'd wanted to stay longer, try harder to convince Karim to leave Harrisburg behind. But his efforts were in vain. Like so many other things.

His scar itched again, kept drawing attention to itself, like an asshole. He shook out his hand to make the tingle go away, the shift of his watch surprising him. It had felt a touch loose when he'd put it on that morning after several days of not thinking about it. It was typical of him to find something else to focus on when he should have been calling Vanessa. As he'd had such great luck with phones in airports, he'd kept his safely inside his messenger bag through boarding. Taking it out, he clicked it on and stared at the screen. Two texts and a voicemail. How had he missed his phone ringing? He listened, his chest filling with the sludge of quick-drying concrete. Her voice was light but brittle. A pitch of disgust at his cowardice rolled over him. Having Pax cover had meant a few more hours to beg Karim to come home. But had it been worth it? A mechanical whirl brought him back to the plane. Vanessa would have been leaving the shop by then. He looked out the window, hoping for some distraction from his inability to keep his life together. He'd be surprised if he still had a girlfriend once he touched down in Detroit.

The way I've been fucking up, I deserve to be single. And Vanessa deserves more than me.

In a taxi, his apartment getting closer, Khalil vacillated between a text, a call, or asking the driver to go straight to Vanessa's. But she might not be there. He could stand on her doorstep, waiting until she got home. He'd look as pitiful as he felt. Opening their chat, his fingers went gummy and useless. There wasn't any way to say what he needed to, to tell her what she deserved. He put the phone down, staring out the window, seeing nothing. Until he got home, and his self-loathing hopped out of the car before he did.

"Hey," Vanessa said, leaning against her parked car in front of the stairs to his apartment.

"Hey." He shifted his duffel to the opposite shoulder as the taxi drove away, leaving a wisp of diesel exhaust that crinkled his nose.

"What's going on, Khalil?" she asked, arms crossed.

The answers were too embarrassing, and he prayed that the shade from the trees was sufficient to hide his flaming cheeks. She waited, watching him. He couldn't look at her for more than a few seconds at a time. The silence stretched too thin, so he said the only word that came to mind.

"Dunno."

"You don't know?" she asked. "About . . . us, maybe?"

And there it was. If she had doubts, it made sense for him to be honest and let her cut her losses.

"About . . ." His bag was too heavy; he let it plop on the ground. He glanced up at her and his useless brain stalled out again. *Game's gone for good.* "I . . . uh. I can't be the boyfriend you deserve right now." The words stung, but at least he was clawing his way toward truth.

"Why do you say that?"

"I . . ." He paused for a breath, sorting emotions. "I can't keep my life straight anymore. You deserve more . . . than I . . . am." The lump that rose in his throat cut off words and air.

Vanesa shook her head, arms still crossed.

"Is that really for you to decide?" she asked.

He wasn't sure what to say.

She pushed off her car, taking a few steps toward him. She stopped just out of arm's reach, cocking her head to the side.

"A couple weeks ago you were the boyfriend that I deserve. Now you're not? That doesn't make sense. Unless you don't want to be," she said.

A small part of him, somewhere deep, tried to cling to her logic. But a much louder, stronger part pulled up his shame and disgust with himself, blasting the feeling through every pore of his skin. The burn made him shaky.

"It's just better—" He needed a breath. "If we—"

"Break up?" she asked.

"Yeah," he said, swallowing the "no" that had almost escaped. The air bent, sharp and ugly. There was no pull to get closer to her. If anything, he needed to run.

"Is it something—"

"It's me," he said. "I . . ." He bent, collecting the straps of the bag. "I'm sorry. I have to go. It's this." He mangled a gesture meant to connect them. "It's too hard. I can't keep fighting to be who I should be for you."

Sliding her hands into her pockets, she nudged at a pebble on the ground with the toe of her shoe. When she looked up, the shimmer in her eyes made Khalil want to crawl into a hole.

"I don't think you're . . ." Her voice cracked. "I don't believe what you're saying about yourself. And I think you're wrong about us. But I can't force you to see things my way." She stopped, looking away, and sighed. "I'll always be there for you. As a friend, okay? One day, when you're ready."

He nodded wordlessly, then he was moving on heavy, wooden legs, past her car, up the stairs. Mortification kept him from turning back, and inside he crumpled to the floor, self-loathing knocking the breath and the thoughts out of him.

CHAPTER TWENTY-EIGHT
December

The landing in Detroit was bumpier than Vanessa liked, the back of the plane shifting to the side as the wheels touched down. Her heart snapped once in her chest, but the woman sitting next to her had the armrest in a death grip, and Vanessa put her hand over hers, squeezing.

We're fine, she mouthed over the roar of the engines as the plane slowed.

The woman looked at her, chest heaving, but managed a smile, squeezing Vanessa's fingers back.

"Yeah?" she asked.

Vanessa nodded. "Promise."

She faced forward again, holding the woman's hand until they'd taxied to the gate.

It was only a little white lie, Vanessa said to herself, tucking her chin into her scarf as she wheeled her carry-on out to the row of waiting taxis. She wasn't fine. Hadn't been for ages. Detroit had turned bitterly cold, but it fit Vanessa's feelings. The cold on the outside matched the cold sadness within. She was home but hadn't felt happy about it in a while. After all her team's hard work, the Alphastone project had fallen through. Thankfully, her company's reputation was still intact, but it was another loss to go along with her personal one. Just like coming home from New York that last time, the end of this business trip hollowed her out: Coming back without Khalil to return to killed her a little more each time the wheels touched the tarmac. Time was supposed to heal, but each day without Khalil was getting harder and harder. At least she was sleeping again. Not staying up half the night sobbing anymore.

In the taxi, her notifications pinging away, she took her phone out of her purse to put it on mute as the driver headed into the city. A message from Lisa caught her eye.

> Lisa: I know you're just getting back to yourself. And I don't want to derail that or see you that distraught again. But when you're ready, check out the interview with Darius and Mr. Fine.

Knowing it was unwise, Vanessa clicked the link at the end of Lisa's message. Maybe it wouldn't be so bad with the sound off. She missed his voice too much to put herself through that with a stranger present. An *Under the Radar Michigan* show opened up in YouTube. The Fade Barbershops were part of a segment focused on up-and-coming entrepreneurs creating jobs. After a few moments showing the ambiance at the Original Fade, Darius appeared, laughing with a client. Vanessa smiled. She'd only been by the Original once, but seeing Darius at work brought back a flood of good memories. She took a deep breath, bracing herself for the moment Khalil would appear. When he did, being interviewed by the show host beside the front desk, her heart dropped as she realized that oxygen would never be a sufficient substitution for Khalil. But then, she'd been holding her breath since their breakup. She'd just have to keep doing it.

"You okay, miss?" the driver asked.

Vanessa looked up, lost, then caught the tears rolling down her cheeks. She wiped them away and plastered a smile on her face.

"Yes, thank you," she said, nodding at his reflection in the rearview mirror.

His eyes crinkled in a kind smile, and he returned his attention to the road. Vanessa returned hers to the screen, and her heart lurched again. There were details she'd missed. He was still as beautiful, still as smartly dressed. But his cheeks looked gaunt, his skin sallow. He'd told her he tanned easily, so during the summer he'd been a consistent honey-bronze. Maybe the change in color was due to the change in season. She tried to content herself with that reason, but worry nagged at her as she fished a tissue out of her pocket. She tapped the closed caption button to follow along with what he was saying. Before the words could sort themselves out, he gestured, and his watch and Madison's bracelets swung loosely, rolling out of place. That sucked even more air out of her. She knew his watch fit perfectly. Was he wearing it loose on purpose? She focused on his neck, his shoulders. His clothes were looser too. She pressed her lips together, breathing through the grief her observation provoked, then the words flashing across the bottom of the screen grabbed her attention.

> Interviewer: Any plans to open up a fourth Fade?
> KS: Well, that would be for Darius to decide. He'll be taking over in the coming months.
> Interviewer: Really? Off to bigger and better things, Mr. Sarda?

Khalil shook his head, his sad smile breaking Vanessa's heart.

> KS: Doubt it can get any better than this. But I'm at peace leaving things in Darius's hands. I know he'll make it better than I ever could.

Cold fear flooded Vanessa. The nagging that she'd held back pushed its way to the fore, her skin tingling with a charge she could barely stand. She let the phone fall to her lap, worrying the inside of her cheek as she watched the familiar roads and buildings zip by.

I'm at peace. Three little words and Vanessa was terrified. She looked at her phone again. The segment had changed, so she scrolled the video back and hit pause. He was way too skinny. He was leaving the Fades. And he said he was at peace. She'd respected his wishes and stayed away. But the charge shifted into a rippling fear as the driver pulled up in front of her house. By the time she'd gotten her things inside, her decision was made—no habitual rest and recharge after a long trip. She grabbed her car keys and headed to Fade.

Darius was at the front desk, scheduling an appointment with a freshly barbered client, when Vanessa crossed the threshold, the chime tugging at her heart. He looked up and his smile shifted from warm customer service to relief. She held on to the hope that he was relieved to see her, as she was about to ignore her own rules for breaking up.

"Is he okay?" she asked once the client had gone.

"No," Darius said. "Can we talk?" He gestured to the back. She nodded and followed him out of earshot of the other barbers and clients.

"I'm sorry to just come here like this," she said once he'd slid the door closed.

"It's okay," he said. "I thought about calling you, but I didn't know if that would be out of line; don't really know how you all left things."

Not that she'd expected him to tell Darius everything, but hearing he didn't know she was open to remaining friends came as a surprise.

"I want what's best for him," she said.

"Me too. That's why I wanted to call you."

She pushed aside a sparkle of hope.

"He's leaving the shops? I thought he loved this place."

Darius sighed and looked away, rubbing the back of his head.

"Deep down, I know he does. But he's convinced himself that he's deadweight, that I'm better off without him. I don't even know how he got that idea. Now I can't get him to talk to me. He's stopped playing ball. Missed the finals. Before that, it was like he couldn't maintain a conversation, couldn't focus. Like he just kind of gave up."

"I saw the interview," she said, swallowing against a dry throat. "He said he's at peace. What does that mean?"

"I don't know," Darius said. "I didn't like that either. When I asked him about it, he wouldn't answer; then he got angry, walled himself off."

She sagged against the counter beside the dryers, the memory of their first kiss bubbling up to the surface, melding with the fear.

"Is he at the Original?"

"He hasn't come to work in days," Darius said. "When I go by his place, he refuses to let me in. I was about to call Karim, but with all the shit he has going on, I didn't want to add to it."

"Fuck it," she said.

"I'm sorry?"

"Fuck being appropriate or whatever. I told him I hoped we could be friends. I'm going over there to try to be one." She pushed off the counter, turning toward the door. "What do you think?"

"Please be inappropriate. Be as inappropriate as possible if it gets him thinking straight again."

She nodded.

"I'll text you my number, okay?" he asked as she slid the door open.

"You have it?" she asked.

"Client info, remember?"

"Right. Text me and I'll keep you in the loop," she said.

More doors, more thresholds and lines she was crossing. She rang Khalil's doorbell again, anxious, but trying to look calm so he wouldn't think she was there to bring drama. It took everything in her not to lean against the door and try to hear if he was moving around inside. After glancing back at the parking lot and seeing his Jeep for the third time, she raised her hand to knock as the door opened.

"Sorry," he said, voice gruff. "I was asleep."

Vanessa pressed her fingernails into the palms of her hands to keep from throwing her arms around him. He looked rougher than he had in the interview: cheekbones cutting a stronger line than they should have, skin peppered with multi-day scruff. His hair was a mess, his glasses sitting crooked on his nose. His T-shirt was rumpled and stained, clashing with an ancient pair of basketball shorts and mismatched socks. She didn't know if she'd ever seen anyone more handsome in her entire life.

"I'm sorry," she said. "I didn't mean to wake you. I was just . . . I wanted to come see you. As a friend."

"Oh." He looked down, then threw a quick glance over his shoulder. "The place is kind of a mess," he said slowly. "Maybe—"

"I don't mind," she said. "I'm here to see you, not your apartment."

He darted another look at her, not quite in the eye, and her heart melted. But she was going to stay upbeat. She could throw herself on the bed and weep once she got home.

"Okay, if you want." He stepped back, letting her in.

It was early afternoon, but there was no way to tell from inside. His blinds were drawn, thin strips of light peeking through. The hallway leading to his bedroom was dark. A couple of empty beer bottles clustered together at the end of the coffee table, next to a slouching pizza box. His wallet and keys were in their habitual spot on the bar leading to his kitchen, but tossed in a heap, not neatly placed as they usually were. Khalil wasn't a clean freak, but the layer of dust on everything and the overstuffed trash can she caught out of the corner of her eye told Vanessa all she needed to know: He wasn't doing well at all. She smiled at him, careful to keep her voice upbeat.

"It's good to see you."

He gave her a half-smile.

"You too." He rubbed at his cheek. "Don't have much in the fridge, can I get you a glass of water?"

"Sure." She'd leaned forward, to decipher each word. It seemed he had to focus on forming them. Ignoring another wave of manners, she slid out of her coat and sat down at the end of the couch.

He returned from the kitchen with two glasses, sitting at the opposite end. He glanced at the box and bottles and sighed.

"Told you it was a mess," he said softly.

She shook her head. "I don't care about that. Thanks for the water."

He nodded, scooping up the trash and taking it into the kitchen.

"How have you been?" he asked when he came back.

"Not too bad," she said, running clammy palms down her jeans. "Finally got my staff situated."

"That's good," he said. His gaze never seemed to reach the height of the coffee table. She wanted to lean in and make eye contact, but she was terrified of scaring him off.

"I . . . um . . . I heard you were leaving the Fades," she said.

"Yeah," he said to his water. "Think it's best for everyone."

She swallowed, telling herself again to keep her tone light, in contrast to the leaden slowness of his. "What makes you say that?"

He shrugged, still staring at his glass. "Darius deserves better, a better partner." He gulped and looked away, off to the side. "Like you do." His voice was so scratchy, Vanessa's throat went dry.

"I disagree," she said softly. "About us, but more so about you and Darius. You two make an excellent team."

Khalil shook his head, squeezing his eyes shut.

"He'll be fine without me. You too."

"No, he won't, he misses—"

"Is that what this is about?" His attention snapped back to her, his tone sharp, words fast, eyes narrowed.

"Is that what what's about?"

"Did he send you over here? Is this some sort of pity visit?"

"No—"

"Let me guess. He was all, 'Go check on Khalil' like I'm a baby or something? Some kid who can't handle himself?"

"Not at all," she said, scooting to the edge of the couch, hoping maybe he'd let her touch him, make contact somehow. He bolted to his feet.

"Fine. This is just a pity visit of your own. Look, he doesn't need me, you don't need me, nobody needs me. You'll all be better off without me causing a bunch of drama and needing to be coddled."

Then he was gone, down the hall, slamming his bedroom door. After a deep gulp of water with shaky hands, Vanessa let out an equally shaky breath. After a few more controlled ones, she tried to assess what had happened. Looking around, she had to use the words she was fighting against. She grabbed her phone.

A Harvard Health article was the first result of her search, symptoms of severe depression laid out like tea leaves.

Attention and info processing. Darius had mentioned confusion. *Difficulty making decisions.* Pax said that Khalil had been "nomading," couldn't decide where to work. Plus, there was his change about basketball. Maybe those behaviors ticked a box. *Inability to adapt to goals and form strategies to meet them.* Could that apply to their relationship? To his choice to break up? *Problems with executive function, the small steps necessary to complete a task.* She looked around. Maybe the state of his apartment was a sign of that? He couldn't clean because he couldn't break the work into individual steps? According to the article, it looked like Khalil was severely depressed. Combined with the comment about being at peace . . . She flipped to the text Darius had sent her.

> Vanessa: Has he ever been suicidal?
> Darius: What happened?
> Vanessa: Nothing. He let me in, but he was talking about us being better off without him. That thing about saying he's at peace. I don't want to think this way, but I'm scared.
> Darius: He's had some down times in the past. He always seems sad or gets weird when the days start getting shorter. But I've never heard him talk like this before.

The battle to mind her business raged against the fear that was telling her not to let Khalil out of her sight.

> Vanessa: I'm afraid of leaving him alone.
> Darius: Please don't. I can't come over right now. Can you stay with him?
> Vanessa: I'll try. If he kicks me out maybe we can trade.
> Darius: It's a deal.

She slipped out of her flats and tiptoed down the hall. Holding her breath, she pressed her ear to the door and her heart broke at his muffled sobs. She tempered the urge to throw the door open, hoping a little time might convince him that she only meant to help. She returned to the living room and after reorganizing with her assistant, she searched for recommendations on helping a depressed person. Twenty minutes later, she had a plan. If he'd let her, she'd get him out of the house, get some fresh food. She swallowed down a wave of aversion and put high omega fish on her grocery list. She'd ask him to help her with the shopping, maybe head to the Farmer's Market. She wouldn't push, but making him feel needed was important. His collection of retro clocks caught her eye. He'd offered to help her with the turntable for her dad, getting it to work again. A comment on the article had recommended giving a depressed person a reason to do something they're good at. If he could fix it, that might give him a boost of confidence. But if it didn't work, it might make him feel worse. She took a breath, trying to loosen the knot between her shoulder blades. It would be best to play things by ear.

Kitchen and living room clean, she tiptoed back to his bedroom and tapped on the door. He made an indeterminable noise, so she took a chance and opened it.

"Hey," she said, staying inside the doorway.

"You're still here?" his voice croaked out of the lump of bedsheets.

"Of course," she said, taking a step toward him.

"I was an ass to you." He sniffed, sitting up, pulling his knees against his chest. "I'm sorry."

She shook her head. "I can tell you're not feeling like yourself right now. I didn't take it personally." She perched on the corner of the bed, smothering her Pavlovian reaction to the scent of him and being in his bedroom. But fear subsumed other primal emotions.

"I'm sorry," he said again, voice cracking. Vanessa broke.

"May I please hug you?"

He nodded and she bounded at him, up on her knees, wrapping her arms around him, tucking his head into her shoulder. He hugged back, then a tremor went through him and fresh, hot tears soaked into her shirt.

"I'm sorry," he said into her shoulder. "I shouldn't be—"

"Shh . . ." She smoothed his hair, careful not to pull. "Please don't apologize. It's okay. I don't think you should keep it inside anymore."

Then he squeezed her tight, his sobs wrenching through them both.

CHAPTER TWENTY-NINE

I don't need you," Khalil said, dragging his sleeve under his nose, a disgusting makeshift tissue. He might have cared about how gross it was, if he could care about anything anymore. Vanessa's lip trembled before she took a deep breath, shoulders squared.

"Do you really mean that?" she asked.

His heart screamed "no," the word pressing against his clenched teeth. He crossed his arms tighter around himself and nodded.

She raised her perfect chin.

"Okay, I'll go," she said, by his door, coat draped over her arm. *Please don't. I can't make it alone.*

He nodded again, swallowing hard, and turned to hide in his room. Alone, like he belonged. Then, just before he shut the door, her arms were around his waist and—

His bed was cold. The reflex to cast his arm out, to feel Vanessa's warmth there beside him, sank under the wave of grief that greeted him each time he woke up. Coming out of dreams where Vanessa was back, where she touched him, where he was alive again because he'd felt her skin against his, was the worst form of torture. He couldn't understand why his mind added extra layers of self-loathing. Curling up tighter into himself, he tried to slide back into the safety of unconsciousness where his disgust couldn't reach, but biological needs superseded the desire to run away. He got up, leaving the

dream of Vanessa in his apartment saying she wanted to help. Even
in his sleep he was too stupid to say he wanted her to stay. Lurching
himself out of bed, he fumbled to the bathroom, making his way
with the lights off. The throbbing in his head drove him back under
the sheets. Maybe he'd have a good dream, go back in time and be
with the woman he loved. He was almost there, clambering under,
until he took a deep breath. He was hallucinating. It smelled like
someone was baking something sweet. He grunted his disappointment at his misfiring brain and pulled the covers over his head. He'd
just gotten the little light blocked out when another fragrance registered: fresh coffee. And then a sound. Coming from his kitchen.

"Morning," Vanessa said as he crossed the threshold, her back to
him at the stove. He blinked, unsure if he was also hallucinating her.
Then she slid a pancake onto a plate beside her. There were already
three in the pile. And a pan of scrambled eggs on the stove. And a
pot . . . with grits?

"What are you doing?" He grimaced at his croak of a voice.

"Making breakfast." She turned her attention to the eggs.

"For who?"

"Us. Well, me. Since you said you weren't hungry last night."

Rubbing his eyes with the heels of his palms, he tried to separate
dream from reality. She was there. Standing in his kitchen. And last
night? He took a step back into the hallway and glanced into his living room. It was a blurry mess. Right. No glasses. He went over to his
couch. One of the blankets from his hall closet was draped across it,
along with a pillow. A pair of earrings was on the coffee table next to
her phone.

"You slept on the couch?" he called out.

"Yep."

He lumbered back to the kitchen, scrubbing at his face with his
hoodie's sleeves, hoping he wasn't covered in dried tears or drool.
His beard was loud against the fabric.

"Why?" he asked.

She put the pancakes on the table, adding a spoon to the bowl of
grits as she nodded in the direction of the chair he usually sat in. He
obeyed.

"I was giving you the space you wanted," she said, taking her seat and pouring herself some coffee. "But I stayed in case you changed your mind." She raised the coffeepot at him, quirking an eyebrow.

He picked up the mug beside his plate and held it out. She filled it three-quarters of the way, just like he liked, then handed him the creamer. He added it to his coffee on autopilot.

"Oh," he said. His manners were nudging at him, to say something, but the combination of shame, happiness, and confusion made it too hard to figure out if he should be thanking her, or apologizing, or telling her he loved her. She picked up the grits and scooted closer to spoon some onto his plate.

"Don't know the last time I made cheese grits," she said. "But I thought they made sense with the colder weather." She spooned a little for herself.

"I love cheese grits," he said.

"I know." She took a pancake then handed him the plate.

He took it in both hands, the familiar smell snapping him to attention.

"Are these walnut pancakes?"

Vanessa nodded, chewing.

"Have we . . . ?" Cheese grits and walnut pancakes were his favorite breakfast from his college days. But he didn't remember when he'd told her that.

"Try at least one before they get cold," she said. "I have to report back to Mrs. Clayton."

The pancake landed with the perfect whump on his plate as he glanced back at Vanessa. She was smiling, her usual sweetness there, but she had a determined look in her eye he'd only seen when she'd been talking shop with her project manager.

"You told Mrs. Clayton that I—"

"Could use a little home cooking, and I wanted to surprise you." She paused, popping a bite into her mouth. She narrowed her eyes and he cut a piece for himself. "She was happy to share her recipes for breakfast, and for the red velvet cupcakes if it comes to that."

Khalil groaned at his first bite of pancake. He'd forgotten how good food could taste. The spoonful of cheese grits that followed almost had him in tears. Somehow, Vanessa had made Mrs. Clayton's signature breakfast dishes even better. Then there was the fact that the two women had been in contact, to do something just for him. His breakfast got blurry, and he swallowed hard.

Vanessa frowned. "Did I mess it up? Wasn't sure about the first few. Maybe that one isn't good," she said, gesturing to the pancake on his plate. "Want mine?"

He shook his head, blinked hard so he could focus on her and tried to smile.

"They're perfect, Ness. This is the best breakfast I've had in as long as I can remember." He reached out and squeezed her hand. "Thank you."

She squeezed back.

"You're welcome, ba—" She pulled her hand away, looking down to smooth her napkin on her lap. "Sorry."

He shook his head. He wanted to say it was okay, that he was dying to hear her call him "baby." But if he said anything, he was going to start blubbering again, so he shoveled more of the best food he'd ever tasted into his mouth and tucked his chin to swat away a tear he couldn't hold back.

Twenty minutes and the beginning of a food coma later, Vanessa scooted back from the table, empty plates in hand.

"Finish up, we have to get to the Farmer's Market," she said.

"Why?" He had no desire to leave the house, and how much more food could they need?

"We're having fish for lunch and turkey for dinner." She started the water in the sink.

He blinked and shook his head. "You're staying? And cooking all that?"

She stopped rinsing and looked straight at him. "Do you have a problem with me spending the weekend with you?"

He gulped. "Absolutely not."

"Good." She turned her back to him again, popping the dishwasher open and filling it. "We'll do the shopping, grab a change of clothes at my place, then swing by the shop so you can talk to Darius."

He shot up a silent prayer of thanks that the water was running so she didn't hear the lurch of his stomach at the idea of facing Darius. Searching his addled brain, he couldn't come up with an excuse, a single reason to convince her that he absolutely could not face him. She was going to notice his silence—she was too observant not to, so he just stared at the back of her head, willing a plausible reason to come to mind.

"I can't," he said.

"Why not?" She was focused on scrubbing the grits lining the pot.

"I was . . . horrible doesn't even begin to describe it. I backed out of so many things at the last minute, wasn't there for him—oh God, his dad. I haven't even asked—"

"His dad is fine. They started him on medication and it's working well," she said, still focused on the dishes. He couldn't let her manage that on her own. Standing, he brought the rest to the counter beside the sink.

"How do you know?" he asked.

"We talked last night," she said. "You're low on dishwashing liquid. Got any more hidden somewhere?"

He squatted down, grabbing the extra bottle from under the sink. "You guys talked?"

She nodded. Then she handed him a dishtowel and the washed pot. He focused on removing every drop of water, steeling himself for what she might say.

"Are you sure he wants to talk to me?" he asked.

She stopped washing and looked up at him.

"Khalil Sarda, the people who love you, love you. Especially Darius. He's not mad at all. He was ready to come over last night and sleep on the floor, just to be sure that you were okay." She looked back at the dishes. "Didn't you have another drying rack? I'm running out of space here." She nodded at the drainboard.

He put the towel down and reached over beside the fridge, unfolded the rack, and helped her rearrange the heavier dishes.

"I'm not ready to see him," he said softly.

Grabbing another dishtowel, she dried her hands. She reached up and cupped his cheeks, looking him square in the eye.

"Do you feel better after breakfast?" she asked.

"Yes."

"So I was right to have fed you?"

He nodded.

"Good. Then let's just move forward with the knowledge that I'm right about this too."

He had to be dreaming again. There was no way that his day was going the way he thought it was, so he gave in, expecting to wake up.

But the sun was warm on his face at the Farmer's Market, in spite of the winter breeze. Vanessa's hand was soft in his as they walked from stand to stand. The fruit and vegetables were a riot of color, a bouquet of delicious smells that made his mouth water and his stomach rumble, even though Vanessa's pancakes were still a comforting memory. He was happy to carry the cloth bags she'd brought, heavy with carrots and celery root, squash, zucchini, and apples. She paused at the Brussels sprouts, saying she remembered how much he liked them, but he was never a fan. She asked him to tell her the story again, of the time he'd eaten all of Karim's so he wouldn't get in trouble. He started to correct her, that it was Karim who'd helped him out, and then she winked and he recognized her tease, that she'd intentionally brought up a good memory. And he realized he was smiling.

After a quick stop at her house, she parked up the street from the Fade. She held his hand firm in both of hers until Darius jogged around the corner and spread his arms wide for a hug. Khalil didn't cry as his friend told him he loved him, though everything was blurry.

"Listen, man, you do everything Vanessa tells you for the rest of the weekend, okay?" Darius said.

Khalil nodded, Darius's hand a comforting weight on his shoulder. Darius glanced at Vanessa, his face pinched.

"I'm sorry I can't stay long, got a lot of clients today. And I can't come by tonight—gotta take care of some stuff for my dad. Can I come through tomorrow, just to say what's up?"

"Yeah, that's cool, man," Khalil said through a scratchy throat. "Listen, I just . . . I'm really sorry—"

Darius shook his head as he cleared his throat, thumbing his nose. "Nah, nothing to apologize for. You know that."

Darius gave Vanessa a quick hug, then gave Khalil another before he turned and headed back to the Fade.

It wasn't until they sat down for lunch that Khalil was certain he wasn't asleep.

Picking up his fork to dive into the steamed flounder that smelled buttery, basily, and heavenly, he noticed Vanessa's chicken.

"What are you eating? Wait—what am I eating?" he asked. "You hate fish."

"I do," she said, slicing a piece of chicken. "But please don't let it get cold. Don't know if I got the recipe right."

"But you don't even like to look at it. I remember the sushi place that time: You got queasy at the sight of the tuna."

She nodded, popping a piece of roasted tomato in her mouth.

"You need it," she said. "Well, salmon or bluefish would have been better, more omega-3s. But flounder was the best I could handle for a first time. Please taste it."

He did as he was told. He nearly melted.

"It's delicious," he said. "But I can go eat in the living room, so you don't have to look at it." He scooped up his utensils and plate.

She shook her head. "The tough part was handling it. I'm okay now." She winked at him.

Once again, his world got blurry.

CHAPTER THIRTY

Khalil held his breath as he stepped out of the bathroom, checking that Vanessa was still asleep. The stripes on his blanket shifted just enough to show that her breathing was steady; he hadn't woken her. She'd been on alert all weekend, waking when he was restless in the middle of the night, getting up earlier than he had to make breakfast the past two days. She had to be exhausted. A curving mist of guilt circled its way up, but he tamped it down before it could take shape. She'd repeated again and again that she wanted to help, had proven her words with action. She'd asked him to believe her, so he chose to. It made him feel better about himself than he had in ages. He slipped out of the bedroom, leaving the door open a crack. He had an important task he hoped to finish before she woke up.

After wiping his fingertips on the rag, he tossed it on the drop cloth on the dining room table and picked up the can of compressed air. Two quick blasts and he turned the gear driver over to slide it into place. He grabbed the WD-40 and squirted some in strategic points along the chain he'd fitted.

Okay, time to give it a go.

Returning the top of the turntable to its spot, he clicked the gears together and took one last look at everything before cleaning his fingers off again and sitting up straight. He grabbed the cord, plugged it in, and held his breath. Nothing happened.

It's okay, it's okay.

The self-doubt rose, tightening his throat. He cleared it.

You can do this. You're almost there.

He reached down to unplug it and caught the switch on the side. Flipping the switch, the turntable came to life.

"You did it!" Vanessa said, inside the living room doorway.

He smiled, blushing.

"How long have you been there?" he asked.

"Just a minute or two," she said, joining him at the table, resting a hand on his shoulder. He squeezed his fingertips into his palm, the grease still there making them slip, but he needed to focus on some other touch, something different from the peace that came from hers. She leaned forward, closer to the turntable, watching it move. The curiosity and happiness on her face made his heart soar. He looked away, shy.

"I'm so impressed," she said, taking in every detail. "The guy at the store said he never made any headway." She looked at him. "It only took you a couple hours."

He shrugged, still acutely aware of her touch.

"Two days," he said.

She raised an eyebrow, giving him a gentle side-eye.

"A couple hours last night, and maybe an hour this morning." She bumped his shoulder with her hip. "You better be proud of yourself. I know I'm proud of you."

Plucking the rag off the table to wipe his fingers one more time before turning the record player off, he met her smile with a slow one of his own.

"I guess," he said. "Still gotta try it out with an actual record." The turntable looked like it was moving smoothly, but he wanted to listen to it for at least a couple hours before giving it to Vanessa for her dad.

"Okay," she said over her shoulder, headed into the kitchen. "Before or after we eat?"

"After I guess." He hustled to wash his hands. "Don't have any more forty-fives. And it's my turn to make breakfast."

She smiled at him, hands on those perfect slender hips.

"You want to make breakfast? Wait—are you telling me you're hungry?"

He nodded.

"Excellent. I'll let you get started."

"What do you feel like?"

She leaned against the kitchen counter, fingers curved over the edge. From his angle, the way she squeezed the counter looked painful. It wasn't the first odd gesture he'd noticed over the past two days. Face always pleasant, but from time to time, there was a flash of irritation that peeked out. Maybe she was frustrated with having to baby him.

"Uh-oh," she said, letting her arms go slack. "What was that about?"

"What?" he asked.

She took a step closer, hands behind her back.

"You looked at my hands, then you looked sad," she said.

Unable to maintain eye contact, he went over to the cabinet and grabbed two bowls for cereal. He shrugged.

"Dunno."

"Khalil," she said softly.

He glanced over his shoulder and took a deep breath to face her.

"Yeah?"

"It's hard for me too, you know."

He blew a quick breath out in a stream.

"Then you get why it's better if we just stay fr—"

"It's hard for me not to touch you every time I want. It's hard for me not to push, not to grab your face and keep repeating that I love you until my lips go numb. It's hard for me to hold myself back because I'm afraid of pressuring you into giving us a chance again. I can't rush you. I won't. What I want isn't enough. We both have to want it, and I need to know that I haven't cajoled you into something you aren't ready for.

"So I'm doing my best, but every now and then, you might catch a hint, you might see me resisting the urge to throw myself into your arms because I know you're fragile right now, and I don't want to be—"

He cut her off, pulling her into his chest, his arms tight around her. Then hers were around him.

"Touch me when you want to," he whispered into her crown. "Please. I need you to touch me."

She pulled even tighter, her arms up his back, her breath heating his skin.

"The first time I really got to touch you," he said. "The first time I got to hold you and kiss you the way I wanted, I felt like—"

She looked up at him, resting her chin against his chest.

"I was home," she said.

Then it happened. He looked into her eyes and let go. The past two days, he'd looked at her, at least he thought he had, but he hadn't really. Because for the first time, the very first since she'd held him as he cried, before he'd run away, ended things, and hidden, he let himself fall. Back into those deep pools that made him feel cherished, and alive, and like himself.

"There you are," she whispered.

"Yeah," he nodded. "I'm here." He stroked the curve of her ear, the line of her jaw. He grazed her lips with his thumb. "But why are you?"

She raised an eyebrow and gave him a teasing frown. Stepping away, she caught his hand.

"Come with me."

She led him into his bedroom. Sitting on her side of the bed, she patted the spot next to her, and he sat. After unplugging her phone from its charger, she swiveled to face him.

"So," she said. "You know about The Basic Requirements."

He nodded.

"And the fact that you are the only man I've ever met who checks pretty much all the boxes."

He blushed a little, watching his hand as he slid it down her calf. She tipped his head up with a finger under his chin.

"There's a Second List," she said.

He swallowed.

"And I don't make the c—"

"Shh! Don't jump the gun." She unlocked her phone, swiped and tapped a couple times, then looked back up at him. "I want you to read it for yourself. But first, look at the date the file was created."

She handed him the phone, a note taking app open.

The file that had been created two years earlier was titled List Two—Next Level.

"Next Level?" he asked.

She shrugged. "There's more than just The Basic Requirements. Does it bother you to read it out loud?"

He shook his head. "One: helps others."

She pointed at him. "Creating jobs, fundraising, and helping local businesses. Check," she said.

He swallowed hard, attention back on the list.

"Two: accepting and supportive of my emotions and career," he said.

"Respecting the reasons behind The Basic Requirements. Calling to check on me while I was on the road. Encouraging me when I was having a bad day or difficulty with work. Never, ever asking me to stay home more. If anything, putting my career first." She pointed at him again. "Check."

"Three: honorable. Keeps his word."

"Calling Ma-Max. Asking for the opportunity to apologize to her, even though the situation was beyond your control. Check."

The deep breath pulled itself in all the way from his diaphragm. He moistened his lips.

"Four: willing to share his difficult emotions with me. Willing to let me see him cry." His eyes welled up as he let the phone rest in his lap. He'd reached the end of the list.

"Check," she said, covering his hands with hers.

"But I didn't," he said, gaze intent on their hands. "I ran away, ghosted you."

"You did run away. But you shared before you did. And you're sharing with me now." She turned the phone, so he could clearly see each line. "Where is 'perfection' on either list?" she asked. "You tried, you messed up, but then you tried again. I don't want 'Always Perfect Khalil.' I just want Khalil."

Touching his forehead to hers, he closed his eyes.

"I miss you so much," he whispered.

"I miss you too," she said, her hand on his cheek. "But I'm not going anywhere. You know I got you, Khalil."

She leaned back, pulling him with her as she relaxed into the pillows propped against the headboard. He followed, arms sliding around her waist, head in her lap, resting his cheek against her abdomen.

"I know, but it's not fair to you," he said.

"Fair?"

"My stuff is a lot. I can't put it all on you."

She sighed, running gentle fingers through his hair, grazing his scalp.

He moistened his lips. "I guess it's time for me to listen to Dr. Edwards. My . . . psychiatrist." He held his breath, glad he wasn't looking at her, just in case it made her think he was weak.

"You're already seeing someone? That's great, baby," she said.

Relief slackened his tense muscles. He snuggled deeper against her.

"I was," he said. "I stopped going to appointments, stopped taking my meds."

"Maybe it's time to start again?" She drew soft circles between his shoulder blades.

"Yeah. Dr. E mentioned building a support network. A team. To help me see it when I'm slipping and to lean on before I get too bad. But I dunno. I don't want to bring anyone down."

"You have people in your life who love you. Who want to be there for you," she said, stroking his shoulder.

He caressed her skin with his thumbs. He knew she was right, even if he was freaked out about being that vulnerable.

"Maybe you, Darius, and Karim," he said. "Don't feel comfortable sharing with anyone else."

"Whatever you want, babe. I think a tight circle is wise. We all got you."

He smiled, breathing in deep, filling himself with lavender and her. Nuzzling into her abdomen, he rubbed one cheek along it, then the other. She giggled.

"There you go with my pooch. Like men with their pregnant wives' bellies. You know there isn't anyone in there, right?"

With a fortifying breath, he raised his head and opened his eyes to look into hers.

"I would love it if there was someone in there one day," he said. "If I'm not . . . not too broken."

She smiled, stroking his hair again.

"You're not, baby. I'd love that too."

Two weeks later, Khalil placed his phone, wallet, and keys on the bar leading to the kitchen.

"Looks like Darius was right," he said.

Vanessa leaned back in her seat at the kitchen table, looking up at him from her laptop.

"Right about what?"

"There is a pattern to my moods." He joined her at the table. "Dr. Edwards says it's highly likely that I have something called seasonal affective disorder. That's why I was so depressed at the end of last year and again now."

"Okay. How do you feel about that?"

Khalil shrugged, folding his arms. "Dunno. It's good there's a logic to things, but I feel kind of condemned to having to go through this every year."

He exhaled, pushing the prickly discomfort of not feeling good enough out of his body. Vanessa gave him a slight frown then a shrug of her own.

"Condemned is kind of strong, isn't it? It's good to have a name for what you experience. That way you can manage it better." She scooted forward, typing. After a few moments, she looked back up at him.

"It looks manageable. You have to add some new habits, maybe invest in a light box. Maybe you can change your medication as the days get shorter. Did Dr. Edwards say anything about how to deal with it?"

Khalil scooted his chair to her side, looking at what she was reading.

"He upped my meds, said there were therapies. But I dunno. I still feel . . ." "Broken" was on the tip of his tongue, but he couldn't get it out.

She turned to him, resting her knee against his.

"What's going on up there?" she asked, nodding at his head.

He was stuck, still couldn't say. He'd managed to be okay with having gone through one depressive episode and had accepted that he was in another one. But this, the idea that he'd have to go through it every year, that the dark thoughts would always come back, that he'd have to battle against making another mistake? She scooted down a little, to catch his gaze with hers. He blinked once; the heaviness in his eyes that warned of tears made him want to look away, but he didn't. She'd shown him that it was okay to have the feelings that he did. And he believed her. But it would take time for him to be okay with the idea.

"It's a lot, Ness," he whispered.

She took his hand in hers.

"It is," she said.

He sniffed.

"I—I tried to kill myself last year." He hadn't expected that confession. His voice came out so softly, he wasn't sure she'd heard him. She squeezed his hand with both of hers then looked up at him with tears glimmering in her eyes.

"I'm so glad you didn't," she said.

"What if it gets that bad again?" he asked.

"Were you on medication then?"

He shook his head, squeezing back.

"And you weren't seeing Dr. Edwards?"

"No."

"It doesn't have to get that bad," she said. "Especially now that you have support and tools."

He shrugged, looking away but still holding her hand.

"Is that what the scar is from?" she asked.

He snapped his gaze back to hers.

"You noticed it?"

She ran her fingertips over the knuckles of his left hand.

"I did. Didn't really think anything of it; wasn't sure it was there for a while. Is that why you always wear Madison's bracelets?"

He nodded, looking down at them.

"My watch pretty much covers it. But when she wanted to give them to me, I was happy for the extra protection. You really didn't notice at first?"

She shook her head.

"I love that you wear something she made for you." She rolled her thumb over the largest one. "It's so cute. And so you." She smiled. "Think she'd make a matching one for me?"

He caught himself chuckle.

"You'd like that?"

"I'd love it." She reached up and wiped a tear off his cheek. "Please don't worry about the scar; it's barely visible. Just a little line."

He wasn't sure about that but decided to take her word for it. Since she'd come back, she'd held him down as he clawed his way to a little normalcy. She'd nudged him not to be ashamed and encouraged him as he started taking his medication again and when he reached out to Dr. E. And now he had an explanation, an understanding of what was going on with him and his *stuff*. She was supporting him right now. He'd choose to believe her.

"Maybe you're right," he said. "It's good, knowing it's an actual thing, that it has a name and a pattern."

She glanced back at her laptop.

"And it looks like it means that you don't have to worry about a sudden wave of depression hitting you out of nowhere. You know when it's coming and can prepare for it."

"That's a good point," he said. He didn't have to play defense anymore. But he would need a team. "Speaking of preparation . . ." He stood, grabbing his phone. "Dr. E brought up the idea of a support network, my team again. That it's not to my advantage to keep all of this to myself." She nodded. He turned his phone in his hands, about to unlock it.

"So, Karim and Darius?" she asked.

"Yeah. But . . ." He put the phone back down. "I can't put this on them. Especially Karim. He's got so much on his plate right now. I can't expect him to have the bandwidth to baby me."

She joined him by the bar.

"But what are you asking them to do? Like, to really do?"

He thought for a minute, sifting through ideas.

"Well, just to let me know if they notice my behavior change. If I'm more irritable than normal. Or to step in and remind me what's happening if I start to isolate myself, if things start going bad."

"Okay," Vanessa said. "Don't they kind of do that already?" She quirked an eyebrow.

"Darius noticed a pattern before I did. And Karim's too far to see things on a day-to-day basis, but he's always happy to let me know when I sound like a jerk."

"So you're not asking them to do anything different. Just be themselves with you. I get that it's uncomfortable to open up about the entire situation—which is why I'm so appreciative that you did with me—but I think you can do this."

He picked up the phone again. As he unlocked it, she caressed his cheek and left him alone in the kitchen. While he worked up the courage to call his brother, music started to filter in from the living room. Vanessa had put on one of the records he'd bought to test the turntable.

"You know, babe," she said over her shoulder. "My dad is going to love this. You've given me the perfect Christmas present for him. I hope you're proud of yourself for being so kind and so skilled."

"I dunno," he said blushing. "Don't think it takes *that* much skill."

She returned to the kitchen, hands on her hips. She crooked an eyebrow.

"Okay," he said. "Maybe a little skill."

She frowned. "A lot of skill. I'm on your team too," she said. "I'm not gonna stand around and let you ignore your strengths."

She approached him, sliding her hands around his waist and linking them behind his back. After putting his phone on the counter, he wrapped his arms around her.

"You're kind," she said. "And you're strong. Physically *and* mentally. And you're pretty easy on the eyes."

He smirked. "Is that so?"

"It is." She pushed up onto her tiptoes, biting her lip as she stared at his. He got the message and leaned down to kiss her. He'd expected a light peck, but then her hands were cradling his face, her lips gently coaxing his open. He let himself get lost, in the feel of her on his lips, her body warm and soft under his hands. She moaned, deepening the kiss, and he let himself fall further into the moment, crouching so he could scoop her up and pull her legs around his waist. She giggled into his mouth and he couldn't help but smile as he gently sat her down on the counter. Pulling back, she kept his face cradled in her hands.

"Do you know that I love you, Khalil Ṣarda?" she whispered.

He touched his forehead to hers, closed his eyes, and let her love wash over him.

"I'm so glad you do," he whispered back.

CHAPTER THIRTY-ONE
March, the Following Year

It was official. He was becoming obsessive.

Inching forward on the couch, having finished Sunday Lunch, he counted the pieces in Ma-Max's Lladró porcelain collection again. He was almost sure there'd been three vases and two busts two weeks ago. Now there were three busts and two vases. Maybe she had several pieces and rotated them out. Or maybe he was searching for something to occupy his mind, beyond the reason he'd left his phone charger in his Jeep and asked Vanessa to get it for him. There was one person left to recruit for the next important step in his life. He still wasn't sure she'd be on his side, despite the year she had getting to know him.

Arletta returned from the kitchen with a smile and coffee.

"Thanks," Khalil said, accepting his.

She nodded. "You going to be all right?" she asked.

He swallowed hard.

"I don't know," he said. "What if she says no?"

"There is no reason for her to," she said, patting his knee. "And if she decides to be difficult, you just let me handle it."

He wanted to thank her, tell her that he appreciated the support, but then Ma-Max was back and his throat went dry.

"Well, Khalil," she said, taking her seat. "You seemed rather insistent that Vanessa leave us alone. Is everything all right?"

Glancing down the hall to be sure Vanessa was gone, he took a deep breath.

"I wanted to ask for your blessing," he said. "I'd like to propose to Vanessa, and I know that your approval means the world to her. I hoped to have it before I do."

Ma-Max looked at Arletta beside him on the couch. Arletta tilted her head to one side, an eyebrow raised. Ma-Max raised one back, then turned to Khalil.

"And if I say no?" she asked him.

"Are you serious, Max?" Arletta asked before Khalil even got a breath in. "Why would you say no? He's—"

"I'd still ask her," Khalil said, nervous but interrupting anyway.

Ma-Max laughed, eyes crinkling as she clapped her hands.

"That's exactly the answer I wanted," she said, taking a quick glance over her shoulder. "I know you have a backbone, Khalil, just needed you to show me." She shot a glare at Arletta. "See, I'm not such a pain."

Khalil's heart started beating again.

"Thank you, Mrs. No—"

"Nope!" She cut him off, standing. He stood too. "You call me Ma-Max," she said. "If you're going to be my grandson-in-law."

He smiled and leaned into the hug she stretched to give him.

"If she says yes," he said, hugging back gently.

"Oh, she will," Ma-Max said. "Or she'll have to answer to me."

The door leading to the garage closed and Khalil returned to his seat right after Maxine.

"I don't know if this is the right one," Vanessa called out, joining them. She slowed as she walked through the kitchen. "What are you all up to?" she asked, eyes narrowed.

Khalil looked at the older women, catching Arletta's smile behind her cup of coffee and Ma-Max's quick turn away from Vanessa.

"Up to? Nothing," Ma-Max said. "Come on in here and get your coffee before it gets cold." She winked at Khalil and he shot her a smile back.

Vanessa joined them in the living room, an eyebrow still quirked in his direction. Arletta handed her a mug and started the conversation again. Khalil held back, listening to the warm banter between the women, but he couldn't take his eyes off Vanessa. His pixie who'd held him in her arms when things got bleak and had been holding him down ever since. If she said yes, his single days, the so-called player days, would be beautifully over. Vanessa had him in a whole new game.

ACKNOWLEDGMENTS

I've wanted to write books since I was a little girl, and now, here it is—it's finally happened! But I certainly didn't get here alone. I've been fortunate to have a beautiful village to support me. You all mean so much to me that no simple "thank you" will ever be enough.

To my indefatigable agent, Léonicka Valcius: Mille mercis pour ton soutien, ton courage, et ton esprit. You made me believe when I had my doubts, negotiated when I didn't dare, and guided me when I was lost. Thank you. And go, Eagles!

To my editors, Lexi Batsides and Anne Speyer, and Crystal Velasquez, Jennifer Rodriguez, and the whole Penguin Random House publishing team: Thank you so much for your vision in making my debut novel the best it could be. I am especially grateful for your concern with and support of protecting the heart of this story and its potential impact on readers.

I would be remiss if I did not thank the Pitch Wars organization for giving me the opportunity to grow from a hobby writer into a career-oriented one. A particular thanks goes out to Diana A. Hicks for her mentorship. Likewise, I am grateful for the work of Beth Phelan in creating #DVPit.

I wouldn't be who I am today or have had the courage to write without the support of Melissa "the head cheerleader" Scalzi, and my big little sisters Toushi Itoka and Bibi Gnagno. Thank you for loving me, mothering me, and teaching me who I am.

To The Coven, Janet Walden-West, Anne Raven, and Megan Starks: Your wisdom, guidance, and snark have been invaluable.

Aux Mamans au Café: Merci de m'avoir soutenue et montré comment croire en moi, dans tous mes rôles.

To Alice, thank you for being supportive through my earliest, most awkward, and embarrassing steps.

And to Maud, Audrey, and Jonathan, thank you for showing me that an artist's life is possible.

À Maryline: Merci pour le cadeau de votre disponibilité bienveillante qui m'a permis de poursuivre mes rêves. Et Hervé: Merci pour le nom de plume.

To my Dad: Even though life hasn't always been easy, I'm so grateful that we found each other again and to get to know you on our own terms. Your support in this endeavor has been invaluable, but do me a favor and don't read the middle of the book please?

To my Mother: Thank you for giving me an early love of reading and writing.

To Ladybug and Bubba: Thank you for being understanding when I need to work. Thank you for giving me reasons to laugh and be amazed each and every day. You will always be my poulette and my poulet. You're allowed to read this book in about . . . a decade.

And last, but most certainly not least, to Arnaud. Who knew that when I wrote "my husband is in France" in a journal twenty years ago I was right? There are no words—ni en français, ni en anglais—for me to express what you have meant to me since 2006, and how you've made this dream possible. You're the air that I breathe. Je t'aime.

GETTING HIS GAME BACK

A Novel

GIA DE CADENET

A Book Club Guide

QUESTIONS AND TOPICS
FOR DISCUSSION

1. Khalil continues to see Dr. E as he and Vanessa get to know each other. How do their discussions, in your view, shape the way he approaches his relationship with her?

2. Discuss how gender roles came into play as Vanessa and Khalil's attraction blossomed into a committed relationship. Did the author's choices challenge your perceptions of masculinity or femininity? Why or why not?

3. Vanessa tells Khalil that she's no stranger to objectification, and that she's been treated as an "experiment." Khalil counters, offering his own thoughts. What did you make of this conversation, and how do you believe it influenced the bond between them?

4. Do you think Vanessa's rule about only dating black men is unfair, as she and Jill worry early in the novel, or is it justified?

5. Both Vanessa and Khalil experience challenges in their professional lives as they navigate their growing attraction. Compare and contrast their approaches to dealing with conflict.

6. Vanessa cares deeply about Ma-Max's approval, though she knows that her grandmother harbors certain views about interracial dating. Talk about how their relationship evolves over the course of the novel. Do you have a similar bond with a relative or trusted friend?

7. How do you believe Vanessa's previous relationships affect her relationship with Khalil, and vice versa? Explain.

8. Some of the novel's secondary characters are Khalil's and Vanessa's closest confidants—Darius, Karim, Bibi, and Lisa. How were these characters influential? Did you tend to identify with any one character in particular? Why or why not?

9. Think of a moment or an experience where you realized you could fully trust someone. How did it change your relationship? What does that person's trust mean to you, and has it ever been tested?

10. When Vanessa attempts to help Khalil toward the end of the novel and he rebuffs her, she remains persistent, even if only as his friend. Have you ever helped a friend or loved one in a similar way, and what advice might you give to someone else in the same position?

READ ON
FOR A SNEAK PEEK OF
GIA DE CADENET'S
NEXT NOVEL

NOT THE PLAN

Coming soon from Dell

CHAPTER ONE
Isadora

I *can do this.*

Isadora Maris took a deep breath, squared her shoulders, and maneuvered her luggage into the San Diego airport. Her bags checked and through security, she stopped at a coffee shop before heading to her gate. *Flying is no big deal. How many times a year do you fly? Nothing bad has ever happened.*

She had a few moments, so she took a seat at one of the small tables in front of the shop. Maybe she should buy a magazine. Something light and fun to read? She popped the lid off her cup and tried to ground herself with the aroma and taste of the latte. She tapped her fingertips on the napkin dispenser on the table, grounding herself some more. She was safe; she was fine. *Everything's cool. I've got this. If I can handle stonewalling senators and aggressive lobbyists, I can handle a short flight.*

"Babe, I would totally die for you." Isadora caught a man's voice murmuring a table over. She glanced at the couple just as his blond companion let out a kittenish giggle.

"Kenny, sweetie, you are *so* dramatic," she said.

Isadora suppressed an eye roll as the couple leaned into each other open-mouthed. It wasn't that she was averse to public displays of affection. How long had it been since someone looked at her like that? Touched her like that? But it didn't matter, right now she had too much on the line. In a few short months, her boss would be president pro tempore of the state senate, and as chief of staff, her skill had helped get him there. Next up, managing a successful race for U.S. representative and then she'd reach her childhood dream: becoming a congressional aide in Washington, D.C. She was so close she could almost taste it.

"You know," the guy said after smacking his lips, "after last night, the plane could fall out of the sky, crash, and burn, and I'd die a happy man."

Isadora choked on her coffee, a wave of terror charging over her skin from her scalp to the soles of her feet. She wrenched her phone out of her bag, unlocked it, and tapped on an icon on her home screen. She scrolled down to the most important line in the article.

The odds of dying in a plane crash are one in eleven million. The odds of dying in a plane crash are one in eleven million.

"If we crashed in the water, we—"

Isadora *had* to get away from these people. She grabbed her phone and the cup, pushed her chair back, took one step, and promptly collided with something tall and warm. She watched in slow motion as her latte shot out of the cup, arced into the air, and exploded against a white dress shirt.

"Dammit," a man said.

"Oh! I'm so sorry." She grabbed some napkins out of the dispenser, her fingertips clumsy and buzzing. When she glanced up at his face, she stopped dead. Green eyes framed by dark hair stared back through nerdy-cute glasses. Well over six feet tall, sun-kissed olive skin, and hot. Cover model hot.

She'd just scalded the sexiest man she'd ever seen.

"Here." She offered him the napkins.

"You must be in a hurry," he said, taking them and dabbing at the coffee.

"No. Well . . . I mean, yes."

"Maybe watch where you're going next time." Just her luck, the demigod was pissed at her.

"Maybe *you* should watch where *you're* going," she snapped. "Who walks this close to tables?"

He narrowed his eyes at her, looking her up and down. She wasn't going to give him a pass to talk to her any kind of way, just because he was gorgeous.

"If you'll *excuse me,* miss, I need to go get cleaned up."

She narrowed her eyes at him. She'd taken a step back and was stuck between him and the wall of the coffee shop.

"You're in *my* way," she said.

Waving the hand holding the napkins out and bowing in a sarcastic display of gallantry, he let her by. "Have a nice day," he called after her.

She shot him a dirty look over her shoulder and headed to her gate.

Isadora adjusted her earbuds and started her pre-takeoff ritual. *The odds of dying in a plane—*

"Well, isn't this a surprise?"

She opened her eyes as the demigod's messenger bag slid onto the seat next to hers. Heat blasted into her cheeks as a bright flash of embarrassment crackled over her already frayed nerves when she realized he'd changed into a moss green shirt.

"Uh . . . yeah," she mumbled, tugging at the cuff of her cardigan. "Nice shirt." She snapped her mouth shut. *That's it. I've lost my mind.*

He chuckled, taking his seat. "Thanks. I started the day with a white one, but some crazy lady spilled coffee all over it and I had to change."

Swallowing over the lump in her throat kept her from clapping back. Why did he have to be so hot? She smoothed her cardigan sleeve, trying to ground herself again. She was going to be next to him for nearly two hours. And you catch more flies with honey than vinegar.

"Maybe it's for the best," she said.

He raised an eyebrow.

"That color works better for you than plain white."

"Does it?"

She nodded, proud of the ability to flirt while strapped in a giant steel tube about to be blasted into the air. The corner of his mouth dipped down, and a hint of red crept up his neck as he leafed through his bag, found a magazine, and tucked it in the seat pouch in front of him.

Is the demigod a little shy? She suppressed a chuckle.

"It's also a good cut for you," she said. He slid his bag under the seat. "It fits your shoulders just right."

Demigod raised both eyebrows and gave her a genuine smile. He had a chiseled jaw. And full, crazy sexy lips. And dimples. Literally, the sexiest man she had ever seen. Her heart dipped as his gaze caressed her cheek and the hollow of her throat.

"I'm Karim," he said, offering his hand.

"Isadora. I am sorry about your shirt."

"No, it's nothing."

"At least let me have it cleaned."

"Really, no big deal, I already rinsed it in the restroom. I doubt the stain will set."

"That's good." Unsure of what to say next, she returned her earbuds to their place but didn't turn on her music. The flight attendants were about to start their safety instructions and her pre-flight ritual included following along, even though she knew every detail by heart. At least the earbuds made it look like she wasn't paying *too* much attention. She didn't want to be impolite to Karim, but she needed to get into an acceptable mental space before takeoff. She closed her eyes and took a deep breath. Her ritual did not include basking in Karim's cologne. Or . . . what was that smell underneath? Him? Deep, calming breaths let her conceal her investigation.

Oh God . . . he smells amazing! Deep and woodsy and—something brushed her cheek. She opened her eyes. The curved headrest saved her from utter mortification after she'd leaned toward him. She stole a glance with her peripheral vision, hoping he hadn't noticed. His attention was on the magazine in his lap, but he might have been watching her out of the corner of his eye. Shifting as far over as possible in her seat, she feigned interest in the view out the window while listening to the flight attendants explain what to do if they were facing imminent demise.

She needed to focus on something else. She undid the low bun she always wore for flights. Running her fingers through her blown-out hair, she tried to twist it back into place. Her timing was off, and she had to start over as the pilot announced that they were next in line. In fighting with her hair, she knocked her earbud loose. Karim was unwrapping a piece of gum and offered her one.

"I hate having to pop my ears later," he said.

"Thanks. I hate that too." She focused on the explosion of gooey mint across her tongue as the engines roared. His eyes were shut, so she didn't have to hide the fight to slow her breathing as the plane left the ground. She chewed and chewed and chewed, trying to get back to a calm place. The grating whine of the wheels coming up into the body of the aircraft sent a flash of thick moisture over her skin, and she had to send her mind in a different direction.

"I don't understand your priorities," her mother had sighed on the phone the previous night. "Things haven't been easy for me."

The same call, the same words, the same guilt, every time.

"It's a thankless job, being a parent. Especially when you're on your own."

What do I have to do for it to be enough? Do I have to thank her for raising me every time we talk?

"It's not like he died on purpose," Isadora had said, as always.

Her mother continued, unhearing or uncaring, as always.

"You don't understand my pain. I don't think you'll ever understand."

How could I understand? He was just my dad. It's not like his death hurt me too.

Her gaze fell to the window, but she saw nothing. Pulling in a chestful of recycled air, she willed the tears back down. She pulled her phone out of her cardigan pocket, put the meditation playlist on, and closed her eyes. About twenty minutes into zen, Karim startled her, brushing his fingertips along her arm. She took out her earbuds.

He nodded at the steward, a row ahead of theirs, distributing beverages. "Would you like a drink, Isadora? I'm going to get a coffee, but I'll do my best not to pay you back," he said, smiling.

The depth of his voice sent pleasant tingles through her, the pain she'd dredged up washed away. Smiling, she let herself fall into a present that excluded the rest of the world.

"Guess I deserve that. A sparkling water would be good. It's nice of you to offer."

"My pleasure." He asked the steward for their drinks and handed Isadora hers with care. His casual way of ordering for her was a pleasant surprise. A touch of chivalry, and it wasn't like he made the decision in her place. She thanked him and started to put her earbuds back in, but he spoke again.

"These early flights are tough, huh?"

"Yeah." She sipped.

"Do you usually fly business class?" He put his coffee down and caressed the edge of the tray with the pad of his thumb.

Lucky tray.

"I try. I like to get off as quickly as possible." He raised his eyebrows and she caught how that had sounded. Face burning, she took a quick breath. "You know, um, I mean, the plane. Get off the plane."

"Yeah," he said, smiling a little. "I understand. Always seems to take forever when you're at the rear."

"Yeah," she echoed. *What to say?* He was nice. She didn't want to just pop her earbuds back in and seem rude.

"Um . . . do you like the rear of the plane?" she asked. "I've always had trouble sitting back there. It bounces around too much for me."

He lowered his gaze a millisecond, lips curling in a tiny hesitation. Then he darted a quick glance at her, like he was trying to make a decision. "Really?" he finally asked, meeting her eyes. "I quite like the rear. The bouncier the better."

Um . . . She swallowed. "Is that so?"

"It is."

Is the demigod telling me he checked me out?

"I dunno." She warmed her voice and leaned toward him. "I gotta disagree with you. I prefer it over the wings where you can feel the *thrust* of the airplane. You know? When it's fast and strong and you can't do anything but let yourself go."

"Is *that* so?"

"It is. You don't like the thrust of takeoff?" she asked, eyes wide.

"Oh, I do," he said. "It's . . . exhilarating." He smiled, drawing her attention to his lips. She ran the tip of her tongue along the inside of hers, imagining what his tasted like.

"Exhilarating. Good word choice."

"So what do you do, Isadora?" he asked, raising his cup to his lips.

She frowned inside. Talking about work with strangers was almost always a mistake. She loved what she did, but politics rarely made for good general conversation. After wrinkling her nose, she shook her head.

"Let's not talk about work," she said.

He smiled again and put his coffee on his tray.

"What if I guess?" he asked.

"Guess?"

"What you do. Will you tell me if I guess right?"

She folded her arms, turning toward him. Most people didn't realize that her job even existed, so he'd never guess.

"All right," she said, nodding.

He shifted toward her, then tapped a finger to his lips as though he was thinking. She noticed he wasn't wearing a wedding band. *There's no reason to notice that. No time for men right now.* He glanced back at her.

"Got it," he said. "You're a therapist."

"A therapist?" she asked. "What makes you say that?"

He tilted his head to the side, glancing down to her chin and back up to her eyes. "You seem like a warm, caring person. Easy to talk to."

She raised an eyebrow. That was a lot to assume from their brief conversation.

"And," he said, "I bet you don't like talking about it because people either ask you to break confidentiality for *interesting stories,* or they take one look into your inviting eyes and want to talk about all their troubles."

She flushed a little. Karim-the-demigod thought she had inviting eyes.

"You're very kind," she said. "I'm not a therapist. But—"

The plane slammed downward, and she clung to the armrests until her knuckles burned. A hard shift to the right and the pilot turned on the fasten seatbelt lights.

"Passengers, this is your captain speaking. We've hit a patch of turbulence and there's likely more ahead. We still have a while to go before we reach our destination, and the ride is going to be bumpy. The crew will come by and pick up any garbage you may have, please stow your belongings and put your trays in the upright position."

The steward was next to them in a flash, with a forced customer-service smile that didn't reach his eyes. A woman behind Isadora gasped as the plane shuddered and bounced. The steward stopped a moment, his hand clamped, bracing himself, on the seat in front of Karim. *"Brace." That's the word they use right before we crash.* Roiling nausea splashed through Isadora as she passed the steward her empty cup with quaking hands. Karim tried to make eye contact as she followed the pilot's instructions.

"This part sucks, huh?" he asked.

"Yeah," she said. "It does." She stuffed her earbuds back in, doing her best to show "fine" and "experienced" body language, crossing her arms and repeating her mantra in her mind. He hadn't given her a reason to believe he would judge her, but she had to conceal fear. Raised by a perpetual victim, Isadora had learned to appear fine when she wasn't, lest she take attention away from the person it always belonged to. There was no way for her to stop now.

Karim didn't speak to her again until the plane landed. She wanted to say something nice to him while collecting her things, but she needed to move with as much focus as possible to avoid crying out her pent-up fear. His belongings in hand, he stepped into the aisle and smiled.

"Nice meeting you, Isadora."

"Y-you too," she stammered, avoiding eye contact as he left. She let at least ten people get ahead of her and stayed out of his sight at the luggage carousel. In the privacy of her rental car, a good, long cry released the anxiety and adrenaline. Still shaking, she drove to the apartment that would be her temporary home during the legislative session.

That evening, in bed, grocery shopping done, and bags unpacked, she had time for regret. Karim was nice, attentive, and damn sexy. Flirting with him made her want more.

Nice job, Isa. You could have at least gotten his number. But it's probably for the best. This session is crucial; you must remain focused. No sense in letting a pretty face distract you.

CHAPTER TWO

Karim

Karim waited in the conference room of the Sacramento office of Senator Julian Brown. His potential new boss was in the hallway with Christina, the legislative director he would be replacing during her maternity leave. This second interview had gone even better than the videoconference while Karim was still in Michigan. The only hitch was the length of the position. Covering for someone on maternity leave wasn't ideal; he needed something long term to start his new life.

You're in a rebuilding stage. It's okay. Just get your foot in the door and see what permanent opportunities present themselves.

Once he'd been admitted to the California bar, and with his experience as a senior aide, something would come together. The conference room door snapped open and Senator Brown walked back in, Christina following with a small stack of papers.

"Well, young man, welcome to the team." He offered his hand. Karim stood to accept it.

"Thank you," he said. "Can't wait to get started."

"Excellent, because we need you here tomorrow, bright and early. There's no time to waste, with Christina leaving us who knows when. But that's women for you; they keep you waiting or guessing, or they walk out on you in your time of need."

The remark was a double slap to Karim, inappropriate for work and hitting too close to home.

"Very funny, Julian," Christina said, stapling some papers and handing the stack to Karim. "You know I'll be here as long as possible, and back as soon as possible. Karim, I already took care of your pre-screening. Just fill those forms out and take them to the secretary. She'll get them to Senate Administration, and you'll be clear to start tomorrow."

"Will do," he said. "Thanks again, and I look forward to seeing you tomorrow."

"I won't be here," Julian said at the door. "Gotta head back to the district office for a couple days. Christina will get you set up. There's one bill I want you to focus on—co-sponsoring a highway project with our dear majority leader. It's very important I show my constituents who *really* cares about them."

"Got it," Karim said.

He walked through the glass doors of the senate office building, squinting into the sunlight as he loosened his tie. As he took a deep breath, some of the weight lifted from his shoulders. As he walked down the street, more than one woman's head turned. It was something he appreciated, though he always had to mask a wave of shyness when it happened.

Reaching his rental car, he tossed his jacket on the passenger seat and called his brother back.

"Hey, man, what's the word?" Khalil asked as soon as he answered.

"Hey. I got the job. Start tomorrow."

"Excellent! Not like it's a surprise, though."

Karim shook his head. "You never know. Pass the word around? Don't need Mom to keep worrying." He fiddled with the buttons on the dashboard, trying to get the convertible's top down.

"Like it's possible to stop her," Khalil said. "But yeah, I'll let everyone know. So, I'll see you in San Diego on Saturday."

"You know you don't have to come all this way. I can move in on my own."

"I'm overdue for a vacation. Never been to California. It's the perfect excuse."

"Uh-huh." Khalil wouldn't admit to being worried about him, so Karim wouldn't push. But he could give him a hard time. "One thing," Karim said, admiring the palm trees swaying in the breeze. "You might wanna ease up on the food, man. I didn't wanna say anything before, but you're getting a little soft."

"Hey," Khalil said. Karim could tell he was trying to hold in a laugh. "Don't hate 'cause my girl can throw down. And don't act like you didn't enjoy it when you were here."

"You're right. And I shouldn't complain. It's probably for the best."

"Why's that?"

"People can finally tell us apart."

"Ouch!" Khalil laughed. "I'm glad for you, bro. New city, new start."

"Yeah."

"Now all that's missing is a new girl."

Karim hesitated, remembering his flirtation with the woman from the plane. That Isadora who'd almost scalded him, then made up for it by boosting his confidence. But he wasn't ready to share.

"Don't, Khalil. Gotta go. See you Saturday." He hung up, the phone joining his jacket. As he was getting ready to go to the apartment complex Christina had recommended for a short-term place, his phone rang again. Expecting it to be Khalil, he went to send the call to voicemail but noticed the number before he did. The area code was familiar, but it wasn't anyone in his family.

Who else would be calling from Detroit?

Whatever it was could wait. He needed to get his living situation squared away. Pulling onto the street, he returned to his checklist.

Move to California—check.

Find a job—check.

Place to live in district—check.

Place to live near the capitol—almost check.

Get a life . . .

An hour later, he had his apartment situated and was ready to check out of the hotel. He was loading his bags into the trunk when his phone rang again. It was on the front seat; he didn't reach it in time. The missed call was the same number from that morning, and again, no message.

If you can't be bothered to leave a message, I'm not calling you back.

That evening, he took a stroll through Midtown Sacramento. He was settled in his new place, fridge stocked, and clothes set aside for the next day. His phone rang again, the same number he didn't recognize.

"Finally," a woman said when he answered.

His vision blurred, and he caught his footing with a brief staccato step. But he kept moving forward down the street, just as he was determined to keep moving forward in his life.

"Raniya," he said, his mouth cotton, but his voice strong.

"I was beginning to think you didn't want to talk to your dear sister-in-law." If there was a silver lining to his wife's abandonment, it was that he didn't have to deal with her smug sister anymore.

"As I'm sure you can understand, certain events led me to delete certain contacts from my phone. Had I known it was you, I would have avoided wasting my time and yours by answering."

"Now, Karim. That's no way to speak to your family."

"We aren't family anymore, Raniya. We haven't been for some time." He stopped at the window of an Italian restaurant. Inside, a man who looked like a younger version of himself sat across a table from a woman with long dark hair and golden skin.

Watch yourself, he wanted to warn the guy.

"I must say, we're rather disappointed in you. Running off like this."

His bark of a laugh ricocheted across the street.

"'Running off,' Raniya? Me running off? That's rich. We all know exactly who did the running. And the cheating. The rages, and the gaslighting. And who remained faithful to his vows until he'd had enough of the abuse. Don't call me again."

Raniya was still talking as he ended the call and put his phone in his pocket. He continued walking, trying to discover the neighborhood, to get his bearings in the new place. But it was impossible. His mind was back in Harrisburg, remembering the zombie he'd become once he understood Laila wasn't coming back. At the gated fence, he fumbled with the keys. He got to his apartment and stretched out on the couch, returning to the work he'd done with his therapist in Michigan after staying in Pennsylvania became too much.

Laila's personality disorder is not a justification for her cruelty. She knew it was her problem but demanded that I shield her from the consequences of her actions. But you can't set yourself on fire to keep someone else warm. When she left, I made the necessary choice to protect myself by not chasing after her. She abandoned our relationship when I refused to keep abandoning myself. He drew in the needed breath.

In the shower, washing away the contact with Raniya and the accompanying memories of Laila, he remembered something else he'd discussed with his therapist—the idea of moving on, of trusting another woman again. In Harrisburg, it had been impossible. The town wasn't enormous, the dating pool microscopic. Celibacy wasn't a goal, but his commitment to his vows kept him from anything past a first date. Back home in Grosse Pointe, he'd had zero interest. Despite his family's best efforts, he wasn't up to it, and he never knew when he might run into his in-laws or friends of theirs. He hadn't had the slightest desire until yesterday. Until Isadora. She was beautiful, with dark, almond-shaped eyes to go with her glowing almond skin. High cheekbones, an adorable round nose and full, appetizing lips. Her flash of anger had been sexy. Real sexy. The shock of running into him had tinged the rich depth of her cheeks. He wasn't sure what he'd said to her as she raced away. However, he had a clear memory of checking her out, without hesitation.

Maybe I should have shared with Khalil; he would've been proud. He grinned as he toweled off.

When he'd reached his seat on the plane, he'd asked himself if it was a setup. During the flight, he didn't know what had come over him, once he'd had an excuse to get her to take her earbuds out. It had been *years* since he'd flirted. He wished he'd gotten her number, but he wasn't ready.

Don't beat yourself up. It goes in the "win" column anyway because you sure didn't get onto the plane with the idea that you could flirt. This is a good step—it means you're further along than you thought. Shame not to see her again, though.

In addition to being a Maggie Award finalist and lifelong romance reader, GIA DE CADENET has been by turns a legislative aide, a business school professor, and a translator and editor for UNESCO. She's a coffee connoisseur, celebrates Fridays with champagne, and loves to go to San Sebastián, Spain, for leisurely weekends. A native Floridian, she currently lives in Paris, France, with her husband and children.

giadecadenet.com
Twitter: @Gia_deCadenet
Instagram: @gia_decad
TikTok: @giadecadcnct

ABOUT THE TYPE

This book was set in Garamond, a typeface originally designed by the Parisian type cutter Claude Garamond (c. 1500–61). This version of Garamond was modeled on a 1592 specimen sheet from the Egenolff-Berner foundry, which was produced from types assumed to have been brought to Frankfurt by the punch cutter Jacques Sabon (c. 1520–80).

Claude Garamond's distinguished romans and italics first appeared in *Opera Ciceronis* in 1543–44. The Garamond types are clear, open, and elegant.

RANDOM HOUSE BOOK CLUB

Because Stories Are Better Shared

Discover

Exciting new books that spark conversation every week.

Connect

With authors on tour—or in your living room. (Request an Author Chat for your book club!)

Discuss

Stories that move you with fellow book lovers on Facebook, on Goodreads, or at in-person meet-ups.

Enhance

Your reading experience with discussion prompts, digital book club kits, and more, available on our website.